20/4/2017

D0299656

HERTFORDSHIRE LIBRARY
WITHDRAWN FOR SALE
DATE: _____

R.RD

Please renew or return items by the date shown on your receipt

www.hertfordshire.gov.uk/libraries

Renewals and enquiries: 0300 123 4049

Textphone for hearing or 0300 123 4041
speech impaired users:

L32 11.16

By L. A. Larkin

The Genesis Flaw
Thirst
Devour

Devour

L. A. Larkin

Constable • London

CONSTABLE

First published in Great Britain in 2016 by Constable

This paperback edition published in 2017

1 3 5 7 9 10 8 6 4 2

A CIP catalogue record for this book
is available from the British Library.

ISBN: 978-1-47212-482-1

Typeset in Bembo by SX Composing DTP, Rayleigh, Essex
Printed and bound by CPI Group (UK) Ltd, Croydon, CR0 4YY

Papers used by Constable are from well-managed forests and
other responsible sources.

MIX
Paper from
responsible sources
FSC® C104740
www.fsc.org

Constable
An imprint of
Little, Brown Book Group
Carmelite House
50 Victoria Embankment
London EC4Y 0DZ

An Hachette UK Company
www.hachette.co.uk

www.littlebrown.co.uk

In memory of Marie Colvin and
Rémi Ochlik

1

On the flat, featureless ice sheet, katabatic winds swoop down the mountain slopes, whipping up ice particles and hurling them at a solitary British camp. The huddle of red tents, blue shipping containers, grey drilling rig, and yellow water tanks are so tiny on the vast expanse of white, they resemble pieces on a Monopoly board. Three kilometres beneath the camp, subglacial Lake Ellsworth, and whatever secret it may hold, is sealed inside a frozen tomb.

In the largest tent, used as the mess and briefing room, Kevin Knox stands before Professor Michael Heatherton, the director of Project Persephone.

'So how the hell did this happen?' says Heatherton, dragging his fingers through greying hair.

Knox brushes away a drip running down his cold cheek, as ice, frozen to his ginger beard and eyelashes, melts in the tent's comparative warmth. Outside it is minus twenty-six degrees Celsius but the wind chill makes it feel more like minus forty.

'Mike, we don't know exactly. The boiler circuit's broken. It'll need a new part.'

'Don't know?' Heatherton scoffs.

Knox clenches his pudgy fists. What a thankless little twat! For the last hour he and Vitaly Yushkov, the two hot water drillers, have been struggling to fix the damn thing.

A strong hand squeezes his right arm and Knox glances at

Yushkov standing beside him, whose penetrating blue eyes warn him not to lose his temper. Knox gives the Russian an almost imperceptible nod and Yushkov releases his grip.

Their leader gets out of his plastic chair and paces up and down behind one of three white trestle tables. A marathon runner of average height, he is lean, wiry and exceptionally fit for his age. But, next to Knox and Yushkov, he appears fragile. Knox isn't tall but he is chunky, and likes to describe his wide girth as 'love handles' even if the Rothera Station lads pinned a photo on the noticeboard with his head photoshopped on to the body of an elephant seal. Not that it bothers him.

Yushkov is six foot one. His neck, almost as wide as his head, meets powerful shoulders, and his hands are so large they remind Knox of a bunch of calloused Lady Finger bananas. Knox knows little about Yushkov's past – conscription, ship's engineer, mechanical engineer – and the taciturn Russian doesn't care to share. He is now a British citizen and the most talented mechanical engineer Knox has ever worked with, and that's all that matters.

'The eyes of the world are upon us,' Heatherton says, his Yorkshire accent softened after years working with the British Antarctic Survey in Cambridge. 'Everybody wants to know if there's life down there.' He momentarily looks at the rubber flooring beneath his boots. 'And we're only a kilometre away from the answer. We have to get the drill working again before the hole freezes over.' His voice is high-pitched with agitation. 'So what I need to know is, can you fix it?'

Yushkov speaks, his accent as strong as the day he last set foot in Mother Russia, sixteen years ago.

'Boss, we built the hot water drill. We did not build the boiler. So, we need time to understand the problem. We will talk with manufacturer, get advice. We have spare parts at

Rothera. If we are lucky, we get new circuit in a day or two and all is hunky-dory.'

Yushkov grins, revealing surprisingly perfect white teeth given his heavy smoking. Heatherton opens his mouth but Knox jumps in.

'It's going to be okay, Mike. We'll get it running on a backup element and keep the tanks warm. Stop worrying.'

The taut skin around Heatherton's eyes is getting darker each day. He plonks down into a chair and rubs his hands up and down his face, as if trying to wake up. He looks exhausted.

'Look, Kev,' he says through his splayed fingers, then drops his hands to his sides. 'I'm a geoscientist, not an engineer. But to do my bit, I'm relying on you to do yours. I'm frustrated, that's all.'

That is as close as Knox has heard their leader get to an apology.

Heatherton cranes his neck towards them, frowning, and speaks quietly so nobody can hear through the canvas walls. Not that anyone could anyway, given the blustering winds.

'Could it be sabotage?'

Yushkov shifts from one battered boot to the other.

'Pardon?' Knox says. He can't have heard right.

'Has the boiler been sabotaged?'

'Jesus, Mike!' says Knox, flinging his hands in the air. 'What's got into you? We're in the middle of bloody nowhere trying to do something that's never been done before. Things go wrong. It's inevitable.'

'Yes, quite right.' He sighs. 'But a lot of things are going wrong. Too many. And we all know the Russians are trying to beat us.' Heatherton flicks a look at Yushkov. 'No offence.'

'None taken,' Yushkov replies, but the low rumble in his voice says he is not being entirely honest.

At that moment, BBC science correspondent, Charles Harvey, steps through the door, his black parka covered in snow, like dandruff. He's as blind as a bat without his glasses, which means he's constantly wiping ice off the lenses or cleaning them when they steam up.

'Hear you've had a spot of bother. Mind if I join you?'

Heatherton hesitates. Harvey continues.

'I see a great story here. Engineers struggle in howling storm to save project. That sort of thing.'

'An heroic angle?' Heatherton's hazel eyes light up. He runs his fingers over his smooth chin, the only team member who bothers to shave. Knox knows why: Heatherton wants to look dashing in Harvey's documentary. 'I see. Okay.' He looks at Knox. 'Well, let's get on with it.'

'Fine,' says Knox. 'But if that blizzard gets much worse we'll have to stop work and wait for it to pass.'

'Yes, yes, health and safety and all that,' Heatherton says, 'Quite right. But if you don't get the boiler working soon, this whole project is done for. Ten years down the toilet.'

Knox raises his eyes in exasperation. 'No pressure then.'

As he zips up his black parka sporting the Lake Ellsworth project logo, tugs inner and outer gloves on to his hands, pulls on his beanie and hood and places snow goggles over his eyes, he thinks for the thousandth time what a stupid colour black is for Antarctic clothing. Should have been red, yellow or orange so they can be spotted easier. Through the flimsy door he hears the wind has picked up speed. It will be near impossible to hear each other above the roar.

'Okay, mate,' Knox says to Yushkov. 'Let's get this done as quick as we can. Stay close. Use hand signals.'

Yushkov nods.

'Vitaly, a word,' says Heatherton, gesturing him to stay.

'Right. I'll get started then. But I can't do much without him, so make it quick, will you?'

Annoyed, Knox leaves, letting the fifty-mile-an-hour wind slam the door for him. The field site is a swirling mass of snow. He grips a thick rope, frozen so solid it feels like steel cable, secured at waist height between poles sticking out of the ice at regular intervals. Only thirty feet to the boiler. He carefully plants one boot after another. He staggers a few times. Head down, body bent, he throws his weight into the storm like a battering ram. Where the hell is Vitaly? That bloody Heatherton is probably wanking on about loyalty and reminding Yushkov, in his unsubtle way, that he now works for the Brits. The man is bloody paranoid.

Someone takes him in a bear hug from behind. He thinks Yushkov is mucking about, but when a cloth is held hard over his nose and mouth, he begins to panic. It has a chemical smell he can't place. Confused and disoriented, he tries to turn. He feels light-headed and his eyelids droop.

Knox wakes. He hears a high-pitched buzzing, then realises it's the retreating sound of a Bombardier Ski-Doo. Soon, all he can hear is the buffeting wind. He wants to sleep, but his violent shivering makes it impossible. He opens his heavy eyelids and sees nothing. Just white. Where is he? The hardness beneath his cheek tells him he's lying on one side. Knox tries to sit up, but his head pounds like the worst hangover, so he lies back down. He blinks eyelashes laden with ice crystals, trying to take it all in. Of course. The boiler. He must have fallen. Maybe knocked his head?

This time, Knox manages to sit up and waits for the dizziness to pass. He can't see the horizon or the surface he's sitting on, or even his legs. Like being buried in an avalanche; there is no up or down. He's in a white-out – the most dangerous blizzard. He sucks in the ice-laden air, fear gripping him. Ice particles get caught in his throat and he coughs. His heart speeds up and, instead of energising him, it drains him. He racks his brain, trying to remember his emergency training. But his mind is as blank as the landscape.

Think, you fucking idiot. Think!

It's pointless shouting. He doesn't have a two-way radio. Nobody can see or hear him. Christ! What happened? His jaw is chattering, his body wobbling, and now he can't feel his hands or feet. He lifts his right arm so his hand is in front of his eyes, but it doesn't feel as if it belongs to him. His fingers won't flex and the skin is grey, the same colour as his dear mum when he found her dead in her flat. Frostbite and hypothermia have taken hold of him. What he can't understand is why he isn't wearing a glove. He checks the left hand. No glove and no watch, either. Nothing makes sense.

Knox attempts to bend his knees. His legs are stiff and movement is painful. He manages to bring them near enough to discover he wears socks, but no boots. The socks are caked in ice and look like snowballs. His shivering is so violent that when he tries to touch them, he topples over.

Stunned by his helplessness, Knox stays where he fell. He places a numb hand on his stomach but he can't tell if he's still wearing a coat. He can't feel anything. He blinks away the ice in his sore eyes and peers down the length of his body. He sees the navy blue of his fleece. No coat. The realisation that he will die if he doesn't find shelter very soon is like an electric shock and his whole body spasms. Terrified, he scrambles to a sitting position, battling the blizzard and his own weakness.

'Help!' he shouts, over and over, oblivious to the pointlessness of doing so.

DEVOUR

For the first time since he was a boy, he cries. The tears are blasted by the gale and shoot across his skin and on to the woollen edges of his beanie, where they freeze, as hard and round as ball bearings.

Knox struggles on to his hands and knees like an arthritic dog, sobbing, a long string of snot hanging from his nose. Shelter. Must find shelter. Despite his numb extremities he crawls on all fours, around in a tight circle, hoping to see something, anything that will tell him where there's a tent or a shipping container. Any kind of shelter. But there are no shapes of any kind. Nothing but whiteness. The desperate man decides to go in one direction for ten steps, then turn to his right for ten, then again and again until he returns to his current position. The gusts are so powerful, it's pointless trying to stand. So he stays on all fours.

He tells himself that Robert Falcon Scott walked thousands of miles to the South Pole with frozen feet. Then he remembers Scott never made it back. Knox's head is tucked into his chest and the patches of hair sticking out of his beanie are stiff and white. He peers into the distance every now and again but the view doesn't change. Where is the rope, for Christ's sake? When Knox thinks he's done a full circuit, he stops, but there's no way of telling if he has returned to his starting point. He pants, exhausted. Perhaps he should build a snow cave, as all deep-fielders are trained to do, but he doesn't have a shovel or ice axe, and his hands are useless. Suddenly, he feels on fire all over and claws at his fleece, trying to remove it. But he can't even grip the hem.

Like a match, his strength flares ever so briefly and then vanishes.

He wakes with a start. How long has he been lying here? Minutes? Hours? The snow build-up is now a blanket over him. He pulls his knees to his chest, curling himself painfully into a foetal position.

He chuckles. What a tit! He's going to get such a ribbing when they find him, lost only a few feet from the camp. He'll never live it down. Oh well. Story of his life: always the butt of jokes. He isn't shivering any more and feels warm and cosy. Yushkov will know he's missing. They'll be looking for him. He's so tired. Tired and numb. He can't hear the wind any more.

When he closes his eyes, everything is peaceful. Knox hears his mother tell him it'll be all right. She's reported his bullying to the headmaster. His school blazer is ripped, but she's not cross. His head in her lap, she brushes his long fringe from his eyes. As long as she keeps holding him, he isn't afraid.

2

Kabul, Afghanistan

Olivia Wolfe's head slams into the passenger window, dislodging the scarf that conceals her Western features, as the dented Toyota Corolla – Kabul's favourite car – bounces out of a pothole. Hastily covering her head, she fails to notice she is being watched by an old, bearded Mesher in a black turban standing at the roadside, who raises a mobile phone to his ear.

'Can't we go any faster?' she asks Shinwari.

Her driver and translator is a short man still wearing a Saddam Hussein moustache, who waves a hand at the makeshift market stalls bottle-necking the narrow street ahead.

It's December and snowing. Their progress is slow as they dodge haggling shoppers, bicycles, wooden carts, ancient cars and overburdened, skeletal donkeys. Street vendors in thick coats call out to passers-by, offering pomegranates, eggplants, carrots, cauliflowers, nuts and spices, freshly butchered meat, birds in cages, hot green tea in urns. Cars honk, brakes screech, men shout, chickens squabble. Behind the stalls, ramshackle shops compete for custom. One sign in English and Pashtun, offering a 'Modern Gym', is riddled with bullet holes. She's not surprised; foreigners are not welcome. Snowflakes settle on sand-coloured shattered shops and homes, and the slouching, weary shoulders of a people at war too long. Winter hides the beige city's wounds. But it does not heal them.

Wolfe spots a woman in a head-to-toe pale blue burqa, accompanied by a man she expects is the husband. This is the first woman she's seen in the street.

'Blue Bottle,' says Shinwari.

He glances at Wolfe and grins, but continues to lean over the steering wheel, as if somehow this will make the car go faster. She's heard that derogatory term before, back in her foreign correspondent days when she accompanied the allied troops into war. The troops coined the expression 'Blue Bottle'.

'Where are all the women?' she asks.

'Afraid.'

Accelerating around two boys pushing a bicycle, the horizontal crossbar laden with a bag of wheat they intend to sell, Shinwari then swerves across oncoming traffic to turn left up a mountain road, on either side of which are box-shaped homes that appear to be carved into the sandy hillside. Children pick through the rubbish littering the slopes below.

'I don't like this,' Shinwari says. 'One road in and one road out. Very dangerous.'

Her 'fixer' of many years, Shinwari negotiates their way through roadblocks and no-go zones, offering bribery and banter to officials and warlords alike, so she gets her interview. She trusts his judgement but this one is worth the extra risk.

'I have to do this.'

Shinwari shakes his head. The car lurches and the chassis scrapes across exposed rock. Wolfe fidgets in her seat and clicks the stud of her tongue piercing against her teeth. Earlier on she was freezing – the car's decrepit heating system gave up the ghost years ago. But now, as her heartbeat quickens, she is stifling in her long brown Afghan dress.

'Her husband is not there? You are certain?' Shinwari asks, his voice shaky.

'He's in Tajikistan.'

Shinwari peers through the filthy windscreen as he searches for the right address, the lethargic wipers fighting a losing battle.

'If Ahmad Ghaznavi knows you've been asking about him, this could be a trap.'

'Shinwari.' She turns to face him. 'I know what I'm doing. You know that, right?'

'Yes, yes,' he replies.

'Going after Colonel Lalzad was just as dangerous. We exposed him for the torturer and killer he is. That's why he's now in a British gaol. Because of us.' She squeezes his shoulder. 'But he's still running his organisation from prison and word is the drugs are funding an Isil terror cell in the UK.'

'So why you see Ghaznavi's wife?'

'Ghaznavi is Lalzad's right-hand man in Kabul. He gets the drugs to England. Nooria Zia says she knows how the drug money reaches the man behind this British cell and who he is.'

Shinwari's forehead is slick with sweat. 'But why does she help you?'

'She hates him. He raped her at fourteen. When she went to the police, she was convicted of the moral crime of being raped. Had his son in Kabul's Women's Prison. I did a story, remember? You got me the interview.'

'Yes, yes, but this is big risk for her.'

'Let me finish. Ghaznavi's first wife only gave him daughters, so he pressured Nooria into marrying him, legitimising his son. She wants to be free of him.'

Shinwari nods his understanding and focuses on the narrow road. A hairpin bend. Fewer houses. A steeper climb.

'You always thank me,' he says. 'Other journalists, they use me and leave. I thank you.'

'Any time, mate.'

He scans the street. The houses are bigger, better built.

'That one,' Shinwari says, nodding at a mansion that is about as out of place as exposed cleavage is in Afghanistan.

'A poppy palace. Of course,' Wolfe says.

Shinwari whistles through his teeth.

There is an eight-foot-high perimeter wall, freshly painted cream, and a wrought iron gate, painted gold. Behind the wall, the house façade is dominated by six wide cream columns, the capitals at the top in gold and shaped like scrolls. These support three semi-circular balconies and the floor above. Through vast sliding doors, Wolfe can see a chandelier hanging from the ceiling. The rooftop is flat, supporting a large satellite dish, and is surrounded by a waist-high wall from which to admire the view or shoot intruders.

'I'll turn the car around. Make our exit faster.'

Wolfe tucks wisps of her raven black bob under her scarf, then taps the deep pockets of her loose dress. In one is her smart-phone. She'll record the interview with it. In the other is a long key-chain that holds keys to her hotel room, home, motorbike and a locker at Kabul Airport. She doesn't wear glasses – the sign of a foreigner – and her other body piercings are well hidden. Only her small black field pack strapped tightly to her back suggests she's not a local. The bag usually contains her laptop, sat phone and spare battery, power adaptor, a few items of clothing and a toiletries bag, all of which she left in the airport locker to save weight and bulk. But the backpack stays with her. Always. Attached to it by a clip is a metal water bottle with a long neck and screw-in plastic stopper. Her money and passport are hidden in a money belt beneath her dress. Earlier, Shinwari had asked her why she wore an almost empty pack.

'Protection,' she'd replied.

The house opposite Ghaznavi's is unfinished, the upper level exposed concrete breeze blocks. Another poppy palace. Shinwari parks outside. Wolfe switches on her smartphone's video recorder but leaves it in her deep pocket. Her visit must appear social.

'Let's go,' says Wolfe, getting out of the car.

She waits for Shinwari, then walks a few steps behind him. He tries the golden gate but it's locked. To his left he finds a bell to press. They stay silent and wait. Through the gate's swirling ironwork, Wolfe sees a carved wooden door open. She tenses, ready to run. It is not Ghaznavi or his armed guards who step on to the porch, but a young woman in a pale pink silk dress embroidered with golden flowers, with a simple black muslin scarf over her head. She hesitates and scans the street, then hurries to unlock the gate, opening it a fraction. Nooria looks at Wolfe, her jade green eyes wide with panic. Wolfe stares at the face of a frightened child.

'You must leave,' Nooria says, her accent thick. 'Mina is watching.' Ghaznavi's first wife.

'Can you meet us at the market later?' Wolfe asks.

She shakes her head.

There is a loud crack that seems to echo down the mountainside. Something zips past Wolfe's cheek. Nooria jolts, eyes wide, as blood spurts from a hole in her neck. She collapses backwards.

Wolfe throws herself at a stunned Shinwari and they hit the ground hard. 'On the roof opposite,' she pants. 'Sniper.'

She crawls to Nooria. The girl blinks rapidly in shock, blood pulsing from the wound.

'Help me!' Wolfe calls to Shinwari, but he's frozen with fear.

She grips Nooria under the armpits and drags her behind a column. Wolfe uses the girl's scarf to try to stem the blood flow.

Shinwari scuttles after her. 'What do we do?' he says, cringing behind the pillar.

'Kabir . . .' says Nooria, her voice a gurgle as if she's drowning. Foamy blood seeps from her mouth. 'Kabir Khan.' She chokes.

'Nooria!'

'Bomb London.' The girl's voice dies away then, in one final act of defiance, she spits out the word, 'Da'ish.' The Arabic acronym for Isil or Islamic State.

Another shot booms out. No silencer. The bullet thuds into the snow only centimetres from the column they hide behind. Nooria stares vacantly at the sky. A snowflake lands in her right eye and melts away into a tear.

Wolfe searches for an escape route but the thirty feet between them and their car might as well be thirty miles. There is no cover.

'We gotta run for it,' she whispers.

Shinwari doesn't respond. She shakes his shoulder.

'You hear me? No choice. We run for the car. You understand?'

'Yes.' He's as pale as the murdered girl.

Wolfe peers at the uncompleted roof where she thinks the shooter has set up position. No movement. No glint of metal or scope. She unclips her backpack waistband, wriggles the straps off her shoulders and clutches it close to her chest.

'Car key,' she says.

Shinwari gives it to her, hand trembling. Thwack. A bullet narrowly misses his right shoulder. He recoils.

Ghaznavi doesn't want us to leave, Wolfe thinks. The sniper

could have killed them by now. They'll make good hostages for a high ransom.

'Ready?'

He nods.

'Me first. Stay right behind me. Okay, now!'

Wolfe jumps up, positioning the backpack so that it shields her head and heart. Sewn into the pack is an ESAPI plate designed to protect the body from small arms fire. With Shinwari so close, it gives some protection to both of them. She darts towards the car. But no gunshots. Slipping on some ice, she stumbles and Shinwari literally picks her up by the back of her dress and shoves her forward. They make it to the Corolla and duck low, hoping the sniper's sightline is blocked. Wolfe shoves the key in the driver's door and turns it, just as she is yanked back by two men with Kalashnikovs over their shoulders. Her backpack falls to the ground. One of them grabs it. The other grabs her. She lashes out with her boots as she is dragged backwards, but his grip doesn't loosen, impervious to her blows.

'Get help!' she yells at Shinwari, who is cowering by the car.

Her captor, in a brown coat and dirty white turban, shoves a hand over her mouth. She gags at the smell of tobacco and shit on his fingers. Her heart races and panic threatens, but if she is to get out of this alive, she must think. Every instinct tells her to keep struggling, but her training tells her she's wasting energy. As the gates to Ghaznavi's mansion are locked, Wolfe is dragged further into the compound, her heels sliding through a pool of Nooria's blood. She needs a plan, and to plan she must clear her mind. She shuts her eyes and focuses on calming her heart rate. On the other side of the wall, the Corolla's engine screeches into life and the tyres skid as Shinwari tears off down the road. They'll expect her to be paralysed with terror or weep or beg. Playing the weak female gives her an advantage. She goes limp, surrendering.

They stand her up and give her a shove. Wolfe opens her eyes, taking in her situation: three men, a locked gate and no weapon. Her bag and sat phone are held by the second man with a Kalashnikov, who has the gate keys hanging round his neck. Taller and younger than her brown-coated assailant, he runs a tongue over his thin lips. Both armed men point their guns at her torso. The third man is scrutinising the inside of her bag. He drops it to the ground, then turns to look at her. She recognises Ahmad Ghaznavi. His black beard and hair are trimmed short, Western style. He is dressed head to toe in a long white shirt and white baggy pants. His tasselled loafers are Italian, his watch a gold Rolex.

'You killed your wife,' Wolfe says, trying to keep her voice level.

'She betrayed me. And you, you will make me even richer,' Ghaznavi says. 'Your newspaper will pay well, I am sure.'

'Shinwari will get the police.'

'I own the police.'

He says something in Pashto to his men. The only word Wolfe understands is 'whore'. Ghaznavi turns his back on her and walks up the steps to enter his house. She glimpses a woman, her face hidden by a veil, who follows him down the hall in silence. Somebody closes the front door.

Wolfe checks the rooftop and upstairs windows, but it seems they are not being watched. Her captors lean their rifles against the wall. They laugh and jeer at her. She is their reward. The taller man is playing with his crotch, taunting her with what he will do, as the one in the brown coat laughs, revealing some missing front teeth. Wolfe lifts her left hand up, palm facing outwards, and says in Pashto, 'Let me go in peace.'

There are key phrases she always learns in the language of any country she visits. This is one. Another is, Help me, I need a doctor.

Her right hand is in her dress pocket, gripping her key-chain: a thick cable as long as her forearm, her keys on a ring at the end. She casually pulls it from her pocket. All the while she has her other hand out in front to distract her captors. To them she is saying: back off!

The taller man steps closer, arms wide as if to grab her. Wolfe swings the cable back, then up and over, like a fast bowler, and lunges forward so the sharp keys smack him hard in the side of his face, gouging a deep wound under his eye. He yelps; his hand shooting up to the wound. In one continuous motion, she swings the chain in an upwards arc so the keys collide with his mouth, slicing through his lower lip. His head jolts back. Lifting her leg, she bends her knee and kicks out, the tip of her steel-toe work boot smashing into his balls. He crumples to the ground, groaning.

The brown-coated man is so stunned he fails to react immediately. Then he charges. Wolfe swings the keys at him but isn't quick enough. He grabs her raised wrist with one hand and punches her in the face with the other. She stumbles, reeling from the pain, and lands on the icy ground. He yanks the key-chain from her hand and tosses it away. Disoriented, she scrambles to her knees and blinks away the dizzying light in her eyes. She needs another weapon.

Wolfe pounces on her discarded backpack, unhooks her metal water bottle and grips it by its elongated neck. Her attacker has the advantage: he stands; she is on all fours. He looms over her, shouting abuse, and spits on her. Then, eyes down, he fumbles for his penis. She jumps up and, in a whipping motion, strikes him on the jaw. He sinks to his knees like a lame horse. With all her strength she slams the metal cylinder into the side of his head, the blow propelling him sideways on to the ice. Spread-eagled, he doesn't move.

But it's not over. Her other assailant struggles to get up, still clutching his crotch. Wolfe kicks him in the throat and yanks the gate keys from around his neck, snatches her pack, staggers to the gate, unlocks it and runs.

Someone yells out. 'Here! Olivia!'

Dazed, she follows the sound of the car engine and the cloud of hot exhaust. She sees Shinwari's head sticking out of the window. He's come back for her. Yanking open the back door, she throws herself on the seat to the rapid rattle of Kalashnikov fire.

'Drive!'

3

London, England

A man in his seventies wearing a Barbour coat and corduroys, trailing an overfed Jack Russell, passes me without so much as a glance. Like London's ocean of homeless, I have become invisible. I dress to disappear. My only distinguishing feature – scarring around an eye – is partially concealed behind thick-framed glasses and, today, by the hood of my nondescript, black pea coat, pulled tight. I am no threat. A student? Unemployed? Who else would be crazy enough to sip tea on a park bench on a bone-chilling weekday morning like this?

The dog charges behind the bench, its piercing yap doing my head in as it peers up into the bare branches of a horse chestnut. Conkerless and leafless, the tree resembles an umbrella, fabric torn, spokes broken. The old fella dutifully follows, cursing, splashing through puddles, his back to me, so I look up too, safe in the knowledge he can't see my face. Dangling from the tree is a dead mistle thrush, its neck encircled in what appears to be

17

fishing wire. It swings in the wind, its speckled belly no longer warmed by a beating heart. Further up is an impaled kite, the source of the noose. The man drags the dog away and moves on. I stare at the dead bird, fascinated by its glazed eyes, its mind blank.

I know how it feels.

There is an empty room in my mind. It pulls at me incessantly like the moon on the tides, but every time I return, I find it still barren. There is no window, no furniture, no sound, no people. No me. My diary tells me that my injured brain can no longer hang on to new memories. Yesterday's experiences, places, people, all glimmer briefly and then fade, like mayflies. Yet distant memories of my childhood and early twenties are as clear as a midsummer sky.

I know it is Monday 16 November, 8.26 a.m., because my iPad Mini tells me so. The warmth of it in my lap draws my eyes back to the screen. I gaze at the wallpaper image of the two of us, arm-in-arm, taken when I could function as a normal human being. When I had a future. Your tight-lipped smile, those dark inquisitive eyes, round and questioning like a dumb dog, and that trashy eyebrow stud that cheapened your other-wise pretty face. Of course, you don't have it any more. Since the Pulitzer, you've feigned respectability. But I know you, Olivia Wolfe. I've made it my life's work to know every one of your secrets.

I feel my face flush, my heart race. I crush the paper cup, the warm tea dripping through my fingers. Beads of sweat glue my shirt to my back. The burning fury inside me fights against the frigid air. I know you are responsible for my wretched existence. You have to be. Why else would I be driven to do this?

I smirk at the bitter irony.

There is one advantage to my new state: I recall nothing I inflict upon you and I can, with all sincerity, deny my actions.

How can I be guilty when I truly believe I didn't do it? How can I feel remorse when I can't remember?

I am as innocent as the day I was born.

4

'Wolfe!' bellows the praying mantis from the doorway of his office on the fourth floor of *The Post*'s sparkling new building in King's Cross.

Its exterior reminds Wolfe of an inside-out toaster, with the heating elements protected from the weather by glass. The core is open from the foyer to the roof, bisected by a glass-lined rectangular void through which the 'ant colony', as her editor calls it, can be observed scurrying about on each of the five levels. This set-up makes sneaking out unobserved for a quick fag or an early lunch well-nigh impossible. The interior is littered with sudden bursts of colour, as if the designers somehow imagined that the five-foot-high, shocking pink number two on a meeting room's glass partition, or the lime green chairs, or the intrusive burst of red wall as you turn a corner, might somehow jolt the overworked staff into a renewed flurry of activity.

Wolfe receives nods from fellow journalists as she weaves through the maze of closely packed desks and a sheepish grin from the ambitious rookie crime reporter, Jonathan Soames. The frenetic energy and the babble of voices – urgent, challenging, frustrated, excited, coaxing – revive her after a long flight. When she's out in the field, she misses this convivial frenzy, but after a day or two on the news floor, she can't wait to be in the field again.

'Welcome back,' says Mark Lawn, the political correspondent, as he races by, heading in the opposite direction. He notices her face's purple bruising and stops. 'I heard about the assault. I'm sorry.'

Head down, she continues her journey to Cohen's office, aware numerous pairs of eyes are watching her. Do they know too? She doesn't want to give her boss any excuse to move her to a permanent desk job. She'd go stir crazy.

With a takeaway cappuccino in one hand and her dusty backpack slung over the other shoulder, Wolfe follows Mozart Cohen, editor of *The Post*, into his glass cube of an office. Cohen is six three, gangly, with a long face and a sharp tongue. She's lost count of the number of reporters he's reduced to a trembling jelly.

'You're late,' he growls.

'Just one day, Moz, and the Afghan police might've had something to do with it.'

As he sits, Cohen retracts his bony arms and grips the edge of his desk. Wolfe is convinced that to fit his long legs under there, he must have to bend them in ways not humanly possible. Cohen scowls at a yellow sofa with marshmallow-like cushioned pockets.

'The lemon meringue's all yours.'

Wolfe plonks her bag on the floor and her coffee cup on the circular side table, and sits. She's almost swallowed up by the sofa's squishy pockets. She's wearing head-to-toe black: drainpipe jeans, T-shirt, leather jacket and boots. Her only colour is a gash of pink lipstick and the hideous aubergine discolouration on her left cheek.

'You look like shit,' says Cohen.

'At least I look alive,' she replies.

Cohen nods. They can agree on that.

'Great feature. Well done. Online hits and copy sales are up. For once.'

He chucks the paper at her. Leaning forward, his tone suddenly changes. 'So what the fuck were you doing? Haven't you learnt anything from me?'

Wolfe doesn't reply immediately. She studies his face. Bushy grey eyebrows protrude like ceiling cornices over his deep-set brown eyes, but she thinks she sees a hint of amusement in the corner creases.

'And don't give me one of your penetrating stares,' Cohen continues. 'My soul was damned the day I took up journalism. You'll find nothing's changed.'

She slouches back into the soft sofa pockets, looking like a bruise on a banana. 'Thanks for your concern, Moz.'

He throws his stick-thin arms into the air. 'I *am* concerned! Look! This is me being concerned.' He jolts forward. 'I mean, fuck! Look at your face. You're a mess.'

'Moz, I'm fine. Nooria Zia isn't.' Wolfe stares at the grey flecked carpet. 'I talked her into it. The poor girl died because of me.'

Cohen places his knobbly elbows on his desk and clasps his hands together. 'No, no, no! Stop this, Olivia. Now listen to me.' He waits for her to look up. 'You got too involved. Way back, when you covered her rape and trial. You spent too much time with her. She got under your skin. And I understand, I do. She had a terrible life. But it's your job to expose the truth, to tell the story. It's not your job to get involved. You must never change the story. What's my rule, huh? Rule number one?'

'Report and move on,' she mumbles.

Moz slams a bony hand on the desktop. 'Exactly. Otherwise, you'll burn out. You can't put yourself through the wringer like this. Look at you!'

'I don't normally get involved and you know it. I was foreign correspondent for four years, remember? I've been to war, I've

21

witnessed massacres, seen children butchered, people blown to bloody pieces.' She pauses. 'It's just this one girl.'

'Why this one?'

'I don't know. After all she'd been through, to have enough guts . . . I could never be that brave.' She shakes her head. 'One second, she was talking to me; the next, I watch her die. She was just a child.'

'You have to move on, Olivia.' He cracks the knuckles on his left hand and then the right. 'I need to know you can do that.' He pauses. 'Well? Can you?'

'I must find Kabir Khan. I owe her that much.'

Moz shakes his head, clearly disappointed. 'Wrong answer. This is not about what you owe her. It's about uncovering the truth and printing it.'

Wolfe wishes she'd gone home first, had a shower and something to eat before facing Cohen.

'Had a call from your best mate, DCI Casburn.'

She frowns and the shooting pain it causes reminds her of her battered face. As her editor knows only too well, she and Detective Chief Inspector Dan Casburn don't see eye to eye. She co-operated with Counter Terrorism Command, otherwise known as SO15, during their hunt for Colonel Lalzad, who'd fled from Afghanistan to London on a fake passport, wanted for war crimes. With Wolfe's information, Casburn tracked down Lalzad to a North London flat and arrested him. Lalzad is now serving twenty years on seventeen counts of torture and hostage-taking at a roadblock he commanded on a main route into Kabul.

'What did he want?' she asks.

'Lalzad's got wind you're after his 2IC here and he's using his network to take you down.'

'Does Casburn know about Kabir Khan?'

'He never gives anything away. You know that.'

'Why'd he call you? You're not my mother.'

'Fuck knows. Maybe because a dead journalist is a bloody useless one.'

'Look, Moz. There's a long line of people who want me dead. That's what happens when you expose criminals and corrupt—'

'Yes, yes,' says Moz, cutting her off with a flick of his wrist. He starts typing. 'I'm emailing you your next assignment.'

'I haven't finished this one.'

Cohen sighs loudly, his bony fingers hovering over the keyboard. 'Your source is dead and you have a price on your head. For now, you can't go back to Afghanistan. It's up to Casburn to find this Kabir Khan and prove the Isil connection. Not you. And Soames can keep our investigation ticking over while you're away.' That explains why the rookie crime reporter was looking sheepish. Wolfe opens her mouth to object but her editor raises a long finger to silence her. 'I need you on another story. Something right up your alley.'

'Happy to take on another feature, Moz, but nobody touches the Lalzad-Isil story. That's mine.'

'Hear me out and then we'll decide.' Cohen leans back in his chair.

She takes a deep breath. 'Go on.'

'How does murder in Antarctica sound?'

'Chilly.' Wolfe gives him a closed smile; she's never been one for toothy grins.

'Yeah, very funny. Now listen. British and Russian scientific teams in Antarctica are competing to be the first to discover new life in underground lakes that've been sealed beneath ice sheets for millions of years. As our mob drills Lake Ellsworth, the Russians, headed by a Dr Trankov, are drilling Lake Vostok.'

'I thought the Russians succeeded a while back.'

'Ah, so you do know something about it. Good. Well, the Russians cocked it up. They reached the lake, all right, but the contaminants they used in their drill polluted everything and killed the fucking organisms. It now looks like our chaps at Lake Ellsworth will be the first to succeed. If they do, they could discover ancient life, never before seen by man, that can survive in complete darkness beneath three kilometres of ice.'

Wolfe squints at her editor, wondering if her jetlag has caused a temporary misunderstanding. Cohen has never shown any enthusiasm for the environment or science, giving those editors more leeway than others because these topics bore him 'shitless'.

'You mean microbes?' Wolfe can't prevent her lip curling.

'And what's wrong with fucking microbes?'

'Nothing, Moz, but I don't do science.'

'Let me finish. An old university pal, Professor Michael Heatherton, is heading up the Lake Ellsworth project. He contacted me because he believes his chief drilling engineer has been murdered.'

He pauses for dramatic effect, knowing that murder in Antarctica is virtually unheard of. Until two years ago, when six Australians and one Finnish man were butchered by mercenaries. Wolfe remembers the global news coverage.

'Why does he think it's murder?'

'It's more than murder. He believes there's a traitor, trying to sabotage the project.'

'What? Sabotage bug exploration?' Wolfe can't keep the incredulity from her voice. 'To use one of your sayings, "Who gives a fuck?"'

'According to Michael, the Russians.'

'Oh, of course. Silly me. Putin the radioactive poisoner has turned his evil eye to a bunch of bug researchers.'

'I'm saying if the engineer was murdered, then perhaps these "bugs", as you so disparagingly call them, might actually be worth killing for. Go find out why.'

'Where are you going with this, Moz? Seriously, bugs?'

Cohen flings his arms wide. 'I smell a conspiracy, or at the least, a cover-up. Come on, Olivia, think about it. Or has that blow to your face affected your brain?' Cohen rips a Post-it note from the desk surface and dials the phone number scrawled upon it. 'I'll get Michael to explain.'

'Heatherton? What time is it there?'

'No fucking idea,' Cohen replies, dialling.

5

Heatherton answers Cohen's call immediately and is put on loudspeaker. He's clearly been waiting by his satellite phone. Cohen introduces Wolfe, who now sits on the edge of her boss's desk.

'Michael, can you tell Olivia why you think someone is sabotaging your project?'

Heatherton clears his throat and begins.

'Certainly. On a mission of this complexity and magnitude, at such a forbidding and cold location, I expect there to be problems. But nothing like we've experienced.'

Heatherton clears his throat again. His accent is fascinating: plummy, yet Wolfe thinks she detects the hint of Yorkshire.

'Before coming out here, we tested and retested everything. Particularly the hot water drill. We prepared for every eventuality. I handpicked the team two years ago and everyone gelled. Except Charles Harvey, of course, who joined us here a few weeks ago.'

Wolfe glances at Cohen. She knows Harvey, the BBC science correspondent. This only serves to confirm in her mind that she's the wrong person for this assignment. Heatherton continues.

'But I can't imagine the Beeb sending us a saboteur. I mean, can you?' His levity sounds strained.

Cohen pipes up. 'We know of Harvey. Go on, Michael.'

'Right. George, Bruce, Ed and Trent got here two weeks before the rest of us to finalise camp set-up. All went well. Even the weather was good. Three weeks ago the rest of us arrived, with Charles in tow. The first problem was a hole in one of the onion tanks.'

'Onion tanks?' Wolfe asks.

'Open water tanks, shaped like a kid's circular swimming pool. Made of hardwearing nylon. Each one has to hold ten thousand litres of water at near boiling point.'

'So not easily torn?' Cohen clarifies.

'Exactly. We lost all the water from that tank, and it's back-breaking work shovelling ice in, I can tell you. The hole wasn't repairable, so we had to order a new one to be flown in. In the scheme of things, just a minor delay, but what got me wondering was the nature of the hole. It looked like a cut. A straight line. Not a tear.'

'Did you voice your concerns to your team?' Wolfe says.

'No, no. I didn't want to add to the pressure they were already under. You see, we only have six weeks to complete the mission. Our funding runs out then. Anyway, I had no evidence, so I focused on the project. Then, a few days before Kevin's tragic death, I was riding our one and only Ski-Doo when the brakes failed. Luckily I wasn't going more than twenty m.p.h. I managed to roll off the vehicle and didn't break anything, but I could have been killed.'

'What caused the brake failure?' she asked.

'Good question. The brake fluid had escaped through a tiny

hole. It could have been caused by sharp ice, who knows? Call me paranoid if you will, I just can't help thinking someone wanted me hospitalised so I couldn't lead Project Persephone any more.'

Wolfe nods at the project name: Persephone, the Greek mythological goddess of the underworld.

'And then Kevin Knox was found dead? Tell me about that,' she says.

'Well, just before Kevin's death, the circuit on the boiler failed, which meant we couldn't heat the water in the tanks to the required temperature. It has to be scalding hot to drill through the ice sheet. Kevin and Vitaly were trying to do a temporary fix on the boiler, until we could take delivery of a new circuit. Anyway, the weather was foul and visibility poor. I probably shouldn't have asked them to keep working, but the boiler's housed in a con-verted shipping container, so they were protected from the storm. I was talking to Vitaly in the mess tent, so Kevin went outside alone. He was meant to follow the ropes that lead to the boiler room, but somehow, and this is what none of us can understand, somehow he ended up half a mile away. Poor man froze to death.'

'Is it possible Knox got lost in the storm?' asks Wolfe.

'I don't think so. Kevin might've been a bit unfit, but he's worked in Antarctica three times before. He's done survival training. I mean, he knew.' Heatherton's voice catches, clearly upset. 'It doesn't make sense that he'd wander off like that. And how did he manage to walk half a mile in a white-out? Without his boots or coat?'

'At the extremes of hypothermia, I understand victims feel hot and disoriented. They've been known to strip off. Could he have done that?' asks Wolfe.

'Maybe. I just don't know. But when you can't think, and your hands are frozen and unresponsive, how do you manage to unlace boots and pull them off, unzip your coat and pull that off, and remove your gloves?'

Everyone is quiet, considering this.

'And walking half a mile in a white-out is well-nigh impossible,' Heatherton adds.

'So you think he was taken away from the camp, stripped and left to die?' Wolfe clarifies.

'It sounds crazy, doesn't it? But you must remember that Kevin was a critical member of the team. He helped design and build the hot water drill. There is no other like it. Now he's gone, we have to rely on Vitaly Yushkov. If anything happens to him, we're scuppered.'

'So why would anybody go to such terrible lengths to sabotage your project?'

Wolfe is beginning to suspect there is something more than bad luck going on. But she can't see a motive.

'I would have thought it's obvious. If we fail to bring samples to the surface, then the Russians might do it first. That is, if they haven't contaminated the whole of Lake Vostok.'

Wolfe leans forward, hands clasped. This is getting interesting.

'Who do you suspect?' she asks.

Heatherton lowers his voice, 'There's only one Russian here.'

Wolfe nods. 'If you truly believe that, then why don't you replace Yushkov?'

Cohen chucks her a manila folder with Vitaly Yushkov's name on it. She opens it and is surprised to find only two pages. Yushkov's CV. Wolfe skim-reads it as Heatherton speaks.

'I can't,' he mopes, 'it'll take too long. The new boiler circuit should arrive today. With the boiler fixed, we resume drilling immediately. I have no choice but to keep him here . . . and watch him like a hawk.'

'Has Yushkov actually done anything suspicious? Or is it simply he's Russian?'

'Nothing I can point my finger at—'

Cohen interjects. 'The information you sent us – there's virtually nothing on him. Why?'

Heatherton clears his throat. 'Because there is little information on him. He sought asylum in England and was granted citizenship.'

'Yes, I see that,' says Wolfe. 'Two years ago. But everything prior to that is vague.'

'Ah,' says Heatherton. Silence.

'Michael? Are you still there?' asks Cohen.

'Yes. Look, Yushkov is complicated. There's a lot I don't know. You see, I was asked to take him on as a favour to a friend in the Foreign Office. No questions asked. We go way back, so I helped him out, and placed Yushkov with the maintenance crew in Cambridge. But he proved to be an exceptional engineer and was soon assisting Kevin with the drill design and assembly.'

Wolfe is on the edge of the seat.

'So you're saying he defected, and the Foreign Office is protecting him?'

'Look, I can't say any more, I'm sorry.'

Wolfe chews on the side of her finger. Cohen is smiling. He senses her excitement.

'One more question. Why haven't you called the police if you think it's murder? I gather jurisdictions are complicated in Antarctica, but I thought that if the victim was British, then our police run the investigation?'

'I can't allow anything to stop the project. We have less than a week left here.'

'So why do you want me there?'

'Moz tells me you're his best investigative journalist . . . '

'I didn't quite put it so flatteringly,' Cohen mumbles.

'Professor Heatherton, you understand that if I find a good enough story, I'll publish it?'

'I do.'

'What do you hope to gain from me looking into this?'

'If Trankov is sabotaging our operation, I want it made public.'

'I still don't understand why you don't just wait until you return to England and contact the police then.'

'Damn it! Are you going to make me say it?' Heatherton pauses. She can hear his agitated breathing. 'Off the record, okay?'

'Okay.'

'I've been told there's to be no police investigation. It was a tragic accident.'

'Who told you?' she asks.

'I'm not sure if I should say.'

'If you want me there, you tell me who gave you that directive.'

'The Ministry of Defence.'

Wolfe stands now. The fine hairs on the back of her neck are prickling.

'How fast can I get to Camp Ellsworth?'

'Forty-eight hours.'

'I'll be there.'

6

To get my circulation moving, I shift first one leg and then the other, careful not to lose the iPad on my lap. I blow on my numb fingers and look across the road at a house subdivided into five flats. My view is slightly obscured by two bent oak trees whose gnarled and contorted branches camouflage me, should anyone look out of the window at the park. I've been watching the occupants – my 'lab rats', as I call them – gradually leave for work. Only one remains: Daisy O'Leary, flat one, who is due at her regular yoga class. I need her gone before you arrive.

Her intercom buzzer's label says 'Felicia Savage', in flamboyant cursive script, and this is how she is known to her clients. In a street of elegant Victorian red-brick houses, a conservation zone, in which each windowsill must be painted white, the wrought iron balcony railings black, and the original tessellated Victorian paving tiles cannot be removed, I wonder why your well-to-do Balham neighbours put up with a dominatrix in their midst.

My notes tell me I have had keys to the communal door and Olivia's flat since 23 October. It was warmer then, the leaves golden, the muddy grass littered with prickly conkers. Ditsy Daisy took her rubbish to the bins, leaving her flat door wide open. She got chatting to a good-looking bloke two houses down, who's a graphic artist, and was so busy flirting she didn't notice me slip inside and take the keys marked 'Liv' hanging on a rack just inside the door. I got my own set cut and, within half an hour, dropped hers through the communal letterbox, where they lay on the black and white hall tiles until Daisy found them. She assumed she'd dropped them, and, of course, didn't tell you. She so wants to be a reliable friend, but that takes someone with half a brain and I suspect she has little more than I have left. And if she'd caught me in her flat? I'd have simply shown her my medical ID bracelet and looked vacant, telling her I'm lost. Works every time.

There Daisy is, looking nothing like the photos on her website, except for her waist-length brown hair. No leather, no corsets, no whips, no canes. No sleazy glamour on a weekday morning. She's tall, probably five nine, and takes long strides in baggy yoga trousers and pale pink coat, clutching a purple roll mat as she heads towards Tooting Bec Tube.

I don't have much time. When I rang your office, the recep-tionist told me you had just left the building. Checking my instructions once more, I slide my tablet into my khaki satchel, pull on gloves and, from my coat pocket, take out your keys.

I cross Elmbourne Road at a casual stroll. A female cyclist in yellow reflective jacket rides past, heading towards the low rumble of heavy traffic on the main road, her rusty back wheel squeaking. I wait until she is further down the road, then open the fire-engine red communal door, its top two panels of vintage parti-coloured stained glass. On either side of the doorframe are further panels of red wood and stained glass, making the door appear extra wide. Several copies of the local rag, the *Wandsworth Guardian*, have been shoved through the letterbox. Ahead is a staircase leading up to flats three, four and five, inhabited by two ambitious solicitors, a researcher for the British Museum, and an estate agent. To my right is the door to Daisy's flat. A solid black door. To my left is a plain white one. With a turn of your key, the five-lever mortice deadlock bolt slides back with a solid clunk.

My arm brushes the door chain as I enter. Closing the door, I lean my back against it, calming my breath, inhaling the scent of leather and household bleach and pine-scented shower gel. These smells should be familiar, but I only know that from my notes. It's warmer inside your flat: you leave your heating on timer when you're overseas (two hours in the morning and three at night) so your water pipes don't freeze. Keeps it nice and cosy for me. I savour this moment when the air is still, the house empty, and nobody knows I am here. Even when you're home, you don't have visitors, or dinner parties, or lovers. You only have one love: your job. You used to keep your address a secret and I expect you still do. Hardly surprising given how many powerful and ruthless people you've pissed off. Yet here I am.

To my left is a wall cupboard that's concealed when the front door is open. I look inside. Part hanging space, part shelving. Your coats obscure a deep shelf upon which one black forty-litre backpack, packed and ready to go, lies on the right. Your warm climate bag. On the left, the shelf is empty, because you took your cold climate backpack to Afghanistan. When you are home, which isn't for long, the two Go Bags, as you call them, sit side by side and look identical, like twins in a double crib. And these are your babies, aren't they? One of them is always with you. The contents of each bag are known to me, logged in my diary like every other detail about your life, even the contents of your bathroom cabinet, what food you eat, what brand and size of clothes you wear. But I can't resist unzipping the bag's main compartment and stroking your rolled-up cotton shirt, imagining it on your smooth skin. I inhale the apple smell of your laundry detergent, then put it back just as I found it. Below, next to your motorcycle helmet and leather gloves, is a pile of your post, placed there by Daisy. Twenty-three letters. I've steamed them open, read them all, re-sealed them and returned them to this spot. There are two new letters: one is an electricity bill, the other from the Prison Service. I pocket the second one and close the cupboard door.

The narrow hallway is made barely navigable by your black Harley-Davidson Sportster 883. I run my gloved finger over the seat. Two steps down, and I'm in your sitting room, wondering, as I must do every time I come here, why your home is so strikingly monochrome. I have reams of photos of your flat on my iPad, shot in colour, but they might as well have been taken in black and white. The bedroom has white walls, black wooden platform bed with austere white bedding, white faux-fur rug on floorboards, painted white. In the lounge room, a square-armed, square-backed, Corbusier black leather sofa and matching armchair face a wall-mounted TV and a black and white cube that serves as a coffee table. In one corner is a glass desk, resting on black wrought iron legs, and behind it an Aeron chair. The galley kitchen is grey granite and stainless steel with white cupboards. There are no photographs of you or your family, no mementoes or school certificates or childhood keepsakes. I could only find your birth certificate in a desk drawer, wedged between the pages of a book on journalism. Your home reveals virtually nothing about you.

There is just one collection that hints at what you care about. Behind your desk, the wall is covered in black and white photos, in identical black frames. But you do not appear in any of them, only people you've met on your travels who've touched your heart. They do not smile. Their eyes show fear, grief, pain, desperation. They are the victims you write about. Nooria Zia is on your wall, her face in close-up as she looks straight at the camera from behind prison bars. A child with no hope.

I look around at the security grilles on your windows and French doors; this place feels like a prison. But it is your refuge. Somewhere to rejuvenate between assignments. Drop your guard. Here, your privacy and security are inviolate. But not any more.

I leave you a puzzle.

7

With backpack slung over one shoulder, you jump down from the black cab in your scuffed Harley-Davidson leather jacket, the skull insignia visible when you turn to pay the cabbie. It never ceases to amaze me that, despite your petite frame, you wield such destructive power, whirling through people's lives, leaving misery in your wake.

Your army surplus boots slap the damp paving stones. You open and slam shut the communal door and you're gone, keen to find Ditsy Daisy, who arrived home eleven minutes and twenty-one seconds ago. I bet her text message had you drilling your fingers on the cab armrest, pestering the driver to go faster.

Leaning against a low wall, hood up, busy messaging on my phone, of course you haven't noticed me. As soon as you're inside, I move closer, concealed by a neglected privet hedge that's grown both tall and wide, a hazard to footpath users. To hear you better, I lower my hood. Through the stained glass of the main door, I see you suddenly freeze. It's like I'm peering down a kaleidoscope watching oranges, greens, yellows and blues shift into different patterns as your dark form moves through it. Then you turn and thump on your friend's door.

'Hello, Dais,' I hear you say. 'You alone?'

'Yeah. Come 'ere and give us a hug,' Daisy says.

Your shapes merge and separate, the kaleidoscope turns. Daisy mumbles in your ear something about her text message.

'What happened to your face?' she says, her deep voice androgynous. There's nothing daisy-like about Daisy.

'Got into a spot of trouble in Kabul. At least nothing's broken.' You turn and look at your flat door. 'What happened?'

'Got back from yoga and found that.'

Spray painted across your door in red are the words, 'YOU WILL PAY'.

'You didn't call the police, did you?'

'You asked me not to.'

'How did they get in?'

'Dunno. Must've buzzed their way in, I guess.'

'This wasn't there when you left for yoga?'

'What? You think I wouldn't have noticed?'

'And you've still got my spare keys?'

'Sure.' Daisy goes into her flat and reappears. 'Here.'

You both drop out of sight and must be kneeling near my 'welcome home' message.

'Paint's barely dry,' you say.

Time to move. I sprint across the road and duck behind a parked silver Citroën Dispatch van. You burst out of the main door and stand on the pavement, peering up and down the road and into the park, but you don't see me.

Wolfe knows that insistent intercom ring. He keeps his thumb on the button until she answers. Her search for proof of an intruder is cut short. She scrapes sleep from the corners of her tired eyes, then sniffs an armpit. She'll do.

'All right, Mr Impatient,' she says into the intercom and opens her door. 'Hold your horses.'

Through the stained glass door panels of the communal entrance she sees a man she knows to be DCI Dan Casburn. At five eight and of stocky build, Casburn always stands stiffly, chin up as if he's still in the SAS, even though, these days, he wears suits and ties. His jacket is never creased, his tie is always perfectly centred and his shoes polished – a habit from his army days.

Wolfe opens the communal door.

'You took your time,' she says, forcing a jovial tone. There are few people who make her nervous, and Casburn is one.

Wolfe leans against the door frame, arms folded, as she looks into Casburn's gunmetal grey eyes, which somehow seem fitting, given he was one of the SAS's best snipers. He keeps his hair short with a flat top cut, and has enough stubble on his chin to sand back the peeling paintwork on Wolfe's windowsills. His jaw is in perpetual motion as he chews Nicorette gum.

'Didn't know I was expected,' he says in an East London accent, and tilts his head to one side.

Wolfe doesn't move out of the way. 'Of course you are. You've seen today's *Post* and you want to know everything I've learnt about Lalzad's drugs operation. Right?'

'We both know it's more than that.' He smiles, but his eyes don't.

Casburn's job is to prevent terrorist activity in the United Kingdom and threats to UK interests overseas. Wolfe's article doesn't mention Kabir Khan or Lalzad's suspected link to Isil because she needs proof Nooria is correct.

'You going to let me in or are we doing this on the doorstep?' Casburn asks.

'Just so happens I need a detective.'

'That'll be a first.'

A hint of a smile, then his face muscles resume a neutral position, his expression unreadable again.

Wolfe steps aside and Casburn brushes past her, deliberately giving her shoulder a nudge, asserting his authority. In the communal lobby he turns left. He knows his way, but stops abruptly when he sees YOU WILL PAY scrawled across her door. Casburn bends his knees to take a closer look.

'Shit paint job,' he says.

'Very funny, Dan.'

He frowns. 'Any sign of a break in?'

'I haven't had a chance to look. Just got in myself.'

'Well, do it now.' It's an order.

Casburn inspects the chunky deadbolt without touching it, then steps into the hall, closing the door with his elbow so as not to disturb possible fingerprints, then follows her into the sitting room. The window locks are intact. As he scans the French doors for signs of forced entry, his focus flits to the wall behind her desk where her only photographs are displayed. Some were shot by a professional, others by Wolfe on the fly. But the common theme is conflict. Casburn seems drawn to one of an Iraqi woman and two young children – filthy, frightened, standing in front of a pile of rubble that once was their home.

He shakes his head. 'Cheery, aren't they?'

'They're not meant to be cheery. They're there to remind me why I do what I do.'

'You mean poke your nose in where it's not wanted?'

'I mean write about injustice and oppression, tyranny and terrorism. We're on the same side, Dan. It's our methods that differ.'

He studies the photo taken in 2014 of Hong Kong police clearing a protest camp demanding democracy, a man on the ground being beaten by three officers.

'So why aren't you in any of these?'

'Because they're not about me.'

Casburn swivels on his heels to face her.

'Want to report the vandalism?'

'Not worth the hassle.'

'I warned you.' It sounds more like a threat, than I-told-you-so.

His eyes drop to the backpack she took to Afghanistan, lying on the sofa.

'What did Ghaznavi's wife tell you, Olivia?'

She holds his gaze. 'Tell me what you know about Lalzad's link to terrorist activity and I'll give you what I know.'

He shakes his head. 'Who's Lalzad's right-hand man here?'

'I have a name.'

Casburn nods. Waits.

'But . . . ' she says.

'There's always a but with you, Olivia.'

'You want the name? You tell me what you know.'

'I don't play stupid games.'

'Fine.' Wolfe shrugs and picks up her backpack. 'I need you to leave, Dan. I'm heading for Antarctica tomorrow and I've things to do.'

Casburn doesn't budge. 'You're no longer working the story, Olivia.'

A flush of anger. Did Cohen tell him?

'For now,' Wolfe says. 'Look, Dan, if I can help you bring down a terror cell, I will. But I've done all the hard yards on this one, so give me something in return.'

'Depends what you've got.'

'A name and his intention to bomb London.'

Casburn doesn't seem surprised. Nooria was right. 'And in return?'

'When you find this man, I get an exclusive.'

'Is Nooria Zia your only informant?'

'No. I have another. Local. But I don't yet know if he's trustworthy.'

He chews his Nicorette for a long moment, staring at her white floorboards.

'I'll have to clear it with my superior. And I'll need your source.'

'You know me better than that.'

Wolfe is careful not to fiddle with the chunky ring she wears on the middle finger of her left hand, the three centimetre-long, oblong centrepiece resembling black onyx. Concealed beneath the gem is a USB stick holding the details of all her sources.

'I can get a warrant.'

'You won't find anything.'

There's a flash of anger in his eyes.

'Dan, it doesn't have to get nasty. We've worked together before. Make the call.'

'And there was me thinking our paths would never need to cross again. How wrong I was.' He pulls out his phone and dials.

She heads for the bedroom, dumping her pack on the duvet.

White, fitted, mirrored wardrobes run the length of one wall. She slides back a door and opens her jewellery box, then systematically opens and closes the drawers beneath, checking all her possessions are there. If she keeps moving, she won't betray how shaken she is: first Nooria's murder, now the threat on her door. Casburn's visit is the toxic icing on a bitter cake. He hasn't noticed her hands trembling. Her bravado is a mask.

At the hall cupboard now, she scoops up the mail Daisy collected for her while she was away. She shuffles the letters like cards, searching for anything linked to the threat.

Casburn stops talking into his mobile. Silence. Then he is behind her. Close behind her.

'He's calling back.'

Casburn peers over her shoulder. His cheek is so close it almost touches hers. She smells the mintyness of his breath and feels its warmth on her cheek. He has deliberately invaded her personal space.

'He wants you to arrange a meet between me and your local informant.'

He places a hand on her shoulder and breathes on her neck. He is trying to control her. His touch is light, but she flinches and immediately regrets it. He will think her frightened. Instinctively, she bends her arm and moves her elbow forward, ready to jab him in the ribs. But he knows her too well.

'Don't,' he says, grabbing her arm.

'The last time you met one of my sources, he disappeared.'

'He chose to disappear.'

Sources in law enforcement talk about his ruthless pursuit of a suspect with awe and a touch of fear. He's not a man to be crossed. Rumours abound, but nothing she can prove. He gets what he wants, no matter the means.

'Back off,' she demands.

He releases his grip, but leans closer, their bodies touching as if they were lovers.

'Who punched you?'

Casburn has changed tack. His voice is soft, as if he actually cares.

'Ahmad Ghaznavi. After murdering his wife, his men tried to rape me.'

It is little more than a whisper. The horror of it is still very real.

Wolfe leaves the letters in a neat pile on the shelf and places her hands there to steady herself. She suddenly feels exhausted. She sees Nooria Zia in her mind's eye, lying in a pool of blood, her miserable life ended violently at only sixteen.

'She died because of me.' Wolfe's voice cracks.

She struggles to control her gut-wrenching guilt. Casburn will see her moment of weakness. And once he knows she cares, he'll use it against her.

'It's not your fault.' She feels the scratch of his stubble against her ear. 'Make her death worth something,' he whispers. 'Give me the name.'

Her stomach churns. 'Not without a deal.'

Casburn's mobile rings and he backs away. She steps into the bathroom and locks the door, removes her ring and runs the cold tap, throwing water over her face with trembling hands, blinking hard to banish the image of Nooria's bloody face. She dries her face with a towel and takes some deep breaths. Their relationship is like two bordering countries with similar ideals, reliant on each other for their survival, but history has driven a deep wedge of distrust between them. Even when they have a common cause such as Lalzad, their differing approaches land them on opposing sides. Wolfe doesn't want to go to war with Casburn.

41

Placing the ring back on her finger, Wolfe leaves the bathroom and passes Casburn talking in hushed tones. She searches her desk for anything missing. Everything appears as she left it. Through the French doors, the lawn is a meadow of tall grasses, the patio overrun with weeds. Never mind, she tells herself. I'll deal with it in the spring. At the far end of the garden are four lime trees that have been a source of rows between her and her neighbour at the back. He wanted her to cut down the trees for no good reason and, when she'd refused, he'd tried to cut them down himself when she was at work. Daisy had phoned her. Not only did Wolfe have her neighbour arrested for trespassing, but she also wrote a piece for the *Wandsworth Guardian* with the headline, 'Secret Tree Mutilator'. Shortly afterwards, the man sold the house and moved away.

'Okay,' Casburn says, startling her, his call finished. 'You'll know whatever I'm at liberty to tell you, as long as it doesn't jeopardise our investigation.'

'Ah, weasel words. I'm guessing you won't be at liberty to tell me much at all.'

Casburn knows better than to answer. 'The name?'

'Kabir Khan. Afghani living here. She called him Da'ish. Plans to bomb London. That's all I know.'

She watches his face. Does he recognise this name? He blinks once. In all the time she has known him, she hasn't yet discovered his tell. No twitch, no tugging at an ear, no looking down or clenching his hand. She's often wondered what kind of man is hidden behind such a controlled exterior, a man so mission-focused that nothing else matters.

'Address?'

'I don't have it.'

'Your other informant?'

'Arrest me, Dan, or leave. I have work to do.'

DEVOUR

'I'll get it. One way or another.'

Wolfe ignores him.

'O'Leary still have your spare key?'

Wolfe's head jerks up. 'Yes. What of it?'

Casburn shakes his head. 'She's not reliable. Any one of her johns could've taken your keys and made copies. If that threat on your door is from Lalzad's men, you need to take your security seriously.'

'Daisy's okay.'

'I strongly urge you to get your locks changed and give your spare key to someone more responsible.'

'Don't judge Daisy by her job.'

He sighs. 'Lalzad has a bounty on you. Want my advice? Go to Antarctica and leave Lalzad to the professionals. You understand?'

'I'll do my job and you do yours.'

He stops chewing and looks as if he's going to argue. Instead, he heads down the hall. 'I'll see myself out.'

Wolfe turns her back to her desk and peers at the photos arranged on her wall. One is missing. Bottom row. She touches the vacant spot.

'No. It can't be.'

Casburn is back in the room. 'What?'

'The photo of Nooria Zia is gone. Of when she was in Kabul's women's jail.'

'So?'

'Someone's taken it.'

'Come off it, Olivia. Lalzad's thugs aren't interested in pictures.'

'You think I'm lying?' Wolfe is surprised at her sudden fury.

'I think you're jumping to conclusions.'

'Please go.'

She walks him to the door and opens it. She won't look him in the eye.

43

'Why is it so important to you?' he asks.

'It's like somebody is trying to obliterate her memory.'

8

Sweat pours down Wolfe's temples as she pounds the red punchbag at her local gym. Established in the late eighties in an old Balham warehouse, with industrial fans hung from steel crossbeams and frosted glass windows that do little to remove the pervasive smell of sweat, its equipment is basic, the changing rooms even more so. Wolfe wouldn't have it any other way. The 'fancy-pants brigade' in their state-of-the-art coordinated gym gear goes to a new club up the road offering TVs, hairdryers and skinny cappuccinos. All Wolfe wants to do is get in, do a workout and get out. Only two others are using the equipment, both regulars. With her back to the entrance, she senses a new arrival.

'What's got you so worked up?'

His distinctive voice is deep and hoarse, as if he is recovering from laryngitis. A reformed smoker, his twenty-a-day habit has probably done more to wreck his voice than the Under Twelve Boys' soccer team he used to coach, or all the suspects he'd yelled at over the years.

'Casburn,' she answers.

Wolfe grunts as she rips another punch to the bag. It swings and she grabs it, ready to give it another blow.

'I see,' he says, chuckling to himself as he takes long, steady strides in the direction of the bench press, a towel draped over his neck.

'What's so funny?'

'Some things never change,' he says, shaking his head. 'And if you're aiming at the kidneys, go higher.'

Wolfe pauses, panting, and stares at the retired detective chief superintendent of London's Homicide and Serious Crime Command. In his mid-fifties, Jerry Butcher has coarse, sandy, cropped hair, and a pale craggy face, as deeply etched as ancient sandstone.

'Didn't expect to see you at this time of day,' Butcher says, glancing at the wall clock. It's eleven thirty.

'Needed to let off steam.'

'Then why don't you spar with me?' he asks.

'Maybe. If you avoid my face.'

Butcher leads her to a corner where thick rubber flooring delineates the martial arts practice area. He has studied kali stick fighting in the Philippines and Brazilian jiu-jitsu, and developed his own self-defence system using everyday objects, teaching classes Wolfe attends when she's in town.

'I hear you defended yourself well in Kabul.'

'Not so well,' she replies, gesturing towards the painful bruise across her left cheekbone and eye. 'But it was two against one.'

Her feature in the *Post* doesn't mention the attack on her, but there's no need to ask how he knows about the assault – Butcher keeps in with his buddies at the Met and has a network of informants to rival hers.

He gives her a quizzical look.

'I haven't seen you this worked up in a while. What's going on?'

'Moz wants me off the Lalzad–Isil story.'

'Perhaps you've lost perspective?'

Wolfe blinks twice. Butcher has a way of making confront-ational remarks with such calm, his tone so reasonable, that it wrong-foots her every time.

'Possibly.'

'So what has Moz moved you on to?'

'Murder and espionage in Antarctica. It could be something big, or nothing at all. I leave in the morning. But I can't shirk the weird feeling Moz wants me out of Lalzad's reach.'

'Has it occurred to you he's sending you to Antarctica because you're the best person for the job? I don't see Moz as the motherly type.'

Wolfe laughs. 'Nor do I.'

'Come here a sec.'

He takes her in a hug. Wolfe tenses. If anyone other than Butcher had done this, she would have felled him. Instead, she relaxes in his embrace, listening to his steady heartbeat. Because that's what Jerry Butcher is: a rock. Calm, no matter the situation. One reason why he made chief super. Emotional involvement in a case never blinded him, never interfered with his judgement. Level-headed in a crisis. She closes her eyes. He doesn't talk or move. He doesn't care if others at the gym are watching, drawing the wrong conclusions. When she's ready, she pulls back a fraction and his arms fall away.

Opening a metal cupboard, Butcher hands her a fencing mask and some padded fingerless bag mitts, and takes some for himself. They put them on, then each takes a sixty-six centimetre bamboo cane, moves on to the rubber flooring and faces each other, sticks raised.

'Remember,' Butcher says, 'the stick is an extension of your hand. If you want it to strike me in a particular place, move your hand there.'

They nod at each other and begin.

Wolfe brings her cane down fast, but not quite Jackie Chan. Butcher blocks it with his stick. She tries a different angle but he knocks her arm away, then goes on the attack. Their movements are a blur, cane cracking against cane. When she goes for a low swipe, he grabs the tip of her stick with one hand and slams his cane down hard on her stick's mid-section with the other. Her grip loosens a fraction and Butcher rips it from her hand and throws it to the floor.

'Less anger, more focus.'

Undaunted, Wolfe uses the underside of her forearms to block his cane from connecting with her upper body, then aims a punch at his throat. Butcher smacks her fist away with his hand.

'Nice move,' Butcher encourages.

They spar for a few more seconds until Wolfe knocks Butcher's stick out of his hand. They now exchange punches, circling each other.

'Take a break,' Butcher says, and they stop.

From the metal cupboard, Butcher removes a fake plastic pistol, grips it in both hands, raises it so it points at her face, and walks up to her. Wolfe puts her hands up in surrender. When the gun is only a foot from her face, she uses her raised left hand to push the weapon diagonally across her body and downwards so it points to the floor. Then, with her right hand, she pretends to gouge Butcher's eyes with two fingers. Butcher feigns pain and is distracted while Wolfe uses her left hand to twist the pistol from his grip. Taking a couple of steps back, she aims the gun at Butcher.

'Great work,' Butcher says. 'Fancy lunch? It's been a while.'

Wolfe checks the time.

'Sure. Our favourite?'

Butcher takes a swig of Cobra beer, then stabs his fork into a dish of beef vindaloo, rolls the meat in some pilau rice and shoves it into his mouth. Wolfe takes a bite out of a dosa. This crepe-like dish has made the Bombay Palace on Tooting High Street a London landmark, despite the shabby décor. Wolfe is facing the restaurant's glass-fronted entrance. Condensation drips down the windows. Butcher sits opposite her, his back to the door. The narrow restaurant of orange walls and brown floor tiles is jam-packed with customers seated at cheap pine tables. A few rubber plants line one wall, determined to survive despite an absence of decent soil.

'So how are Chris and Alex?' Wolfe asks.

Her hair is still wet from her shower at the gym and drops fall on to the neckline of her hooded sweatshirt.

'Chris has a conditional job offer. One of the big banks. He hasn't done his final exams yet. But his tutors think he's heading for a first, so he should be fine.'

'And Alex? Still enjoying criminal law?'

'Seems to. He's got a new girlfriend. A solicitor. It must be serious because they're already talking about buying a flat.' He gazes over her shoulder at the slatted swing doors leading to the kitchen and shakes his head. 'He's only twenty-two and already has his life mapped out. When I was his age, I had no sodding idea what I wanted to do. I certainly wasn't thinking of getting a mortgage.'

'You sound disappointed?'

'No, no. Nothing like that.'

'So what's up?'

Butcher shifts on the hard wooden chair. 'We've been lucky, we know that. It's not easy having a dad in the police. I guess it's, you know, they never let their hair down. Never played truant. Never had wild parties. Sometimes I think they've missed out on life.'

'No disrespect, Jerry, but how do you know? I mean, how many parents actually know everything their kids get up to?

Come on! For all you know, Chris could be indulging in drunken orgies. Isn't that what they do at Oxford?'

Butcher smirks at the idea. 'Guess they get their sensible streak from their mother.'

'How is Emma?'

'Well, thanks.'

'So, been keeping yourself busy?'

She spoons some spinach and potato sag aloo on to her plate.

'Yeah, the odd bit of security consulting, you know.' Butcher drops his fork with a clink on the plate. 'I could be busier.'

'You mean they don't need you? Emma has her tennis and ladies' lunches, the boys have their own lives, and you don't have a murder squad to manage any more.'

Butcher smiles. 'Something like that. I'm used to being busy. I miss it.'

He helps himself to some of her dosa. She tries playfully slapping his hand away but he's too quick.

'Still think you're being watched?' Butcher asks.

Wolfe tells him about the missing picture and the threat, spray-painted on her door. Butcher puts down his knife and fork and gives her his undivided attention.

'Casburn reckons it's Lalzad trying to frighten me.'

'I hear Casburn's made DCI. Don't underestimate him, Liv, just because he was a soldier.'

'Oh believe me, I don't.'

'"YOU WILL PAY" could be Lalzad's thugs and the theft of Nooria Zia's photo is an obvious way to rattle you.' Butcher sucks in his lips, thinking. He leans back and crosses his arms. 'Let's recap. Six months ago you first thought you were being followed?'

'Yes, but I could never single anyone out. Just put it down to the jitters.'

'Then nothing until today?'

'Well, not quite.'

'Go on.'

'Shit, Jerry, this feels like I'm at the cop shop.'

He doesn't respond. She knows exactly what he's doing – waiting for her to fill the silence.

'About a week before I left for Kabul, I came home and there was an imprint on my duvet, as if somebody had lain there. I just thought I hadn't made the bed properly.' She shrugs. 'Then weird things happened to my computer diary. Meetings disappeared. Luckily I have a good memory, so I didn't miss much. And, before you say it, no, I didn't delete them by mistake.'

'Go on.'

'On the day of my flight, I realised one of my diamond stud earrings was missing. I turned the flat upside down. Couldn't find it. Because only one was missing, I thought I must've knocked it to the floor and vacuumed it up, so I emptied the vacuum and combed through the dust, but found nothing.'

'Who gave them to you?'

'Davy. When I was fourteen. On the day he left for the Army.'

'I see.'

'Those earrings mean a lot to me.'

'I know they do. We met not long after. Remember?'

How could she forget? Butcher led the raid on the shared house she lived in. She was hiding under the bed when he entered the room, his pace unhurried, his large-sized polished lace-ups suggesting he was a tall man. Downstairs, doors were being kicked in, people were screaming, glass exploding. 'It's all right, miss, you can come out now,' he'd said, his tone soft and reassuring. She'd frozen, so he'd kneeled on all fours. 'No need to be frightened. Give me your hand.'

Lost in the memory, Wolfe doesn't hear Butcher's question. He clicks his fingers to get her attention.

'I said, why didn't you tell me this before?'

His already lined brow is now etched with deep furrows.

'Because . . . oh, I don't know. I thought I must've dropped it.'

'Knowing how meticulous you are, I'd hazard a guess you haven't. A thief takes two earrings, not just one of a pair.' He pauses. 'When did you last change your locks?'

'I haven't. Casburn asked the same question.'

Butcher nods. 'Do it today before you leave and give me a key. I'll keep an eye on the place. And now you've got evidence, report the threat. Make it official.'

'Ah.'

'Ah, what?'

'I cleaned it off. Wanted it gone.'

'Did you take a photo?'

'Yes, and Casburn saw it too.'

'That's enough to work with. I'll come with you to Wandsworth nick.'

'I don't have time, Jerry. I've got a medical at two and I can't join the BAS team without passing it. And I've got to prepare for the trip.'

'BAS?'

'British Antarctic Survey.'

'How about I call a locksmith I know? He's actually an ex-con. Straight now. He owes me a favour.'

He pulls out his wallet and puts a twenty on the table. She adds two tens and a tip. They leave.

'Put a suspects' list together,' says Butcher.

Wolfe glances at him and collides with a man smoking just outside the door. She apologises, then bends to massage her knee.

'Still giving you trouble?' Butcher asks.

'Always will.' A torn meniscus injury that never fully healed.

As they walk down Tooting High Street, Wolfe considers her suspects' list.

'Apart from Lalzad and anyone who works for him, how about Judge Simms, or should I say, the retired Judge Simms? He'd gladly have me hung, drawn and quartered. Then there's former MP Simon Redmond – the paedophile who murdered a twelve-year-old boy at one of his sex parties. Oh, and any of the four soldiers found guilty of rape in Iraq. One of them threatened to cut my throat—'

'What about someone you come into contact with more regularly?'

'Nails would love to see me fail.'

'Who's Nails?'

'Eric Lowe. Works for the tabloid *UK Today*. We've been competitors for years and he's a nasty piece of work.'

'I know that name. Was he involved in the *News of the World* phone-hacking scandal?'

'Sure was. Got off, mind you.'

'Ever threatened you?'

'He's told me to fuck off and die a few times, but I don't think he actually meant die.'

'This may not be about revenge. What about someone you've rejected? Angry ex-boyfriend; someone who's asked you out and you've refused? One-night stands who wanted more?'

As they weave past people on the crowded pavement, they are forced to separate by a woman pushing a pram. When they come together again, she looks askance at him. 'Do you really want me to answer that?'

He turns his head to look at her. 'Of course.'

Wolfe focuses on the pavement ahead. It's like she's talking to her dad about her sex life. Feels wrong. 'I'll write them down but my boyfriends are few and far between. Anyway, I never bring them to my flat.'

'Doesn't matter, Liv. One of them could've followed you home.'

Wolfe frowns at him, uncomfortable with the thought. They are silent for a while.

'From what you've told me,' ruminates Butcher, 'he doesn't sound like a sexual predator. It's unlikely he'd take this long to attack you.'

'Jees, that's reassuring.'

'Who else has threatened you?'

Wolfe considers the question for a moment. 'Davy's wife? She swore she'd get her revenge.'

'Yup, I can see her doing it. But I'm not sure she's the subtle type. She's more likely to throw a brick through your window or try to run you over.'

'True.'

'Anyone else?' He scrutinises her face.

'Jerry, just go through my features. There's a long list.'

They turn right down Trinity Road, passing Tooting Bec Tube station on the corner.

'You're missing someone obvious.'

Wolfe chews at an already stunted fingernail. 'He's in prison.'

'Yup,' nods Butcher, 'but that doesn't mean he can't get to you.'

'I just don't think he'd do it.'

'Really? You helped put your brother away for seven years. Don't you think he's a little angry?'

9

Your pale body flashes by the camera like a ghost. Then you are gone. I lean back in my swivel chair, rest my socked feet on the desk and plough into a packet of ready salted crisps. I'm bathed in blue light from my monitor. The rest of the room has fallen away into blackness. Nevertheless, I sense Dr Sharma's report, calling me like a siren to doomed sailors. Each one of six photocopied pages is neatly Blu-Tack'd to the wall facing me, the paper barely visible as ghostly shapes hovering in the gloom. There's a copy in the bathroom. And my bedroom. Mustn't forget the kitchen either. And my underwear drawer. And taped above a shelf in the garden shed. The good doctor and I are locked in an embrace from which I can't escape. I resist the urge to switch on the light and read it again, my finger tracing each line, as I mouth the words. A partial truth. One day, I will discover what really happened.

Through the locked door I hear a burble of voices, a TV blaring, clanking pots in the kitchen, a creaking floorboard above. They know better than to disturb me. They've seen what happens. Boiling water poured over a hand sorts out these mis-understandings rather effectively, I find. An accident, of course, and I was so very sorry. But I don't want anyone poking around. This place is mine. It's the only thing that really is. Mind you, it's not that the fuckwits will ever get to read my diary. My iPad automatically locks after five minutes of inactivity and my fingerprint alone unlocks it. Only I have a key to my study, if you can call a room too small to fit a bed, which used to be full of junk, a study.

Bored, I divide my screen-viewing in two, and log into a hackers' chat room under the name H5N1. Invisible, always morphing, and, usually, deadly. Scanning the online conversations,

I'm not at all surprised to find Slave Trader – otherwise known as my computing and systems development tutor, Warren Butler – online, boasting he'll soon have a new 'slave' for sale. I can still smell his vinegary sweat and see his pudgy fingers on my keyboard. When he's at my house, we use my old laptop. I can't risk him using my iPad. The sneaky fat twat could install spyware in the blink of an eye. I'm pretty good at this stuff, but I'm still learning. And re-learning.

Warren has a weakness, or perhaps I should call it an obsession: he likes spying on attractive women, watching them inside their homes, ideally the bedroom, but that depends where the computer is located. One lunch break at college, I caught him doing it, and in return for my silence, he's teaching me all I need to know about cyber-stalking. It's slow going. But when I've finished with you, Olivia, Warren gets full viewing rights. Of course, he'll sell them. If only you knew the number of sad gits who'll be wanking off watching you from the comfort of their homes. I make a note to hack the voyeurs and anonymously email you some footage so you can see how thoroughly your privacy has been violated. But for now, you are my very own private Olivia Wolfe Show.

You are back on screen again, unaware of the Remote Access Trojan, or RAT, you unwittingly downloaded earlier today. That email wasn't really from Mozart Cohen. Lurking inside the attachment was a nifty little piece of code that gives me control over your computer, including your webcam. I read every email, see every website you visit, watch you write. I guess the end of your sentences. I'm usually correct. And now I can switch your webcam on and off whenever I choose and you have no way of knowing I've invaded your life, your home and your thoughts, because the malware has deactivated your webcam's green 'on' light.

Wearing a white, towelling bathrobe, you lean over your desk to adjust the position of your monitor, your face monstrously large, your eyelids – framed by thick dark eyelashes – heavy with tiredness, your black bob tucked behind your ears. Along your cheekbone, almost hidden by the purple bruise, is a semi-circular cut. Your smartphone rings. You answer. All I can see is your torso.

I catch my breath.

Your robe isn't tied and has fallen open. Warren boasts that some of his slaves use their computers in their underwear. Some webcams even face the bed. I have hit the jackpot. Your dark pubic hair is shaped like a postage stamp and the pearl on your bellybutton ring catches the light from your desk lamp. I reach out and touch the screen, brushing my fingers across your pert B-cup breasts, and trace small circles around your dark areolae, each marred by a sluttish silver ring.

You sit, pulling your robe around you so you're covered again, arguing with Cohen. I hear your side of the conversation only, but I get the gist of it: Cohen is furious about your deal with Casburn. He wants you to leave the Lalzad-Isil story alone. You stop speaking and stare, wide-eyed, at the phone. I'm guessing Cohen has slammed it down on you. You ring him back. Contrite. Apologise. Promise that while you're working the Antarctic story, you'll pass Casburn's intel on to Soames. But I can see your face. Moz can't. Nooria means too much to you; you're lying. Moz wishes you a safe trip. You sip at your green tea, deep in thought.

'Come on, Olivia, do something!'

As if you're responding to my command as effectively as your laptop does, you lean forward, touch typing fast, never glancing at the keyboard. It's as if you are looking straight at me, but your eyes move very slightly, following the words as they dance across the screen. My skin tingles.

Cohen has forwarded to you Professor Heatherton's emails, along with the CVs of his team; what the drilling project entails; and a detailed timeline of mishaps and death that have ground the project to a halt. You skim-read, devouring the data, and so do I, almost keeping up, missing the last phrase or two. You hone in on Vitaly Yushkov. No record of his birth, no school photos. He would have done conscription, but you cannot find anything to suggest he stayed in the military. His CV says he spent thirteen years as a ship's engineer but nothing about where he got his training. No social media or mainstream media or blogs about his defection. His life history has more holes than a sieve.

'Who censored you?' you ask aloud.

Your eyelids droop. A yawn. You swivel in your chair and stare at the wall behind you. Where Nooria's picture used to hang, there is now a bare white space amidst black square frames. I imagine you frowning; perhaps you feel some discomfort, like heartburn? You are plagued by her death, aren't you? How distressing to find her picture stolen. Closing down your computer, we part company for the night.

I look down into my bin. There Nooria lies, the glass shattered.

10

Wolfe has been cooped up with Trent Rundle in the tractor's cabin for four hours as they traverse the Ellsworth Mountains to reach the camp. She's sixteen thousand kilometres from London and feels she has truly reached the end of the Earth.

Rundle is the most junior member of Heatherton's team and, Wolfe suspects, the most garrulous. By now, she probably knows as much about the twenty–eight-year-old Rundle as his girlfriend, Miranda, twenty-six, who wants to get married and if he doesn't propose when he gets home, she'll probably dump him. Miranda won't move in with him until they're engaged, he says, rolling his eyes, so he still has Sunday lunch at his mum's house and she washes his dirty laundry. None of this helps Wolfe further her investigation. She steers the conversation to the hot water drilling, which has resumed, now the boiler is working at full capacity. As machinist and water probe design engineer on secondment from the National Oceanography Centre, Rundle is clearly proud of his contribution to Project Persephone.

'Aren't you needed at the drill site?'

'The probe isn't used until the drilling's over, and we estimate twenty-four hours before we reach the lake's surface. Besides, I know this route like the back of my hand, where all the crevasses are. Michael doesn't trust the old girl with anyone else.' Rundle pats the tractor's steering wheel, then gives Wolfe a cheeky grin. 'Or its precious cargo.'

But when she broaches the subject of Kevin Knox's death and rumours of sabotage, he goes very quiet.

'Poor sod,' is all Rundle will say.

Earlier, at Union Glacier, she'd watched Rundle and the pilot carry the dead man, shrouded in a white body bag, into the plane's cargo hold to be flown home to his grieving family in Lancashire.

Wolfe stares ahead through the tractor windscreen, which extends from the footwell up to the roof, the headlights illuminating the swirling ice particles that slam into the safety glass. Long windscreen wipers sweep them away and the heater inside the cabin helps to keep their view clear, even if it's like peering through fog. Out front, the huge curved blades of the snow-plough are raised. From front-on they remind Wolfe of a scorpion's pincers. The tractor crawls forward on caterpillar tracks, like a military tank, and the cabin vibrates as the engine roars, rattling her bones. Even so, she's managed to grab some much-needed sleep.

'Not long now,' Trent says, glancing her way. 'We're through the worst of it.'

'How many times have you done this?' she asks.

'Twelve, towing eighteen tonnes of equipment each time.'

Since landing on the ice runway at Union Glacier, vicious winds do their best to harry them and impede Wolfe from completing her interminable journey. She sits up straight and moves her stiff neck from side to side, and tries raising her arms above her head to stretch, but there isn't enough room.

'So tell me about hypothermia,' she says, having one last go at getting Rundle talking about a potential traitor. She knows about hypothermia's effects first hand, having suffered from a mild dose herself in the Safed Koh mountains of Afghanistan.

There is reluctance in Rundle's mahogany brown eyes, the same colour as his wavy hair and beard.

'I'm not a doctor, Olivia.'

'Oh, come on, Trent. Help me out here. I know jack-shit about this stuff.' Pleading ignorance often encourages people to talk.

He nods, then gives her the kind of boyish grin that would melt hearts.

'You're a whole lot more interesting than Charles Harvey, and a whole lot prettier. It's nice to have some female company for a change.' His cheeks flush red. 'Apart from Stacy, of course. But she's one of the lads.'

He is referring to the only woman on the ten-person team: Dr Stacy Price. Rundle gives Wolfe a cheeky grin. He's good looking and uses it to cover his gaffes.

'So tell me why you think Kevin threw his coat and boots away.'

He shrugs once. 'I dunno. They say when hypothermia is really bad, you feel like you're overheating.'

'Did you find them? His coat, boots and gloves, I mean?'

'Nah, never did. But his gear would've been buried in the storm.'

'How did he manage to get half a mile from camp?'

'No idea.'

Wolfe scratches her head. 'Did he use the snowmobile?'

'Nah, we checked.'

'Who noticed him missing?'

'Vitaly. I'm told he was talking to Michael, so he didn't get to the boiler for about five minutes. When he got there – no Kev. He searched the obvious places, then sounded the alarm.'

'And how long was Vitaly out searching, before he reported Kev missing?'

Rundle glances at her. 'You sound like Agatha Christie or something.' She smiles and waits. 'Jesus, you've got amazing eyes.'

Wolfe ignores his deflection from the topic. 'So was Vitaly gone long?'

'Dunno. I was in the workshop. Knew nothing until Toby came to get me.'

'Dr Toby Sinclair, the environmental microbiologist?'

'Yup, that's him. You've done your homework.' He nods at the windscreen. 'Weather's clearing. Knew it would once we got into the valley.'

Even though the tractor still grunts and grinds, it's quieter outside. The wind has slowed and visibility has improved. Wolfe stares ahead at what looks like a sea of frozen waves.

'What causes that rippling effect?'

'Sastrugi,' Rundle says. 'It's the wind that does it. Beneath the ice is a long and narrow lake, approximately twenty-nine square kilometres. About the size of Lake Windermere.'

Wolfe can't help looking down at the tractor floor, imagining the subglacial lake beneath them. 'How thick's the ice?'

'We think three kilometres. But I guess we're about to find out.'

'Thick enough to support this, then.' She sounds relieved.

'Thick enough to make drilling, without using antifreeze, about as difficult as it's possible to get. As fast as we drill, the bore hole freezes up, unless we keep shooting boiling water down it.'

'Is that what happened at Vostok?'

'Yup, Trankov's team used antifreeze to keep the hole open and then the kerosene drilling fluid leaked into the lake. They're out to win at any cost, but it backfired on them, didn't it?'

'They contaminated their samples?'

'Sure did.'

'And you think Lake Ellsworth is liquid?'

'Yes, warmed by geothermal heat from the Earth's interior.'

Ahead is nothing but windswept waves of ice. No colour. No penguins or birds in the sky. No life. It's as if even Mother Nature has abandoned such an inhospitable place. The jagged white peaks of the semi-circular Ellsworth Mountains curve around the ice-covered valley. The sky above them is a soft pink and the mountains cast sharp shadows. She has no idea what time it is at Camp Ellsworth, just that it's evening. Rundle has warned her about the permanent daylight of summer in Antarctica and how difficult it can be to sleep. Wolfe leans forward. In the distance she thinks she sees red pyramids and some dark rectangular shapes protruding out of the whiteness, and something colourful, raised high and flapping in the wind.

'Over there. Is that the site?'

'Sure is.'

Soon Wolfe sees a huge Union Jack. It seems to dwarf everything else beneath it, as if the flag somehow protects the people below. As they approach the camp, Wolfe makes out red marker flags and several dark blue boxes she guesses are the converted shipping containers. Rundle explains that one is a laboratory, another is the drilling operations centre and communications room, and the last container stores vehicles and equipment. At the centre of the camp is a long red tent known as a Weatherhaven, shaped like a cylinder cut in half, which faces two rows of red pyramid tents – the sleeping quarters – and, behind them, three large circular pools of steaming water, contained by what look like yellow, oversized children's paddling pools. The onion tanks.

Rundle blows the tractor horn. Three orange figures are huddled around a small crane and what looks like a six-foot-high yellow cotton reel lying on its side. They wave in response.

'What's that yellow spool?'

'The hose. Kevlar reinforced. Three point four kilometres of it, so we should have enough.' He grins. 'See the crane? It keeps the hose centred above the bore hole and feeds it down.'

He cuts the engine near one of the container sheds.

'Time to see history being made,' Rundle says, clearly happy to be back in the action. He pulls on his black windproof parka and woollen hat, then pauses.

'Don't be surprised if they ask about your face.' His gaze moves to her now purple and yellow-green bruise. 'See you later.'

Wolfe watches him jump down from the cabin and race off. Grabbing her backpack from the seat next to her, she opens the door and jumps, landing with a crunch on the ice. It's a relatively mild minus twenty-two degrees Celsius. She's wearing one of the Lake Ellsworth branded parkas. It's a man's small size, which is big for her, but she has a fleece and thermal vest underneath. She looks around and sees the three men handling the hose are wearing orange coveralls and hard hats over black beanies. The noise from the crane supporting the giant hose jars like a digger scraping the asphalt off a road. Someone steps out of the middle shipping container, then strides in her direction.

'Olivia! Welcome to our humble camp. Michael Heatherton.'

Neat and clean-shaven, he gives the impression he has every-thing under control, except for his mop of grey wiry hair that springs out from beneath his beanie, threatening to dislodge it. He is about to extend his hand when he notices her bruise.

'Got punched in Afghanistan. Guess he didn't like my story,' she jokes.

Heatherton's eyes open wide. He recovers himself and offers his hand. His grip is strong, as if he is trying to assert his dominance.

'Perfect timing,' he says, beaming at her. 'We're still drilling. Come with me.'

A tall man in a yellow and black woolly hat, bushy beard and a creased face like a Shar Pei bursts into their conversation.

'Professor Gary Matthews, aquatic biogeochemist,' he says breathily, as if he's been running. They shake hands.

'Cambridge United?' she says, nodding at his hat.

'Well spotted,' Matthews says, beaming. 'So you're from the *Post*? Read your articles. Very thought-provoking they are, too. Never imagined I'd find you in Antarctica, though. No tanks, no Taliban, no political coups—'

'Yes, yes, Gary, another time perhaps?' Heatherton interrupts. 'This way.'

Wolfe has to jog to keep up with Heatherton as he charges across the expanse of slick ice.

He leans close and drops his voice. 'Told everyone your science correspondent couldn't make it, so you volunteered. You've always wanted to see Antarctica. A bit lame, but it's all I could think of.'

'I can work with that.'

'We have two teams,' says Heatherton, talking fast. 'One, at the drill site, is led by George Beer, with Ed Ironside, plant engineer. Bruce Adeyemi stepped in while Trent was gone.'

'Adeyemi is your electronics and software engineer, right?'
'Correct.'

They approach the container Heatherton left earlier.

'Vitaly moves between the two teams, but right now we need him driving the drill, so he's with me at the control centre. He manipulates the speed and direction of the drill through a joystick and by observing sensor readings on a computer.'

Trying to keep pace with Heatherton, Wolfe stumbles and almost slips over. She steadies herself.

'Put that out, for God's sake!' Heatherton snaps.

Wolfe looks up to see a tall man with a wrestler's neck and muscular torso, leaning against the container in grease-stained orange overalls. Dangling from the corner of his chapped lips is a cigarette. He gives Heatherton the kind of stare she's seen Taliban prisoners give their American captors.

'Boss, there is nothing flammable here.' His Russian accent is pronounced. Vitaly Yushkov.

Matthews flicks a worried look at Heatherton.

'And the fuel bladders?' says Heatherton, nodding towards grey rectangles the size and shape of waterbeds, some hundred metres away. 'Now put it out.'

The Russian's sapphire blue eyes languidly move from Heatherton's face to the fuel containers. Wolfe is near enough to smell the bitter, raw smoke, and guesses the brand he's smoking: Belomorkanal. No filter, cheap, and a favourite of soldiers in the Russian Army. The brand was introduced to commemorate the construction of the White Sea – Baltic Canal, known as the Belomorkanal. She knows their distinctive aroma well from her time reporting on the Russian annexation of the Crimea.

Yushkov slowly takes the cigarette from his mouth and pinches the burning end between his fingers. His hands are huge, like baseball gloves, and given his muscular arms, she suspects are very powerful. The cigarette is only half smoked so he pulls a packet from his overall breast pocket, opens it, places the remainder of the cigarette inside, and shoves it back in the pocket. It's only then that Wolfe notices everyone is watching him.

11

The drill has been going non-stop for twenty-two hours as jets of scalding hot water force a twenty-inch-diameter circular hole deeper and deeper into the ice sheet. Wolfe has been seated on a plastic chair at the back of the operations room for four hours. Rather than bored, she is fascinated by their Herculean efforts and finds their excitement contagious. She has stretched her legs outside once, observing Yushkov having a brief smoke, despite Heatherton's scowls. Yushkov's closely cropped fair hair and stubble of a beard suggest he normally keeps both shaved. Perhaps a habit he picked up in the Russian Army, along with a taste for Belomorkanal cigarettes?

Nobody has slept. Empty coffee mugs litter surfaces. The stale air is ripe with sweat.

'Final approach,' Yushkov says to Beer through two-way radio. 'I'm slowing it right down. I don't want to blast our way in.'

In front of the seated Yushkov is a computer screen and his hand rests on a joystick. His concentration is intense. Because of the harsh conditions in the bore hole, there is no camera on the drill itself. Yushkov must infer what is happening almost three thousand metres below, using telemetry. One sensor counts the revolutions on the spool reeling out the drill hose; another measures the weight of the dangling hose, with minute changes indicating the resistance from obstructions; a third monitors pressure to detect if the water level in the hole rises or falls – evidence that the lake has been reached.

'Copy that,' says Beer, from the bore hole site. He sounds tired. In the background, the generators thrum.

Seated next to Yushkov is thirty-three-year-old Dr Toby Sinclair, who, next to the large-framed engineer, looks like a boy. Sinclair is little over five foot four. According to her notes, he was a child prodigy, and is considered a genius in the field of environmental microbiology, probably the most brilliant mind in the camp. Sinclair has barely said a word to her or anyone since her arrival. His warm, clammy handshake and his avoidance of eye contact tell her he's not good at social inter-action. His cheeks are a web of broken blood vessels, his mouse-brown hair looks as if it hasn't been brushed for a while, and his beard is long and unkempt. He is clearly not bothered about his appearance.

'Stop!' says Yushkov, peering at the depth reading. 'We should have reached water. Pull up the nozzle, slowly. Then get the camera down there.'

'Copy that.'

'Shutting down is a race against time,' Heatherton says for her benefit, as well as Harvey, who sits next to her. 'It can cause clots of ice to form in the hose, which blocks the power of the water jet. It's the mechanical equivalent of a blocked coronary artery.'

Harvey is as thin as a whippet and wears thick glasses which, needless to say, are not very practical in a freezing environment. He stops tapping away at his laptop keyboard.

'So we could see the lake any minute?' Harvey asks.

Heatherton nods.

Even from inside the metal container, Wolfe hears the crane outside grinding as the hose is dragged out of the hole, and wound back around the giant spool.

Dr Stacy Price, the senior sediment scientist, paces the room, flicking her thick bunch of wavy auburn hair on each turn, much like a beaver's tail slapping water. Her weather-beaten face and leathery neck adds at least ten years to her thirty-five.

'Hurry up,' she mutters.

As soon as the hose is out of the hole, Yushkov remote-controls a camera as it snakes down the white narrow tunnel of ice, illuminated by a single light. Apart from the hum of the machinery and the growling of the generator, it is as if everyone is holding their breath.

'Almost there,' says Yushkov.

'Mike,' calls Beer through the radio. 'Get a move on. The diameter of the hole is shrinking already.'

'Look!' says Yushkov, drawing everyone's attention to the monitor.

'I don't believe it!' says Heatherton.

It's clear from the camera feed that it lies on a floor of white. Of ice. The hole has dead-ended and it hasn't reached the water yet.

Sinclair tugs at his straggly beard and mumbles, 'The lake's got to be deeper than we think.'

'Has to be,' agrees Matthews.

Yushkov shakes his head. 'I think the sensor data is incorrect.'

Heatherton voices Yushkov's concern through his two-way radio to Adeyemi, who's helping manhandle the hose outside.

'No way,' says Adeyemi. 'I calibrated them myself.' There's a hint of a Nigerian accent.

Yushkov points at the screen, his gravelly voice raised, a touch of irritation. 'Bruce, I do not see water. I see ice. I think you must look at the sensors on the drill hose. We have not drilled deep enough. I go for a smoke. Then I will take a look at the drill hose with you.'

'Not again,' moans Heatherton.

'Give him a break,' says Matthews into Heatherton's ear. 'The poor man's been driving that drill for almost twenty-three hours.'

Heatherton ignores the remark. 'Bruce?' he calls through the radio. 'Double-check the sensors, will you?'

'Okay, boss,' he replies, sighing.

Nine minutes later, Adeyemi enters the control room, followed by Yushkov.

'My mistake,' says Adeyemi, shaking his head. 'A sensor wasn't calibrated properly and has overestimated the length of hose fed into the hole. We're at least thirty metres short of the lake. We need to keep going.'

Minutes trickle past as the drill is lowered down the bore hole once again, driving deeper and deeper into the seemingly never-ending ice sheet.

'Cable just went slack!' yells Beer into his radio.

'Stop drilling!' shouts Heatherton.

Wolfe's heart has sped up. Everyone crowds around Yushkov to get a closer look at the monitor. She watches the camera as it's lowered through the circular tunnel of white.

'Twenty-five metres,' Yushkov counts down.

'Twenty metres.'

'Fifteen . . .'

' . . . ten . . . five.'

The image on the monitor darkens to a murky brown.

'What's that?' says Matthews, pointing.

The picture blurs as the camera shakes.

'Keep the camera still,' says Heatherton.

'We must wait for it to stop swinging,' Yushkov says.

The fuzziness clears. The camera's light pierces the blackness to reveal murky water, the colour of black tea.

'My God!' exhales Sinclair.

'Is that what I think it is?' says Price.

'Keep going,' says Heatherton, wiping sweat from his forehead with his sleeve. 'But very slowly.'

In the narrow cone of light they see tiny particles, stirred up by the camera, like loose tea leaves swirling around. Suddenly, the camera shakes violently, and everything goes black. There's a collective sharp intake of breath.

'What just happened?' asks Price, her voice tight with panic.

'Vitaly?' asks Heatherton.

Before Yushkov can do anything, the camera jolts back into life. It lies on its side, the lens gazing across a muddy floor, strewn with tiny bits of rock.

Silence. Wolfe looks to Heatherton, desperate for confirmation.

'My God! We've done it,' he breathes, white-faced with shock. Then he remembers the men outside and uses the radio. 'Lock everything down, guys, and come and take a look. We've breached Lake Ellsworth! We've found it!'

Both teams erupt into loud cheers and whoops of joy. The control room crew is high-fiving, hugging and laughing. Matthews slaps Yushkov on the back.

'Well done, mate. Top work.'

A snow-covered Rundle bursts through the door first and launches himself at Yushkov, almost toppling him from his chair. Beer, his blond beard caked in ice, drags down his fur-lined hood and shakes the snow off his back like a bear just out of hibernation. Matthews steps aside so Beer can get near to the monitor.

'Thank Christ!' Beer says, leaning on the console, clearly exhausted. He wipes his face roughly with his gloved hands. There are tears in his eyes. 'We finally found you.' He taps the screen. 'You little beauty!'

Wolfe finds herself laughing, enjoying their moment of victory.

'We're making history,' says Price, mesmerised by the camera feed. 'It's liquid. It really is liquid.'

Ironside, whose facial features remind her of Bill Clinton when he left the White House – relaxed affable smile, short grey hair, bulbous nose – whistles through his teeth. 'Lucky we had that extra bit of hose. We were this close to falling short.' He holds his hands shoulder width apart.

'And I was that close to freezing my bollocks off!' Blond-haired Beer laughs heartily, head thrown back.

'Okay, everyone,' calls Heatherton, clapping his hands together, trying to get attention above the chatter. Harvey is recording his speech on a tripod-mounted video camera. 'This is a momentous achievement. We have reached Lake Ellsworth! We are the first people to lay eyes on it.' Cheers erupt. 'We have a lot still to discover, but we know one thing for sure; it's liquid, which means—'

Price yells out, 'There could be life!' and punches the air.

Heatherton momentarily loses his smile at the interruption, but regains it quickly, looking straight at Harvey's video recorder. 'Congratulations to all of you here and everyone at British Antarctic Survey who have worked tirelessly to make this dream a reality. I'm very proud of all of you.'

Wolfe snaps a few photos, but through her camera lens she's zooming in on the faces of his team, watching their reactions. If Heatherton is right about sabotage, then someone in this freezing-cold shipping container has failed in their mission. Someone should look disappointed, or at least worried. Harvey nods incessantly, like one of those nodding toy dogs you see on car dashboards, leaving the video camera to run on its tripod as he shakes everyone's hands. Beer can't stop grinning, hugging anyone he can grab. Price fidgets, eager to get moving on the sediment collection. She starts wriggling into a white Tyvek all-in-one protective suit. Sinclair's eyes are glued to the screen, his mouth slightly open, gawping, in a world of his own. Matthews slaps Ironside on the back, who then gives Matthews a jovial shove, laughing like kids in the playground. Adeyemi laughs, as if at some private joke. Rundle mumbles 'Fuck me!' several times, as if he can't believe his own eyes. Yushkov has swivelled round to face Heatherton, so has his back to the monitor. His arms are folded, his expression like a poker player's, giving nothing away. But Wolfe thinks she detects a hint of amusement in the slight upturn of his lips and the outer edges of his eyes.

Wolfe tunes back in to Heatherton's speech.' . . . But we must keep going. The bore hole is already refreezing and will reduce its diameter by point six centimetres each hour, so we need to get the water-sampling probe down there right now. We aim to capture fifty millilitre samples from various depths in the lake. Then we'll send down the corer to recover sediment from the lake floor. I know everyone's tired and cold, but in a few more hours we'll have the samples and know if we have found ancient life forms or not.' Heatherton receives supportive nods. 'Gary is in charge of the probe, Stacy leads on the corer. Any questions? No? Okay, let's go to it.'

Matthews and Sinclair hurry to join Price, changing into Tyvek suits with hoods, sterile latex gloves and face masks, worn to minimise the possibility they will contaminate the samples with dust, skin, hair and even germs.

The team disperses, as they prepare for stage two. Initially, Wolfe joins Matthews and Rundle at the bore hole as they guide the water sampling probe into the hole in the ice. It looks like a steel bicycle pump with a glass cylinder. Then she goes back to the control centre to watch through the camera-feed the delicate process of taking a fifty-millilitre sample at the lake's surface, using computer controls. The surface sample appears grainy but a lighter colour than the opaque water near the lake's floor. The very first sample rises through the ice tunnel. Wolfe has butterflies in her stomach.

'Steady,' says Heatherton to Matthews, also in a Tyvek body suit. 'I'm going outside,' Heatherton adds, pulling up the hood. 'I want to see it come to the surface. Charles, will you film this?'

Harvey follows Heatherton out of the control room, as does Wolfe. Adeyemi is at the control console. There is no sign of Yushkov. She asks Adeyemi where Yushkov has gone.

'Probably getting something to eat,' he replies, uninterested.

Wolfe joins the small crowd at the drill site and watches the bottle rise into view, the liquid a weak transparent brown. If they had been watching the dead rise from their graves, they couldn't have been more transfixed.

'This water hasn't seen daylight for millions of years,' says Heatherton as the bottle hangs suspended a metre off the ice surface.

Matthews, face and hands covered, carefully removes the bottle from the probe. Sinclair leans in, legs bent, as if ready to catch it should it fall. Matthews carries it to the laboratory in a sterile protective pouch, a silent following close behind.

'We'll take a quick look at this one, then get on with collecting others,' Heatherton explains.

They enter a second shipping container decked out like a biohazard laboratory. Nobody can enter without protective booties or face masks. At least this space is heated. Under the bright strip lighting the lake water looks a very pale honey colour. It is decanted into a clear test tube, then placed in a brace, and Matthews dips a salinity meter into the water.

'Fresh water.'

Next he uses an electrode. A number flashes on an LCD.

'It conducts electricity strongly, evidence this sample is laden with mineral salts that could serve as food for microbes.'

Matthews uses a pipette to deposit a water drop on a slide, which he places under a microscope. He zooms in. Despite the cold, sweat trickles down his temples and he has to ask Price to wipe it away.

'What the hell?' says Matthews, readjusting the microscope.

'What do you see?' asks the normally taciturn Sinclair.

'Take a look.'

Sinclair peers through the microscope and gasps, pulling his head back suddenly, as if he's been stung. 'Good God!'

The suspense is too much for Heatherton. Sinclair steps aside. Heatherton takes one long look, then jolts his head up.

'Never seen anything like it.'

'What's wrong?' asks Wolfe.

'Nothing. Nothing at all.'

'Well, what do you see?' she persists.

'It's teeming with life.'

12

Inside the lab it is quiet but, when the door is opened, bursts of laughter from the rowdy celebrations in the mess tent reach Stacy Price and Toby Sinclair, who are still working in their protective gear. Even though their rudimentary analysis of the lake's samples is complete, neither can tear their eyes away from the microscopes. The lab is basic – microscopes, autoclaves, computers, Petri dishes. The focus is on preventing contamination of the samples, rather than protecting the scientists from contamination, which Wolfe finds unnerving, given they are handling a life form never before seen. Having been to a Biosafety Level 4 research facility when she was reporting on a new, deadly strain of avian flu, the Tyvek suits and masks don't seem adequate protection. Wolfe tries asking Sinclair a question, but he either doesn't hear or will not be distracted. She tries the sediment scientist instead.

'Dr Price?'

'Call me Stacy.'

'Stacy, I'm still not clear what you've discovered. Michael's talked about micro-organisms and how "alien" they are, but in what way are they alien?'

Price swivels on her stool to face Wolfe.

'This lab is pretty basic, as you can see. The real work starts when the samples reach Cambridge. But I'm in no doubt we've discovered a new species of bacteria. Given it's survived for thousands, if not millions of years, cut off from the rest of the biosphere and in total darkness, it's not surprising it's unlike anything we've seen before.'

Professor Matthews walks in.

'All water and sediment samples are safely stored. I'm off to join the others. Coming?'

'Later,' says Price.

'Come on, Stacy. Enjoy the moment,' Matthews urges. 'You too, Toby.'

Both shake their heads.

'What about you, Olivia? Dinner's almost ready.'

It's three in the morning, but Wolfe is hungry. She promises to join him shortly and Matthews leaves.

'Why are the samples in cylinders in an ice cave?' Wolfe asks. 'Are you worried they're hazardous?'

'Not at all. Here, let me show you.'

Sinclair momentarily looks up from the microscope and gives Price a hard stare. She is so focused on the grey cylinder she's holding up, she doesn't notice. The cylinder looks similar to a small diver's air tank, but no larger than a thermos flask.

'The subglacial lake's under a lot of pressure from heavy ice above,' Price says. 'So we have to maintain that same pressure at the surface, otherwise the organisms will get the bends, like divers. Such a sudden change in pressure will kill them. So these titanium cylinders were designed just for this expedition – to keep the microbes in the dark and at the right pressure.'

'But why in an ice cave?' Wolfe persists.

'Best way to keep them at a temperature they're used to.'

But not very secure. Wolfe doesn't know how much, if anything, Heatherton has conveyed to his team about his sabotage theory.

'They're precious, one of a kind. What's to stop someone tampering with them?'

'I see,' says Price, nodding. 'Michael's spoken to you about that then.' She looks down at the floor for a moment, considering her words. 'The two chests are padlocked and weigh a tonne. They're going nowhere.' She pauses. 'I think his concerns are unfounded.'

'The cylinders travel to the UK in these locked chests?'

'Yup. They'll be flown at low altitude to Rothera, then get loaded on to our research vessel, the *James Clark Ross*, and kept inside a hypobaric chamber.'

Wolfe nods, then peers over Sinclair's shoulder.

'So if all the samples are locked away, what is Toby looking at?'

'At lake water left behind in the probe. The leftovers.'

'Can I take a look?'

'Sure,' says Price, and then lays a hand gently on Sinclair's arm. He jumps and looks up. 'Huh?' he says, pulling down his mask.

'Olivia wants to take a look. Can you move away for just a moment, Toby?' She coaxes him as if she's talking a child out of a sweet shop.

'Oh, of course. Didn't see . . .'

Wolfe watches his lips. Sinclair barely parts them when he

speaks so he's hard to hear. She knows he's from Edinburgh originally, but his accent is swallowed up by his straggly beard.

Sinclair gets up and moves aside. He appears tubby, mainly because his short limbs make his torso seem out of proportion.

'Mask and goggles first, though,' Price says, handing them to her. Wolfe sits on the stool and peers down the microscope. She instantly pulls back.

'They're darting about so fast. Like they're angry or something. Is that normal?'

Sinclair and Price exchange glances.

'Nothing about it is normal,' Price says. 'That's what's so exciting.'

Wolfe looks through the microscope again.

'Shouldn't they be dying, given their exposure to surface pressure?'

'Yes!' says Sinclair, enthusiastically. 'But, instead of slowing, they're speeding up. Incredible, isn't it?'

Price glares at him and he blushes.

'So it's never had contact with mankind?' Wolfe asks.

'That's right,' says Sinclair. 'We believe the valley froze over two million years ago.'

'So we have no immunity because our ancestors have never had any contact with it?'

Without realising it, Wolfe has pulled further back from the Petri dish.

'I can't see how a microbe that existed before we did will know how to attack our system, so I doubt there's any threat,' says Price. 'And anyway, we're taking all the right precautions.'

'Don't worry, Olivia, I've dealt with extremophiles many times,' says Sinclair.

'Extremophiles?'

'Microbes that survive extreme conditions. I've worked with

bacteria that live inside a volcano, or can survive without oxygen, or endure unbelievable water pressure. Did you know bacteria are eating away the *Titanic*? And with all these extremophiles, I've never had a containment issue.'

'Do you have a name for our particular extremophile?'

'Just a code at the moment: LE31S.'

The mess tent is buzzing with banter and the clatter of spoons on plates as the hungry crew chows down on beef casserole, followed by cans of beer. Price is the only one absent: she's eating her meal in the lab. The long Weatherhaven has a basic kitchen set up near the door with butane-powered stoves; three white trestle tables and folding plastic chairs in the centre of the space; and at the far end is a freestanding whiteboard with scribblings on it. Beyond the whiteboard, a rope has been strung up between either side of the tent's frame, from which is hung an open sleeping bag to provide some, albeit limited, privacy. This is Wolfe's sleeping quarters. There are no spare pyramid tents and Dr Price refused to share, claiming she needed her privacy. Wolfe doesn't take it personally, appreciating the pressure the scientist is under. She's slept in far worse places; with a butyl rubber ground sheet, inflatable airbed, and beneath her down-filled sleeping bag, a sheepskin; she'll be snug. However, with the celebrations in full swing, she doubts she, or anyone else, will get any sleep.

Wolfe is next to Heatherton at the top table. Opposite her sits Beer, who raises his beer can.

'We haven't been properly introduced. George Beer, programme manager and engineer. And before you start with the jokes,' he says with a wide grin, 'I've heard them all.' He looks around the table. 'A toast. To new life!'

Wolfe and Heatherton join in. Beer drinks half the tin. His fair features look Scandinavian, but his accent is Cornish. He has deep laughter lines and Wolfe likes him instantly. Harvey, also seated at their table, is still finishing his meal. The steam from the stew fogs up his glasses, so he removes them and wipes them with a lint cloth.

'I've got great footage,' Harvey says. 'It's being aired as we speak. Not often we discover new life on our planet.' He looks at Wolfe and grins. 'Not often a science story gets priority.'

'That's great, Charles,' she says.

'What about the *Post*? Will Cohen bury the story at the back, as he usually does with science copy?'

'We'll see,' she replies.

Harvey has no idea what her angle is, and she wants to keep it that way. Thankfully, Matthews distracts Harvey. He sits at the farthest table with Yushkov and Sinclair, facing her. Matthews screws up his jowly face and lets rip with an almighty beery belch. He receives appreciative applause from Rundle and Adeyemi.

'I'm getting another drink,' Wolfe says. An excuse to move groups.

She grabs another beer from a bucket on the floor, then sits opposite Yushkov. Three crushed beer cans are on the table in front of him.

'I wanted to say congratulations, Vitaly, and properly introduce myself. I'm Olivia Wolfe from the *Post*.'

She offers her right hand across the table to the Russian, who pauses mid-swig, then swallows, his blue eyes twinkling with amusement. He breaks into a big smile.

'You sure you want to shake my hand?'

Yushkov holds them palms-up for her to see. They are filthy, but even under the grease stains, the second and third fingers of his right hand are stained yellow from nicotine.

She keeps her arm outstretched. He takes it and her hand is engulfed in his, but his shake is surprisingly gentle.

'A man do this to you?' he asks, nodding at her bruised face.

'Yes, in Afghanistan. He ended up with a broken nose, and his balls so battered he won't be fathering any children.'

Vitaly guffaws. Loud, head thrown back, like the bark of a fur seal. Other conversations pause, as they wonder what has set Yushkov off. 'This is very good!' As his laughter dies away, his features harden. 'I not like men who beat women.'

'I hear you're the man to cadge cigarettes off,' she says, marvelling at the man's perfect white teeth, which, unlike his fingers, are stain-free.

'I not think you like my cigarettes. They are very strong.'

'Belomorkanal? I've smoked them before. I was foreign correspondent during Russia's invasion of the Crimean peninsula in 2014. I've shared a few smokes with your soldiers.'

He nods, as if she has gone up a notch in his approval rating. Then he looks serious. 'I am not Russian any more. I am British citizen.' His eyes scan the room. 'I want to be clear.'

Yushkov gets up suddenly. 'We need vodka,' he announces, and leaves the mess tent.

'Good idea,' says Matthews, slurring his words, eyes closing.

Rundle bounces over, like a gangly excited puppy, followed by Adeyemi. 'Did someone say vodka?'

Sinclair stiffens and stares into his can of beer, clutching it with both hands.

'Vitaly's gone to get some,' Wolfe replies.

Rundle grabs a chair next to her. Adeyemi sits opposite, but doesn't take the chair Yushkov has just vacated. She's had very little contact with the Nigerian-born engineer, but knows he was going to study medicine, then switched to engineering. He produces a pack of cards.

'Poker, anyone?' he asks.

'What do you play for?' she asks, assuming that money isn't easy to access in Antarctica.

He grins. 'Not biscuits or toothpicks, if that's what you're thinking. The real thing. I keep tabs.'

Nobody's interested so the cards go back in his pocket.

'Can you believe it?' he adds. 'We've discovered aliens!'

Sinclair speaks but doesn't look up. 'It's momentous. Not just what we've discovered here. It also means there could be life on other planets.'

'Who gives a shit about other planets?' shouts Rundle. 'I'm talking about what we did today. And we were first. Like being the first man on the moon,' he adds, stabbing his finger on the table.

Sinclair clams up, clearly intimidated.

'Tell me more,' Wolfe encourages.

Sinclair shakes his head.

'Really,' she says. 'I'd like to know.'

'Take Europa, one of the moons of Jupiter.' His voice is faltering and, given the noise in the tent, she has to lean close to hear him. 'It has an icy crust with a liquid ocean underneath, so you can see the parallels to Lake Ellsworth. Some astrobiologists think that life might be able to survive there. Our discovery today makes this hypothesis more likely.'

Sinclair pauses, eyes lowered, undoubtedly expecting Rundle to lay into him.

'Bugger me! That's amazing!' says Rundle, slapping Sinclair on the back.

Yushkov returns, clutching a vodka bottle.

'Vitaly! Over here!' Rundle yells.

'Get some mugs,' Yushkov tells him.

As soon as Yushkov is seated, Sinclair's hunched shoulders relax.

He stops gripping his can and leans back in his seat, even making eye contact. He reminds Wolfe of a sea anemone that closes up into a ball when in danger, but opens when the danger passes.

Yushkov generously fills mugs with vodka.

'*Za milyh dam,*' he says, raising his mug at Wolfe, smiling at her. She knows it translates as 'To lovely ladies', one of many traditional vodka toasts, but she doesn't let on she understands.

'What does that mean?' she asks.

He tells her what she already knows.

'Hold on,' says Rundle, 'I can do way better than that.' He leans in. '*Tu es la plus belle femme du monde!*'

Wolfe laughs. 'Okay, given the state of my face, I know you're lying.'

Rundle, clearly used to wooing and winning the ladies, looks put out and pouts.

'Okay, I have a toast,' says Adeyemi. 'To fame and fortune!'

'Amen to that,' says Matthews, who tries to drink and ends up with most of it down his chin.

'Fame? Pah! You can have your fame. I will take the money and run,' says Yushkov, chuckling.

Wolfe pretends to drink, but doesn't swallow. She wants to stay sober and alert.

'And you, Olivia, what is your toast?' Yushkov asks, giving her the kind of penetrating stare that feels invasive, as if he is searching her soul for the answer. She looks straight back at him, determined not to be intimidated.

She suddenly remembers Nooria Zia, the girl's eyes wide in shock the moment she died, the perfect circular hole in her head and the single trickle of blood running down her young face. Wolfe looks down at the Formica table top because she doesn't want Yushkov to see her guilt. She swallows something lumpy in her throat, then holds up her mug.

'To those brave enough to speak the truth.'

Wolfe swallows the vodka this time and gazes into the depths of her cup. She wonders where the poor girl has been buried, if she was buried at all. Would the shamed family take her out into the mountains and leave her in a shallow grave? Her energy dissipates like a punctured tyre. Should she have ignored Cohen and tried to locate Kabir Khan? She has contacts. At least then Nooria's death wouldn't be in vain. The boisterous chatter washes over her. She looks up and is taken aback by Yushkov's intense stare. It reminds her of a husky she got to know in Alaska when writing a story on the impact of shrinking sea ice on the Inuit villages. She had fallen from a sled. The dog, part wolf, had the palest of blue eyes that slanted up at the outer edges, as Yushkov's eyes do. It had peered deep into hers, as if confounded by her ineptitude. She had never had an animal study her quite so intently before. Now the Russian is studying her too. Gone is the lopsided grin he usually wears, as if the world never ceases to amuse him. Does Yushkov see the fleeting pain and uncertainty as her eyes dart from mug to mug? Or is he sizing her up as an adversary? She cannot tell.

She recalls Jerry Butcher once telling her that for every detective there is always one case that haunts them, however good that detective is at staying detached from the job. For him it was the unsolved murder of a five-year-old girl. Even in his retirement, the memory haunts him. Wolfe wonders if Nooria Zia's death will follow her to her grave. She feels suddenly hot and tugs at the tight neckline of her thermal top.

'Sometimes the price is too high, I think,' says Yushkov in a hushed tone. 'Sometimes it is best to walk away.'

Shocked, she looks up. Wolfe has walked away from Nooria Zia's assassination and left it to Casburn to make the guilty pay. Or is Yushkov talking about himself?

He blinks, their connection broken, and stands abruptly. 'We need more vodka!' he shouts, deliberately engaging Rundle and Adeyemi, who have been deep in conversation. 'I will bring my friends a new bottle.'

Even though Yushkov has drunk more of the vodka than the others around the table, he isn't affected. He strides out of the mess tent, pulling a packet of cigarettes from his pocket.

'I'm going for a smoke,' Wolfe says. She gave up years ago, but it gives her alone-time with Yushkov.

'You break my heart,' Rundle protests, clutching what he thinks is his heart but his hand is too far over to the left.

'I'll be back,' she says, in her best Arnie Schwarzenegger voice, and zips up her coat.

Only then does she notice Price in huddled conversation with Heatherton. Harvey is nowhere to be seen and must have gone to bed. Wolfe makes a point of walking past them slowly.

'When did you first notice this?' Wolfe hears Heatherton say.

'I was trying to identify similarities with known bacteria,' Stacy replies. 'They haven't slowed or died as we expected. Quite the contrary. They've grown more aggressive. A few minutes ago, they started to attack each other.'

Heatherton's eyebrows shoot up.

'Get Matthews sobered up and bring him with you.' Heatherton spots Wolfe within earshot. 'Keep it to yourself,' he says to Price, then heads for the door.

'Michael?' Wolfe calls, as she follows him through the exit.

'Not now, Olivia,' he snaps, and heads for the lab.

The sub-zero air claws at her scalp and gives her an instant headache. Yushkov is lighting up and nods at Wolfe. She decides to give Heatherton time to calm down before she finds out what has him so worked up.

'May I have one?' she asks Yushkov.

'Sure.'

He lights the non-filtered Russian cigarette and hands it to her. He watches her inhale, expecting her to choke. It's been a long time, but she manages not to cough.

'What do you want to know, Olivia?'

Wolfe is surprised by his directness. She studies his face and cannot read it.

'You are journalist. Journalist always have questions.'

She exhales loudly, relieved.

'You were a soldier,' Wolfe says, taking a punt.

Yushkov nods, an amused smile on his lips.

'Which regiment?'

'It was a long time ago.' He takes a deep drag on his cigarette. 'I get more vodka.'

As he walks away, he says something in Russian under his breath. His back is to her, so he doesn't see her eyes widen. Wolfe watches him take long, steady strides in the direction of the rising sun. She is unsure whether Yushkov has issued her with a warning or a threat:

'Watch your back, little lady.'

13

You look straight at me, but you cannot see me. I have my screen divided so I watch both sides of your Skype conversation with Cohen.

'Gotta keep my voice down,' you say. 'I think they're finally asleep but I can't be sure.'

It's ten past five in the morning at Lake Ellsworth and London is three hours ahead. Your laptop must be balanced on your legs because you look down at the monitor. Behind you, the white ceiling of your tent billows in the wind and I imagine you are sitting in your sleeping bag. With a black beanie on your head and half your face a dark bruise, you look like a member of a tragic tribute KISS band. You rub your bloodshot eyes, revealing fingerless gloves on your hands.

In the other half of my screen, Cohen's long face and deep-set haunted eyes remind me of The Silence in *Dr Who*. While you waffle on about the day's events, I google The Silence, which, I'm told, were modelled on Edvard Munch's *The Scream*. Cohen sits too close to the webcam and I get an uncomfortably microscopic view of the open pores at the end of his long nose and wiry nostril hairs. He really should trim them.

'So is there a story?' Cohen asks, yawning. It's 8.10 a.m. GMT, and he needs another coffee.

I look away. His foul yellowing teeth are full of amalgam fillings.

You lean closer to your laptop and drop your voice. 'I've already emailed you "It's Life Jim, But Not As We Know It", but don't get too comfortable. That's the last science story I'm doing.'

I catch my breath. Cohen checks his emails.

'When? It's not here.'

'Must be. I sent it hours ago.'

The look of bewilderment on your face is a delight. You shake your head.

'I don't get it. It's disappeared. Not even in my Sent items. How on earth did that happen?'

'Check the satellite link.'

You move away from my view. 'Connection's fine.' You sit and pull the laptop to you once again. 'Am I too late?'

'For today's paper, yes. Online, no. Send it again.'

'Shit! I wanted it in today's edition.'

Why isn't Cohen more annoyed?

'I'm re-sending now.'

You've just spoilt my fun.

I can hack your computer and delete an email once and get away with it, but twice is pushing it. You're smart. You'd work it out. On another monitor I see every word you type and the attached document you send.

'And the conspiracy slash murder angle?' Cohen asks.

'Any one of them could've killed Knox, if he was indeed killed, and I'm not convinced he was. You should've seen the euphoria when the drill hit water and they discovered the freaky bacteria. I don't think anybody here wants to stop the project.'

'"Freaky" a technical term, is it?' Cohen jokes.

'It's the best you're going to get, given how knackered I am. The celebrations went on most of the night.'

'And the Russian?'

'An enigma. Dislikes authority. A survivor. A man of secrets. Yet he's exceptional at his job and has some surprising friendships.' She's thinking particularly of Sinclair. 'Seems genuinely proud of their success here. I've managed to establish he's ex-Army and he clearly doesn't want to talk about it, but that in itself doesn't mean he's guilty of murder.'

'A soldier would know how to kill a man without raising suspicion.'

'True. Anyone who survives the Russian Army has to be tough as old boots. But if I'm right about why he defected, there's no way he'd work for the Russians.'

'Go on.'

'Most of the Russian Army is made up of peasants and conscripts. They're mostly cannon fodder. Bullying and torture are rife. It's a brutal life. Hundreds desert every year, seeking asylum in nearby countries. Yushkov's possibly one of them.'

'So how are you going to prove this theory?'

'I'll ask Jerry Butcher if he can help, and if he can't, I have a contact at MI6. Although I'd rather not use her unless I've run out of all other options.'

'Jerry still got his fingers in the right pies?'

'He has, but there's a limit to how many favours he can call in.'

'How long before the bacteria are moved?'

'Weather permitting, a Rothera plane should be here tomorrow.'

It's your turn to yawn and I catch a glimpse of the metal stud in your tongue.

'Well, that means you've only got a day left to find out what's going on.'

'I know. I know. One more thing,' you say. 'Heard anything from Casburn?'

Cohen shakes his head. 'Leave it alone, Olivia. You've got an assignment. It cost a fucking fortune to get you there, so show me it was worth it.'

You nod, ending the Skype connection with your editor, but you are still connected to me. Like an invisible umbilical cord, your webcam remains switched on. Deep in thought, your jaw moves as you play with your tongue stud and your eyes wander around the interior of your tent. I hear the click of the metal against your teeth. It irritates, like a squeaking wheel or a screaming baby. Really irritates. Stop it! Just stop it!

There's an explosion of white light in my head. I am no longer at home. I'm on my back, my body contorted in odd angles. A tangled mess. I cannot breathe, crushed by the weight of something I cannot see. Only one eye half opens. You lean over me, blocking out a blinding light like a solar eclipse, your face close to mine. Your lips move but I am adrift in a terrifying silence. Then you are gone. I try to move. My body doesn't respond. I try calling your name. My voice is a gurgle and I choke on metallic blood. I don't want to die alone.

I jolt suddenly, limbs flailing, and almost fall from my chair. My shirt is soaked in sweat. I suck in rapid shallow breaths, eyes darting around the room. What the fuck was that? I stand on unsteady legs, desperate to be in the here and now. There's a dark blue stain in the crotch of my jeans and a wet smear on the fake leather seat.

Did I fall asleep? Have a nightmare? A mug of tea is on the floor, a star-shaped stain on the carpet. I check the time. Less than a minute has passed. You are still on my screen, emailing that tosser, Butcher. Your world hasn't shifted in that minute. Mine has burst wide open.

I knew the psych report was a lie. I knew there had to be a reason for this loathing, this rage, this frenzy I have for you when everything else in my world is colourless, odourless and tasteless. You abandoned me. When I needed you most. My neuropsychologist would call it a breakthrough. Well, fuck him! The lying piece of shit! I claw at Dr Sharma's pages stuck to my wall, tearing his words to shreds.

Start again, it said. You were always good with computers, so get some training. Get a job. Integrate. Move on. Forget the past. Fuck that! The past is everything. Those missing months are all I think about. And you.

I need to change my jeans and wipe the piss from my chair, but I mustn't break our connection. Peeling off my sodden clothing, I use a dry section of fabric to wipe the chair and sit.

You are reading an email from Butcher that's just arrived.

I smile.

'Got mugged last night,' says Butcher. 'Hit from behind. Feel like a right twat. He took your keys, but don't worry. There was no address on them and I've got the locks changed again anyway. Your home is safe.'

I watch your eyes widen. You email Butcher immediately.

'Are you sure you're OK?' you type. 'Any idea who did it?'

Good question. Do tell.

I have no recollection of striking him on the back of his head and leaving him unconscious, but my diary entry for that day makes quite a thing of the adrenalin high. For a so-called self-defence expert, Butcher was pretty easy to take down. But that's what happens when you have a nagging bitch of a wife chewing your ear off down the phone as you're racing home in the dark. He was distracted. He turned too late. A large Maglite torch can be a handy weapon.

'Concussion, that's all,' Butcher replies. 'No idea who attacked me. Should have been paying attention.'

'I can't believe you teach me self-defence and get taken down by a mugger! However did that happen?!' You include one of those round smiley faces.

'Rub it in, why don't you?' Butcher adds a winking smiley face to his email.

Can you believe it? Fucking smiley faces?

'I need some information. Are you up to it?' you ask.

'Shoot.'

'What can you dig up on a Russian, Vitaly Yushkov, an engineer with British Antarctic Survey? Two years ago he was made a British citizen. The Foreign Office fast-tracked his application, and got him a job. Prior to that, it's as if he doesn't exist. He's ex-Army, but that's all I've got. Any chance you could ask one of your spook mates? I'm guessing it's pretty sensitive.'

Butcher replies, 'Happy to ask but I won't get far if it's classified. If I'm reading this right, you think he may be a spy, either
for us or for Russia. If so, tread very carefully. The SVR are not
to be messed with.'

Russia's Foreign Intelligence Service, formerly part of the
KGB, is now known in the English-speaking world as the SVR.

Butcher's warning gives me an idea. It's time to prod the
Russian bear. I select a dummy email address set up under a false
name. It's practically untraceable. I email Vitaly Yushkov at his
British Antarctic Survey address:

'Beware. Olivia Wolfe is not what she seems.'

That should spice things up a bit.

14

A gloved hand uses bolt cutters to break the padlocks on each
wooden crate containing the precious Lake Ellsworth samples.
There's no danger the loud crack of the metal snapping will
penetrate the thick walls of the ice cave or be heard above the
moaning, thirty-knot winds.

The cave entrance is barely wide enough to fit a man on all
fours. It slopes down gently to a metre's depth and then widens
into a circular shape, the ceiling high enough to give a man
crouching room. His tracks are already covered, the winds whipping up surface ice particles and blowing them along the ground
through gaps between tents and storage containers, like ghosts
using the site as a race circuit. The figure in the ice cave is insu-
lated from the wind's battering and kneels next to the first chest,
hood raised, white lab mask over nose and mouth. Underneath,
thermal gloves are latex ones to protect his skin from the boxes'

contents. Over thermal leggings, waterproof trousers are sealed tight at the ankles with tape. Over his rubber boots are two layers of sterile blue booties.

Inside the first chest is a large, blue plastic cool box. He flicks up the four clips holding the lid down and carefully places it on the floor, then stares down at the fifteen pressurised titanium cylinders containing the living water samples. They are stacked like miniature torpedoes. With both hands, he reaches into the box and lifts the first of the thirty-centimetre-long containers and, cradling it like an injured animal, he wraps it in clothing and places it inside a draw-stringed kit bag. He then picks up the next cylinder, shuffles a few feet away and places it on the ice floor. There is a moment's hesitation as the thief glances behind, through the tunnel-like cave entrance. Everyone else is asleep, dead to the world through exhaustion or alcohol or both. Alarms are set for eight. No need to rush.

The pressure valve is slowly opened and the air hisses out. Then the cylinder's plug is unscrewed. There's an initial pop and more hissing. The pressure gauge's needle drops rapidly. Once again his hands cease their movement, a moment of reflection. But not for long. He knows what has to be done. The cylinder's watery content is tipped on to the ice, freezing almost instantly, leaving only a pale stain, a distant memory. He's careful to avoid any direct contact with the organisms. The saboteur re-seals the empty cylinder, placing it on the ground. He repeats the same exercise thirteen times, until all the Lake Ellsworth water samples are destroyed, save for the very first cylinder safely concealed in his kit bag. Then the fourteen empty canisters are stacked back in the blue cool box. The stolen cylinder is replaced with a brand-new one, which brings the total number back up to fifteen. The cool box is clipped shut and the wooden crate closed. The broken padlock is pocketed and an identical one takes its place.

Now for the twelve sediment samples in the next crate. Trickier to cover his tracks as the muddy sediment will stain the white cave floor. To make it less likely somebody will notice the gritty residue, the destroyer of ten years' planning and preparation – of ancient life forms never before seen – decides to carry each sediment-filled cylinder out of the cave and dump the alien contents behind the generators, where very few ever go.

After twelve trips back and forth, his muscles ache. The now-empty cylinders are returned to their crate and padlocked. With any luck, the destruction won't be discovered until the crates are opened on British soil.

Wolfe wakes and sits bolt upright, momentarily confused by the restrictive nature of the bedding. The tent fabric, though taut, ripples as it is assaulted by the relentless wind. She moves her head from side to side, trying to hone in on the clank that woke her, but all she can hear is the wind wailing and the thrum of generators. She's bleary-eyed with sleep, but there's no mistaking the sour post-party stink of old beer. Reluctant to leave her warm, silky cocoon, she hesitates, but knows better than to ignore her instincts.

Grabbing her heavy, black aluminium torch, the same kind used by the British police that doubles as a weapon, Wolfe checks the time: 6.06 a.m. Unzipping her sleeping bag, she hastily pulls on coat, hat and gloves, and considers wearing her backpack for protection, then berates herself for being paranoid. What's she afraid of? The Yeti?

Shoving aside the makeshift curtain that separates her sleeping space from the rest of the dining area, she passes tables strewn with dirty plates, empty beer cans and vodka bottles and an over-flowing rubbish bin. One of the plastic chairs is tipped backwards.

Outside, the wind blows diagonally across her, tearing at her outer wear and almost ripping off her beanie. She tugs it down. Ice swirls around her legs but visibility is clear enough at eye-level. No movement, apart from the flapping of the Union Jack and guy ropes vibrating in the wind. She coughs on the frigid air and pulls up her hood for warmth, which restricts her vision and ability to hear, but the cold is piercing. The ice beneath her feet is glassy like a rink so she moves slowly, feeling her way around the Weatherhaven's exterior, careful not to trip over guy ropes. Having done a full loop, she is about to go back inside when she catches a glimpse of a dark figure disappearing behind the laboratory container, some ten metres away. It's impossible to tell who it is: they, like her, have their hood up and are wearing BAS-supplied clothing. What could be so important it warrants attention at six in the morning? She tries to remember the camp layout. Where are they going? Isn't the ice cave behind the lab?

Wolfe approaches the lab with caution and finds the door locked. She listens through the door, but all seems quiet. She squeezes through a narrow gap between the lab container and the next one, which is used for mechanical repairs and housing the Ski-Doo and tractor.

Wolfe stops dead. It's unlocked. The door is slightly ajar.

'Hello? Anybody there?'

Wolfe opens the heavy steel door and fumbles for the light switch. Finding it, she peers inside the container and sees nothing unusual. A well-equipped mechanical workshop is set up at the rear of the container, with anything from saws and spanners and drills to spare machinery and vehicle parts. The tractor and Ski-Doo are parked at the front, where they should be. Just as she leaves the workshop and shuts the heavy door, she sees a person crawl out of the tight entrance of the ice cave. They move fast and the visibility is too poor for her to recognise them. She darts between the two containers and hides, hoping she hasn't been seen. She needs to wake Heatherton. Something is very wrong.

Peering in the direction of the pyramid tents, she desperately tries to remember which one is Heatherton's, when she sees someone leave their sleeping quarters. Only one man is crazy enough to walk about bare-headed in such cold, and his bulk and height is unmistakable. Yushkov. She flattens her body against the container's exterior wall, then sticks her head out to watch him. He moves three tents along, stops, and looks around. Wolfe pulls back and holds her breath. She counts to ten then peers around the corner. Yushkov is outside Harvey's tent. He bends and begins unravelling Harvey's drunken attempt at tying up the entrance. The tubular fabric chute is designed to prevent snow and ice from entering. Wolfe's heart is pounding. Should she challenge Yushkov? Harvey could be in danger. Is he working with whoever she saw leaving the ice cave? Before she can decide what to do next, she's shoved from behind and thrown to the ground, hitting her head on the hard ice. A gloved hand shoves a cloth over her face that stinks of chemicals, and in one horrifying second she knows it's chloroform. Wolfe struggles, trying to turn her mouth and nose away from its soporific effect, but it's too late.

Wolfe blacks out.

15

Light penetrates Wolfe's consciousness. Her head is pounding and bile rises up her throat. She opens her eyes and sees Adeyemi looking down at her, smelling of disinfectant. The surface she's lying on is flat and white but not cold: a Formica table. Near her, a first-aid box lies open.

'Tell Mike,' Adeyemi says to someone.

Her brain feels two sizes too big for her skull. She closes her eyes, hoping the room will stop rolling up and down like a boat in rough seas.

'Can I have some water?' She barely recognises her feeble voice.

He moves out of her line of vision and returns with a beaker. 'Sit up.' His tone is sharp. He won't win a Mother Teresa Award. 'You may feel dizzy. You've banged your forehead.'

Wolfe uses her arms to push up into a sitting position. The tent roof, the walls, the table, the door, the floor sway up and down. A moan escapes her lips. Adeyemi grabs her and holds her up.

'Deep breaths,' he says.

'You a doctor?' She slurs her words. Shit! What happened to me?

'Nothing like it. I did the advanced medic course, that's all.'

Wolfe gulps down some water and doesn't even register Beer leading Heatherton into the Weatherhaven.

'Do you have any idea what you've done?' Heatherton demands.

'Sit forward,' says Adeyemi. 'Hang on to the table.'

No longer willing to prop her up, Adeyemi lets her go. She sways but manages to keep herself upright, crossing her legs for stability. Heatherton is clearly furious – his eyes have almost disappeared under a deep frown and his mouth is clenched into a slit – but Wolfe has no idea what he's talking about. She looks for Beer's cheery face but sees only fury.

'I . . . I don't know . . . what happened?'

Heatherton and Beer glance at each other.

'Really? Well how about this? You've destroyed every last one of the samples we've worked night and day for.'

'But I didn't . . . What? All of them?'

'Yes!' Heatherton shouts, puce in the face. 'Even the sodding lab samples.'

Wolfe frowns, bewildered, but frowning sends a shooting pain through her head. She shuts her eyes, trying to remember. The noise. That was it. She went outside to look.

'Something woke me,' Wolfe says. 'I went out to see what it was.'

'Sure you did,' says Heatherton, his voice dripping with sarcasm. 'What do you think I am? Stupid?' He turns his back on her and rakes his fingers through his messy hair, clearly trying to control his rage.

'Why, Olivia? Why?' says Beer, his voice pleading.

'But I didn't. I saw someone going into the ice cave. It looked suspicious, so I hid between two containers and watched. Then I looked away for some reason, and I was shoved forward. Hit my head. I must've passed out.'

Heatherton turns abruptly. 'So how come Toby found you lying in the cave with samples strewn around you? Explain that!'

'What? I have no idea. No. That can't be right. Unless I was dragged there.'

'Then tell me who you saw.'

'I didn't get a good look.'

'Perfect!' Heatherton says, throwing his arms up.

Wolfe gingerly runs her hand over her brow and winces. There's a small bump beneath a cut. Her face is really taking a pummelling.

'Oh for God's sake, Michael, I've got the bloody Eiffel Tower sticking out of my forehead! How did I manage to do that to myself?'

'I don't know, Olivia. What I do know is that everything we've worked for over the last ten years is gone. Every tedious, arse-licking meeting, begging for financial support; every team member, painstakingly selected; the years it's taken to develop the drill; the nightmare logistics getting us here . . . all that, for nothing!' Heatherton's voice cracks.

'It's all right, mate,' says Beer, placing a hand on his shoulder. But Heatherton shrugs it away, turning his back on everyone so he can wipe his wet eyes with his hands.

A flash of memory. A smell of chemicals. Wolfe looks down, trying to hang on to the image. 'Somebody used chloroform. A cloth over my face. After they'd forced me to the ground. I remember now. I was between two containers.' She looks up. 'I most definitely was not inside the ice cave.'

'I don't know what to believe,' Heatherton sighs.

'Think about it, Michael. You invited me here. I didn't kill Kevin, I didn't sabotage your snowmobile or the boiler. So why on earth would I destroy the bacteria? Can't you see? Somebody tried to kill me because I caught them in the act.'

Beer stares, open-mouthed. 'What's she talking about?'

Heatherton looks up, his eyes sunken. 'I invited her here and Christ, I wish I hadn't. I thought Kev's death was suspicious, you see. Of all the people to have a fatal accident, it just happened to be the most critical member of the team. I don't believe in coincidences, George. All the technical problems, they were deliberately engineered.'

'What?' Beer is wide-eyed with incredulity. 'Who would do such a thing?'

'I think someone here is working for Trankov.'

'What?' Beer blinks several times.

'It's all about being the first.'

'My God, Mike! Why didn't you tell me? We could have

taken turns at guarding the cylinders. Why didn't you confide in me?'

'And what about me, boss? You think I'm a traitor?' Adeyemi asks, his presence forgotten.

Heatherton slumps back against the kitchen workbench and looks defeated. He shakes his head.

'No, Bruce, I don't think you are and I'd appreciate you keeping this to yourself.'

'This is very bad,' says Adeyemi. 'This kinda thing can tear the team apart.'

'Mike, answer my question,' Beer snaps. 'Why didn't you tell me you thought the security of this project was compromised? Why? I, of all people, had to know. I'm logistics, remember?'

'Because, George, you already thought me obsessed about beating Trankov, and if I'd told you I thought the Russians had a spy here, you'd have thought I'd finally lost the plot.'

Beer is speechless for a long moment. 'So who is it?'

Heatherton looks up. 'Not you, mate.'

'Then who?'

'Isn't it obvious?'

'You're joking? Because Vitaly is Russian? Or was. That man has worked his arse off for this project. He's dedicated to it. No wonder you've been treating him like crap since Kev's death.' Beer shakes his head. 'Everyone takes their lead from you, Mike. They've picked up on your animosity towards him. Which is bad for teamwork, bad for morale.'

Heatherton stares at the floor.

Beer focuses back on Wolfe. 'Can you recall anything about the person you saw?'

A fuzzy memory of Yushkov outside somebody's tent. When was that? It was very quiet. People were sleeping. She remembers the cold metal of the container at her back. Yushkov was trying to get inside a tent. Not his own. That's it! Harvey's tent! Wolfe is about to tell them, when Yushkov pokes his head in.

'I not want to interrupt, but this is urgent,'Yushkov says.

'What now?' Heatherton sighs.

Yushkov steps inside and glances at her. His look is threatening. 'I no want to talk about this with her.'

Heatherton rubs his brow. 'Vitaly, whether we like it or not, there are no secrets here. Tell me what's so important.'

Yushkov gives Wolfe a warning look.

'The drill and sediment probe, they are damaged.'

'Damaged! How?'

'We drill into ice as hard as concrete,' says Yushkov.

'Hold on. Before we go any further, I want Stacy, Gary and Trent with us at the bore hole,' says Heatherton, heading for the door.

They leave. There is no way Wolfe is going to miss out on this conversation. She stands and stumbles through the Weatherhaven, clinging to handholds like a drunken sailor. Her jacket lies on her sleeping bag. She puts it on. The exertion makes her nauseous again. She waits for the feeling to pass, then heads for the bore hole site, planting each step carefully. The horizon moves, she stops, then starts again. Frustrated, she takes some deep breaths and locks her eyes on to the crane.

By the time she gets to it, Heatherton, Beer and Yushkov have been joined by Price, Rundle and Matthews. The steel and titanium probe, as tall as a man and shaped like a pencil, has had its protective plastic covering removed so it can be inspected. It is suspended above the bore hole by a mechanical winch.

'So what's the problem?' asks Heatherton.

Yushkov holds up two fingers. 'Two problems.' He points to the very tip of the probe. 'Number one, the sediment corer. It is corroded very bad. I do not think we can bring the sediment back to surface using this.'

Price grabs the middle of her thick bunch of hair and flicks it out behind her, then kneels down to take a closer look. She wears latex gloves and runs her fingers over the steel tip.

Rundle, also wearing sterile gloves, takes a look. 'It's taken quite a battering.'

'Okay,' Heatherton asks Rundle. 'But can it collect samples?'

Rundle shakes his head. 'I don't think so. Look here. The tip is partially closed, as if the sides have been squeezed together. You're not going to get much through that.'

'I agree,' says Price. She looks at Rundle. 'Do we have a replacement?'

'Not here or at Rothera. It'll have to be flown from England.'

'Shit!' says Heatherton.

'If Grantham Engineering gets it on a plane today – and that's really pushing it – then the best-case scenario is four days. That's based on good weather,' says Beer.

'In eighteen hours there will be no hole,' says Yushkov.

'Which means we'll have to start all over again,' says Beer.

'What about the water sample probe? Will that work?'

'Hold on, Michael,' says Price, shooting up from her squatting position. 'This project is about both sediment and water, not one or the other.'

Heatherton raises his hand to pacify her. 'I'm simply asking the question. Trent?'

Rundle scratches his head. 'The water probe includes three rosettes of eight bespoke hundred-millilitre titanium water sample bottles. I've inspected them, and they all seem fine. The mechanism to open the bottles once they're immersed is also working perfectly.'

'Sensors? Camera? Sonar? They all okay?'

'That's Bruce's baby,' Trent replies, glancing in the direction of the control room. 'He's testing all that right now.'

Heatherton and Matthews both nod. Price frowns, her freckled neck flushed with anxiety.

'I don't like where this is heading,' she says. 'If we don't take sediment samples, we could miss out on the most critical evidence of microbial life in the lake. We can't just rely on water samples.'

'I take your point,' says Heatherton. 'But something is better than nothing.'

'I disagree,' Matthews chips in. 'We should wait and retrieve both.'

'Can the drill cope with making a second bore hole?' Beer asks Yushkov.

'This is problem number two. I show you,' says Yushkov. He pulls away the drill nozzle's plastic covering to reveal the circular brass and steel head, with jet holes around the circumference and at the tip.

Yushkov points. 'Look at the screws. They hold the nozzle together. They are rusting. See. This is big surprise to me.' He pauses as Heatherton and Rundle peer closely at the screws. 'And two of the jet holes have got bigger. This mean the bore hole on that side of the head will get more hot water than the other.'

'He's right,' says Matthews. 'It'll force the drill to swing from side to side. Instead of focusing the impact on boring down, we'll get an ever-widening hole.'

'It needs replacing?' Heatherton asks, but it's clear he already knows the answer.

'*Da*,' says Yushkov.

'Fucking hell!' says Heatherton. 'Replacements will take four days to get here. Will the boiler even last that long?'

'It should do,' Beer replies.

'And fuel? Do we have enough left?'

'Again, we should have,' says Beer. 'But I need to check.'

All eyes are on Heatherton.

'Make the calls. You've got four days to get everything here, then we drill again.'

'And if it doesn't get here in time?' asks Beer.

'We go home empty-handed.'

16

As Heatherton, Yushkov, Beer and Rundle finalise logistics with Grantham Electronics for the replacement parts, Wolfe sits on the edge of one of the waterbed-sized fuel bladders at the far end of the camp, keen to avoid the glares she's been getting from the team. Even the morning sun looks like an angry eye hovering above the horizon.

Through their Skype link, Cohen scrutinises the cut just above Wolfe's right eyebrow. 'I send you to fucking Antarctica on a cosy little research trip. And look at the state of you! Sheesh.'

'Keep it down, will you? My head's ready to explode.'

'Adds some balance at least,' he says, his bony finger wavering between the cut on the right and her black eye on the left.

The painkillers are finally kicking in and as long as she keeps her head still, she can just about think.

'Turns out Heatherton was right,' Wolfe says, keeping her voice low. The wind has died away and sound travels easily across the ice. She's wearing earphones so nobody else can hear Cohen's booming voice. Wolfe gives him a rapid summary. 'Someone here wants this project to fail, and I now think Knox was probably murdered. What I don't understand is why they didn't finish me off.'

'Maybe they will.'

'That's comforting. Thanks, Moz.'

'I'm just saying,' Cohen shrugs. 'You want to come home?'

'No way. It's just getting interesting.'

Cohen leans back in his chair, hands behind his head, nodding his approval. 'Well, if an RPG-7 can't shift you, not sure what can.'

Wolfe remembers the convoy of Isil militants entering Mosul, Iraq, in June 2014. Hidden from view, she'd watched, horrified, as a rebel prepared to fire an anti-tank rocket-propelled grenade launcher at the abandoned shell of a house where she and Annabel Maine, CNN journalist, and her cameraman, Joe Rossi, were hiding.

'Heard anything from Annabel?' Wolfe asks.

'She's a vegetable.'

'Jesus! You can be a bastard. Have you forgotten she used to work for you?'

'She defected to the Yanks. So why should I give a fuck?'

Wolfe shakes her head. 'You always gave her such a hard time.'

Cohen juts his head forward, as if about to head-butt the monitor. 'She had no fucking talent! Worse, she thought everything she wrote was gold. Expected accolades for mediocrity.'

'She wasn't that bad.'

'Yes, she was, even when you helped her. She only got the CNN gig because she was blonde and pretty.'

'She was a friend, Moz.'

Cohen views her in silence. 'I went to see her once. In hospital, a few weeks after she'd been airlifted to London. See! I can be nice.'

'Last I heard, she was recovering well. Working from home.'

'Bully for her.'

Wolfe remembers the exact moment the grenade exploded and Annabel flew into the air. 'I was lucky. Just a damaged knee.'

'Bullshit! You kept your wits about you. She ignored the danger.'

'Let's move on, shall we?'

'No, you've missed my point. You're still working for me after all these years because of your instinct for a good story, your sheer bloody-mindedness, and, most importantly, your courage. What you did for Annabel . . . it was nothing short of heroic. Me? I'd have fucking run like the wind.'

'No you wouldn't.'

'Oh yes I fucking would! And don't tell me what I would or wouldn't do. You sound like my bloody wife!'

'In that case, when I get back, you can take me to dinner to celebrate our eight-year work anniversary,' Wolfe teases.

'Hey! I never take my wife out, so why the fuck would I take out one of my godforsaken reporters?'

He's trying to cheer her up, and it's working. Moz has more heart than he likes people to realise.

'Could you talk to Michael? He's convinced I destroyed the samples.'

'Someone's done a good job of making it look that way. I'll send an email. Remind him why you're there.'

Wolfe's laptop pings. She divides her screen so she can still see Cohen's ugly mug, and also view her Inbox. The subject is 'Your traitor'.

'You just sent me something?'

'No, but I'm waiting for you to send me something along the lines of "Sabotage – alien life destroyed".'

'Christ, Moz! You should be on a tabloid. I was thinking more like, "A Race to the Death", focusing on the rivalry between the two teams and posing the question of a traitor sabotaging the British project.'

Cohen chuckles to himself.

'Ah,' she says, 'you're winding me up. I should've known.'
Wolfe has opened the email. It is unsigned, and brief.

**It is not difficult to guess your traitor. He has betrayed
his birth country and now betrays yours.**

'Shit! It's from your email address.'
'What are you banging on about?' says Cohen, leaning in.
She hesitates for a moment before opening the pdf, wary
that the attachment might be infected. Written in Russian
Cyrillic, the document is only one page of nine. There is a photo
of four men in the mottled khaki uniform of the Russian Army.
The photo is a little grainy but, as she peers at each man in
turn, she sucks in a sharp breath as she recognises a younger and
slighter Yushkov.
Cohen has lost patience. 'What the fuck are you looking at?
Send it to me!'
'Okay, okay, keep your shirt on.'
Wolfe forwards it to Cohen.
'Yushkov can't be more than twenty,' she says.
His hair is shaved so short, he looks bald. His wide smile of
white teeth and piercing blue eyes are unmistakable. He has his
arm draped over a comrade: shorter, darker, and laughing.
'Bollocks! It's in Russian,' comments Cohen. 'I'll get a translator on to it.'
Wolfe doesn't respond. She is transfixed by the photo.
All four men lean against a BTR–80 – an amphibious armoured
personnel carrier in camouflage khaki – and behind them is a
convoy of off-road camouflaged trucks that look to be Ural-
4320s, but one is definitely a BM–21 rocket launcher. They are
on a rocky, mountainous road. A high bank on one side of the
road is covered in thick tree cover. She tries to translate the copy,

but struggles, the complexity of the sentences and the military jargon are mostly beyond her limited knowledge. Under the photo is a date, 25 March 2000, and a location.

'A bit before my time,' she says. 'Ring any bells?'

'I know about this,' Cohen says. 'The photo would've been taken just before the Zhani–Vedeno ambush. I was a correspondent back then. The Second Chechen War. Mujahideen forces ambushed a column of Russian troops from the Interior Ministry. It was carnage. Few survived.'

'Well, Yushkov did.'

'You know some Russian. What does the bloody thing say?'

The next few sentences are beyond her but she recognises the word for bomb disposal expert in reference to Yushkov.

'He was clearing landmines ahead of the convoy. Dangerous job.'

Wolfe skim-reads. She recognises a word in the last sentence that surprises her.

'This document accuses Yushkov of cowardice.'

'Does it, indeed?'

'He doesn't seem cowardly to me. In fact, quite the opposite.'

'And the word stamped diagonally across the page in red means Confidential?' Cohen guesses.

'Top secret.'

On her way back to the mess tent, Wolfe passes the back of the lab and overhears Price and Heatherton.

'Somebody unlocked the tool shed last night,' Price says.

'That's the least of our worries.' Heatherton sounds irritated.

'Wait!' Price says. He must be walking away. 'If we get a chance to drill again, we must be more careful. And I don't just mean security. I mean, we don't know what life form we're dealing with.'

'Keep your voice down, will you?'

'But it's so aggressive.'

'You're overreacting, Stacy.'

Wolfe hears no more because Charles Harvey yells at her.

'You're a disgrace!' He is doing his best to storm towards Wolfe, but his clumsiness on the ice makes him look like an under-stuffed scarecrow. 'How can you even face these people?'

'Come on, Charles. You know me.'

'You're no better than the worst hacks. If you can't find a story, you make it up. Well, I've just filed one of my own. It's about a journalist sabotaging a British Antarctic project.'

'That's ridiculous. Your producer will never run it.'

Heatherton and Price intervene.

'Break it up, you two,' Heatherton says. 'We don't have time for this. Charles, come with me.'

He leads Harvey into the lab. Price gives Wolfe a poisonous glare, then leaves her feeling stunned at the ferocity of Harvey's outburst. He can't seriously believe she destroyed the bacteria? Is everybody going mad?

Left alone, she heads for the ice cave's narrow entrance and crawls inside, hoping to find a clue to her attacker's identity. Whoever knocked her out must have dragged her unconscious body into the igloo-like interior. Being of light weight, almost anyone on the team could do it, even Price. The cave is empty, the crates and canisters removed. She uses her torch. A few drops of blood near the entrance have frozen solid like tiny rubies. Her blood. She must have lain there. Near the back wall, blobs of gritty sediment are strewn like bird seed. She systematically searches every bit of the ice cave's floor and finds nothing helpful. Wolfe is about to leave when she sees a blemish on the concave wall. Kneeling, she finds a white downy feather stuck to the ice. Odd, given there are no penguins or birds of any kind for miles.

She blows warm breath over it several times and carefully peels it off the wall. Was it buried beneath the ice for years or carried in on somebody's clothing? She tucks it in an inside pocket.

'What are you doing here?' The accent is unmistakably Russian.

Wolfe turns to find Yushkov bent forward, his spine pressing against the cave roof. He fills much of the central space and blocks her exit. Unsure of his intentions, she swings the torch up and over her right shoulder and points the beam straight into his eyes, making it hard for him to see her. She's also in a position to swing the torch down hard on his head or clavicle if he attacks her. But Yushkov doesn't even blink at the light.

'I thought coming here might jog my memory, but I can't remember a thing.' She keeps her voice level and calm. She doesn't want to antagonise him.

Wolfe takes a step towards the exit but Yushkov doesn't shift out of the way.

'Why are you here? Tell me the truth.'

'Get out of my way, Vitaly.'

'You answer my question.'

His eyes have that hard glint in them she's seen before. Even if she screams, she doubts her voice will carry beyond the thick ice walls. She's going to have to talk her way out.

'Okay. How about this for an idea? For every question of yours I answer, I get to ask you a question of my own. Deal?'

'I don't play games with traitors.'

'I'm no traitor, Vitaly. I'll answer your questions, providing you answer mine.'

'Lower the torch.'

She lowers the beam, pointing it at the floor, but she still holds her only weapon above her shoulder. The Russian kneels and straightens his back. He is no fool, though; he still blocks her exit. He nods his agreement to their dialogue.

Wolfe decides to come clean.

'I came here because I don't believe Kevin Knox's death is an accident and nor does Heatherton, who invited me. I also don't believe the multiple equipment failures are down to bad luck. Since somebody has destroyed the lake samples, there's no doubt we have a traitor amongst us, somebody willing to kill to ensure this project fails. I intend to find out who.' Yushkov doesn't give her any response. He just watches her face. 'Now it's my turn to ask a question. What were you doing at six this morning, entering Harvey's tent?'

Yushkov's gaze never falters. Wolfe searches for a tell. Nothing. He doesn't blanch or flush or tug at an ear or cover his mouth. God, he's good. It takes training to control facial reflexes. A spy's training.

'You are mistaken.'

'I am not. You and I were the only people awake, except the person who smashed me over the head. Did you see who hit me?'

'That's two questions,' says Yushkov, his eyes creasing at the edges, but they don't lose their steeliness. 'I have answered your question. It is not my problem if you do not like my answer. I now ask you: who are you working for? And please do not insult my intelligence and tell me a newspaper.'

Wolfe senses he has an agenda. Has somebody been filling his head with lies?

'You find this question difficult?' Yushkov asks.

'Why are you so determined to believe I am the saboteur?' He doesn't reply. 'Talk to my editor. I have a sat phone in my bag. Will that satisfy you?'

'Who sent you here to destroy our work?'

'Look, Vitaly, I work for the *Post*. I'm not working for any government organisation, either British or foreign. If anyone has said otherwise, it's probably someone with a vendetta against me. A lot of powerful people would like to take me down.'

He calls her a liar in his native tongue. She keeps her eyes glued to his and hopes she hasn't given him any indication she understands what he's just said.

'If you're testing me, you're wasting your time,' Wolfe says. 'It's my turn to ask a question. How do you feel about your mother country, Russia?'

Yushkov raises his chin. 'That is a stupid question. I am British citizen and am loyal to my new country. One thing you will learn about me, Olivia Wolfe, is that I am a man of honour.'

'Why don't you want people to know you were in the Army?'

'It is not relevant to my work here and it is not your business.'

'Are you a deserter?'

Wolfe has never seen a bear roar, but she has heard it's truly terrifying. He is up and leaning over her in one step, bellowing into her face, his eyes slits of fury.

'You know nothing of me! How *dare* you judge me! I was protecting the innocent.'

Yushkov stops suddenly. He's said more than he should. He spits on the ground, then crawls out of the narrow entrance. Wolfe is trembling. She thought he was going to rip her head off. She waits a minute or two, trying to calm her heart rate, then she too leaves.

'Olivia!' calls Heatherton, jogging over, his face muscles taut with anxiety. 'Please tell me you didn't phone Dr Trankov and let him in on our little mishap.'

'Of course I didn't. I can't believe you think so poorly of me. Speak to Moz. He'll vouch for me.'

Heatherton is pacing the ice, hands on hips.

'Then how the hell does he know exactly which parts we need for both the probe and the drill? Huh?'

'How would I know? Anyone could've contacted him. People here, someone at BAS, or Grantham Electronics.'

'Never! They all know how hush-hush this is.'

'You use the VSAT satellite system for your voice and data links, don't you?'

'Yes, why?'

'All it takes is a quick email to Trankov from the privacy of their sleeping quarters. Anybody here could have done it. But I didn't.'

Which might explain what Yushkov was doing trying to enter Harvey's tent. Perhaps he didn't want an incriminating email trail from him to Trankov, so he opted to use Harvey's sat phone instead? Is Yushkov making her the scapegoat? Last night, Harvey was so drunk he wouldn't have woken even if a charging elephant seal had entered his tent. Wolfe considers telling Heatherton her suspicions, but doubts he'll believe her. In his eyes, she has shifted from ally to potential enemy.

'What did Trankov want?'

'He claims he's developed a drilling system that doesn't use contaminants, a drill he can't use because it's unseasonably cold, even for Vostok. At minus seventy Celsius, he can't drill and he can't keep the bore hole open. He's offered it to us.'

'Why would he do that?' Wolfe asks.

'Because it's better to share first place with us than to come a miserable second. In return for giving us his drill, this project becomes a joint British-Russian venture and he gets equal credit.'

'And Trankov can get his drill here faster than four days?'

'Eight hours. But it makes no difference.' Heatherton's eyes rest on the silent drilling equipment. 'I'm not having a bar of it. This is a British project and it's staying that way.'

17

They have only been given an hour's warning, too late to demand the pilot turn back. The Russians know that, of course. The Ilyushin Il-76 four-engine, strategic airlifter, with a fifty-metre wingspan, is spotted by Sinclair first, as it appears over the top of the Ellsworth Mountains, ripping through the wispy clouds and belching out fumes that stain the sky murky brown. Landing a plane on the Lake Ellsworth ice sheet has never been done before. With little time to prepare, the British team has done its best to set up a temporary runway. Using the tractor's snowplough, Rundle has flattened the worst of the undulating surface. Then the tractor is positioned on one side of the makeshift airstrip and the Ski-Doo on the other, leaving the headlights on and facing in the direction of the plane's approach: from ninety degrees east.

Only Ironside has any experience of guiding planes to land on ski-ways, having done a season at Rothera Research Station and learned aircraft marshalling signals. Multi-skilling is just part of life on Antarctic stations. He stands in a yellow reflector jacket, facing the approaching airborne beast, right arm raised, giving the pilot the all-clear. The scientists scurry around like squirrels hoarding nuts, locking away research data and computers. Yushkov and Beer ensure the drill head and probe are secured inside a padlocked shipping container.

'So much for the spirit of scientific co-operation,' grumbles Matthews, who clearly does not regard Trankov's team with the same degree of suspicion as Heatherton.

'Oh, give me a break,' says Price. 'Trankov gave us the finger when we begged them not to pollute Lake Vostok. He doesn't believe in co-operation. He wants to take over our project and steal the glory.'

The grey and white airlifter, with its high tail and bulbous glass nose, lumbers towards the tiny British camp, dropping lower and lower in the sky, its enormous wheels like vulture's talons ready to grip the hazardous ice surface. The screaming engines are so loud, Wolfe covers her ears. She feels the throb of its engines vibrating through her ribcage. The icy ground shakes as the 190,000-kilogram plane touches down, the perilously uneven terrain barely causing the plane's wings to dip, the wheels holding the ice just as well as if it had landed on concrete and asphalt. It thunders past the waiting team, who watch in stunned silence as loose ice is sucked into the air behind it, rendering the giant plane almost invisible. Ironside has to squat behind the bright orange Ski-Doo, pummelled by the backdraught. The Il-76 rumbles off into the distance, then makes a wide arc as it turns towards the camp – the vulture circling its prey.

Heatherton grinds his jaw, his shoulders hunched with tension. Sinclair can't keep his feet still and shuffles nervously from one boot to the other, hands in pockets. Wolfe is surprised to see Yushkov standing next to Heatherton, his feet wide set, his hands gripped behind his back, his expression wary, as if protecting his leader. Perhaps, as the only Russian speaker, he's been asked to provide the introductions, but her research tells her that Trankov speaks English very well.

'What the hell are they up to?' says Beer to himself, but it's loud enough for Wolfe to hear. 'We said no, yet the buggers came anyway.'

'Trankov must've got permission from his government to land on such a dangerous ice runway,' Wolfe says. 'Which means he has approval from the highest level.'

'How do you know that?' Beer asks.

'I did my homework,' Wolfe tells him.

The Il-76 seems to move painstakingly slowly as it completes the circle and follows Ironside's signals. The engines' roar makes further conversation difficult. Finally, some hundred and fifty metres from the camp's outer perimeter, the plane grinds to a halt.

'It's bloody enormous,' Matthews shouts.

The engines are cut but still whir, whipping up ice fragments, blurring Wolfe's view. But she can just make out the detail of the Il–76's nose. It has a grey bulbous point, like a snub nose, surrounded by panes of glass, so the pilots can see ahead, above and below. A side door is opened and the steps are lowered.

The first to walk down the steps is short and dumpy. He wears a red parka, but no hat or hood; his hair and beard are white. From photographs she's seen, she knows this must be Dr Trankov and, if he has come bearing gifts, he's going to find no takers. Three others disembark, also dressed in red, carrying backpacks.

The first is very tall, well over six foot with square shoulders. He walks with the surety of a man used to difficult terrain. His hair is blond and fine and cut short.

The second man is shorter and wiry. He strides, almost in a march, towards them. The third, who walks with shoulders forward and arms wide, has short brown hair and the body of a shot-putter. As the third arrival draws near, Wolfe realises she is a woman. She doesn't wear her red parka, just a fleece, and Wolfe can't take her eyes off the width of the woman's arms and neck, imagining that in an arm-wrestling match with Yushkov, she could give him a run for his money.

Ironside drives Trankov to them by Ski-Doo. The others follow on foot. The leader of the Russian group offers Heatherton his hand, smiling jovially, his cheeks puffing out like a hamster chewing food. Heatherton shakes the proffered hand, his smile forced.

'My friend!' says Trankov, 'It's good to see you. A long time, I think.'

114

Before Heatherton can respond he is gripped in a hug by the rotund Russian, and it is all Wolfe can do not to smirk at Heatherton's sour expression. Releasing Heatherton, Trankov chats jovially about the flight until his companions have joined him.

'Anya Snigir. Our chief drilling engineer.'

Snigir has downward-slanting, hooded brown eyes that make it difficult to see their expression. Her wide, pudgy face is androgynous. She nods her head at the welcoming party.

'She does not speak English,' Trankov adds.

Wolfe takes a sideways look at Yushkov, who is studying Snigir closely. Heatherton glances nervously at both Yushkov and the woman. Perhaps Heatherton still suspects Yushkov is a spy and doesn't like the idea they can speak to each other in a language he doesn't understand.

'Sergey Grankin,' Trankov says next, gesturing to the tall man whose patchy beard is relatively new, probably a week's growth. 'Engineer.'

As Grankin moves down the line shaking hands, Heatherton provides the introductions to his team, and to Wolfe and Harvey.

'Ah, the great British press,' says Trankov, with a hint of mockery.

When Grankin shakes Wolfe's hand, she notices his defined cheekbones and his long bony nose has a kink in the middle. It's been broken in the past. His smile reveals a crowded mouth with teeth that stick inwards.

'Do you speak English?' she asks.

'Yes, a little.'

When he shakes Yushkov's hand he stands a fraction too close, eyeballing the man who is no longer a Russian citizen. It is subtly threatening. Yushkov doesn't flinch.

'Demitri Magnitsky. He designed and built our drill. He is machinist,' Trankov says.

The dark-haired wiry man stands stiffly, but smiles as he says, 'It is very nice to meet you.'

'And your pilot?' Heatherton asks. 'Does he need any help?'

'No, no. Mikhail will secure the plane and join us later.'

Harvey steps forward and introduces himself.

'I'd like to see the cockpit, if that's all right with you? Always been fascinated by these big birds.'

'Of course,' Trankov nods. 'Mikhail will show you.'

'I'll take him,' says Ironside. 'Need to sort out the runway.'

'Let's get inside, then,' says Heatherton. 'Follow me.'

It has been agreed that only Heatherton, Beer, Price and Matthews will meet the Russian delegation until the exact purpose of their visit is established. After much argument, Wolfe has been allowed to join them, but no recordings, no notebooks. Harvey is apparently more interested in the plane than in the impending showdown.

'Ah, it is tropical here, I think,' says Trankov. 'You British are too soft to cope with the temperatures at Vostok.'

Heatherton flinches at the jibe. Inside the mess tent, the four Russians are offered tea and coffee; in honour of their arrival, the last packet of chocolate biscuits is opened. As the Russians sit on one side of the trestle table and the hosts on the other, it reminds Wolfe of the many peace talks she has reported on.

'So, Alexey,' says Heatherton, 'it's always a nice distraction to have visitors, but I'm sure this is not a social visit. Do you mind telling me what you're doing here?'

Trankov has removed his red puffa and put on metal-framed glasses. He smiles warmly. 'We have come to help you with your problem.'

'Really?' says Heatherton. The sarcastic tone appears lost on Trankov. 'But I have already made it clear that we don't need your help. We have made our own arrangements.'

Trankov nods. 'You did, my friend. That is why I fly thousands of kilometres to ask you to change your mind. You must wait three more days for replacement parts. This mean the bore hole, it will freeze tight.' He twists his hands as if throttling a small animal. Wolfe's mind is spinning with questions she's dying to ask, especially how he knows about their arrangements for the new parts. 'This means you must drill a new bore hole, which is a big risk for you. You may run out of fuel. Many things can go wrong. But if you start to drill now, with our drill, you can use the bore hole you have. No problem! So!' Trankov pauses for dramatic effect, his arms raised high like a magician about to reveal that his assistant has disappeared from the box. 'Our drill is sterile. And no pollution.' Trankov winks at Dr Price, who flushes, livid. 'I think you will like it.'

Beer leans forward and places a clenched fist on the white Formica table top. 'What makes you think it'll take three days for us to get new parts?'

'There are no secrets in Antarctica. Everybody knows your first samples have been destroyed. I tell you this. Somebody here is sick in the head.' Trankov scrutinises the faces of the four people opposite.

'Hold on a second,' Price says. 'Are you saying you've developed your own hot water drill?'

'This is correct. We had, how do you say . . . a few problems with our last drill. Using Freon and kerosene to lubricate the bore hole and antifreeze to keep it open upset many scientists and killed our living samples. We learn from our mistakes. So we develop a sterile hot water drill.'

'But it's already too late,' Price retorts. 'You've contaminated Vostok, one of the last totally pristine lakes in the world. You should be ashamed.'

'Stacy!' warns Heatherton.

'We have not contaminated the lake, Dr Price. Just our samples.'

'Rubbish,' Price replies. 'Why do you refuse to allow other countries to test the water?'

Heatherton intervenes. 'Let's not beat around the bush, Alexey. Your drill design has been a closely guarded secret. Likewise, we have kept ours under lock and key, because it's one of a kind, developed specially for this project. Are you seriously going to share your unique design with us?'

Trankov nods.

'But why? If it gets damaged, you can't use it at Vostok.'

'Because we cannot progress. We are hindered by very cold weather. The forecast is bad. It says it will stay minus sixty or seventy for the next two weeks. You will have completed your mission by then. I do not want to come second. But, I am happy to be joint-first. With you.'

Price mutters, 'It's not a fucking race.'

Trankov raises a white eyebrow. 'I think you are being naïve, Dr Price.'

'How dare you—'

Beer cuts in. 'Can we see the drill? Then we decide if we want it.'

'No way!' Price blurts out. 'And anyway, this is pointless without a sediment probe.'

Heatherton glares at her. 'I think you've said enough, Stacy.'

She looks away, mortified at her mistake.

'I can help you, once again,' says a smug Trankov. 'Our probe is on the plane. And, yes, you can inspect both. But if you decide to use our equipment, then we get equal credit for whatever is discovered in Lake Ellsworth.' Trankov peers over the top of his glasses at Heatherton.

'It does no harm to look,' says Beer.

'No way,' says Price. 'This has taken us ten years. I'm not giving equal credit to someone who shows up at the last moment offering a solution we don't need.'

Matthews has listened quietly until now. He unfolds his arms. 'I agree with George: it does no harm to have a look. But, and here's the big but. We'd have to be convinced it carries no contaminants. It needs to be absolutely sterile.'

'But we don't know how to use it,' says Heatherton.

Trankov pipes up. 'That is why I have my engineers with me.'

'Alexey,' says Heatherton. 'I'm happy to see your drill and probe. I will then talk in private with my colleagues. If we decide we do not want to use it, we ask you to get back on your plane and leave. Today.'

'What kind of hospitality is this?' asks Trankov, again with a dramatic gesture. 'It is a long journey from Vostok. We must refuel. My people are weary. We must stay the night.'

'We'll see,' says Heatherton. 'Shall we take a look?'

One by one they leave the Weatherhaven. Beer turns to Wolfe. 'It's going to be an uncomfortable night.'

18

Their boots clatter on the steel floor of the Il-76, the sound amplified within the tunnel-like confines of a cargo hold that can carry four armoured trucks and fifty soldiers, no problem. Wolfe follows Yushkov inside. Before entering, he glances around at the brightly lit interior, then stands near the exit, well away from the rest of the group.

The big man has waited until all the Russians are inside the plane's belly. He has not spoken since the visitors arrived, but his eyes are watchful and his body as tense as a drawn bow. The Il–76's ceiling is padded insulation, exposed pipes, electric cables and a few down–lights. It's in need of some TLC. Running the hold's length, on both sides, are overhead lockers, and beneath them, folding metal chairs, screwed to the floor. It is a workhorse. No comfort provided. The cargo hold is almost empty, except for two long crates, secured by straps. Wolfe can guess their contents: the Russians' drill head and probe. Beyond the crates, a rectangular bladder of aviation fuel, as big as a family swimming pool, is strapped to the floor.

'It is time for the . . . how do you say? Unveiling?' says Trankov, who is clearly a bit of a performer.

Snigir and Magnitsky take control of unstrapping the first crate. Grankin assists. They speak in hushed Russian.

'What are they saying?' Wolfe whispers to Yushkov.

He is observing them so intently he doesn't even register her question. Grankin uses a crowbar to carefully lever open the crate's lid. Magnitsky releases the second crate from its bonds and, also, forces open its lid. The Lake Ellsworth engineers – Beer, Ironside and Rundle – move closer, drawn to the boxes' contents like children to presents under a Christmas tree. The rest of the British team follow suit. All except Yushkov, who holds back.

Snigir squats next to the box containing their hot water drill nozzle. The seams of her waterproof pants strain as the flesh of her strong but chubby legs swells. As she points out the key features of the drill, Grankin translates.

Rundle kneels next to Snigir.

'Fuck me!' Rundle says, interrupting Snigir's fast talking. 'It's like ours.' He looks up at Yushkov. 'Vitaly! You've got to look at this.'

All eyes are on Yushkov. He takes careful steps towards the open crate as he pulls on latex gloves and kneels opposite Snigir.

He asks her in Russian if he can pick it up and she nods. He is much easier for Wolfe to understand as he speaks slowly and deliberately. Yushkov lifts the drill nozzle a few centimetres and peers at the circular drill head through its protective cover.

'The nozzle assembly is brass and steel, 1,400 millimetres long, has forward-facing jets.' He looks at Snigir and reverts to Russian. 'Has this sterile bag been opened?'

'*Nyet*,' she replies firmly. 'Sterile,' she adds proudly in English.

'I cannot be certain until the bag is open,' Yushkov says to Rundle. 'But the design looks . . . ' He chooses his words carefully, aware Russian and British eyes are on him. ' . . . almost identical. It is a miracle.'

He gently places the drill nozzle back in the crate.

'See!' says Trankov. 'I tell you we have sterile hot water drill, and it is true!'

'But that's just not possible,' says Rundle. 'Our drill is one of a kind. There's no way another design team could've come up with something like it.' Rundle shoots up from his squatting position, his tone indignant.

Beer has been quietly inspecting the bagged drill nozzle. He shakes his head. 'I don't know how you did it,' he says to Snigir. 'But that's our drill you've got there.'

Heatherton takes a closer look.

Grankin translates and Snigir's eyes disappear under her puffy brows as she fires out words like machine-gun bullets, pointing a finger at Beer in angry emphasis.

Grankin speaks. 'This is not your drill. It is our design and engineering. It is arrogant to assume that we have copied your design. Perhaps you have copied ours!'

Rundle jumps up and opens his mouth to retaliate when Heatherton speaks up.

'We're not accusing you of anything, but you have to admit

it's extraordinary.' It's clear from his troubled expression that he thinks the coincidence is more than extraordinary. 'Let's move on to the probe, shall we?'

Rundle and Beer focus on the next open crate: the probe is sealed in plastic but clearly visible.

'So how does it operate?' Rundle asks, trying to keep his cool. He gives the female engineer his most winning smile, but she's unimpressed.

Snigir flicks a look at Trankov, who nods. Grankin translates. 'The probe consists of two pressure cases. The lower contains the majority of the instrumentation, and the upper the power and communications demodulation systems. These two vessels are separated by the water samplers. Data is delivered in real-time, and water and sediment samples are recovered for post-retrieval analyses.'

Beer gawps at Snigir. Rundle, young and not prone to diplomacy, storms over to Heatherton. 'Michael, for fuck's sake, it's the mirror image of ours!'

'Dr Heatherton,' says Trankov. 'I urge you to control your people. These accusations are unfounded. This will not end well.'

The tension in the confined space is like static.

'Vitaly!' says Rundle. 'You haven't said a word. Come on, man, what do you think?'

Yushkov takes a deep breath. He looks into Grankin's eyes and Wolfe swears she sees Grankin shake his head almost imperceptibly. Yushkov stares at the floor, his jaw muscles tense. Wolfe recognises the look of a man faced with a terrible dilemma. A dilemma that could have dangerous repercussions. She has watched whistle-blowers with that same look in their eyes as they decide whether or not to destroy their lives and careers to do the right thing. A mix of terror and weariness, pride and doubt.

'Well?' demands Heatherton.

DEVOUR

Yushkov looks at his project leader. 'I cannot be certain until I inspect the machinery. It is possible for separate teams to produce similar designs.'

Rundle yells at Yushkov. 'That's a cop-out and you know it. You're on their fucking side!'

Wolfe looks round at Grankin and catches him smirking. Yushkov holds his ground for a few seconds and then turns his back on Rundle and leaves.

'You're meant to be on our side!' Rundle shouts after him.

Heatherton clears his throat. 'Dr Trankov, I think our teams should go about their duties, while you and I have a talk in private.'

19

Your Skype conversation is with Jerry Butcher. My spyware enables me to watch both of you. Behind Butcher is a bookshelf so neat, so ordered, it's as if the books are cardboard cut-outs for a show home. On the middle shelf there's a framed photograph of him shaking hands with none other than the biggest piece of filth of all, the Metropolitan Police Commissioner.

'Aren't you well connected, Jerry, old boy? Not that it will do you any good.'

You, Olivia, are multiple layers of clothing, like a robin puffing out its feathers to keep warm. But I want you stripped. Exposed and vulnerable, as I was when you left me to die. Dr Sharma is delighted with my progress. Almost did a little jig when I described the flashback. This is the first new memory I can hang on to, recall over and over again, even if it is sometimes so painful I want to throw up. So I guess it is progress.

You are wearing headphones, sitting at a table, your back to the tent wall so your screen can't be seen by others. I don't hear voices, so guess you are alone. The coffee mug you drink from has left a circular stain on the table's white surface.

'Did you find out anything?' you ask Butcher.

'I have something. Wasn't easy to get, mind you. Met with an old mate from the Foreign Office. Retired now, keen to chat about old times over a few beers.'

You look around, checking nobody has entered the Weatherhaven. 'What did he tell you?'

'Turns out Yushkov is a bit of a hero.'

You frown.

I frown.

I'm as surprised as you.

'Do you remember two years ago when some maniac, Robert Zhao Sheng, blew up a massive Antarctic glacier?'

'Of course I do. It was a big story. But the man who tried to stop him was Australian, wasn't he?'

'That's right. Luke Searle and an American, Maddie Wildman. But there was one other whose identity was kept secret. At the time, he was engineer on an Antarctic tourist ship.'

'You're not serious? Vitaly?'

You say his name out loud, then realise your mistake. For a moment you appear to be listening for something, then your shoulders relax.

'According to my source, yes,' Butcher says.

You shake your head in disbelief. I immediately google the media coverage at the time. Searle and Wildman are hailed as heroes. No mention of Yushkov. No mention of a third person.

'But Searle and Wildman nearly died. Are you saying he helped them?'

'I am.'

You run your finger round the table's circular stain, lost in thought. 'He helped an Australian and an American? Why? This flies in the face of an email I received yesterday.'

'What email?'

'I'll send it to you now.'

Butcher receives the one-pager on Yushkov's army career and cowardice.

'Sent anonymously. Moz is getting it translated,' you say.

Good. That would be helpful.

'I'd regard anything anonymous and untraceable with a great deal of suspicion,' Butcher says. 'Perhaps someone is feeding you misinformation?'

Not me. Not this time. Someone is treading on my patch.

'Maybe,' you say. 'But if he's the hero you say, then why on earth would he keep it quiet?'

'I've been racking my brains about that – or what's left of them, anyway.' Butcher grins. 'To achieve a media blackout like this needs government intervention at a very senior level. If the British Government did this, then MI5 would've been involved. Probably Six too.'

'If that's true, he must be extremely valuable.' You shake your head. 'It doesn't make sense. What could he possibly know that's worth all that trouble?'

'Yushkov may well be a spy, Olivia.' A pause. 'One of ours.'

'So what's he doing here, in the middle of nowhere?' You chew a fingernail, thinking. 'Can your friend give us anything solid? Documents? Photos?'

'You know me better than that, Liv. I'm helping you because I think you're in danger, but everything I've just said is off the record and I certainly won't give you confidential documents.'

Nice try, Olivia, but Butcher is a real by-the-book kind of guy.

'Did your source say anything else?'

'He talked about a cable between the Australian ambassador in Argentina and the Foreign Office in London. He claims they agreed that Yushkov's involvement in what they refer to as the "Robert Zhoa Sheng incident" will be kept secret. The Ambassador confirms that both Searle and Wildman have agreed not to disclose Yushkov's identity.'

'Argentina?'

'Yes, the Argentinian Navy was part of the rescue mission.'

'I'm beginning to think our Russian friend might be the one in danger. No wonder our visitors are making him nervous.'

You are both silent for a while.

'Any news on your mugger?' you ask.

'Nope. No witness, no street cameras and I didn't see him. Makes him hard to find.'

'Was your wallet stolen?'

'Yes, but I think that it was just covering up the real motive. It was found in a bin. Cash and cards still in it.'

'You think it was all about my house keys?'

I hold my breath.

'Come on, Liv. Isn't it obvious? It was your stalker.'

I whoop with delight and punch the air. Well done, Mr Detective!

'If that's true, then he's escalated to direct violence,' you say.

'When you're back in London, be vigilant.'

You frown. 'My computer may be compromised,' you say. Bonus points to Olivia! 'An article I emailed to Moz just disappeared. No record of me ever sending it. And I swear my files have been rearranged.'

You noticed? My mistake.

'Get your laptop checked out when you get home. Until then, be careful what you write. Someone may read it, or even make it public.'

Fuck off, Jerry! You're raining on my parade.

'I'll use my phone instead.' You pause. 'I think we can rule out Lalzad,' you say. 'I can't see one of his goons deleting stuff just to be annoying.'

Butcher clears his throat. 'Look, Olivia, I have some news you're not going to like.'

I'm all ears. Has this news something to do with the letter I stole on my last visit to your Balham flat? You give Jerry one of your penetrating stares and I can tell from your jerky jaw movements that you've started to play with your tongue stud.

'Just tell me, Jerry.'

A slight pause. 'Davy has been released.'

'What!' Your eyes are wide as walnuts. 'Why wasn't I warned?'

'I checked with Prison Services. You were sent a letter, as is the rule, with details of his imminent release.'

'But I never got it. Shit! When is this happening?'

'He got out eight days ago.'

You cover your face with your hands and say something barely audible.

'Say again?' says Jerry.

When you remove your hands, the colour has drained from your face. You look horrified. I wish I could get that reaction from you.

'To think Davy could've been watching me, and I didn't even know,' you say. 'He knows I value my privacy, the security of my home.' Then your face brightens. You sit straighter. 'But weird things have been going on for the last six months. So it can't be him.'

'But it could have been Claire. She blames you for putting Davy away. Maybe he asked her to scare you, and now he's out of gaol, he's doing it himself? Payback.'

I've already looked into the manslaughter conviction of David Wolfe. Did it as soon as I read the Prison Services letter. It got big media coverage: an ex-Second Tank Regiment squaddie-turned-nightclub-bouncer beats a nineteen-year-old punter to death. In the *Daily Mail* there's a great photo of eighteen-year-old, pink-haired Claire Spiers, clutching newborn Joe, outside the court just after sentencing, telling everyone who'll listen that Davy is innocent and Olivia is a liar.

In the *Guardian*, there's a longer piece on David Wolfe's family life and background. The reporter describes Davy as 'a time bomb waiting to go off'. An angry boy, never finished school; he joined the Army at eighteen and spent five years with the Second Royal Tank Regiment. Accused and acquitted of the unlawful killing of an Iraqi man in Basra, he left the Army shortly after and worked as a security guard, then nightclub bouncer.

Harry Coleman, the nineteen-year-old victim, had been goading Davy all night. A fight broke out when Coleman tried to leave the club with some beer he'd bought at the bar. Coleman wandered off but a few minutes later returned and spat in Davy's face. CCTV footage shows Davy dragging Coleman down a laneway. But the CCTV camera covering the laneway wasn't working that night, so the prosecution relied on witness statements to convict him.

'But doesn't an early release mean he's subject to recall for any breach of conditions?' Wolfe asks.

'Yes. One of the conditions is he stays away from you.'

'So stalking me is a big risk.'

'Maybe he thinks it's worth it.'

'How did he get out early?'

'Good behaviour and found God, apparently.'

'Found God? How can the parole board be so gullible?'

'Got some shrink to testify on his change of heart and his remorse.'

'He'll never forgive me.'

20

The decision has been made. The Russians fly back to Lake Vostok early in the morning and take their equipment with them. Trankov is doing a great job of pretending not to be upset, but Snigir ate her dinner in sour silence and left the mess tent in a huff. Wolfe imagines her guarding the re-crated and controversial drill nozzle and probe, sleeping between them in the cargo hold. The other person to leave the Weatherhaven quickly is Yushkov. He's received the cold shoulder from the Brits and Russians alike. As the evening progresses, Wolfe notices the visitors take turns eating dinner so that at any one time there are always two of them inside the Il-76.

The pilot, Mikhail Nikolaev, has been the most affable, probably because he is not directly involved in the Lake Vostok project. He works for TransAVIAexport Airlines, a Belarusian cargo line. Nikolaev's anaemic pallor and gaunt features belie his outgoing personality. He regales whoever will listen with his aerial Antarctic adventures, in stilted pidgin English. Heatherton and Matthews listen politely. Ironside, his cooking duties over, has joined them. Wolfe is seated at another table, next to Sinclair.

'Toby, any idea what's really going on?' she asks.

He stares down at his bowl of chilli con carne. 'Your guess is as good as mine,' he mumbles.

'But there's got to be more to it.'

'I have a theory. Well, a kind of a theory, but I don't want you quoting me.'

He blushes and scoops another spoonful into his mouth.

'Off the record, then,' Wolfe says.

Sinclair avoids eye contact as usual. 'Nobody has been allowed near Vostok Station – other than Russian personnel – since they first drilled into the lake,' he whispers. 'My guess is they have already drilled a second bore hole using their new drill, and found they've destroyed the lake's pristine environment.'

'Can kerosene and antifreeze contaminate the whole lake?'

'Ah, no, that's not what I mean. I was talking about them introducing microbes from our world. Easily done if the equipment isn't kept sterile. It's possible an ancient life form will be vulnerable to attack from modern-day bacteria or viruses.'

'So Trankov needs another subglacial lake to drill?'

'It's just a theory, of course.'

Sinclair lapses into silence. As Wolfe mulls over his idea, Sinclair unexpectedly pipes up again. He shifts his chair closer to hers and keeps his voice low. But he needn't worry: Nikolaev's booming voice fills the tent.

'Dr Trankov is under enormous pressure, you see. The Kremlin is watching his project very closely.' Wolfe can't help staring at Sinclair. Where did he get this information? 'A major scientific breakthrough will bind the federation together with nationalistic pride. You know, like putting a man on the moon. Apparently, Putin believes such a momentous discovery would help his re-election.'

This is news to Wolfe, who prides herself on keeping up to date with world politics.

'But Putin can't be President again. He can only be re-elected once.'

Sinclair shrugs. 'I don't know. You'll know more about politics than me. I'm just telling you what Vitaly said.'

'Vitaly?' Of all the people for Yushkov to confide in, she finds it hard to understand why it should be the shy and awkward Sinclair. 'What does he think our Russian friends are up to here?'

'Ah, he hasn't said. But I think he's quite upset. Trent was out of order laying into him like that. He put Vitaly in a really awkward position. Antagonising Russia at the best of times is a risky business, but when you're a defector – well, pissing off someone as well connected as Dr Trankov is a really bad idea. If I were in his shoes, I'd have done exactly what he did. Tried not to rock the boat.' Sinclair looks furtively at Trankov and Grankin eating. 'The sooner they're gone, the better.'

Wolfe tries to keep a poker face. 'Do you know why Vitaly defected?'

Sinclair stares at his lap. 'N . . . no. I don't. He's talked about the Second Chechen War and the atrocities on both sides . . . Maybe he just couldn't stomach it any more.'

Sinclair clams up. Wolfe tries to keep the conversation going.

'I did some reporting on the Ukraine crisis in 2014. I met locals who'd survived the Battle of Grozny during the previous Russian–Chechen war you're talking about. Vitaly's right: it was brutal. What often gets forgotten are the innocent people in the way. The women and children. I wanted the rest of the world to know what the war was doing to them.'

Sinclair looks up at her, eyes wide, as if he's seeing her in a whole new light.

'You know, I think I remember your article: it was about the Russians bombing civilians queuing for bread.'

'That's right. You've got a good memory.'

'I do. Almost photographic.' He frowns. 'Didn't you report in Afghanistan too? On drone attacks killing civilians?'

'I did. A great and brave journalist, Marie Colvin, once said that the "truth of history demands witnesses". I believe that's our job: to bear witness,' Wolfe says.

'But nobody cares, Olivia. What do the military call the women and children killed by drones? Collateral damage. How very compassionate.' For the first time, Sinclair looks her straight in the eye. He is no longer whispering. His face is flushed with indignation. 'Drone strikes are inaccurate and data on casualties is kept secret. It's only through people like you that we get any information at all, because you're there, witnessing murder.'

Price has been deep in close conversation with Harvey. She turns round at Sinclair's raised voice.

'You all right, Toby?' Price asks.

'Yes, um. Been, you know, a stressful day.'

He gets up. Wolfe and Price watch him leave.

'Highly strung, is our Toby,' Price says. 'Brilliant mind, but very sensitive. He likes order, routine. And today is anything but.' She looks at Wolfe. 'What was he saying about murder?'

'We were talking about my war reporting. I didn't mean to upset him. I might go after him and make sure he's okay.'

Before Price can ask anything else, Wolfe leaves the mess tent. Outside, the light is muted, the sun hidden by grey cloud. The wind is little more than a murmur. She scans the two rows of red pyramids, then the shipping containers, all locked up, and further in the distance, the drill site, now cloaked in a tented structure to keep prying eyes off the equipment. Rundle has volunteered to sleep in the container with the damaged drill and probe, so 'those thieving bastards can't touch them.' In the opposite direction, the Il-76 squats on the ice, its side door open. Someone in a red parka, hood raised, sits on the top step, smoking. His legs are long. She guesses, Grankin.

Wolfe heads for Sinclair's tent and spots a second smoker, his identity obscured by the row of red pyramids. She sniffs the air and recognises Yushkov's brand – Belomorkanal. Wolfe hesitates. Is this an opportunity to talk to Yushkov in private? There's a flash of red clothing as someone moves along the row of tents towards him. Wolfe ducks down and waits. She hears two male voices speaking Russian. The men can't see her crouching on the other side of the tent. She listens, wishing her Russian was better.

Yushkov's greeting to Grankin is short, his tone wary. Seconds pass as the men smoke in silence.

'Why do you work with these people?' Grankin asks. Wolfe is fairly certain she has understood correctly. 'They treat you like the enemy.'

Yushkov spits. Is he going to ignore the jibe?

'Russia made me an enemy. The British gave me asylum, gave me citizenship. I owe them much.'

Grankin laughs, tilting his head back, and his hood falls away, revealing fair hair.

'You owe them nothing. They cannot operate the drill without you and yet they shun you, ignore you. Treat you like a . . .'

Wolfe cannot translate the last word but she suspects it must be something like 'outcast'.

'I am here to do a job and I will do it.'

'They think you killed Kevin Knox, yes?'

'I don't care what they think.'

'Tell me who killed him.'

Grankin speaks with authority. This is not an engineer in idle gossip.

'He died in a blizzard. It was an accident. Nothing more.'

'My friend, you are blind if you think that.' Grankin makes clicking noises with his tongue, as if reprimanding a child. 'You should be working with us. Russia still wants you.'

Does he mean the Russian Arctic & Antarctic Research Institute, or something more sinister?

'Russia wants me in a military prison.'

'Perhaps you will be pardoned?' Grankin says. 'Perhaps I can make this happen?'

Pardoned for what? Defecting? Or is Yushkov really a deserter? And how can an engineer pave the way for a man with Yushkov's past to return to Russia?

'You are *Sluzhba Vneshney Razvedki*?' Yushkov asks if he is with the Foreign Intelligence Service, known as the SVR.

Wolfe's heart beats so loudly she swears Grankin will hear. She doesn't move an inch. If Grankin is SVR, the Russian equivalent of MI6, he will be armed. She holds her breath, listening for Grankin's response.

'Come, come, my friend. You are paranoid.'

'What do you want?' Yushkov demands.

'Come, let us walk.'

'So I end up dead like Kevin? I don't think so. We talk here or not at all.'

'Walk with me to the plane. It's not far. What I have to say is for your ears only.'

'I do not wish to hear it.'

Yushkov's head appears to the left of the pyramid. He's heading for the mess tent. If she stays where she is, he will see her. But if she moves and makes a run for it, Grankin will see her.

'Your sister wants to see you,' Grankin calls out.

Yushkov stops dead. He turns on his heels and takes angry strides back towards Grankin.

'Leave my sister alone,' he roars in Grankin's face.

21

Grankin doesn't flinch at Yushkov's fury. Now he's hooked his prize, he walks away.

Yushkov follows, trailing Grankin a fraction, a reluctant participant. Their conversation is muted. Wolfe cannot follow them to the cargo plane. There is nowhere for her to hide. Instead, she lies on her stomach and peers around the tent's edge. She pulls out her camera and waits for Grankin to turn her way. Yushkov suddenly stops.

'Shut up!' he shouts, rubbing his bare head roughly, clearly agitated.

Wolfe takes a couple of photos of both men, then zooms in on Grankin's face. Grankin places an arm around Yushkov's shoulder. Yushkov flinches, but he allows himself to be led on.

Wolfe races back to the Weatherhaven and darts behind the makeshift curtain of her sleeping space. Is Grankin SVR? How does he know Yushkov's sister? Why would Yushkov end up in military prison if he went home? Unlocking her backpack's padlock, she pulls out her laptop and searches the Web for any images of Sergey Grankin, engineer. It appears he does work for the Russian Arctic & Antarctic Research Institute in St Petersburg. He's been to Antarctica four times, twice to Vostok, once to Novolazarevskaya Station and once to Bellingshausen Station. But is the man with Yushkov the real Grankin? She finds a photo taken during the Antarctic summer in 2012 of 'Crew Bellinghausen' posing outside a red hut raised on stilts above the ice. Each person's name is listed. She scans the faces searching for Grankin and finds a tall man with a thick beard in blue work overalls and black beanie. But she can't tell if the man with Yushkov right now is the man in the picture. She keeps searching the site and finds a corporate-looking headshot of a slightly chubbier Grankin. Again, a bushy beard. His eyes are blue but his nose isn't broken. It could be an old image. Wolfe can't be sure.

It is approaching midnight and Wolfe can't rest. The daylight doesn't help: it's like England on a dull winter's day but bright enough to disturb sleep. She can't stop replaying the conversation between Yushkov and Grankin over and over in her head. Outside, the wind has picked up. The tent occasionally creaks but otherwise the camp is quiet. She's emailed Butcher the photos she took earlier and told him she believes he could be an SVR agent, just as Butcher suspected.

Her stomach churns, but not from hunger. There are too many unanswered questions and the Russians' presence is unsettling. She turns on to her side and runs her hand underneath her improvised pillow – a fleece rolled into a sausage – to reassure herself that the knife is where she placed it. It is. Made from an extremely strong black plastic, Wolfe always sleeps with it for protection when on assignment. The ten-centimetre blade is sharp enough to slice flesh and passes through airport metal detectors unnoticed.

She tucks her head down into the sleeping bag and closes her eyes. Wolfe drifts off but wakes with a jolt, unsure if she has slept for a minute or for hours. She listens. A clunk, like a door unlatching. If somebody is in the kitchen she'll hear the squeak of boots on the rubber floor, but she hears nothing. The wind whistles through the campsite and the tent is buffeted by its force. Sitting up, Wolfe wriggles her arms free of the sleeping bag and removes the knife from its sheath. With her other hand she holds her Maglite torch, but she doesn't switch it on. If there is someone on the other side of the partition, she doesn't want them to know she is awake. As quietly as possible she wriggles her legs out of the sleeping bag and kneels. If she stands, her damaged knee will click. She tilts her head and listens. Can she hear breathing? She imagines Butcher yelling at her to stand up so she can defend herself. She risks it. Click.

Someone charges straight through the dividing curtain, knocking her backwards. It's like being hit by a snowplough, front on. She lands hard on her back, flattened by her attacker's body weight. He grabs her knife-holding hand and slams it into the floor, forcing her to drop it. While he's focused on the knife, Wolfe tries to smash the metal torch into his head, but he blocks her arm. He rips the torch from her fingers and throws it away. It hits the tent fabric with a dull thud. She has to get out from under him, otherwise she is lost.

Wolfe slides her right arm under his chin and pushes upwards. At the same time, she puts her left hand on his hip and uses her left elbow as a stilt, forcing his hip up a fraction, giving her a little space to move. She locks her legs around one of his and then wriggles her hips out from beneath him so that she lies on her side, her knee in his groin, her right elbow in the crook of his neck. He can't now use his weight against her. Her right knee slides across his stomach and she twists her body, forcing the man off her. He now faces away from her. A Brazilian jiu-jitsu move she'd learnt from Butcher.

Wolfe scrambles to stand but her attacker spins around and lunges at her again, covering her head with the sleeping bag. Disoriented, she stumbles. He sits on her chest, pinning her arms down with his knees. With ferocious force he presses the padded material over her nose and mouth. She desperately tries to shift her head to find an air pocket, but he forces the material into her open mouth. She gags, sucking in fabric. Her lungs begin to burn. She's going to die.

Wolfe has one move left: she jerks her hips up into a bridge position and manages to shift to her side at a forty-five-degree angle, unbalancing her attacker for a moment. She feels in the darkness for the knife. Her fingertips touch the handle but she can't quite grip it. Wolfe bends a knee, forcing her attacker's leg away from his body, giving her more wriggle room so she can stretch her hand out further. Gripping the knife, she plunges it into the man's arm. He grunts. Wolfe shakes the sleeping bag off her face and gulps in air.

But her attacker raises a flattened palm above her nose. In one horrifying moment, she knows what he is about to do. It's a technique Butcher has showed her and warned her never to use, unless it is literally a matter of her life or death – the palm heel strike. The killer is going to ram his palm into her nose in an upward motion, forcing fractured bones into her brain. A quick and certain death. Wolfe has run out of options. She screams.

But the killer's open palm never reaches her face. Someone literally picks her assailant up by his coat and throws him on to a trestle table. The table cracks and collapses under the man's weight. Chairs topple. But he is quick to recover. He picks himself up and runs from the Weatherhaven, the door slamming behind him.

Yushkov kneels beside Wolfe.

'Did he hurt you?'

She gulps for air. 'He . . . was going to kill me.'

She feels something wet under her nose and wipes the blood away with her hand. Her knuckles are raw where he stamped on them.

'These are dangerous people, Olivia. You spy on them and they will come after you.'

22

Beer rushes into the dining area, his blond hair flying. He sees the smashed table and toppled chairs and the back of Yushkov leaning over Wolfe and charges at the Russian, tackling him from behind. Beer has Yushkov's neck in an arm lock as he drags him backwards.

'No! Stop!' Wolfe cries, but her voice is hoarse. 'Not him!'

'What?'

Yushkov elbows Beer in the ribs. Beer winces and lets go.

'I was attacked. Vitaly dragged him off me. He ran out that door.'

'I didn't see anybody,' says Beer.

Heatherton runs in, followed by Adeyemi.

'What happened?' demands Heatherton. 'I heard screaming.'

'What the hell?' says Adeyemi, staring at the broken furniture.

'Someone tried to kill me,' she coughs. 'Vitaly scared him off.' Wolfe grabs her boots and shoves them on, not bothering with the laces. 'He mustn't get away.'

'Who?' asks Heatherton. When he doesn't get an answer, he asks Vitaly, 'What's going on?' Vitaly also ignores him.

'Olivia, do not chase this man,' Yushkov says. 'It is too dangerous.'

I bet you know how dangerous, too.

Wolfe stumbles to stand and dodges past her stunned onlookers as she hurries outside, forgetting her coat. The door slams in the wind as she peers out over the camp, searching for a man running away. But all she sees is people running towards her.

'Where did he go?' she mutters, then focuses her attention on the ice beneath her boots, searching for blood. She stabbed his arm. Ice particles swirl around her, making it hard to see the ground clearly.

'Olivia!' says Beer. 'You'll get frostbite. Here's your coat.'

Already shivering, she hurriedly puts it and her gloves on, then gets down on her hands and knees searching for blood.

'Tell us what you're looking for and we'll help,' Heatherton says.

'I stabbed him in the arm. There must be a blood trail.'

'What with?' asks Beer.

'A knife. My knife.'

The men exchange looks.

'Search for blood,' Wolfe persists.

'But why attack you?' asks Beer.

'You think it's those Russians?' asks Adeyemi.

Wolfe glances at Yushkov, who is examining the icy ground next to her. She'd lay any money her attacker was Grankin. Yushkov saw her spying on them so Grankin probably did too. But if she tells them what she overheard, she will open a can of worms for the man who has just saved her life.

'I don't know.' Wolfe stares in the direction of Il–76 searching for movement, but the plane is little more than a blurred outline through wind thick with ice.

'Vitaly, you must've seen who it was?' asks Heatherton.

'*Nyet!* He wore a balaclava.'

'But was he in red? How tall? There must be something you remember?' Beer interjects.

'It was fast. I just pulled him off her and threw him on the table. Then he ran. I do not remember.'

'A man?'

'*Da.*'

'Look!' Wolfe says, a few paces from the mess tent. 'Blood.'

Woken by the ruckus, Price, Sinclair and Matthews join the search. Wolfe's nose and ears burn with cold but she keeps following the trail until it disappears beneath shifting ice, like sand drifting in a desert.

'This is hopeless.' Wolfe stands. 'Michael, we need everyone accounted for, including on that plane. Someone has a stab wound.'

'Now wait a second,' says Heatherton. 'I can't just go over

there in the middle of the night and demand they show me their arms. It's bad enough we've rejected their offer of help. I'm not going to accuse them of attempted murder without some evidence.'

'You have two witnesses, Michael!' She explains what her attacker was about to do when Yushkov tackled him. 'As leader of this expedition, you have to investigate. And that includes Trankov's team.'

'Look, I can't—'

'Mike!' says Beer. 'She's right. We have to find who did this. And we've got to alert BAS.'

'Christ!' says Heatherton, dragging his fingers through his hair. 'Anything else!'

Wolfe has had enough. 'Michael, I'm going over to that plane. If they refuse to co-operate, we know they have something to hide.'

'No, no, don't do that,' says Heatherton. 'It'll cause an international incident. We should at least check our team first.'

'You check your team. I want some answers from those Russians.'

Wolfe leaves.

'Wait, Olivia! I go with you,' says Yushkov.

'Olivia!' calls Heatherton, running after her. 'I'll get everyone into the mess. If my team gets the all-clear, then I'll come with you to see Trankov.' She stops walking away. 'They're not going anywhere till the morning.'

'Okay. Your team first, but hurry.'

Heatherton sends Beer to wake up Ironside and Harvey, as everyone else moves into the Weatherhaven.

Wolfe leans close to Yushkov. 'You know who did this, don't you?'

Their eyes meet.

'I cannot be certain.'

'Sergey Grankin?'

He shakes his head. 'It is better for you, you never know.'

Despite the hubbub at the camp, the doors to the cargo plane remain resolutely closed like a castle under siege. Everyone on Heatherton's team has voluntarily shown their arms to Wolfe. Rundle has an old cut on his right forearm, just above his wrist, but his fellow engineers can vouch it happened during the drilling process.

'Well, that leaves us with the four men and one woman on board that plane,' she says.

'Oh dear me,' says Heatherton. 'This is very awkward. I mean, we can't just go over there and accuse them of murder. I should talk to our director first, but I'll have to wait a few hours until she's awake.'

'Mike, they're due to leave at seven. We can't delay any longer,' says Beer.

'But why you?' asks Harvey, sipping a black coffee and blinking rapidly behind smudged lenses. 'I mean the only person they've been less than friendly to is Vitaly.'

'I don't know.'

'Oh, come on, Olivia! Why would engineers want to kill a journalist reporting on a drilling project?' scoffs Harvey.

Wolfe wants to slap him. 'I'm not waiting any longer.'

'No, really, I must talk to . . .' pleads Heatherton.

Yushkov follows her out of the door.

'I'm going with her,' says Rundle. 'Those bastards stole my designs.'

'Mate, I don't think going over there looking for a fight is the best idea,' says Matthews.

'They started it,' Rundle snaps.

Beer glances at Heatherton, then follows too. The crosswind is now strong enough to make walking in a straight line difficult.

'If this gets worse, they may have to delay their departure. The wind's already thirty-five knots,' says Beer, jogging to catch up.

'No way,' says Rundle. 'They're leaving.'

'Amen to that,' says Yushkov.

'Look! The side door's open,' says Wolfe, pointing. 'Maybe they're expecting us?'

'Oh shit! Someone's moving the wheel chocks,' says Rundle.

A hundred and fifty metres away, a figure leans down and picks up a red wedge that has been keeping one of the sets of tyres from rolling on the slick ice. The other chocks have already been removed. The figure runs up the steps two at a time and then scrambles to shut the side door. The four turbofan bypass engines rumble into life.

'They're leaving!' shouts Wolfe, running towards the plane, waving her arms in the air. 'Wait! Stop!'

The others follow. 'Make them see us,' pants Wolfe, her arms flailing.

'They see us,' replies Yushkov, running with her.

'Get a flare,' Beer says to Rundle.

The young man turns and bolts for the equipment shed. The other three still have fifty metres to go. Wolfe coughs on the frigid air.

The engines are warming up fast and the earlier rumble is now a deafening roar. Wolfe is close enough to see movement through the glass of the cockpit. The giant bird starts to shift.

'No!' she breathes, accelerating, her leg muscles burning.

The mountains cast long shadows across the temporary runway, due to a low midnight sun. Trankov must be desperate to take off on a makeshift runway, in strong winds and poor visibility. Her assailant is on that plane and she must stop him leaving. Suddenly, the engines scream and the heat haze appears to melt the Ellsworth Mountains. The plane accelerates and its long wings dip slightly to one side as the crosswinds attempt to push it off course. As the bird lifts its nose up to the sky, she sees a man waving at her from inside the cockpit. He is so tall, he has to bend down, as if in a bow: it is Grankin mocking her.

She has no choice but to watch an assassin fly away.

23

Twenty-nine hours after the delivery of the replacement parts to Camp Ellsworth, thirty sealed, pressurised canisters of water and sediment samples are loaded on to a British Antarctic Survey Twin Otter plane, watched closely by Beer, Sinclair and Matthews. Since they extracted the samples, the canisters have been guarded non-stop by a tag team of at least three people.

Heatherton has been in hushed phone conversations. Wolfe and Harvey have been kept in the dark about their content, as have the crew. People speak in whispers. Conversations are short. Tension is high. Wolfe squints at the brilliant blue sky – her last day in Antarctica. Putting on her sunglasses, she heads for the Twin Otter, backpack slung over her shoulder. She is leaving with Heatherton, Sinclair, Matthews, Price and Harvey. Destination: Rothera Station. At Rothera, the crated samples will be loaded on to a ship bound for England. The engineers and Beer, as head of logistics, stay behind to close down the camp.

But there is one engineer travelling with them: Vitaly Yushkov.

Doug Whetton, the pilot, asks Yushkov to sit in seat 2A, at the front. Heatherton is directed across the aisle to 2B, Price to

2C, Matthews to the seat behind. She guesses it must be to do with even distribution of weight. She is in 5B, next to Harvey. On the other side of the aisle, in 5A, is Sinclair. The small plane bounces and shudders on take-off. It's like being inside a cocktail shaker. A sheepskin on the seats cushions some of the jolting. The engine noise is a constant drone, loud enough to make conversation difficult.

'Why do you think Vitaly is with us?' she says, leaning in close to Harvey's ear.

Harvey has the window seat and is watching the disappearing ice sheet below with relief. He turns, but looks across the aisle at the back of Yushkov's head. Single seats are on the left of the aisle as you face the cockpit, and the twin seats are on the right.

'Odd, isn't it?' Harvey replies. 'Did Michael ask you to stay behind too?'

'Yes. But there were spare seats so I insisted.'

The Twin Otter takes twenty passengers. Only six are on board.

Between the gaps in the seats, Wolfe can see Heatherton at the front, fidgeting constantly.

'Michael seems anxious,' she says.

'Fair enough, considering,' says Harvey. 'Good of you to keep schtum about the attack. Didn't think you would. It would've made one hell of an article.'

'I've agreed to sit on it until I get home. That's all.'

'You contacting the police?'

'I don't know.'

Wolfe closes her eyes and drifts off to sleep. She's woken by an announcement they will soon be landing at Rothera.

Wolfe leans over Harvey in the hope of seeing something of Adelaide Island, but she only sees blue sky. She sits back in her seat and turns to look out of the window to her left, where

Sinclair grips his arm rests, his knuckles white. Sinclair stares ahead as if he's seen a ghost, his lips clamped in a taut line.

'It's all right, Toby,' she shouts across the aisle, 'we're nearly there.'

'Hate little planes,' Sinclair says.

The small aircraft jerks upwards suddenly and the content of Wolfe's stomach almost leaves her mouth.

'Sorry, folks,' says Whetton over the intercom. 'Just an air pocket.'

Sinclair clenches his eyes shut until the juddering subsides. He glances her way, embarrassed. 'Thank God I'm going by ship,' he jokes.

'You're on the *James Clark Ross* with Michael, Stacy and Gary?'

'Yup.'

The aircraft lurches upwards again and Sinclair's right hand shoots forward and grips the edge of the seat in front. He swallows hard.

'The ship has a fully equipped biology lab, doesn't it? So you can do more tests?' Wolfe is trying to distract him.

'Five weeks of pure bliss. Just us getting to know the new life forms.'

Through Sinclair's window, Wolfe spots an island of low-lying snow-covered mountains with meandering brown rocky shorelines. An inky blue ocean is dotted with floating slabs of ice, like broken bits of polystyrene floating in a can of navy blue paint. The runway's perfectly symmetrical stretch of grey asphalt is the only part of Rothera Point totally clear of ice.

Wolfe leans across the aisle, as far as her seatbelt will let her. 'So why go by ship? I mean, why not fly to Cambridge and study the microbes there?'

'Because a commercial airline flies at an altitude that could affect the pressure inside the containers. To keep the microbes alive, we have to keep them at the exact pressure they're used to beneath the ice.'

'And this plane?'

'It's flying low. Especially low.'

As the Twin Otter lines up with the runway, Wolfe catches a glimpse of the hundred metre-long red and white research ship, RRS *James Ross Clark*, docked at the wharf, to the right of the runway. The aircraft's nose dips slightly and Sinclair leans back into his seat and stares ahead, unblinking, their conversation over. The cabin rattles as they get lower and the pilot has to fight to keep the wings level. The plane bounces as the wheels hit the asphalt, pulling up just before they reach the end of the runway. The captain pulls up near a fuel tanker, then cuts the engines. Wolfe and Harvey unclip their seatbelts and stand, keen to get out and stretch their legs.

Heatherton also stands and says something to Yushkov, who is up and stretching his back. Yushkov frowns, hesitates and sits back down.

'Change of plan, everybody,' announces Heatherton. 'Nobody leaves the plane, sorry. We're simply refuelling and taking off immediately, so if you need the loo, you'll have to use the one at the back.'

'Mike! We can't,' Sinclair objects, shooting out of his seat. 'What about the canisters?'

Heatherton runs his hands through his hair. 'Toby, I haven't been able to level with you for security reasons. All I can say is that the samples will be perfectly safe. I promise you no harm will come to them.'

Sinclair looks at his fellow scientists for support. Matthews, who sits next to Heatherton, and Price, in seat 2C, remain seated, heads bowed.

'Ah,' says Sinclair, his pale face flushed with anger. 'What do they know that I don't, Mike? Don't you think I can be trusted?'

Matthews unbuckles his belt and turns in his seat so he can address Sinclair.

'Toby, don't take it personally. This is out of our hands.'

Heatherton gives him a warning look.

'Given all the . . .' Heatherton clears his throat, ' . . . problems we've had with equipment and other things, there's been a change of plan, which means greater security for our precious cargo.'

Wolfe is feeling uneasy. Only she, Harvey and Yushkov were meant to stay on board and fly on to Punta Arenas, where they were boarding commercial flights. Why the change?

'You think Trankov will try to steal the crates?' Yushkov mocks. 'I do not think so.'

Heatherton ignores him.

'So what is going on?' Wolfe stands in the aisle. 'Who is telling you what to do? Your director?'

'I can't go into it, Olivia.'

'So the samples are going by ship without you? You're prepared to hand over everything you've worked for to complete strangers? I don't believe it,' she persists.

Sinclair is quivering with rage. 'Mike, for God's sake! We've been to hell and back to prove subglacial life exists. And now we've finally got it, you're going to let others examine it?'

Heatherton drags his palm across his face, wiping away perspiration. 'The samples are staying with us. All right?'

'What?' Toby's jaw drops.

Whetton comes out of the cockpit and unlocks the side door. As it opens outwards, a gush of cold air enters the aircraft and a man in orange high-vis overalls wheels some steps up to the exit.

'Refuelling should only take twenty minutes or so,' the pilot says before skipping down the steps.

'Everyone, please sit down,' says Matthews.

'No way,' Wolfe says, moving down the narrow aisle. 'I want to know exactly where I'm going and on whose orders.'

Matthews and Heatherton glance at each other.

'Oh, for Christ's sake!' Price snaps from her seat, her exasperation obvious. 'You can at least tell them we're flying to Mount Pleasant. At low altitude all the way.' Price stands and gives a horrified Sinclair a reassuring smile. 'Don't worry, Toby. I won't let anything happen to our babies.'

Mollified, Sinclair sits, but Wolfe isn't so easily won over.

'Is this because our cargo is dangerous?' she asks Heatherton.

He looks down, avoiding her gaze. 'We're taking a few extra precautions, that's all.'

She doesn't believe him. 'Why the Falklands? Mount Pleasant is an RAF base.'

'Olivia, please,' says Heatherton. 'We don't even know what'll happen when we get there. These orders have come from the very highest level.'

'How high?'

'The Home Office.'

24

The Falkland Islands

Windswept, desolate and rocky, the sub-Antarctic Falkland Islands are not for the faint-hearted. Through the Twin Otter's small window, Wolfe sees moss-green mountains, coastlines strewn with boulders and boggy lowlands devoid of habitation.

'Approaching Mount Pleasant,' announces the pilot. 'Buckle up.'

The RAF air base is in the middle of nowhere, near a mountainous area suitably named No Man's Land. Surrounding the base is flat, boggy, open land, with only a smattering of lakes and access roads to break up the featureless terrain. Port Stanley, where most of the island's three thousand inhabitants live, is thirty miles away, and from what Wolfe can see from the plane's cabin, it might as well be thirty thousand miles away. But the air base has its own community of two thousand troops and a small military town of housing, shops and sporting facilities. Closer now, Wolfe spots two Sea King helicopters on the tarmac, not far from a series of huge khaki green aircraft hangars. The Voyager K2 air-to-air tanker is nowhere to be seen, nor are four Eurofighter Typhoons – either in the skies or the hangars, she guesses.

In contrast to the Rothera landing, this one is a breeze. They taxi towards the hangars on smooth asphalt. The cabin is quiet, faces anxious. Sinclair has a hand under his chin and his fingers tap his cheek nervously. Harvey is cleaning his glasses for the fourth time. Ahead, Price's head snaps from side to side, desperate to see what is happening outside. The plane heads for the biggest hangar, built to take the air-to-air tanker with its sixty-metre wingspan. Inside is a Lockheed C-130J 'Hercules' tactical transport aircraft, which fills almost a third of the space. Its hinged loading ramp at the rear of the fuselage is down and the activity surrounding it suggests it is being readied for take-off. When she spots two men in disruptive-pattern operational uniform, carrying MP5 submachine guns, approaching the Twin Otter, she knows something is seriously wrong.

The hangar's steel doors grind electronically to a close and the knot of apprehension in her gut twists tighter. They have been brought to one of the most isolated British military bases in the world; the classic strategy of anti-terrorist spooks wanting to interrogate a suspect away from prying eyes or, worse, make them disappear altogether. Wolfe looks down the aisle and watches Yushkov. Is this about him? She turns her gaze on the back of Heatherton's thick mop of hair. What has Heatherton done?

Wolfe drags her backpack from under the seat in front and leans over it, ensuring Harvey, who sits to her right, can't see what she's doing. But Harvey looks the other way, peering through the window, seeking answers to their bewildering situation. From her wallet she removes something credit card sized. It is not a bank or membership card but a tiny stainless steel tool kit for picking locks, which looks like a rectangular pattern of metal holes until you snap off the lock-pick device you need. It contains a ball pick, a hybrid feeler pick, a tension wrench that can also be used as a handcuff shim pick, and a diamond pick. She pushes it inside the cuff of her jacket. Up the other sleeve she shoves her plastic knife, safely sheathed. She's not taking any chances.

The pilot kills the engines and then scrambles to open the side door. Heatherton grabs Whetton's arm.

'What's happening, Doug?'

'Haven't got a clue. Been told to open the door and wait for further instructions.'

As soon as the door is open, two men in red berets, their batons extended, enter the cabin. On the arm of their khaki uniforms is the unmistakable insignia of the Royal Military Police: the initials MP on a red background.

'Are you Vitaly Yushkov?' asks one of the officers.

'I am.'

'Undo your seatbelt. Then put your hands on your head. Nice and slow.'

So that's why the pilot directed Yushkov to seat 2A. Vitaly nods, as if he's expected this, and stands, hands raised above his head, leaning forward because of the low-ceilinged cabin.

'Everyone else, please stay seated.'

'I don't believe it,' Wolfe says to herself.

Why doesn't Heatherton object, or Matthews or Sinclair? Instead, they watch in silence.

'Turn around,' orders the officer.

'Will somebody please say something,' Wolfe says aloud.

Yushkov turns to face the tail section. He may appear calm, but his jaw is clenched and his eyes cold with fury. An officer grabs his hands, drags them behind his back and handcuffs him.

Wolfe can't stand it any longer. She undoes her seatbelt and gets up.

'Where are you taking him?'

'That's need to know, ma'am. Let us do our job.'

'But he's a British civilian. You're military police. You have no right to do this.'

The tension in Yushkov's face dissipates for a moment as he smiles a thank you. It's little more than a creasing of the eyes and the mouth, but it conveys genuine warmth.

'I have done nothing wrong, so I have nothing to fear,' says Yushkov.

'Bullshit!' says Wolfe. 'Too many innocent people have disappeared under extraordinary rendition, just like this. I repeat, Yushkov is a civilian.'

'And under Section 24(A) of the Police and Criminal Evidence Act 1984, we can arrest any person we have reasonable grounds to believe is committing, or has committed, an indictable offence.'

'What offence?'

'I'm not at liberty to say.'

Wolfe moves down the aisle.

'Stay where you are, ma'am,' the second officer commands, raising his MP5.

'What offence?' she demands.

'Olivia, it is okay. I go willingly.'

'Sit down, ma'am. Now!'

Between her and Yushkov stands one of the arresting officers. The other military policeman steers Yushkov out of the plane.

'Michael, why don't you say something?' she says.

Heatherton shrugs helplessly, 'What can I do?'

'Anybody?' she asks. 'He's your friend. This is wrong.'

Price grabs Heatherton's arm. 'Dear God, Michael! What on earth have you done?'

A stocky man with a crew cut, in grey suit and a long, black woollen coat that looks totally out of place on a military base enters the cabin. He moves casually, chewing gum, hands in pockets, as if Yushkov's arrest is boringly everyday.

'You?' says Wolfe, taken aback.

'Good to see you too, Olivia,' he says, giving her a nod. He addresses the whole group. 'Listen up, everybody. I am Detective Chief Inspector Casburn from Counter Terrorism Command.'

There are rumbles of surprise throughout the cabin as the passengers digest this information.

'This officer,' Casburn says, looking at the man hovering in the doorway, 'is agent Nic Flynn.'

He's been followed by a man in his late twenties, also in civilian clothes, but his are all about blending into the background: jeans, sweatshirt, olive green zip-up jacket with hood, with scruffy black shoulder-length hair and dark, watchful eyes. Wolfe recognises a spook when she sees one. MI5, probably, and almost certainly not named Nic Flynn.

'We have reason to believe that Kevin Knox was murdered. To further our investigation you'll all be interviewed.'

Heatherton pipes up. 'You think Vitaly did it?'

Wolfe detects a hint of self-satisfaction in his tone and it sickens her.

'Yushkov will be questioned, as will all of you.'

'So he's not under arrest?' she asks.

'Don't interfere, Ms Wolfe.'

'Why's SO15 involved?'

'You don't really expect me to answer that.'

'I thought you were searching for—'

Casburn gives Wolfe a warning look and she stops herself just in time. So whatever is going down here is more critical than finding Kabir Khan.

'Because of your special cargo,' announces Casburn, 'you are being flown direct to Brize Norton. You'll board an RAF Hercules and your statements will be taken on board. We have clearance to fly at low altitude. Dr Heatherton and Dr Matthews, please come with me. I imagine you would like to supervise handling of the crates.'

'Yes, certainly would,' says Heatherton, but hesitates before he undoes his seatbelt. 'Now?'

'Yes, please go with Nic. Your bags and equipment will be transferred across too.'

As Heatherton and Matthews head for the exit, Price stands up.

'And what about me?' she demands. 'I'm Dr Stacy Price, senior sediment scientist. I must be with the canisters at all times.'

'Of course, Dr Price. Please go with Nic.'

Wolfe watches the three scientists leave. Sinclair clutches his scruffy daypack to his chest as he stands. He's trembling. A tiny bear dangling from the bag's handle jiggles.

'And me?' he squawks, barely able to speak. 'I . . . I'm T . . . Toby Sinclair. Environmental microbiologist.'

'I'm sure three supervisors are enough, sir. All the rest of you, please come with me. There's food and drink on board. You'll be quite comfortable.'

Wolfe slings her backpack over her shoulder and charges down the aisle. She grabs Casburn's shoulder as he turns to leave.

'Dan, what are you doing here?'

'My job, Olivia.'

'Which is?'

He tilts his head and stares hard into her eyes. 'Investigating the murder of a British subject overseas.'

'Don't give me that flannel! You're counter-terrorism.'

'Keep moving, Ms Wolfe, you're blocking the way.'

She steps aside to let the others leave and watches them cross the hangar's floor and board the Hercules. She and Casburn are the last to exit the Twin Otter.

'It's about the bacteria, isn't it?'

'Time to move, Olivia. We're on a tight schedule.'

As Wolfe reluctantly leaves the BAS plane, the Hercules's engines roar into life. She spots the RAF circles of blue, white and red at the tail end and the back is open as the wooden crates are loaded into the cargo hold. Her path from the Twin Otter to the Hercules is hemmed in by two rows of armed military personnel. Wolfe stops.

'And Vitaly? Please tell me you're not leaving him here.'

Casburn jerks his hand towards the Hercules, his irritation beginning to show. Wolfe reluctantly walks on. He escorts her.

'Are you taking him to another county?' Where torture is normal interrogation practice.

Casburn chews his Nicorette loudly and doesn't answer.

'Yushkov saved my life.' She stops, unsure how much of the conversation between Yushkov and Grankin she should tell him. Will he then suspect Yushkov is being blackmailed by the Russian SVR? 'If there's a killer amongst us, I don't believe it's him.'

Her voice trails away as she notices men in camouflage gear, carrying heavy packs and M16s, jogging over to the same Twin

Otter she's just vacated. The small plane is being refuelled and a new pilot is already doing a pre-flight inspection.

'Where's the SAS going in a British Antarctic Survey plane?'

Tight-lipped, Casburn shakes his head.

'Are they going to Camp Ellsworth?'

His expression doesn't alter but he lifts his chin slightly, as if somebody standing just behind her has made eye contact. Finally, she's found his tell.

Wolfe has her answer.

25

RAF Brize Norton

Vitaly Yushkov is not on the RAF Hercules. Nor are Casburn and Flynn. After an eighteen-hour flight, with one stopover for refuelling on Ascension Island, a gruelling police interview, and several fruitless attempts to extract information on Yushkov from the officers on board, Wolfe just wants to go home, take a shower and sleep. But she knows she has a story to write. Unless she can engender a public outcry, she fears Vitaly Yushkov may never be heard of again.

It is dark when they land at RAF Brize Norton, Oxfordshire. Wolfe and Harvey are escorted across rain-soaked tarmac to a silver BMW saloon, inside of which sits a plain-clothed officer who will drive them home. He doesn't need their addresses; he knows where they live. Wolfe watches Heatherton, Matthews, Sinclair and Price wearily climb into a mini-van for their journey to Cambridge. The samples are in a transit van, accompanied by two plain-clothed officers, heading for the Clinical Microbiology and Public Health Laboratory in Cambridge. Her mobile rings: it's Casburn.

'I'm asking you nicely not to make public Yushkov's detention or the escort you've just received.'

'I didn't sign the non-disclosure agreement,' Wolfe says. The scientists with her on the flight caved and signed.

'If you want my help in future, it would be wise to co-operate with me now.'

'I can't do what you ask.'

'Don't make me your enemy, Olivia.'

The threat is clear. She swallows.

'Why are you holding a civilian at an overseas military base?' Casburn sighs. 'Moz will hear from us.'

'Moz will back me.' She barely takes a breath. 'Does Yushkov have a lawyer? He has the right to legal representation.'

Casburn snorts. 'Yushkov's really got under your skin, hasn't he? Tell me, Olivia, is it his rights you're interested in, or have you fallen for the Russian's biceps?'

'A cheap shot, Dan, even for you.'

He cuts her off.

Harvey leans close to her in the back of the car. 'I didn't sign it either. The Beeb can deal with legalities. The story's too bloody good.' He counts on his fingers. 'Treason, espionage, murder by a former Russian. This is the career break I've been waiting for.'

'You assume Vitaly is guilty. He may be innocent.'

'Well, the police obviously think he is. That's good enough for me.'

'How did they get a gag order so fast?' Wolfe paces up and down Cohen's over-heated office. 'Wake up a judge?'

She hasn't been home yet. She asked the driver to take her straight to the *Post* in King's Cross and called an emergency meeting with Cohen and Negus, their general counsel.

'That's exactly what Counter Terrorism Command has done,' says Margaret Negus, nodding, her centre-parted mousy hair so fine Wolfe can see her pink scalp. 'Which means that whatever they suspect Yushkov has done, or was planning to do, it must be pretty serious.'

Negus might look like the cliché of a spinster librarian in her black round-neck cashmere sweater, pearls, and her grey wool skirt and wire-rimmed glasses, but she is tougher than old boots. She's got Wolfe out of tricky lawsuits in the past and Wolfe trusts her judgement.

'On what grounds?' Cohen asks, slapping his palms down on the desk.

'A threat to national security.'

'That old chestnut,' mutters Cohen.

'How restrictive is the order?' Wolfe asks.

'Very. We can't publish anything about Yushkov's detainment, your escort to the UK, or what you saw at Mount Pleasant, which includes the SAS boarding a BAS plane,' Negus replies.

'Sheesh!' says Cohen. 'And the BBC?'

'The same,' Negus says.

'So, no story,' says Wolfe, folding her arms and leaning against Cohen's desk. 'It must be big, though, otherwise why interrogate him overseas?'

'The Falklands are British territory, so if Yushkov is still there, he's technically on British soil,' Negus points out. 'But I get your point. They won't be scrutinised in quite the same way as if they held him here.'

'I've tried to find out where he's being held – the Foreign Office, Home Office, Ministry of Defence, SO15, RAF. Nothing. I'm being stonewalled.'

'Let's face it, Olivia,' says Cohen, 'the poor sod has the word terrorist tattooed on his forehead, whether he's guilty or not.

A loner, a defector, ex–military, loyal to God knows who. Nobody's going to fucking believe him. And, you know as well as I do, he can be held for up to forty days for questioning, without access to a solicitor.' He takes a breath. 'What you need to find out, Olivia, is why they're holding him.'

'I can guess. If bacteria LE31S is a pathogen and therefore a potential biological weapon, they'd want to stop Yushkov giving it to the Russians. But the first batch was destroyed and the second constantly guarded so I can't imagine how he has any of it.'

'Where there's a will, there's a way,' says Negus.

Cohen holds the tips of his long fingers together as if in prayer, but prayer couldn't be farther from his thoughts. 'If Grankin is SVR, I'm guessing the SAS soldiers you saw were, indeed, going to Camp Ellsworth. Probably to stop the Russians getting their mitts on it.'

'But Casburn's SO15, not MI6. Where's the terrorism link? Surely they don't think Russia would sponsor a terror plot against this country?' asks Negus.

'We condemned Russia's annexation of the Crimea,' says Wolfe. 'Could be payback?'

Cohen crosses his lanky, crane–like legs and leans back into his swivel chair. 'We're wasting time guessing.' He stares pointedly at Wolfe, 'I want you to find out what makes the Lake Ellsworth bacteria so special. Why do the Russians want it? Why is SO15 involved? What's Yushkov's role in all this?'

'Will do.' Wolfe stands. 'Heatherton was right, by the way. Knox was murdered.'

'How do you know?' Cohen asks.

'Dot Simons did his post-mortem. She and I go way back, from my crime-reporting days. I phoned her on the way here. Trouble is, what she told me is off the record, so I can't use it.'

'Which is?' says Cohen impatiently.

'She found traces of midazolam and an injection point in Knox's neck. He would've been out in seconds. I'm guessing he was then dragged on to a snowmobile and driven away from the camp. Remove his outer clothes, dump him and, hey presto, tragic blizzard accident.'

'Do you think Yushkov did it?'

'No, but he's hiding something.'

'Stay ahead of the pack on this one,' says Cohen. 'The BBC may have delayed broadcasting, but they'll chuck Harvey off the story and put someone like Minkley on it, and you know he's bloody good.'

'Yes, boss.'

Her mobile rings. She doesn't recognise the number.

'I'll get on to it right away,' she says, leaving Cohen's office to answer the call. 'Hello?'

'Olivia? Is that you?'

'Speaking.'

'It's Stacy Price.'

She's whispering.

'What's the matter, Stacy? Something wrong?'

'Um, look, I have to speak quietly. I don't want my husband hearing. The less he knows, the better.'

'Go on.'

'Look, I don't know if I should tell you this, but George called Michael, Michael called me.'

'Why? Something happened at Lake Ellsworth?'

'Yes.'

'What?'

Price is silent but Wolfe can hear her agitated breathing.

'Maybe I'm doing the wrong thing. It's just, well, such terrible news.'

'Please tell me, Stacy. Is someone hurt?' Wolfe thinks of the men left behind: Beer, Rundle, Ironside and Adeyemi.

'Michael told me not to talk to you or Harvey. Casburn wants a lid kept on it. But . . . well, I don't trust that man.' Silence. Wolfe waits. 'This can't come from me, okay?'

'I won't name you, I promise.'

'Trent was using the tractor when it stalled, blades raised. He got out to check them and they fell. Crushed his leg. Bones shattered.'

'Oh, Stacy, that's terrible! Where is he now?'

'On his way to Rothera, then a hospital. George says Trent's in really bad shape.'

'How did it happen?'

'I don't know. The blades were locked, so they shouldn't have fallen.' Price pauses, then drops her voice further. 'Sabotage?'

'But why? The mission's complete. It doesn't make sense.'

26
Cambridge, UK

Before placing the titanium cylinder inside a hyperbaric chamber at his home laboratory, he drops a minuscule sample of the bacteria's watery solution into two Petri dishes. One he positions under a hydroponic light, blinking at the ferocious brightness. His gloved hands tremble. He adds something to each dish, convinced the aggressive bacteria, given the right stimulation, will attack. The second dish is placed inside a fridge that's had its light removed. Now he must wait.

After taking off his surgical mask and gloves, protective eye-wear and coverall, he leaves the basement to make a cup of tea.

He spills milk on the kitchen bench – his hands won't stop shaking. Wiping up the mess, he then sips his tea, acutely aware of the silence that embalms the empty house. His eyes rest on the rainbow-coloured, alphabet fridge magnets arranged so they spell DADDY. He opens a package delivered to his neighbour while he was away, unwraps the portable CCTV camera he bought online and plugs it in to charge the battery. Leaving his tea half drunk, he heads upstairs, showers, shaves and changes his clothes. He removes his equipment from a backpack–style camera bag and carries it downstairs. Each vial fits neatly into the padded pockets.

It's time to check the dishes. He slowly descends the basement stairs, his heart thumping, and clambers into his protective gear once again. He takes a hesitant step towards the Petri dish under the hydroponic light. Then stops. Part of him wants to be proved right. Part of him is horrified at where this will lead. He takes another step and leans in, peering into the dish.

'Oh – my – Lord!'

As if on the receiving end of a defibrillator discharge, he leaps back from the bench. He slowly turns to the fridge, removes the twin from its dark confines and lays it on the workbench where he can see it better.

'Yes!' he shouts, elated.

It's just as he expected.

But it won't be long before others discover what he now knows. He must act, and act fast. First, he will say goodbye.

There are few places left in England where light pollution doesn't stain the night sky a sepia brown, hiding the stars. But on the low-lying marshland of the Cambridge Fens, the sky is punctuated with millions of dots of light that seem to welcome him back. He stops for a moment, remembering the black paint on his little boy's ceiling and the fluorescent stars he'd stuck there. He shakes his head, pushing away the memory, and moves his hand behind his back, gently tapping the backpack's outer pockets. The foam that protects the five glass vials compresses slightly at his touch but the vials are intact. Satisfied, he keeps walking.

The reflection of the moon in the water appears to follow him along an overgrown path edged with reeds. He wears the hood of his coat up, and keeps his head down, focused on the beam of light from his torch pointed a few feet ahead. For a stranger to this boggy area, a night walk is fraught with potential mishap: at best a muddy tumble, at worst a drowning. But he has made this trip so many times, he hardly needs a torch. To his left, tall meadow grasses whisper as if trying to soothe away the pain of their deaths. But their faces are always with him. If only he'd known that the goodbye would be so final. If only he could turn back time and undo his mistake.

The ground is muddy and his boots squelch. The meadow is in darkness, but he hears a short-eared owl call out as it hunts, its unusual sound like the braying of an angry pony. He glances round and catches a glimpse of the owl's round yellow eyes. Not long now. He spots the peg, hammered deep into the ground, then the mooring rope, and lifts the torch beam so he can follow the rope to the narrowboat's stern.

His fifty-foot narrowboat has been moored here for the last two years, alone, no other boats for miles. She is dutifully maintained, in perfect working order, the engine turned over regularly, but the moorings are never untied. Made locally of steel, by a family business that's built narrowboats for five generations, she was designed to outlast him. When they'd commissioned the build, they knew they wanted the motif on the boat's sides to be of two swans, because they mate for life, and being married for life was how it was meant to be.

As he approaches his narrowboat, he's convinced he hears children's laughter. He stops and peers into the darkness, but knows it cannot be. This neglected stretch of water is silted up and seldom used, and no children live nearby. His head is pounding like a migraine; he rubs his temples. It's a memory, so clear and so dazzlingly bright, he can barely look at the two skipping figures chasing a Red Admiral butterfly, the sun warm, their arms and legs bare. She's in her favourite yellow summer dress; he's stumbling after her, the younger of the two, in shorts and a Winnie-the-Pooh T-shirt.

The cry of a fox startles him. He must hurry. The tarpaulin covering the cruiser stern has become detached at one corner, and that corner has blown into the muddy water. No matter. He throws it over the roof of the main cabin, then steps on board. He touches the swan's neck – the S-shaped steel bar welded to the rudder post – and pats it as if patting the arm of an old friend. Then he unlocks and opens the saloon-style cabin doors.

The haunted man steps down into the cabin. Two fixed single berths, the beds hugging the hull, with a narrow aisle between them. He aims his torch at the kids' paintings stuck to the walls, curled with damp. On one bed, a white floppy-eared toy bunny. On the other, a hot water bottle, covered in a big-bellied Winnie-the-Pooh. He stops, unable to go any further. Picking up the bunny and the yellow bear, he hugs them. A tear runs down his cheek. Minutes pass. He is lost in reverie, so lost, he forgets why he is there.

The narrowboat creaks. Taking a deep breath, he wipes his eyes. This is their shrine; where he can grieve, away from friends and relatives and colleagues who think it's time for him to move on. But what would they know about loss? He takes the toys with him into the main cabin and sees his wife's coat hanging on a hook, her gloves still sticking out of the pockets. He takes hold of one sleeve and holds it to his lips.

'Goodbye, my love,' he says.

On the table is a paperback novel she was reading. It lies open, the bookmark in the crease between pages 153 and 154. He sees her clearly, relaxing into the cushions, a steaming cup of tea next to her, lost in her reading. He gently closes the book, their story together over.

From his backpack he removes a portable battery-powered CCTV camera, which he screws to the cabin's wood panelling so that it faces the main living area. He switches it on and checks he's receiving the camera's images on his phone. Pulling on latex gloves, safety glasses and face mask, he takes a foam-wrapped test tube from an outer pocket and removes the airtight seal. Opening the hatch to the engine bay, he pours the test tube's contents into the cavity.

Then, as gently as if they were made of the finest porcelain, he places the book, the toy bunny and the Winnie-the-Pooh in his bag and leaves.

27

It's almost midnight when Wolfe switches on the hall light, closes the door to her Balham flat and latches the chain. Eyes closed, her back to the door, she breathes a sigh of relief. She's surprised to smell rose, vanilla and white almond, and the fragrant gum resin, benzoin. It's her favourite perfume: Keiko Mecheri's Loukhoum Parfum du Soir. But she hasn't worn it for weeks. How can the scent still be in the air? Has Daisy used it? Or dropped it by mistake? But the purple glass bottle that looks like a black tulip on fire is in her bathroom cabinet, just as she left it.

Her stomach rumbles. She last ate something on the flight from Mount Pleasant. Wolfe moves from room to room, switching on the lights and then the central heating, the timer having turned it off hours ago. The sitting room radiator rattles as hot water is forced by the boiler through old pipes with noisy air pockets. A familiar and somehow comforting sound. Wolfe heads for her galley kitchen and pulls a curry from the freezer and takes a packet of jasmine rice from the pantry.

Wolfe fills the kettle and gets the rice boiling. She heads for the bedroom, strips off her Antarctic gear and wraps herself up in a dressing gown. It's then that she notices her plantation shutters are open.

She freezes. Only Daisy and Jerry have been inside her flat while she was away and both know she keeps the shutters closed, otherwise people on the street can see straight into her bedroom. Wolfe snaps them shut, embarrassed that a passer-by may have seen her naked. Standing with her back to the window, she tries to control her growing unease. There are new locks on windows and doors. But the fine hairs on the back of her neck prickle. She fears she's not alone.

Wolfe races to the hall and takes the Maglite torch from her backpack and holds it up as a weapon. She heads back to the bedroom. She slides back the doors to her fitted wardrobe and sees only clothes, bags and shoes. She jumps at a hissing sound from the kitchen, then remembers her saucepan of boiling rice. It's bubbled over on to the hot gas ring. Turning off the burner, Wolfe takes a kitchen knife from its wooden block, holding the torch in the other hand. In the sitting room, she double-checks the French doors are locked and draws the curtains.

'There's nobody here,' she says. 'You're being paranoid.'

But a knot of anxiety in her gut kills her appetite, and after a few mouthfuls she throws the food away and heads for the shower. The hot water is relaxing and Wolfe begins to unwind. She hardly notices the phone ringing above the loud splashing. When she does, she decides to ignore it. If it's urgent, the caller will leave a message. She's almost towelled dry when her mobile rings again. She runs from the bathroom naked and snatches it from the coffee table. It's a blocked number. She answers.

Silence.

'Hello?' she repeats.

She hears breathing and thinks it might be Price having second thoughts.

'Stacy?'

The breathing doesn't sound the same. Price's was fast and feminine. This is slow and loud, as if the caller is holding the phone too near his mouth.

'Can you speak up? I can't hear you.'

Just breathing. Wolfe ends the call, frowning at her phone. Aware of her nakedness, she pulls on her dressing gown and ties it tightly.

The phone rings again. Another blocked call.

'Yes?' she answers sharply.

This time she knows what to listen for. The same slow, deep breathing.

'Whoever you are, piss off! Go and annoy someone else.'

The voice is androgynous, metallic and distorted, as if somebody is speaking through a megaphone from inside a corrugated-iron shed.

'I like your flat, Olivia.'

Wolfe gasps, betraying her shock. The caller laughs, the sound like pans clattering. Her stalker is using a voice distorter, which means they've prepared for this call. Clearing her throat, she speaks slowly, determined not to betray her fear.

'Are you going to tell me your name?' she asks.

'You know who I am.'

'Okay, well, I'm pretty tired, so help me out here. Who are you?'

The voice tuts at her. It sounds like a mechanical chicken clucking. If it weren't so creepy, she'd find it funny. But Wolfe isn't laughing.

'Where's the fun in that?'

'If you want me to guess, then turn off the voice distorter.'

'You've been a bad girl, Olivia, and you're going to pay.'

His taunting makes her angry. 'I don't do phone sex, you jerk. What do you want?'

'I want you. I'm coming for you.'

Wolfe's eyes dart around the room. In the background, a car engine starts. The line goes dead. Wolfe is trembling. It takes a few precious seconds to realise the significance of the car engine. She heard it both through her phone and outside. Her stalker is in Elmbourne Road. She seizes the kitchen knife and bolts from her flat, flinging the communal door open. The entry light flicks on, illuminating the path, front garden and pavement outside the house. A car disappears around the corner. She's too late to clock the number plate. Peering into the shadows of the park opposite, there is no movement. A young couple sway up the street, giggling, arm in arm, a little drunk. Wolfe shuts the door.

Light creeps from under O'Leary's door and Wolfe hears the pulsing rhythm of Whitesnake's 'Still of the Night'. Daisy is awake. Upset by the call, Wolfe is about to knock when she hears a male voice begging for forgiveness.

'I've been a very naughty boy,' he says. 'I deserve to be punished.'

The words chill her.

Back inside her flat, Wolfe bolts the door. Despite the cold night, she has broken out in a sweat. She squats down with her back against the door and toys with the idea of calling the police. They could try to trace the call, but if he's careful enough to use a voice distorter, he'll be using a burner phone too.

What did he say? She's been bad.

How?

She's going to pay.

For what?

Refusing to lie to keep her brother out of prison? Giving SO15 Kabir Khan's name? Eavesdropping on Grankin and Yushkov?

Wolfe heads for the freezer and takes out a bottle of vodka. She pours a shot and drinks it neat. The burning in her throat feels good. Glass in hand, she sits, but is up and pacing a moment later, going over the caller's words. She starts to pull apart what she knows, as though investigating a story. The stalking started six months ago, which rules out Grankin. Unless that call wasn't from her stalker.

Davy was still in gaol then, but it has escalated since she got back from Afghanistan, which coincides with his early release. Her brother would know the significance of the diamond stud earrings. But why take Nooria's photo?

Lalzad, on the other hand, has the money and connections to employ someone to intimidate her and to hack her system. Perhaps he doesn't know she's off the story?

She momentarily considers Eric Lowe, the reporter. He's phone-hacked before, and blackmailed. But why target her if he wants gossip on the Lake Ellsworth story? Wolfe takes another gulp of vodka, as her mind returns to Davy.

She hadn't seen the fight with Coleman. She'd dropped by

the nightclub on her way home because Davy said he needed to talk. When Wolfe got there, another bouncer nodded towards the alley, where Davy was sorting out some trouble. When she rounded the corner, it took her a few moments to spot them in the dimly lit passage, but she did see Davy draw his arm back and lay an almighty punch at Coleman's face. Coleman dropped, she found out later, dead almost instantly. Davy sunk to his knees, then collapsed on his side. As Wolfe cradled her brother, he had a seizure. When the paramedics arrived in the dark alley, they used the ambulance's headlights to light up the scene. The police found a small bag of cocaine in Davy's pocket. Later, he begged her to say Coleman had thrown the first punch. Wolfe did everything possible to help him, even paying for a top QC to take his case, but she couldn't commit perjury.

Pouring another glass, Wolfe heads unsteadily for the bedroom. She puts the heavy torch under the bed and her mobile on the bedside table. As she slides her sheathed knife under her pillow, she smells something sour, like morning breath. It can't be. The pillowcase was clean when she left for Antarctica.

Doubting herself, Wolfe places her nose near the pillow again. She gags. Pulling back her duvet cover, she sniffs the top edge. Sweat. Not hers. Stumbling backwards, she races to the toilet, heaving up the contents of her stomach.

28

Her Majesty's Naval Base, Portsmouth

At five in the morning, the HMS *Queen Elizabeth* is a floating city of lights. It is the largest warship ever built for the Royal Navy, and is only three days away from full 'operational military capability', due to depart for the Arabian Sea, mission unknown. The 65,000-tonne aircraft carrier has taken ten years to build, is as long as twenty-eight London buses parked end-to-end, and will carry thirty F35B joint strike fighters and four Merlin helicopters. As the rest of Portsmouth sleeps, the vessel is a hive of activity as carpenters, electricians, plumbers, technicians, engineers, painters and two hundred of the thousand-strong naval crew dart along the decks and up and down gangplanks, illuminated like an ant colony for a David Attenborough documentary.

But there is one man within the security perimeter of the base who shouldn't be there. He leans against someone's Volkswagen Transporter, pretending to smoke. To calm his nerves he recites in his head everything he knows about the warship.

Made of 17 million parts, features 250,000 kilometres of electrical cables, and 8,000 kilometres of fibre-optic cables. Around 250,000 litres of battleship-grey paint.

He checks his pocket for the hundredth time, and finds the glass vials there: four of them, each encased in bubble wrap. His backpack is in his car, parked a few blocks away.

Security surrounding the naval base is tight, but the sentry on duty is tired and cold and the Royal Navy credentials he presented are real, if a little out of date. He is not in uniform, just civvies, as if off duty. His Royal Fleet Auxiliary ID has got him this far, but it's unlikely to get him on to the ship, so he'll need to rely on others who do have access.

The quay is a car park of tradesmen's trucks and vans, most unlocked, some with doors flung open, the assumption being that nothing is going to get nicked on a well-guarded naval base. The noise level is astounding: the slap of waves against the quay is drowned out by the shouting, hammering, drilling, clanking, and roar of engines. Above his head, a seagull screeches from atop a lamp-post, head jutted forwards, as if furious at the racket.

Through bloodshot eyes he peers through the drizzle, searching for his first 'carrier'.

The intruder pulls his jacket collar up high and tucks in his chin, his woollen hat pulled down low. There is not much time, so he moves on, weaving in and out of the parked cars and vans until he finds what he's looking for: the fibre-optics contractor's truck. Three men push a mechanised spool of blue cabling on to the truck's electronically controlled ramp. The spool is taller than the men and as wide as a family car. Once the ramp has reached ground level, the spool – on wheels – is rolled into position. The leader of the group, a rotund man in blue coveralls, talks into a two-way radio, liaising directly with one of the many crane operators in a cabin suspended from the crane's trolley. The scratchy voice of the operator crackles through the radio.

'Get in line, mate. There's six ahead of you.'

'How long?'

'Half-hour.'

'Right you are then.'

The rotund man shrugs his shoulders and suggests a tea break. Two of them get back in the truck, switch on the engine, and enjoy the warmth from the heater as they sip tea from a flask. The third man wanders off for a fag break.

The observer checks the truck's wing mirrors. If he stays directly behind the vehicle, it's unlikely the driver will see him approach the cabling. He walks up to the spool, removes a vial from his pocket, empties its contents over the exterior of the cabling and walks away, without anyone noticing. One vial down, three to go.

His breath is ragged and he trembles from the adrenalin rush, but his initial success spurs him on. He searches for his next carrier as he lists what he knows about the warship.

The on-board bakery can bake a thousand loaves of bread per day. Rations can last forty-five days. They include 66,000 sausages, 64,800 eggs, and 12,000 cans of baked beans. That's a lot of hot air, he thinks, smiling.

There is a whole army of painters on board. Truck-loads of paint cans have just been delivered to the quay. One of the crates is open and there's an argument over some missing cans. The two men race over to another with a clipboard, clearly expecting him to resolve the issue. While they are distracted, the trespasser pours the contents of a vial over the lids, and moves on.

Two down, two to go.

From the keel to the top of the tower is the height of Nelson's Column.

He's much closer to HMS *Queen Elizabeth* now, and looks up, almost overwhelmed by its massive bulk, a tsunami of steel. It's equipped with the latest Phalanx CIWS radar-guided Gatling guns mounted on a swivelling base, used for defence against anti-ship missiles. He frowns, but refuses to get distracted. A man, also in the obligatory blue coveralls, carrying a welder's helmet, heads his way. He steps into the man's path, deliberately colliding with him. The welder drops his helmet and the intruder apologises, picking it up and handing it to him. The man grumpily tells him to look where he's going and strides off, unaware that his helmet is now covered in the contents of the third vial.

It takes him a while to find the recipient of the fourth and final vial. Crates of food, including large cans of oil, are being loaded on board. He approaches the latter container, but a navy officer spots him and heads his way.

'Sir! Can I see your security pass?' the officer shouts.

Before the man reaches him, the vial's airtight seal is unscrewed and its contents poured over the crate containing hundreds of baked-bean tins.

'Hey, you! Stop!'

He runs, weaving in and out of parked vehicles, passing the giant spool of fibre-optic cable as it's lifted into the sky at the end of a crane's hook.

In three days the warship will be escorted from Portsmouth Harbour by a flotilla of navy vessels and spectator boats, seen off by well-wishers and the crews' families. But it will not return. He is certain of that.

29

The Met's Cyber Crime expert looks no more than eighteen, but Wolfe has been told that Jwala Ponnappa is, in fact, twenty-five, and worked with Butcher on his last case. Ponnappa's delicate frame and child-like fingers make even Wolfe seem big-boned. Bangle-sized gold hoop earrings, long black hair that reaches the seat of her chair, spangly pink T-shirt and torn designer jeans only serve to make her look younger than she is. Butcher has asked her to help out unofficially because Wolfe is adamant she doesn't want to make an official complaint. The officer's fingers dance across Wolfe's laptop as she sits at Wolfe's desk.

'Yup, you've been hacked.' Ponnappa holds up the laptop and places her eye right in front of the inbuilt webcam. 'Hey, you! Pervert! I'm going to track you down and lock you up.'

Ponnappa grins at Wolfe and continues tapping away.

'There, the fucker can't see you any more. I've killed the RAT.' She explains a Remote Access Trojan and how it enables the voyeur to switch on and off her webcam whenever he wants. Her eyes remain on the monitor. 'These creeps collect what they call "slaves", then sell the viewing rights to other weirdos.' Ponnappa looks up at Wolfe. 'Do you ever walk about in the nude?'

Wolfe is taken aback by the question. Then the penny drops. 'Yes.' She can't help shuddering at the thought of being seen naked. 'Can you find him?'

'I'll do my best. Depends how clever he is.'

Butcher wears latex gloves and is up a stepladder, unscrewing the smoke detector on her sitting room ceiling. He's searching for bugs and hidden cameras and has already checked her table lamps, behind her framed photos and beneath chairs and tables.

'Ah-ha!' says Butcher, peering up into the guts of the smoke detector. 'There's a tiny camera in here. Whoever did this is pretty savvy.'

Wolfe hugs herself.

'He knew I'd get my laptop checked out once I got home,' says Wolfe, 'so he installs that spy camera. You remember we talked about it on Skype?'

'I do, and he must've been watching us,' says Butcher, bringing the whole smoke detector with him down the steps and handing it to Ponnappa. 'The camera was pointing at Olivia's desk but I'm guessing it had a pretty wide field of vision.'

'What do you mean "had"?' says Ponnappa. 'It's still on. Probably connected to his computer or smartphone via Wi-Fi.'

'Christ!' says Wolfe. 'Switch it off!'

'There you go,' Ponappa says, flicking a tiny switch. 'Nice bit of gear. Quality.' She removes an SD memory card. 'It's all recorded on here, which means we know what he's seen. Let me take a look. It'll tell us the time and date of the footage.'

'So we'll know when it started recording?'

'Yup.' Ponappa scrutinises the device's innards. 'Heat sensing, passive infrared motion activated, the hidden camera not only records movement during the day, but has night-vision capabilities. Impressive.'

Wolfe feels light-headed with lack of sleep and too much caffeine.

'You really shouldn't have washed your bedding,' says Butcher.

Last night, she'd stripped the bed and thrown the bedding in the washing machine.

'I couldn't bear it. I had to get rid of it.'

'He wants to dominate you. To show you he can get to you. His next move may be more direct.'

'You mean a physical attack?'

'Possibly. You have to make this official, Liv.'

Ponnappa nods.

Wolfe plonks down on the sofa. She looks around at the one place she had always felt safe. But now she sees a threat around every corner.

'Your safety is more important than your job, Liv,' Butcher urges.

'Okay, but I have to go to Cambridge today. I'm already behind schedule.'

'I'll phone DI Overington,' says Butcher. 'Women's Crime Unit. I'll ask her to come round.'

Wolfe nods. Butcher makes the call.

'She'll be here within an hour.'

Ponnappa raises her arms and has a big stretch. 'This is going to take time. I'll need to keep your laptop, go through your emails, everything.'

'But all my work stuff is on there. Confidential data. I don't want strangers trawling through it.'

Ponnappa glances at Butcher, her eyes encouraging him to say something.

'Can work provide you with another? At least temporarily?' asks Butcher. 'You've backed everything up, right?'

Wolfe reluctantly agrees.

'Any other smoke detectors?' Butcher asks.

Her hand flies up to her mouth.

'What?'

'In my bedroom.'

Butcher picks up the stepladder and quickly disconnects the bedroom spy camera.

'Who is doing this?' says Wolfe. She feels sick.

'You already know who's top of my suspect list,' says Butcher.

Wolfe snaps. 'Why the hell would Davy watch me in bed, for Christ's sake?'

'It's not about that, Liv. It's about keeping tabs on you. Where you are. Who you talk to. Come with me.'

He leads her to the hallway where he's dumped his holdall.

'Let's take a walk.' Butcher picks up his bag, then calls out to Ponnappa. 'Will be back in a tick.'

He leads Wolfe across the road to a park bench facing her flat. They sit. Butcher pulls from his holdall a manila folder, concealed beneath his gym towel, and gives it to her.

She opens it. Inside is a six-month-old medical report on David George Wolfe. Clipped to the front is a photo of her brother, unconscious, propped up in a hospital bed, one eye closed, the other swollen shut, slack mouth, a tube in his nose and a myriad of tubes in his arm and beneath his hospital gown. Stitches hold livid skin together from the middle of the left eyebrow, around the left side of his head and into his hairline. She hardly recognises him.

'My God!'

Wolfe reads the description of his injuries. Someone cracked

177

his skull, gave him a couple of broken ribs and a smashed foot, breaking some of the bones in his toes.

'Who . . . ' Her voice trails away. There are tears in her eyes. 'Who did this?'

'Good question. As usual, in prison, nobody saw anything.'

'Then why?'

'Another good question. He must've pissed off somebody important. From the report, he was found like that in the showers.'

'How is he now? Do you know?'

'Medical report the day before he was released is at the back.'

She finds the printout and reads it aloud.

'Multiple minor closed head injuries. As a result has moderate frontal lobe impairment . . . David is impulsive, unaware of the consequences of his behaviour, has anger management problems, and will find it difficult to integrate back into society . . . His drug addiction has exacerbated his condition.'

Wolfe's jaw drops. 'Drug addiction? In prison?'

'It's how many cope.'

She looks at the photo again.

'I had no idea. I feel terrible.'

'It *is* terrible, I agree. But this is not your fault, Liv.'

'I should go and see him.'

'I'd think very carefully about that. You won't be welcome and you most certainly won't be safe. And, if he's not your stalker, you'll land him in a whole load of shit. Any contact with you is in breach of his conditions of release.'

She is quiet for a moment, thinking about her brother. How has it come to this? They were so close as kids. She'd looked up to him, four years her senior. When her dad left home and her mother had a mental breakdown, Davy was her rock, her best friend.

'There's no way he's my stalker.'

'I'm not so sure about that. Traumatic events can trigger stalking behaviour.'

She stares at him, incredulous.

'Read the rest of it. The bit about job prospects.'

She skim-reads fast, something as a journalist she's learnt to do by necessity.

'He did a course in computer programming. So what?'

'Okay, there's a piece of this puzzle you don't know, so let me fill you in. His cell mate was Freddie Glenn. In for murder – his ex-girlfriend. But that's not the important bit. This guy stalked the poor woman for over a year. He stole her mail, killed her cat, hacked her computer. Then he breaks in, rapes her and slits her throat.' Butcher pauses, so it sinks in. 'Davy could've learnt to hack from Glenn.'

30

My pills are in a Perspex box with a transparent lid, delivered to my door every month by the local pharmacy. There are sixty-two little square receptacles and each one is labelled with the days of the week, a.m. and p.m. As long as I take them every morning and evening, my life just about holds together.

'No!' I scream at my blank monitor, the camera feeds cut. 'Fucking cunt!'

That Indian bitch thinks she's better than me. Mocking me.

My arm sweeps the open pill box off my desk. It flies through the air and lands on the carpet, spewing white, yellow and blue pills all over the floor. I pick up my water glass and hurl it at the wall. The glass shatters and water drips down the pages of Dr Sharma's report, as if the typed words are weeping.

I am blubbing like a baby. I can't be without you. If you go to Cambridge, I can't follow. I daren't travel that far. This city is familiar, Cambridge isn't. I'll get lost and then have to explain what I'm doing there. Panic grips me. I can't breathe.

I charge at the door and I turn my shoulder so it'll take the force of the impact. I want pain. I need pain. I turn my face away as I slam into the door with an almighty thud. I hear the faint crack of wood splitting. I take two steps back. My shoulder aches. I pull back a clenched fist and smash it into the top right door panel. The impact reverberates up my arm, through my shoulder, and I cry out. My knuckles burn and I stare at the torn skin, fascinated. I try flexing my fingers. They are stiff and blood oozes from my knuckles. Taking deep breaths, I wait for the throbbing pain to override my fury, for the moment I'm calm enough to think clearly. It doesn't happen.

I look down at the sodden carpet and the shards of glass, some large, some no bigger than a pin head. I home in on a triangular piece, about as long as my thumb. I pick it up then pull up the loose sleeve of my long-sleeved T-shirt and I dig the point into the pale flesh of my inner arm. The glass bites. I exhale. Ah, that's better. Keeping the pressure up, I drag the makeshift blade from the crease of my arm towards my wrist. Blood blooms along the gash and I wonder if the quacks of the Middle Ages might have been on to something when they used bloodletting to balance the humours and cure apoplexy. I breathe deeply and relax. I stop before I reach my wrist. This is not a suicide. As long as you live, I have a purpose. I bring the jagged glass close to my eye and marvel at the vibrant red of my blood.

There's a tentative knock at my door.

'You all right in there?'

'I'm fine. Go away.'

A momentary hesitation, then the sound of shuffling feet receding.

31

The Laboratory of Molecular Biology in Cambridge is the hub of one of the largest clusters of healthcare-related enterprises in Europe. It reminds her of a glass cruciform cathedral, with stainless-steel-clad towers above the transept. When Wolfe's train sped past the building on her way to Cambridge Station, the afternoon sun illuminated the mid-section, turning the steel a shining gold. Now, as the lobby's glass doors slide back and she enters the atrium of Bavarian Jura beige limestone floors and four-storey-high glass walls, she's met by a flurry of young scientists and university students. Six hundred people pay homage to the God of Science here, including some of the world's best microbiologists.

She clocks two guards in black and white uniforms and a door marked 'Security' to the right of the reception desk. Somewhere in this building, Heatherton, Price, Matthews and Sinclair are working with the lab's most brilliant microbiologists on the unknown bacterial life. But she doesn't know their exact location; her phone calls have been met with silence chillier than anything she experienced in Antarctica. Casburn has put the fear of God into them.

The receptionist is in her fifties with a blonde French twist and a cheery smile, wearing bifocals from which a little gold chain hangs so she doesn't lose them. The woman sits behind a mono-lithic rectangular limestone-clad desk that reminds her of an altar. Wolfe is handed a clipboard with a questionnaire attached.

'Can you fill this in, please?'

It's for the LMB international PhD program. Wolfe hands it back.

'I'm here to see Dr Michael Heatherton.'

'I'm so sorry. I assumed you were here for an interview.' The receptionist glances at Wolfe's biker jacket, torn jeans and biker boots, backpack slung over her shoulder. She assumed Wolfe was a student. 'Do you have an appointment?'

'I don't. It's a personal matter.'

The receptionist smiles sweetly and makes an internal call.

'I'm sorry, he's not available.'

'Can I speak to him, please?' says Wolfe. 'It's important.' She points to the receptionist's phone.

'I'm afraid not.'

'Can you possibly find out when he'll be free? I've come down from London specifically to see him.'

'I see,' she says. 'Why don't you get yourself a coffee,' she says, gesturing to a café at the far end of the atrium, 'and I'll see what I can do.'

Wolfe thanks her and shuffles off to the café. She needs another coffee anyway. Making a statement to DI Overington was distressing, but tougher still was the realisation that Wolfe can no longer sleep soundly in her own home. A night in a Cambridge hotel will do her good and staying locally gives her a better chance of snagging an interview. Her coffee ordered, she sits at a table that gives her a full view of the atrium. Olivia's cappuccino has barely arrived before the receptionist walks over.

'I'm so sorry,' she says, looking genuinely apologetic. 'I've been told Dr Heatherton can't see you and he isn't available for visitors. He's in the middle of a big project, you see.'

Wolfe tries to keep the annoyance from her voice. 'And what about Dr Stacy Price? She'll have time for me.'

After all, Price did call her about Rundle's accident.

'I'm afraid none of his team is available to talk to the media.'

'Who told you I was media?'

The woman's eyelashes flutter in agitation.

'Look, please don't take it personally. Nobody's allowed near them.'

The receptionist scuttles back to her desk. Somebody other than Heatherton is refusing her access. Is Casburn back in the country?

Near the café is an escalator. Wolfe looks up. The layout of each floor is identical: from what she can see, the offices and labs are glass-fronted and face on to the void. Security cameras are everywhere, but if she looks as if she belongs, she shouldn't raise the alarm. She needs a white coat to blend in and a security pass around her neck. When she's sure the receptionist is busy with a well-dressed visitor, Wolfe takes the escalator.

Wolfe goes up to the third floor, keen to put some distance between her and the security guards. Avoiding eye contact with people, she glances into each lab through the glass walls, hoping to see someone she recognises, or, at the very least, a spare lab coat. In one room, a female lab technician drops tiny amounts of cloudy liquid from a pipette into a tray of test tubes. She is alone, her back to the door, and is wearing earphones, an iPod in her pocket. Wolfe opens the door as quietly as possible, steps into the lab and lifts the white coat off the hook and leaves. She puts it on: it's a little bulky over her jacket, but it'll have to do. Trying to hurry without looking rushed, Wolfe searches for the Lake Ellsworth scientists before Security finds her. Distracted, she almost collides with a guy whose chin bum-fluff and acne suggests he's an undergraduate. He's chatting to somebody on his phone. This could be her chance.

'Oh, I'm sorry,' says Wolfe, deliberately knocking his arm so he drops his phone.

He picks it up, checks it's not broken and shrugs, still talking on the phone.

'Can you help me? I'm new. Looking for Dr Heatherton.'

He points up. 'Fourth floor,' he mouths, then continues with his phone conversation. He hasn't noticed she's taken his security pass.

As soon as Wolfe arrives on the top floor, she realises all the labs are Biosafety Level 4 facilities, designed to contain potentially lethal biological agents such as smallpox and anthrax. Each lab has an electronic, vacuum-sealed door. Peering through the reinforced glass panels of the nearest facility, she sees changing rooms, and then another door, through which researchers can pass only when fully kitted out in protective gear. There are lockers and piles of gowns in varying sizes, as well as male and female shower rooms.

Wolfe hesitates. Is Heatherton being overly cautious, or is LE31S potentially hazardous? She doubts the student's pass around her neck will get her inside one of those labs, and, given the risks, she's not sure she really wants to. Perhaps she should wait until one of Heatherton's team takes a break?

Moving quickly, she works her way along the corridor, peering into each lab as she goes. No Heatherton or Matthews or Price or Sinclair. She stops when she sees a technician in an airtight suit with breathing apparatus working at one of three sealed transparent cabinets with Perspex fronts. Each cabinet has two arm spaces to which thick white rubber gauntlets are attached: entry points that enable technicians to work with the dangerous microbes inside. At the corner of the room is the kill tank, where all the lab's liquid waste is destroyed. It's heated under pressure to 121 degrees Celsius. Wolfe waits for the person to turn around. She doesn't recognise him, so she keeps searching.

Wolfe glances down through the void. The two security guards she saw earlier race up the escalator from the ground floor. She starts to run. At the very end of the corridor, two men in dark suits sit outside the entrance to a lab. One holds his hand to his ear, and looks straight at her. Both men stand. Their loose-fitting jackets tell her they are carrying firearms. The taller officer charges at her. He's fast. The other officer places a hand inside his jacket and stands with his back to the door. She's caught in a pincer movement between the armed officers and the security guards. There is no point running. If she does, she might get shot. She stands her ground.

'Ma'am, you have to leave. Now,' the officer says, grabbing her arm.

'I'm here to see Dr Heatherton,' Wolfe replies.

'No, you're not. You're coming with me.'

'You can let go now. I'll leave quietly.'

But he doesn't let go. He grips her arm until he has escorted her down the escalator and out of the building.

'Drove here?' he asks.

'I can find my car without you.'

'What are you driving?'

'A silver Fiat 500.'

'Hired from?'

She gives him the details.

'I'll take you to your car.' He holds her arm again, but his grip is lighter.

An ITV outside-broadcasting van has set up in the car park, and an ITV reporter is trying to gain access to the building. They weren't there when she arrived, so who has tipped them off? She spots Minkley from the BBC, on the phone and sounding furious, his cameraman by his side. He's clearly irritated that news of the alien bacteria has got out. Wolfe wants to talk to him, to find out what details have leaked.

'Ignore them,' says the armed officer. 'You're leaving.'

Crowd control fencing is being hastily erected across the entrance to the main building, as security guards refuse entry to the reporters. A short man with a cocky walk in a Burberry rip-off trench coat heads for a gap in the fencing: Eric Lowe from the tabloid, *UK Today*. He's blocked by Security. Known in the business as Nails, he's a hard-bitten, old-school journalist who always carries a bundle of fifties in his inside pocket, should his attempts at intimidation or blackmail fail to elicit the sensationalist story he's after. Lowe clocks her being manhandled, and mocks her with a royal wave.

'Why does Dr Heatherton need a protection detail?' Wolfe asks her escort.

No answer.

As Wolfe unlocks the Fiat, Heatherton runs through the car park in shorts, trainers and a singlet, despite the cool, crisp weather, heading back to work after a lunchtime jog.

'Michael! Over here!' she shouts. 'Michael, it's Olivia Wolfe.'

At first he doesn't hear her. She calls his name again.

Heatherton looks her way, stops abruptly and leans forward, panting. He is only a few feet away. 'I . . . I can't talk to you,' he says, his eyes fixed on the police officer.

'Yes, you can,' she says. 'Tell this buffoon to let me go.'

'In the car, now,' says the buffoon.

Heatherton won't look at her. 'I . . . I just can't. I'm sorry.'

Finally his eyes meet hers. Gone are the arrogance and naked ambition. In their place is wide-eyed fear.

32

It's six in the evening and Wolfe chews on a stick of licorice as she sits in her Fiat 500 outside the Laboratory of Molecular Biology. Even though she's at the back of the car park, there is a good view of the security-fenced main entrance. She's left messages for Casburn, who, unsurprisingly, hasn't called back. Since none of the scientists will talk to her, she's rung Beer on his satellite phone, keen to know how Rundle is doing in hospital, but as soon as he heard her voice, he disconnected the call. To alleviate the boredom she's unpacked and then re-packed her Go Bag: temporary laptop, smartphone, toiletries, notebook and pen, torch, knife in sheaf, key chain, lock pick, water bottle, as well as warm clothing, her Afghan dress, headscarf and passport, which she always carries, just in case she's sent overseas at a moment's notice.

The car park's sodium lights cast an orange glow on the building's exterior and distort the colour of cars, hair and clothing, making it harder to identify the people she's waiting for. She has their home addresses. An easy exercise, since three are in the local phone book and Matthews, although ex-directory, has been photographed outside his renovated, super-energy-efficient, low-carbon-footprint home for the local paper. Naturally, the year-old article didn't reveal his house number, but by using Google maps Wolfe managed to locate it. Her mobile rings.

'Where the hell are you?' Cohen barks.

'In Cambridge, doing what you asked me to do. Except nobody's talking.' She suppresses a yawn.

'Boring you, am I?'

'Stakeouts aren't exactly exciting, Moz.' Wolfe tells him about the scientists' protection detail. 'I'm going to follow Stacy Price home. I think she's the most likely to talk.'

'Why the police escort?'

'I'm guessing whatever the bacteria does, it isn't good. It's in the lab's Level 4 facility.'

'Is it now? That's a story in itself. I want an article tonight. Apart from Harvey, who's as useless as a kick up the bum, you're the only one who has a relationship with the team, so don't let me down.'

Wolfe recognises Price's wavy auburn ponytail poking out from her navy bobble hat. She's in a matching down jacket, and she tucks her chin into her scarf to hide her face. 'Gotta go, Moz. Stacy's leaving.'

The media still hanging about don't recognise Price, so she is undisturbed as she walks to the bus stop. Wolfe turns the ignition, reverses out of her spot, catches up with Price and winds down the passenger window.

'Stacy! It's Olivia. Get in!'

Price speeds up. Wolfe keeps up with her, leaning across the passenger seat so she's sure Price will hear her.

'Stacy, I just want to talk. Hop in and I'll buy you a drink.'

Price approaches the car and bends so she can see Wolfe through the open window. 'I'm sorry. I've been told not to talk to anyone. Not even my family.'

'But Stacy, you called me, remember?'

A bus is approaching. Price takes off and jumps on board just as the doors are closing.

'Shit!'

Wolfe does a U-turn and drives back into the car park, wondering if one of the many security cameras has recorded her accosting Price. Deliberately parking in a different spot, she waits. There's a steady stream of people leaving the building, but from her new parking spot it's difficult to see their faces.

A man of short stature with a plodding walk leaves the

building. As he gets closer, his bedraggled beard confirms he's Sinclair. He's wearing the style of duffel coat that reminds her of Paddington Bear, even if Sinclair's is brown. He gets into a dark-coloured Volvo XC90. Nobody else but Wolfe follows him, so it seems the protection detail is for the bacteria, not the scientists. He turns on to the A1134. She memorises his number plate in case she loses sight of him, but manages to tail the Volvo all the way to Mill Road in the suburb of Sturton Town. Sinclair parks in the Co-op supermarket's car park and gets out. Wolfe trails him inside. Sinclair struggles to free a wire basket jammed tightly into the one beneath, then sets off down the first aisle, grabbing a couple of Granny Smith apples. Two aisles over, he selects a pack of three lamb chops.

'Toby!' Wolfe calls.

He almost drops his basket. 'Jesus!'

He looks past her to the exit as if he's considering doing a runner. She raises a placating hand.

'It's okay, Toby. I just want to talk.'

Sinclair shakes his head.

Wolfe steps closer. He takes a step back.

'How are you, Toby?'

'W . . . what are you doing here?'

'I want to talk.' She nods at his shopping basket. 'How about I take you out to dinner? Save you having to cook.'

Sinclair glances at the exit again.

'I've been told not to talk to you or Charles or anyone.'

'Who says you can't? I thought we were mates.'

He clenches his jaw and glares at her. There's a ferocity she hasn't seen before. 'You're not my mate. You're a journalist.'

'Yes, that's my job. But I've grown very fond of you guys and I'm very sorry about Trent's accident. Do you know how he's doing?'

'No. No, I don't.'

For a moment Sinclair is distracted, lost in his thoughts. Wolfe moves closer.

'Should I be worried, Toby? Could the bacteria make me ill?'

Wolfe stands between Sinclair and the six self-service check-outs, so he walks quickly to the back of the store. She runs after him, grabbing the back of his coat.

'Wait!'

He stops and faces her. His eyes are bloodshot and his lids heavy, his skin taut and flaky. He's exhausted and his body odour tells her he hasn't washed for a while.

'Toby, please tell me what's going on. I never betray a source. You're perfectly safe.'

His shoulders droop. 'I'm a prisoner.'

'How do you mean?'

'All my life, I've marvelled at our beautiful world, how magnificent it is and how little we really know about it. To discover new life, cut off from the rest of the world for millions of years – well, that was truly amazing. Finally, I could make a real difference.'

He shakes his head.

'Go on,' she says.

'I'd hoped we could learn something about life on our planet, and possibly on other planets too.' Sinclair looks straight at her. 'But how could I forget how destructive we are? We use our brilliant minds to find devastating ways to kill. Did you know that the most deadly pathogens known to man, the ones we have spent decades eradicating, like smallpox, are kept alive in maximum-security facilities in the USA and Russia? Do you know why? Do you, Olivia?'

Sinclair has raised his voice. He's drawing attention from shoppers.

'I'm guessing germ warfare,' Wolfe replies, keeping her voice low.

'Precisely. Instead of eradicating them for ever, we keep them, to be used as a weapon against some future enemy, potentially killing millions of innocent people. Collateral damage, they call it. I call it murder.'

He clams up, flushed with embarrassment. A young mum near the dairy fridges scurries away, dragging her two little girls with her.

'What's this got to do with the bacteria?' Wolfe asks.

'Nothing. Nothing at all. Leave me alone.'

Sinclair drops his basket on the floor. Wolfe watches him go.

33

The man who answers the door to Heatherton's four-bedroom, thatched cottage in the village of Abbotsley isn't Heatherton. Wolfe is fairly certain that he and his wife, Patrice, are home; there are three cars parked on the gravel drive: a blue Volkswagen Golf, a silver Land Rover Discovery and a white Mazda 6 estate. She guesses the Mazda belongs to the undercover cop who has just answered the door and told her, in no uncertain terms, to leave Dr Heatherton alone. He knew about her conversation with Sinclair, which explains why the four scientists now have an officer with them twenty-four/seven.

Frustrated, Wolfe heads for her hotel on Trumpington Street in the Cambridge city centre, plonks her bag on the single bed and rings room service, ordering beer-battered fish and chips and a Kronenbourg 1664. She sits at a tiny faux mahogany desk, wondering what on earth she's going to write for Cohen. She looks around the narrow room for inspiration, but the plain cream walls, faded striped bedspread with padded navy blue bedhead, and the tiny TV on wall brackets too high to see the picture clearly, aren't helpful. But she can't grumble: she chose this room because she can see her car in the rear car park, there's a fire escape walkway beneath her window, the window locks, and there's a spy hole in the door. Wolfe likes to have an escape route.

The sagging desk chair is uncomfortable so she shoves her backpack to one end of the bed and sits cross-legged, her temporary laptop balancing on her knees, and taps out the bones of an article titled 'Police Guard Alien Bacteria'. It doesn't mention Sinclair, both to keep her promise and because she doubts his outburst is anything more than paranoia. It asks why such intense security is necessary for apparently harmless bacteria. She knows the article is weak. Worse still, there's a twinge of guilt: will it make the Ellsworth scientists' lives even more fraught than they already are? Wolfe prepares an email to Cohen, asking for another day. But her message won't send. No internet connection. Her personal wireless modem appears to be working, but she tries the hotel's network, just in case. Still no internet access. Frustrated, she copies the article on to a USB and uses her smartphone to send the email.

Cohen's response is fast and brief.

Email article now, as is.

Wolfe attaches the document, but doesn't send it.

Leaning back into the bedhead, Wolfe is torn between her job and the people she has come to like and respect. There's a knock on her door and a man calls out 'Room service'. Wolfe peers through the spy hole before opening the door. She sees a painfully thin teenager with glasses, in a burgundy waistcoat, carrying a tray. She opens the door and he puts it on the desk. He takes the top off the beer bottle, gets her signature on the docket and leaves. The bottom edge of the door drags across the carpet as it shuts in slow motion thanks to the mechanical closer. At last she can relax. As she picks up the bottle, there's a thud. Wolfe turns fast, sees a black leather boot and part of a leg jamming the door open. She instinctively hurls her shoulder into the door so the boot is stuck, then slams the thick glass bottle down on to the intruder's knee. Beer explodes from the open bottle.

'*Ebat!*'

Grankin!

Beer pours down her arm, the wall, the door and the assailant's jeans, but the bottle hasn't broken. Using all her strength to keep the door shoved tight against the boot, she raises the bottle again for a second hit.

'Olivia! Stop!'

She knows the voice but doesn't believe it.

'Who are you?'

She cannot hold the door any longer.

'Vitaly,' he says. 'I must speak with you.'

She releases the pressure a fraction. It slams back into the doorstop with such force, the stopper is ripped from the floor. Yushkov stands in the doorway, clutching one knee.

'They torture me, and now you try to break my knee. Fuck!'

Wolfe has the bottle raised above her head, ready to strike again.

'Stay where you are.'

'Olivia, please. I must speak with you.'

'Why me?'

'On the plane, you spoke for me.'

Yushkov remains in the doorway, waiting to be invited in. How did he know where to find her?

'What the hell?' Wolfe lowers her weapon. 'Come in, quickly.'

As Yushkov hobbles to the desk chair and sits, she takes her knife from her backpack pocket and points the sharp blade at the man SO15 and MI5 believe is a killer.

'Casburn let you go?'

He nods. 'I stink like a drunk,' he says, touching his sodden jeans.

Yushkov is wearing a thigh-length black leather coat with fleece lining, dark blue jeans and shiny leather steel-capped boots. His shirt still has the front crease marks, as if it has just been removed from the packet.

'You react very fast. You surprise me,' Yushkov says.

Wolfe stays near the door, so she can escape if needs be.

'How the hell did you find me?'

'Easy. I rang the *Post*. Asked for you. The first person was not helpful. I rang again. Some guy told me you were in Cambridge. It was easy to guess where. The laboratory.'

'You mean you've been following me all day?' She is stunned. Why didn't she notice?

'This evening, yes.'

'Damn.' She gives Yushkov a hard stare. 'I don't like being predictable. It'll land me in trouble.'

'Michael, Toby, Stacy? They tell you nothing, yes?'

She nods. 'Why the boot in the door? It wasn't necessary.'

'I think you will not speak to me now I am a terrorist.'

'Are you a terrorist?'

'I am not. But what are you?'

'What?'

'I had tip-off you are not what you seem. Maybe you are a spy. Your job is the perfect cover.'

She laughs. 'God give me strength!'

Yushkov touches his knee and grimaces. 'You have ice?'

Wolfe opens the minibar and finds a tray of ice cubes. She empties the entire tray into a white hand towel, wraps them up and hands the bundle to Yushkov, whose body seems to fill the tiny room.

'You want me to take my trousers off?'

'Vitaly, I've seen it all before. I don't care.'

He shrugs. 'Okay, I not strip for a lady in a long time.'

Yushkov removes his leather coat, places it on the back of the chair and then kicks off his polished boots. He undoes his belt and peels off his jeans, dropping them to the floor, revealing muscular legs and raw rings around both ankles. His wrists have the same circular flesh wounds. What has Casburn done to him? Oblivious to her scrutiny, he lifts his sore knee and rests his foot on the edge of the bed, then presses the towel full of ice on to his kneecap.

'You got another beer?' he asks. 'I wear the last one.' He grins up at her.

'What did your last slave die of?'

But her sarcasm is lost on Yushkov, who frowns, confused. Sighing, she offers him a Budweiser from the minibar.

'American beer! Tastes like piss.'

'Then have this.'

She chucks him a miniature bottle of Absolut vodka. 'Fussy for a suspected terrorist, aren't you?'

'Ha! You are very funny lady.'

He opens the bottle's red screw-top and swallows the vodka in one gulp. Wolfe picks up his discarded jeans.

'I can't believe I'm doing this,' she mutters. 'I feel like your frigging mother.'

In the bathroom, she runs water over the beer-stained jeans, squeezes them out and puts them on the radiator to dry.

'What's with the new gear?' she calls.

'They bug my clothes, my boots, my home.'

Yushkov has her food tray close and is eating her dinner.

'Not bad,' he says, waving a piece of golden battered cod in the air.

'Hey! That's my meal.'

'Then eat.'

She sits on the bed and tucks into what remains.

'What happened to you?' she says, chewing on a chip.

'They fly me somewhere. A white, empty room. Tie my hands and ankles. Question me. Deprive me of sleep, water, food. Let me piss myself. More questions. Threats. Then I am released.'

'This was Casburn and Flynn?'

'Yes, and others. They take turns.'

SO15 and MI5, she guesses. Wolfe is no longer interested in food. 'Where did they take you?'

He looks up, irritated. 'I don't know. They make sure I do not know. They put a hood on my head, drag me from one plane and shove me in another. I am in a sealed room. No windows. The lights are very bright and they play loud music, so loud I want to cover my ears but I cannot.'

'My God!'

'Then bang!' He claps his hands. 'They fly me to England.'

'Why let you go?'

He shrugs.

'Did they beat you?'

'They slap me about. It is nothing.'

'What did they want, Vitaly?'

He swallows. She watches his Adam's apple bob. 'They want to know where I take the missing bacteria.'

'Missing?'

'That's what they said.'

'How?'

He takes the last chip. 'They tell me one canister is stolen. They were very certain of this. They think I give it to Sergey Grankin.'

'Did you?'

Yushkov gives her a cold stare. 'I did not. Russia has made me an enemy. Why would I help my enemy?'

Wolfe studies Yushkov's worn, weather-beaten face for any sign he's lying. She sees none, but if he is SVR, he has been trained to be convincing.

'So why does Casburn think you did?'

'Because he is an idiot,' he says, tapping his forehead with a finger. 'He thinks because I was born a Russian, I am a traitor to my adopted country. Easy to blame me. Easy to frame me.'

'Is it a pathogen?'

'I don't know.'

'Did he tell you why the Russians want it?'

'*Nyet.*' He looks at the sash window. 'You okay if I smoke? I open the window.'

He pulls out a packet of Marlboro's.

'Blow it away from the smoke detector,' she says, pointing at the ceiling.

Yushkov nods and leans over to the sash window, flicks the latch and opens the lower half. The night air rushes into the over-heated room.

'You want one?'

'I keep telling myself I've given up,' she says. 'But what the hell.'

With the knife still in her right hand, she takes a cigarette with her left and Yushkov lights it. She shuffles around the seated Russian so she can smoke near the window.

'They took your fags away?'

'*Da*, and they did not give them back. Not very good hosts, I think.'

Yushkov smiles and inhales deeply, then studies the cigarette with disapproval. 'Like American beer. Piss weak.'

She watches him for a moment, unable to make up her mind about him.

'So why are you here, Vitaly?'

He flicks his head to the window and blows a plume of smoke at the night sky. 'I need your help.'

'My help? How?'

'They let me go, but do not believe me. They hope I will lead them to the canister, but I do not have it.'

'Were you followed here?' she asks, peering into the floodlit car park.

'I lost my tail.'

Wolfe frowns. 'How? They're surveillance experts.'

'From Brize Norton they drive me home. They sit in their car and wait and watch. I find bugs in my flat, in my mobile, sewn into my coat and in the heel of my boots. So I ask a neighbour: can I use your car? I ask him to go to a cashpoint and withdraw all my money. Seven hundred pounds. I say, you do this and I give you a hundred. He does this for me. I pay him. I leave the back way and drive to shopping centre. Everything new.' Yushkov waves a hand up and down, gesturing to his new gear. 'Very cheap.' He nods approvingly. 'This Casburn, he forget something important. I know how to disappear.'

'Why did you disappear, Vitaly?'

Wolfe remembers the top-secret document that describes Yushkov as a coward in Chechnya. Yushkov takes another deep drag on his cigarette and puffs out smoke circles.

'It is not relevant.'

'I can't help you if you're not honest with me,' says Wolfe, stubbing out her barely smoked cigarette in a glass tumbler.

'I want you to help me prove my innocence.'

'And how do you propose we do that?'

'By finding the real terrorist.'

34

Wolfe leans against the windowsill, studying the man everyone else has given up on. 'And why would I help you?'

Yushkov draws on the last of his cigarette and extinguishes it between two fingers, dropping it into a glass tumbler at the bottom of which is Wolfe's barely smoked cigarette, bent out of shape.

'Because you want to know the truth. You have to know the truth.'

'Don't presume to know me.'

Her eyes flash an angry warning. She moves away from the open window and takes from the bar fridge a half-bottle of shiraz that'll cost her twice as much as a full bottle from the local off-licence. Gone are the days when bar-fridge expenses went on journalists' company credit cards. She pours it and takes a swig, her back to Yushkov, annoyed she has let him get under her skin. He seems to know her too well.

'If you want my help, you have to be honest with me.' She faces him. 'Otherwise, get out of my room.'

'You do not trust me?'

Wolfe laughs. 'Are you kidding me? Nobody trusts you, Vitaly. Nobody but me would have you sitting in their hotel room. Casburn thinks you're a murderer involved in some kind of terror plot. You want me to trust you? Then tell me the truth.'

He is silent for a long moment, then glances at the knife she still clutches.

'If I wanted to kill you, you would be dead by now. That knife would not stop me.'

Her breath catches but she won't let him see her fear. 'You presume to know me, and you underestimate me.' Wolfe raises the knife. 'Get out.'

'I am trying to make a point, Olivia. I am a soldier. I know how to kill. But I will never hurt you.' He pauses, scanning her face. 'Remember, I stopped Sergey.'

Her eyes open wide. 'Stopped Sergey, what?'

'From killing you.'

'So you knew all along it was him, but you never said. Why?'

'It's complicated.'

Wolfe sits on the bed and chugs down some wine. It's one step forwards and two steps back with Yushkov. Yet his secrets intrigue her as much as the truth – his truth – terrifies her.

'I have a rule, Vitaly. It's how I survive in this business.' She looks him in the eye. 'Never get involved. I broke it in Afghanistan. I wanted to help a girl who'd been raped, imprisoned and forced to marry her rapist. I told her story, then I went after her husband and the drug trafficking ring he's part of. I realise now she was more to me than a source . . . ' Her words trail off. She finds her way again. 'You want me to prove you are innocent. But my job is to report what I see, not change the outcome.'

Wolfe looks down at the glass she's clutching.

'Why was it wrong to help this woman?' Yushkov asks.

'Because instead of writing the most powerful story I could, a story that helps victims like Nooria, I got mixed up in it and got her killed.'

Yushkov studies her face as if he is trying to read her mind. 'Tell me about this girl.'

'Why?' Her stomach churns. She doesn't want to remember.

'Please. I would like to hear it.'

Wolfe tells him about Nooria's short life and death, but finds it difficult to control the tremor in her voice.

'She was very brave,' Yushkov says. 'But you? You are angry with yourself, I think?'

'In Antarctica you told me that sometimes it's best to walk away. What did you mean by that?'

'You have a good memory.'

'Was it about walking away from the Army?'

Yushkov moves the ice-filled towel aside and stands. 'My knee is good now.' He goes into the bathroom, leaves the damp towel in the basin and pulls his jeans off the hot radiator. Wolfe stands in the bathroom doorway.

'Vitaly, do you want me to help you or not?'

He pulls on his damp jeans and does them up. 'I cannot talk about it.'

'Are you a deserter?'

A pause. The extractor fan hums. 'Yes.'

He takes a step towards her but she doesn't budge.

'Get out of my way,' he says quietly.

She can see the muscles in his thick neck tighten.

'What drove you to desert?'

'*Nyet.*'

'The truth!'

Yushkov's eyes are as hard as blue ice. He looks down, his jaw muscles tensing. Seconds pass.

'We sit.'

He takes the chair, she the bed. He won't make eye contact. 'It is March 2000. I fight in Second Chechen War. I was with 160th Tank Regiment, commanded by Colonel Gerasimov.'

'Gerasimov? I know that name. Something to do with a rape trial?'

'Yes. A brutal man.' Yushkov shakes his head as he stares at the worn carpet. 'Gerasimov claimed the girl was a sniper. The truth is he saw her in the village of Tangi Chu and that night he went back with the duty crew, raped and strangled her in his vehicle.' He looks up at Wolfe. 'I was not one of the duty crew. But I was coward, too afraid to report him. Who would believe a soldier against a colonel?'

'Then what?' asks Wolfe.

'I was recalled. Both Andrei and me.'

'Andrei?'

'My friend.' The expression in his eyes has softened.

Wolfe remembers the group shot: Yushkov with his arm around a smaller, dark-haired soldier.

'We think the Colonel send us away to die. He volunteers us for a suicide mission. In Afghanistan.'

'But the Russian military hasn't been in Afghanistan since 1989.'

'Really?' Yushkov rubs his bruised knuckles across his lips. 'If you print this story, I am a dead man. You understand?'

'I understand.'

'You must not speak of this to anyone. If Casburn or MI5 find out, I will be sent back to Russia with the certainty I will be executed.'

'I won't tell anyone, unless you give me permission. You have my word.'

'My life depends on your silence.'

She nods. He looks down again.

'I am sent to assassinate a Taliban leader. No firearms, no noise. I am to strangle him in his sleep.' He watches her reaction.

She gives him none. 'This leader is well protected. Gerasimov, he has sent me to my death.'

'I'm assuming the Afghani Government had no idea?'

'None. Russia cannot attack the Taliban inside Afghanistan. Instead, it supplies arms to anti-Taliban forces. But Russia conducts secret airstrikes on Taliban positions. Of course, they deny it. But then the new President, Putin, decides he must do more to control the threat of the Taliban on his border. He is angry the Taliban helps train the Chechens to fight Russia. Did you know about this?'

'I'd heard rumours.'

'So we are sent to assassinate a Taliban commander named Fazi. He is outspoken about his support for the Chechens. He supplies them with weapons to kill us. We have information Fazi hides in a mountain village with twenty men. The intelligence is wrong and we are led into a trap. Our guide takes us into a minefield and abandons us. We are fired on. We run. I watch men blown to pieces. Andrei steps on an IED. He dies, I live.'

He is still, lost in his memories.

'Did you kill Fazi?' she asks.

Yushkov shakes his head. 'Only three of us reach the village, including my captain, Razin. Our target is not there. He has been tipped off. Captain Razin, he orders us to round up the villagers. They are forced to their knees in the street.' Yushkov's voice cracks. 'Razin demands of each person: where is Fazi? An old woman is first. She weeps and says she does not know. He shoots the old woman in the head. Then he kills a teenage boy. Then a young girl, no more than nine or ten …' Yushkov is barely audible. 'It was murder. Stupid and pointless. These villagers, they know nothing or they are too afraid to tell us. I could not be a coward again, so I shout at my commander to stop. I say they are civilians and we must not kill civilians. He shoots me.'

Yushkov touches his right collarbone and moves his shoulder stiffly. 'I was lucky. But the villagers were not. He shoots them, one by one. Only a boy escapes.' Yushkov shakes his head. 'Just one. It is then that I know I cannot stay in the Army. But I am bound by a contract – I will never be free. So I turn my gun on my commander and kill him. I have been running ever since.' Yushkov leans back in his chair and exhales loudly, relieved he's come to the end of his confession. 'My country wants me dead. Why, Olivia, would I do Russia's bidding?'

'Forgiveness?'

'Ha!' he laughs bitterly. 'The Army never forgives.'

'A chance to return to your homeland?'

Yushkov shakes his head.

'I tell you, I step foot in Russia and I am dead.'

Wolfe pauses. 'To see your sister again?'

His head snaps up. 'How do you . . . ? Ah, you hear Grankin.' He smiles. 'I must watch you very carefully.'

'How does Grankin know your sister?'

'You are a smart woman. You tell me.'

'You like your games, don't you?' she says. 'Okay then, Grankin is blackmailing you?'

'Very good.'

'He promises safe passage for your sister if you give him the bacteria.'

'Also correct.'

'And? There is something else,' Yushkov says.

'And, the man we met, claiming to be Sergey Grankin, isn't the real Grankin?'

Yushkov nods.

'Are you working for the SVR?' Wolfe asks.

'I am not. Will you trust me now?'

35

Yushkov's stare never wavers as he waits for an answer. There are too many questions pinging around Wolfe's head like a pinball machine. Should she believe him?

Wolfe's phone rings. The caller ID says it's Cohen.

She ducks into the bathroom and answers. Yushkov watches her, his wide shoulders slouched, as if his confession has drained him.

'What the fuck is going on?' Cohen yells down the phone.

His voice booms out. Even Yushkov hears him and frowns the question: who is that?

'Moz, hold your horses! What do you mean?'

'What I mean is, I tell you to email me your story and you send me fuck-all while your mate Nails beats you to it. Go to *UK Today*'s site. I'm sure you'll get a kick out of reading his so-called first-hand account, "Police Guard Alien Bacteria".'

'What?'

It's her headline. Exactly.

Yushkov stands, worried by the alarm in her voice. 'What is happening?' he mouths.

Wolfe mutes her phone. 'It's my editor.'

'Who's there with you?' says Cohen.

She takes it off mute. 'Nobody,' she lies. 'Sounds like Nails stole my story.'

'And how the fuck did he do that?' Cohen sneers. 'Telepathy?'

'Give me a chance, will you? Let me read it.'

'I'll tell you what it bloody well says,' Cohen snaps. 'Unnamed sources at the Laboratory of Molecular Biology have confirmed that the Lake Ellsworth bacteria is a deadly pathogen. So deadly that the lab and the scientists are under twenty-four-hour police guard.' Cohen pauses for breath, 'You're in fucking Cambridge, you're the only reporter to get inside the lab, you've even talked to the scientists. So tell me how that fuckwit writes the story you promised me!'

'I'll call you back.'

'Oh no, you don't!'

She cuts him off and uses her phone's internet. On *UK Today*'s site there is a photo of the Cambridge lab, an exterior building shot, and a pretty scary-looking photo of tuberculosis bacteria in close-up, subtitled, 'Tuberculosis was the most deadly bacteria on Earth. Until Antarctic scientists brought something more sinister to our shores'.

She skim-reads the article and calls Cohen back.

'My words, verbatim. Except he's made up the TB stuff.'

'Magnificent!' says Cohen. 'So what am I going to print?'

'Moz, listen to me. I'm telling you this is exactly what I have written. Look, I'll email it now.' A few seconds later it's sent. 'See what I mean.'

Cohen is silent for a minute as he reads. 'If you wrote this, how come I'm reading it under Nails's by-line?'

'My computer's been hacked, so this phone could've been too,' she says. 'Nails may well be behind the weird shit going on at my flat. The prick!'

Yushkov moves to the open window and lights another cigarette.

'Moz, I'm not using this phone again. I'll send you a story tonight with a better angle.'

'How?'

'I'll get a new phone.'

She ends the call, switches it off, removes the SIM and pockets it. She doesn't want to lose her day-to-day contacts. When this is over, perhaps she can retrieve them. She glances at the chunky ring on her finger: at least she still has her sources' details stored safely.

'My phone's been hacked,' she says to Yushkov. 'Probably a rival reporter.'

Yushkov frowns. 'Is there anything about me on there?'

'Yes, I made notes in Antarctica. You were in them.'

'Including my argument with Sergey?'

'Yes, it was easier to use—'

Suddenly, he is in her face. 'Did you say Sergey is Russian agent?'

'It is one of my theories, yes.'

'What if this Nails prints this theory? Says I talk in secret with SVR? Casburn does not know these things. If Nails makes it public, I will have SVR hunting me, and Casburn.'

It seems to happen in slow motion. One moment she is looking up at Yushkov's anxious face, the next there is a faint pop, his head twitches sideways and he throws her to the floor. Glass shatters. The bullet hits the wall. She screams. He lands partly on her, partly next to her and covers her mouth with his hand.

'Quiet!' he whispers.

She nods her understanding. The window has a jagged hole. One shot. The sniper is waiting to take another. Yushkov crawls on his elbows across the glass-strewn carpet and stretches a hand up to the light switch, killing the lights. Another bullet zips past Yushkov's head. Shattered wall plaster falls on his head.

The laptop still illuminates the bed. And them.

'Shut the laptop. Keep low.'

Wolfe nods, rolling on to her belly, and crawls closer. Tiny shards of glass crunch beneath her. Head down, she runs her hand blindly across the bedspread, finds the laptop, closes the lid and drags it to the floor. The room is plunged into darkness, except for a jaundice yellow glow from the car park lights.

'The fire escape,' Wolfe whispers, 'outside the window. He could use it.'

'Then we go now.'

Wolfe and Yushkov creep towards the strip of light under the door. They listen out for an accomplice on the other side of the door, but hear nothing.

'I open it. You crawl through first. Okay?'

'Yes.'

Yushkov reaches up to the door handle. More glass explodes, he collapses, and her heart almost stops.

36

Yushkov is motionless. The slit of light seeping under the door is enough to see a dark wet patch on his ear. Wolfe reaches out and touches warm blood.

'Vitaly?'

Yushkov slowly shifts his hand to his bloody ear. 'Grazed me.'

Tufts of carpet jump before her eyes as another bullet shreds it.

'He's up high. We stay here, he will kill us,' Yushkov whispers. 'We must run for it. You ready?'

She nods. Yushkov takes a deep breath, jumps up, throws open the door and dives for the corridor floor. Bullets smash into the corridor wall, sending plaster and wallpaper flying. Wolfe darts through the opening.

'Run!' Yushkov yells.

They charge down the corridor. The top of Yushkov's ear has been cut and blood drips down his neck. There's a tray of half-eaten room-service food outside a guest's door. Wolfe seizes the cotton serviette.

'Here.' She flicks it to him. 'You're bleeding.'

They hurtle down the red-carpeted stairs.

'Can't use my hire car,' Wolfe pants, working hard to keep up with him. 'In my name.'

'Use mine.'

They burst through a fire door into the reception area and get a stunned gasp from the receptionist and disapproving stares from a man checking in.

'Sir? Madam?' calls the receptionist. 'Wait a moment, please, we've had complaints . . .'

Ignoring her, Yushkov takes Wolfe's hand and they run from the hotel and down Trumpington Street. Except for a few passing cars, the street is almost empty. It's bitterly cold and their heavy breathing creates a fleeting mist around their faces.

'There!'

He points to a Seat Ibiza: his neighbour's car. Yushkov pulls the key from his pocket and remotely unlocks it. He is about to open the driver's door when Wolfe sees a shadow shift behind the car. Yushkov doesn't see the man steal closer, knife in hand. Wolfe charges him and swings her backpack at his hand, knocking the knife into the gutter. But their assailant reaches inside his jacket. Yushkov recovers himself in time to punch the man in the stomach, then slams his attacker's hand into the car door, forcing him to drop the gun he's pulled. Wolfe grabs it and points it at the killer as Yushkov throws him on to the car bonnet and pins him down.

'Who are you? Who do you work for?' he demands.

Before the man can answer, he convulses and blood spatters over Yushkov's face. The sniper has followed them, ensuring their captive doesn't talk. Immediately, Yushkov ducks low, dragging Wolfe between two parked cars.

'Over the road!' Wolfe says, and takes off.

They dodge a bus heading for the city centre, sprint down Lensfield Road and take an immediate right into Brookside.

It's a narrow, poorly lit residential street. Beech-tree branches obscure the cars parked beneath. The newly built terraced houses opposite are shut up for the night, curtains drawn, lights mostly out. She slows.

'We need a car,' Wolfe says. 'An old model. Watch my back.'

They race past Audis, Fords, Volkswagens, Fiats and the occasional Volvo.

'This one,' says Wolfe, stopping at a twelve-year-old Vauxhall Astra.

She drops her backpack on the ground and pulls out her wallet, removing her lock-picking kit. She finds the pick she wants, inserts it in the driver's door lock, jiggles it around until it clicks. She lifts the handle and the door opens.

'Get in,' Wolfe says.

Chucking her pack into the back, she leans across and unlocks the passenger door from the inside. Yushkov fills the space, his head brushing the car roof. Wolfe crouches over the steering wheel, yanks off the cover, pulls down the ignition wires, strips the ends and gets them to touch. The engine comes to life.

'So, we have something in common,' Yushkov says, grinning.

'How do you mean?' she asks, as she drives off down the street, taking a sharp left down Pemberton Terrace.

'A misspent youth.'

Wolfe glances at him. 'My brother taught me.' She looks around, trying to get her bearings. 'I've no idea where we are. How do I get to London?'

'Why London?'

'We have to disappear and it's easier in a city of nine million. And I'm paying Nails a visit.'

He shrugs. 'My flat is being watched. So I guess I go with you. But I think this reporter is the least of your problems.'

'How do you mean?'

'You should be more worried about the men who just tried to kill us.'

'SVR?'

'I think so.'

'We need burner phones. One each. What'll be open at this time of night?' She glances at the car clock. It's just gone ten.

'I know supermarket that opens late.' He gives her the directions. She drives. 'We need a gun. I have friends in London who can help.'

Wolfe's head snaps round. 'No way. No firearms.'

'Have you forgotten what just happened? They are armed, so we must be armed.'

Wolfe doesn't like where this is heading. 'You know gun dealers?'

'I would not call them dealers. They are men who need to defend themselves. With a past, like me.'

'Who are these men?'

'It is best you do not know their names. They are Chechen. Russian. Afghani.'

'Jesus, Vitaly! Are you out of your mind? MI5 and SO15 think you're a terrorist and you're going to buy a gun from the Russian and Chechen mafia, or – even worse – an Afghani who's probably on a terror watch list.'

'I will be careful, Olivia.'

She slams the palm of her hand down on the steering wheel.

'You do this, you'll get picked up and you'll never be heard of again.'

'SVR will not stop hunting us. This is the only way.'

Wolfe shakes her head. 'I don't want to know who you call. I'm having nothing to do with it.'

Thirty minutes later they are on the motorway heading for London, with new pay-as-you-go phones in fake names, and woolly hats and scarves to keep their features hidden from prying eyes and CCTV cameras. Yushkov has a large plaster on his ear. They've filled the car with petrol, bought snacks and drinks, and paid for everything in cash. Yushkov has made several calls and left cryptic messages. The only man he's succeeded in speaking to – a Russian – is unwilling to help.

'Was the sniper after you or me?' Wolfe asks, gunning it down the motorway.

'I think both. We are lucky to be alive. The assassin was a professional.'

'What makes you so sure?'

'A kill shot at night is very difficult.'

'You heard him fire? How?'

'I know the sound.'

They are silent for a while.

'So, you decide to help me?' Yushkov asks.

'I guess I have.'

He stares at her profile as she drives. 'I thank you.'

'Don't thank me yet.'

Yushkov throws a handful of crisps in his mouth.

Wolfe overtakes an Audi R8 that's barely doing sixty m.p.h. 'What a waste! Look at those sleek lines. Gorgeous car.'

'You are not like other women I know.'

'You can be sure of that.' She flicks him a big smile.

'Why you have metal in your tongue?'

'Cause I want to,' she replies, the smile gone. 'Hey, do I get any of those? You ate my dinner, remember?'

He holds out the bag of salt and vinegar crisps and she takes a couple.

'So let's say Grankin tried to kill us tonight,' she says.

'Presumably because you know too much and he doesn't want you blabbing to me or Casburn.' Yushkov's loud crunching makes it hard to think clearly. She takes a deep breath. 'But Grankin wasn't at Camp Ellsworth when Kevin was murdered, or when the accidents happened. So who on the team is working for Grankin?'

'I don't know.'

'Come on, Vitaly. You lived with these guys. You must have an inkling. Anyone do or say anything weird? Ask strange questions?'

Yushkov screws up the empty crisp bag and squeezes it into one of the cup holders recessed into the dashboard.

'Hey,' she says, 'that's got your DNA all over it. We're taking it with us and wiping down the car when we get to London, okay?'

He nods and folds his arms. 'Michael was with me when Kev left the mess tent. So was Harvey. No,' Yushkov pauses. 'Harvey left shortly after Kev. He was embarrassed at the way Michael spoke to me. He told me this later.'

'Where was everyone else?' Wolfe asks.

'I can only guess. Engineers in the control centre. The others in the lab.'

'So pretty well everyone at the camp had the opportunity to kill Kevin, except Michael.'

'Michael would have had to walk past me and then take a snowmobile. I didn't hear the engine start.'

'Would you have heard it in a blizzard?'

'Maybe not.'

'That doesn't narrow it down much. What about motivation? It's a big deal to betray your country. Huge, if you have to kill. Why would someone do it?'

'Perhaps they have a secret. Maybe criminal record? And SVR blackmail this person?'

'As Grankin tried to do with you?'

'As Grankin tried to do with me.'

Wolfe glances at Yushkov's side profile. Has he told her the truth? If Yushkov is SVR or has been recruited recently by Grankin, she is playing a very dangerous game.

'Everyone has secrets but few will actually kill to avoid exposure,' she says. 'Anyone spring to mind?'

'Kev was my friend. I did not get close to the others.'

'Gossip?'

'I not like gossip.'

'Yes, but there's often a grain of truth behind it.'

He stares out of the window into the night. 'Before we arrive in Antarctica, there was talk about Michael.'

'What about him?'

'People say he was having an affair and she wanted him to leave his wife. Gary saw this woman at BAS reception, demanding to see him.' He shrugs. 'That is all I know.'

'I can't see Heatherton sabotaging his own project, can you?'

'*Nyet.* He is obsessed. I think he would prefer to lose his wife than this project.'

'Okay, what if somebody on the team needed money badly. Does anyone have a gambling or drug addiction?'

'Bruce, he likes to go to the casino. Plays blackjack. And Trent talks a lot about gambling, but it is small bets on horses.'

'Have you heard Trent's injured?'

'No, what happened?'

'All I know is the tractor blades came loose and crushed one of his legs. He's in hospital.'

'How did they come loose? This is not possible.'

'I don't know, I'm sorry.'

'I do not think it is an accident.'

'Nor do I.' She glances at Yushkov. His features are hard set in anger.

214

'What about financial difficulties, medical bills, anything like that?'

'Stacy has two sons at university. Both at Cambridge. She complains about the fees, but I think she is paid well and so is her husband.'

Wolfe picks up a can of V energy drink and takes a swig. 'All right, then what about somebody with a grudge? Hates this country for some reason?'

'Bruce talked about growing up black in London. But he said he was determined not to let other people's prejudices spoil his life.'

'Was he bitter about it?'

'No, I did not see this. I think he is proud he has a good career and a beautiful girlfriend.'

Wolfe catches his eye.

'Are you angry at the way your new country is treating you?'

'I am not angry. I am afraid.'

37

Yushkov rests his calloused hands on the armrest of an opulent, purple velvet wingchair and rests his boots up on a matching velvet footstool. The ex-soldier looks as out of place as a fish and chip shop on an iceberg.

'This is nicest hotel I ever see,' he says, stroking the velvet as if it were a cat.

Theirs is one of the spacious rooftop rooms with views through recessed windows along Great Russell Street and over the twinkling lights of the city. It's one in the morning and Wolfe is curled up on a matching velvet armchair, her head resting on its wing, barely able to keep her eyes open. She can see into the marble bathroom. The claw-footed bath with gold taps looks inviting.

'Why you choose this place?'

'Because they know me. I bring whistle-blowers here. Sources who want their identities kept secret. The staff are discreet and they let me book by the hour, no questions asked.'

'So they think you are prostitute?'

'I don't care what they think.' She flushes pink and looks away. 'I pay in cash, no questions asked.'

'But we have this room for the night, yes?'

'Yes. Except we have a sleeping issue,' she says, nodding at the king-size bed. There had been no twins available.

Yushkov smiles. 'There is no problem, Olivia. I take the bed and you sleep on the nice soft carpet. I give you a blanket.' He watches her face darken and then bursts out laughing. 'It is a joke. I will sleep on the floor.'

'Yeah, very funny.' She gets up, weary. 'I'm taking a bath. I need to be up early.'

'Where are you going?'

'To find Nails. Then tee up an interview with the Russian ambassador. I want answers.'

'He will deny everything.'

'Of course, but, sometimes, provoking the beast can be revealing.'

'And very risky.'

Wolfe picks up her backpack and takes it to the bathroom.

'You still don't trust me, do you, Olivia?' he says, nodding at the bag.

'I don't trust anyone.'

She locks the bathroom door and leans against it, enjoying her solitude. She needs time to think and she thinks best when alone.

Part of her knows that Yushkov may be lying, but to discover the truth, she must stick with him. Wolfe turns on the mixer tap, adds some bubble bath, and strips. As she waits for the bath to fill, she brushes her teeth. If Yushkov is the enemy, then why has he saved her life twice? Why would he even want her help? If he were a spy, wouldn't he lie low and avoid contact? When the bath is full enough, she gets in, enjoying the relaxing warmth and the rose-scented bubble bath. She closes her eyes and runs through the day's events: has she missed anything important? Her eyes suddenly open wide and she sits up sharply, splashing water on to the hexagonal mosaic tiles.

'That's it!'

She dries herself quickly with a white bath towel so huge it's like a sail, and throws on her PJs: black with a tiny repeating pattern of white skulls. She opens the bathroom door, her face flushed from the heat.

'Vitaly, I think I've got it.'

But Yushkov isn't there.

Why would he leave? Her alarm dissipates when she notices that the silk purple paisley throw is missing from the bed, as are two of the four pillows. On the other side of the bed, Yushkov is asleep on the floor, curled up under the throw. She kneels down and gently touches his shoulder. A hand shoots out and grabs hers so tightly she squeals.

'Let go! It's me.'

Yushkov keeps his eyes shut but releases her hand. 'You can't have me. I'm too tired,' he mumbles, his mouth twitching into a grin.

'That's never going to happen,' she says. 'Listen, I think I know how we can trap the killer.'

Yushkov rolls on to his back and opens his eyes, blinking away his tiredness. 'What is this idea that can't wait until morning?'

'I interview you, the man questioned by SO15 about the stolen bacteria, the man accused of being a Russian asset.'

'How does this help us?'

'Because in it you'll claim you know who really stole the canister and who murdered Kevin Knox. We'll flush out the real traitor.'

Yushkov sits up. 'But I do not know this. I tell Casburn I do not. I tell MI5 I do not. Now you want me to say I do? They will arrest me and, this time, they will not let me go.'

'Not if we keep you hidden.'

Yushkov runs a hand over his head. 'So you want me as bait?'

'We will both be bait.'

'You make an assumption that could get us killed. You presume the man who killed Kevin and stole the canister is also the sniper. Maybe not. If too many people come after us, we will end up dead.'

'Think about it this way: this is your chance to tell your story, how your rights as a British citizen have been violated, and you're in hiding from the very authorities who should be protecting you.'

'Are you crazy?'

'Probably.'

'If we do this, our enemies will try to hurt you. I do not know if I can protect you.'

'Vitaly, I'll be fine. I'm a born survivor.'

It's seven in the morning. Lowe always starts his day with bacon – nice and crispy; two eggs – nice and runny; baked beans – cooked to mush, and two slices of white toast laced with oodles of margarine, washed down with a sweet cup of tea. The Greasy Spoon is a block away from the offices of UK Today, where he works. Lowe sits in a booth at the back on a red, sticky, plastic bench as he shovels his breakfast into his mouth with the gusto of a starving mutt, then uses his toast to mop up the oil. No pauses, no interruptions, until his plate is empty. Satisfied, he leans back, pulls his paper napkin out of his shirt collar and screws it up into a little ball, before tossing it on to the empty plate.

'Bloody lovely, Barry! As always,' Lowe shouts to the lard of a man who can be glimpsed in the kitchen through the serving hatch.

The cook salutes him, then wipes his runny nose with the back of his hand before he flips the bacon.

Wolfe watches Lowe unobserved through the grimy, steamed-up windows. She knows there is a rear exit through the kitchen that leads to an alley. It's where Barry goes for his smoke breaks behind two overflowing, industrial bins. Yushkov has used one of these giant bins to jam the back door shut, and now waits at a safe distance, standing at a bus stop. They've agreed Yushkov cannot be seen by Lowe, who may recognise him. Wolfe opens the café's front door, enters and heads along the line of booths. Lowe notices her instantly. He slides out of his seat and dives through the double swing doors into the kitchen, almost slipping on the greasy floor tiles. Wolfe is right behind him. Lowe twists the door handle to the alley but the door doesn't budge.

'Hello, Nails,' Wolfe says. 'Thought we might have a little chat.'

Barry watches the two of them as he flips a burger. 'You all right there, mate?'

'Yeah, he's just fine, aren't you?'

Lowe's worried face breaks out into a toothy grin. He has egg stuck in his teeth. 'Sure. Always happy to talk to me fellow journalists.'

'Let's sit, shall we? Two more teas, Melissa,' she calls to Barry's long-suffering wife and the café's only waitress, who is as thin as Barry is fat. They sit in the same booth Lowe has just bolted from, but she makes sure she is nearest the door so she can stop him if he makes another dash.

'You're looking tired, Nails,' Wolfe says. 'The weight of all those lies wearing you down?'

She hasn't seen him in a while and, even though he's late thirties, he looks twenty years older. His thick mop of dark hair is receding fast and has turned pepper and salt. His yellowing teeth are too large for his mouth and seem out of place on his gaunt face. Lowe's hand slowly creeps down to his trench-coat pocket.

'No, you don't,' Wolfe says. 'You're not recording this.'

Lowe brings both hands up to the table. In his coat's deep pockets he keeps an old-fashioned voice recorder, spiral-bound notebook and pen, and his tablet. His wallet, crammed with bribery money, is in his inside pocket, kept close to his heart.

'You're not looking too hot yourself,' says Lowe. 'Heard you pissed off somebody who used you as a punch bag. Nasty! Can happen when you stick your nose in where it's not wanted.'

'Well, you'd know all about that.'

Melissa shuffles over in UGG boots and slams two mugs of tea on to the table and shuffles back to the counter, without even looking at them.

Wolfe leans forward. 'Let's cut the friendly chat, shall we, and get to the point. Who gave you my story?'

Lowe folds his arms. 'Funny that. There's me thinking it was in yesterday's paper and has my name all over it. Still, I must be seeing things.'

'Cut the crap, Nails! Somebody gave you my copy. I bet you didn't even bother to verify it.'

'Bollocks, I have me own sources.'

'Like who?'

'Like I'm going to tell you! Get real.'

'You didn't even bother to change the copy. You're getting lazy in your old age.'

'Look, Liv. It's my story, aw right. I wrote it, it was printed. The end. Now stop your whining and let me get to work.'

Lowe starts to shuffle along the sticky seat.

'I haven't finished.'

'Tough!'

Lowe stands. She gets up and blocks his path.

'The cops are all over my laptop and phone. Once they find it's you, I'm going to make damn sure you go down. You're not getting away with it this time.'

Lowe screws up his face as if he smells something rotten. 'What you talkin' about? I ain't done no hacking.'

'Then how did you get my copy? Cyber Crime will prove you did it, so you might as well spit it out.'

Lowe chews the inside of his cheek as he weighs up his options. The sucking noises make her feel sick. He sits.

'Look, Liv. It was emailed to me, aw right. That's all I know.'

'Who sent it?'

'Anonymous. Email address that'll probably lead to some web server in the middle of bloody China somewhere.'

'So you paid a hacker to get into my files?'

'No way,' says Lowe, holding his hand across his heart. 'I don't have no clue who your hacker is. And, quite honestly, Liv, I have better ways to spend me money than getting someone to hack your stuff.'

'Like hacking a murdered child's mobile? Or the PM's phone?'

'Ouch! That's below the belt and has never been proved. All conjecture.'

Wolfe shakes her head. 'Not good enough, Nails. I need to know who hacked me. Show me the email.'

He tilts his head as if he is about to refuse, and then pulls out his Note Pro and opens his emails. 'There,' he says, pointing at an email from someone calling themselves MysteryMan334.

'"Come on Eric," it says, "you're missing the story of the century. Keep up, will you? Olivia Wolfe is about to publish this article, and I thought you might enjoy pipping her to the post. She has no idea you have it and she'll never know how you got it."'

'Forward it to me.' Wolfe writes down a new email address on a napkin and hands it to him.

'And what do I get in return?'

'Oh, let me see. You avoid a police investigation and lots of unwanted publicity for your paper.'

'You drive a hard bargain,' he says, tapping his long fingernails on the Formica table top. 'That's what I like about you, Liv. My life would be so dull without your condescending moral superiority.'

She watches him forward the email.

'So I done you a favour. Now you do me one. I bet you know where that Russian spy is holed up, hey?'

'I have no idea, Nails. And if I did, you'd be the last person I'd tell.'

She gets up.

'Come on, Olivia. The fucker's trading in germ warfare.'

'You should write a novel, Nails. You've got a vivid imagination.'

'I'll be watching you,' he says, tapping his nose. 'That Russian bastard killed one of our own. The British public want justice.'

'Funny that. There was me thinking in this country you're innocent until proven guilty.'

38

Wolfe peers through the glass case at Gebelein Man, a 5,500-year-old mummy on display at the British Museum. Ginger, as he is known because of his red hair, is not wrapped in cloth and lying regally on his back, as are many of the other mummies at the museum. He is curled up into a tight foetal position, his skin shrunken and leathery, surrounded by earthenware pots once filled with food for his journey to the afterlife.

'Turns out the poor guy was killed,' says Butcher, his croaky voice only just audible above the loud chatter of museum visitors. 'Stabbed in the back.'

Some Chinese tourists play with the touch screen, exploring the inside of Ginger's body in 3D, to discover more about how he died.

'One of my forensics team worked on Ginger. The scans confirmed it was murder.'

Butcher is wearing a blue striped scarf and navy blue blazer, and carries a satchel-style briefcase. He looks more like the detective he used to be.

'That must be your oldest cold case,' Wolfe says, smiling.

He smiles. 'Let's walk.'

They move away from Ginger and meander at a leisurely pace through the Egyptian mummies. Wolfe tells him about Yushkov asking for her help and the sniper attack. She doesn't tell him Yushkov is with her in London.

'I've had a little chat with Eric Lowe. I now know MysteryMan334 hacked my phone and sent him my article. Why, I have no idea. I'm getting the feeling my stalker is MysteryMan, and the sniper who tried to kill us in Cambridge is SVR. Different people with different motives. I've tried the Russian ambassador but his PR people are stonewalling me.'

The many lines of Butcher's face deepen as he frowns. 'This might explain why the Russians aren't talking to you.'

Butcher hands her a rolled-up copy of *UK Today*. Two head-and-shoulders shots sit side by side on the page: Yushkov and Wolfe. Fortunately, because she hates her photo being taken – one reason why she never ventured into TV reporting – it's a stock shot from years ago when she had long hair and was into red lipstick. She looks nothing like that photo now.

'"British journalist protects traitor",' Butcher reads aloud. 'Lowe claims you know where Yushkov is and you're protecting him. Apparently SO15's confirmed Yushkov has gone missing.'

He scrutinises her face. She doesn't look up.

'Liv, I'm not going to ask you directly if you know where he is, but, if you do, I urge you to tell Casburn. If you're harbouring him, you're guilty of assisting an offender.'

'I never betray my sources.'

'What if you're wrong about him? What if he is a Russian asset? Have you considered that?'

'Don't believe that crap,' she replies, handing back the newspaper. 'Vitaly has saved my life twice. Why would he do that if he's working for the Russians? Why would he ask me to help prove his innocence?'

'Because he's clever? Because through your articles he can persuade the public he's innocent. You buy him time.'

'I'm doing an exclusive interview with him and, before you say anything, it was my idea, not his.'

Butcher smacks the paper against his leg in frustration. 'Do you have any idea what a difficult position you're placing me in?'

It's rare for Butcher to raise his voice. There's a fierceness to him she hasn't seen since he arrested her brother.

'I'm sorry, Jerry. You've always been so good to me, and you know I love you, but I have to do this.'

'You're in way over your head.'

'Don't worry, I'll leave you out of it.'

Wolfe gives him a peck on the cheek. Butcher watches her walk away through the Great Court, still flicking the rolled-up paper against his leg. He catches up with her on the museum steps on Great Russell Street.

'Hold your horses, will you?' Butcher calls out.

Wolfe slows. Butcher leads her behind one of the Portland stone, Ionic pillars, away from a security camera. 'Why did you want to see me?'

'I was wrong to involve you.'

'I'm here now. You might as well tell me.'

Wolfe hesitates. 'You sure?'

'To be honest, Liv, no. But if there's anything I can do to stop you landing in gaol or ending up dead, I will.'

A chilling wind gusts through the Greek Revival portico, blowing his scarf in his face. She still doesn't know why he saved her when she was fourteen, and now he's trying to do it again. His faith in her is unwavering.

'I don't deserve you.'

'Don't be daft.' He gives her a fatherly hug. 'So tell me what you need.'

'Background checks on everyone at Lake Ellsworth. I'm looking for aptitude and motive.'

'Including Yushkov?'

'Of course.'

'You seriously think one of them is a traitor?'

'I need to know their secrets, Jerry. Affairs, debts, addictions, marriage problems, criminal records, political leanings; any reason they'd feel aggrieved.'

'Jesus, Liv!' Butcher shakes his head.

'I shouldn't have asked.'

'Don't you think Casburn has done that already?'

'I think Casburn's already made up his mind.'

'Christ!' Butcher turns away from her and appears to be watching the traffic. 'I can get it. Some of it, anyway. The problem I have is Yushkov reading it.' He rounds on her. 'For God's sake, Liv. He's using you!'

'I could help save an innocent man.'

'You'd better be right, Liv, because, if you're not, we're both in a pile of shit.'

'Thank you.' But she knows words are not enough. She'll find a way to repay him some day, she has to.

Wolfe hands him a scrap of paper. 'My work email is compromised. Use this.'

'This may take time. I'm not as in as I used to be.' He squeezes her hand. 'Be careful, Liv. Don't go near your flat. It's being watched. And, please, stay away from Yushkov.' He opens his wallet and hands her all his cash. 'Take this. If you use your bank card, not only will Casburn find you, but, if you're right about the SVR, they will too.'

'No, Jerry, you've done enough.'

He shoves the money into her hand. 'Take it.'

Wolfe hesitates, then puts it in the inside pocket of her leather jacket.

'Don't get yourself killed, you hear?'

39

Wolfe leaves the museum through Sydney Smirke's twenty tonnes of cast iron gate, the gilt ornamentation glistening in the damp air. With her chin tucked into her scarf and her hands deep in her jacket pockets, she dodges people and pigeons. Wolfe turns to look up at the pediment over the main entrance depicting The Progress of Civilisation with allegorical figures. She wonders whether Sir Richard Westmacott, who created the sculptures in 1852, would think mankind's great achievements – such as vaccines and putting man on the moon – outweigh the development of more and more horrifying ways to destroy, from the atomic bomb to biological weapons.

On the way to the hotel she calls Cohen.

'Congratulations! You're about as popular as Attila the Hun. Your Yushkov exclusive has sent traffic and sales through the roof. I could kiss you!' Cohen almost sounds happy. This is a first.

She laughs, but it fades fast.

'Moz, your line could be tapped so I'll make this quick. My mobile and email are compromised.'

'Okay, but I need a second piece. Different angle. Yushkov's past?'

'As soon as I have something worth printing, I'll get it to you. I promise.'

'Don't let him out of your sight. You're the only journalist he's talking to. Keep it that way.'

'Heard from Casburn?'

'*Heard* from him! We've been raided. Fuckwits!'

'Anything else I should know?'

'Harvey rang. Said it was urgent. Says he has information on Knox's killer. But watch him, Olivia. Bet he's looking to piggyback your success.'

'Okay. I've got to go.'

Wolfe hesitates before dialling the BBC. But Harvey is at the bottom of her suspect list so she dials anyway.

Harvey is breathy. He sounds panicked. 'We need to meet. Something's happened.'

'I can't meet you, Charles. Just tell me.'

'I can't talk, I'm at work.'

'Then find somewhere private and call me back.' She gives him her number.

A few minutes down Great Russell Street, her mobile rings.

'Where are you? I have to see you.'

'Charles, I have to keep a low profile right now so just tell me what's so urgent.'

She hears snuffling sounds and for a moment she thinks Harvey could be crying. 'I . . . I think I know who murdered Kevin.'

'Who?'

'I . . . please, I need to see you. It's complicated.'

She sighs. 'Are you alone?'

'Most definitely.'

She tries to think of a public place to meet. Somewhere familiar.

'Meet me on York Bridge in Regent's Park. Enter through York Gate. I'll be on the bridge, but come alone.'

'Give me an hour.'

'Okay, but don't call this number again.'

She ends the conversation, making a mental note to buy another phone. Turning up Gower Street, Wolfe heads towards Euston Road and calls Yushkov.

'Now is not a good time,' says Yushkov, curtly.

'Why?'

'I'm with a friend.'

With a sinking feeling Wolfe realises what Yushkov is doing – buying a gun.

'I'm meeting Harvey in Regent's Park. He says he knows who killed Knox.'

'When I am done here, I will come with you,'Yushkov says.
'No need. It's only Charles. I'll see you back at the hotel.'

The SO15 detective, sitting in a crowded 'natural' fast food café, is bored. Peter Jones sips an organic coffee, resenting the fact it was twice the price of a normal coffee, on a circular wooden stool he swears is deliberately uncomfortable so customers move on quickly. Pretending to read his smartphone, he watches nineteen-year-old law student, Samad Sayyaf, pick at some chopped fruit in a plastic container, seated on a high stool, facing a wall, alone. On the bench top is a brown paper bag with the distinctive logo of the café, containing a sandwich Sayyaf bought earlier, prepared for him by a man of Middle Eastern appearance the detective doesn't recognise.

A Caucasian man of big build in a leather jacket sits in the vacant seat next to Sayyaf. He hasn't bought any food or drink and, without looking at Sayyaf, says something brief. Jones almost drops his phone when he recognises the newcomer. He snaps some photos but both men have their backs to him. Vitaly Yushkov takes Sayyaf's paper bag, leaves what looks like a car magazine behind and, without another word, slides off the stool and heads for the exit. At the precise moment that Yushkov turns around, Jones takes more photos. He immediately phones his boss, DCI Casburn, and updates him.

'You sure it's Yushkov?' Casburn asks.

'Yes, sir. Who do I follow?'

A moment's pause. 'Yushkov. I'm getting back-up.'

Jones ignores the still-seated Sayyaf, a known associate of suspected terrorist Kabir Khan, and races from the café into the busy street, hoping he's not too late. But Oxford Street is chock-a-block with the lunchtime crowd and Yushkov is nowhere to be seen.

40

Wolfe leans over the wrought iron railings of York Bridge in Regent's Park and peers down at mallards drifting between the fingertips of a willow dangling over a muddy lake. In one direction is Regent's University. In the other, York Bridge Road connects with the Outer Circle, which runs around most of the 395 acres of one of London's most central open green spaces. At either end of the narrow bridge, ornate Victorian streetlamps with birdcage-shaped glass cages are dusted with snow, as are the glistening black-painted railings running the bridge's length. Sleet falls from a leaden sky and even though it's only midday, it feels as if night is approaching. Wolfe cups her takeaway tea with both hands, enjoying the warmth on her numb fingers. The fierce wind chases the steam away from her drink and blows wet snow in her face. Beneath her, two white swans huddle under the bridge, reluctant to swim into the open. The lake hasn't frozen over yet, but it will tonight. Is it the sleet they're avoiding or the slick of bottles, plastic bags, chocolate-bar wrappers and cigarette packets so kindly dumped there by visitors?

Wolfe checks her watch: Harvey is late. In the distance, a dog barks and she sees it chasing a grey heron at the lake's edge. Apart from some students and a cyclist, very few people are brave or mad enough to endure the park in these conditions and she feels, suddenly, very alone. Wolfe checks her watch again. Harvey is ten minutes late. Perhaps it was missing breakfast, but her stomach squirms. Something is wrong. She chose this location because it's in the open, and from the top of the bridge's hump she can see people approach, but she's forgotten how deserted the park can be in winter. She downs the last of her drink, screws up the cup and drops it in a bin just beyond the bridge. There's a crack of twigs nearby. She jumps, but it's only a grey squirrel searching for nuts. She should leave. Instead, she undoes the carabiner on her backpack and takes her water bottle in hand – ready for a fight – then walks back to the middle of the bridge. She'll give Harvey a few more minutes.

Whippet-thin Harvey waves as he approaches from Marylebone Road. He's wearing a trilby, a paisley scarf and mackintosh. He's panting when he reaches her.

'I'm so sorry. I got delayed. I . . . ' He catches his breath and peers at her through lenses smudged with melted sleet.

'Shall we walk? I'm freezing,' Wolfe says.

'No! I mean, no.' He realises he is shouting. 'I'm out of breath.'

Wolfe tries to read his eyes through the wet glasses but she can't see them clearly. It's like peering into a car windscreen in the rain.

'Let's make this quick then. Who do you think killed Kevin Knox?'

'I . . . well, you see . . . '

A drip reaches the bottom of his right lens and clears the glass. Wolfe sees Harvey look over her shoulder. His eyes widen. It's not surprise. It's fear. She spins round as two men in dark coats, hats and sunglasses walk towards them. Who wears sunglasses on a day like this?

'What did you do?' she yells, grabbing Harvey's coat lapels.

'I'm sorry.'

The men are walking faster, their eyes on Wolfe. She shoves Harvey away, disgusted.

'You stole the canister?'

'Not me. Someone got there first.'

Harvey lunges at her. Wolfe darts around him and bolts towards Marylebone Road, but another man blocks her escape, arms wide. Harvey tries to grab her leather jacket.

'Just do as they say.'

Wolfe shoves Harvey away and he staggers into the railings. She's trapped. Her nearest assailant reaches inside his coat. A gun. She clambers up on to the bridge's handrail and jumps, falling fifteen feet. Wolfe curls into a ball to protect her arms and legs. As she disappears beneath the murky surface, she exhales with shock. Icy water seeps under her clothing and into her boots. Eyes open, she tries to get her bearings. The churned-up mud, rotting leaves and plastic bags look like soggy ghosts swirling around her. Visibility virtually nil. Webbed feet paddle frantically.

It won't be long before her pursuers scramble down the banks and come in after her. Her boots connect with sludge and a broken umbrella as she struggles to stand. The water is less than four feet deep, but it's enough for them to drown her. The swans are honking with fury and shoot off across the water. Ducks scatter, squawking with alarm. She has silt in her eyes. The man on the Marylebone Road side of the bridge is first to head for the grassy bank. On the other side of the water, a wrought iron fence runs parallel to the lake's edge and the two other attackers are navigating its awkward spikes. Her best chance of escape is to bypass the single man, who has just leapt into the water. Her finger is still looped through the metal flask and she prepares to hit out with it.

'Oy! Get out of there! You lot! Out!' somebody shouts.

A Royal Parks ranger in a green motorised buggy is racing along a footpath in their direction.

Her pursuers stop, exchange looks, but they don't draw their guns. The leader shakes his head and they sprint away in opposite directions. One of them grabs hold of Harvey on the bridge. The ranger is out of his buggy and scrambling down the bank towards her.

'Call the police,' Wolfe calls to him. 'They attacked me.'

The ranger splashes through the water and takes her frozen

hand and leads her up the bank to his buggy. Soaked, muddy and shivering, she coughs up stagnant water. Her sodden pack weighs a ton.

'Are you all right, miss?'

She nods but her teeth chatter. The ranger steps away and phones for the police and an ambulance. Wolfe looks up at the bridge, expecting Harvey to have fled, but sees him slouched over the snow-covered bridge railing, like a rag doll flopped over a washing line. Blood slides down the handle of the knife deep in his eye socket and drips into the dirty water below.

Wolfe runs and doesn't look back.

41

Her feet numb, her boots sloshing with freezing water, Wolfe stumbles across Marylebone Road, aware she is making a spectacle of herself – the last thing she should do. But all she cares about is getting away. Her beanie lies at the bottom of the lake, her hair is sodden, her face smeared with mud. She probably stinks. A businessman in a pinstriped navy suit and French cuffs steps out of her way and purses his lips in disgust. Water seeps from her backpack leaving a wet snail-trail behind her in the settling snow.

Who were her attackers? The SVR?

She stops to get her bearings, gasping for breath. She looks back across the thrumming lanes of traffic. Is she being followed? She decides to avoid main roads and the myriad of embassies in the area, especially those along Portland Place, where security cameras grow like mushrooms from embassy walls. She ducks down a lane so narrow it doesn't even have a name and tucks her face into her wet scarf as she runs until she can't run any more. She's heading for the hotel without thinking. But she doesn't know where else to go. Her drowned-rat appearance is attracting too many looks. She has to get changed and then find somewhere else to stay. But do those men know where she is staying?

The lane ends. Wolfe takes a right, passing shops, avoiding eye contact. She looks behind so often, her wet collar chafes her neck. Darting through an archway of cream stone, she arrives in a cobbled mews lined with expensive terraced houses – a momentary haven of calm. Hidden from street view, she pulls out her mobile phone. It's sodden and useless. She wants to warn Yushkov. She must find a payphone or buy another mobile.

She keeps moving, if for no other reason than to try and warm herself. Her shivering has become more violent. She passes boutiques, cafés, delicatessens and expensive furniture shops. Further up the street are two currant-red phone boxes, their St Edward's Crowns reassuringly familiar. She can't believe her luck. Thank God they haven't all been scrapped. She opens the heavy door and fumbles in her wallet for some change. She pops a coin in the slot and dials. The phone swallows her coin but fails to connect. She slams the receiver down and heads for the second booth. This time it connects but Yushkov doesn't pick up. Why isn't he answering? Surely he's back at the hotel by now. She leaves a message: she's on the way to the hotel but watch out for SVR agents, who, she believes, killed Harvey.

The snowfall lies thicker on pavements, cars and windowsills. Her breath steams up the phone box's windowpanes. She made herself a promise she wouldn't ask Butcher for anything else, but she's desperate.

'Give me a chance,' Butcher says, wrongly anticipating the reason for her call. 'I can't work miracles.'

Wolfe tells him about Harvey's death and the men chasing her.

'Call the police. You're witness to a murder.'

'If I do that, they'll never let me go. I have to find out what the hell is going on.'

'Now listen to me. A man is dead. The park ranger doesn't know if you did it or someone else. You have to turn yourself in.'

'CCTV will prove I didn't do it.'

'If there's a camera pointing in the right direction, and if it's working.'

'But Vitaly? He's in danger.'

'Forget him. Think of yourself. Whoever these men are, they want you badly. And if they're SVR, they will find you.'

'Jerry, Harvey might've killed Knox. My God, why would he do such a thing?'

'It doesn't matter.'

'It doesn't matter?' she shouts. 'People are dying because of this bloody bacteria! I have to know why.'

Butcher softens his tone. 'Liv, tell me where you are and I'll come.' Her teeth chatter, her fingers are white, her ears burn with cold. 'Liv, whatever you do, don't go back to wherever you've been staying. That's the first place they'll look.'

'Jerry, the information I asked for is now more important than ever. Please hurry. I'll call you. Soon.'

'Where are—'

Wolfe replaces the receiver and leans her back against the misted glass. Her body aches. She tries recalling her attackers' faces, but she is having trouble thinking straight. None was as tall as Grankin, she's sure of that at least. Furious she didn't see the trap Harvey set for her, Wolfe kicks out at the booth.

'Think!'

She can't go to her Balham flat. She can't go to Jerry's place. The hotel is only around the corner and Yushkov could be in

235

danger. Perhaps there's a back entrance? Dialling the hotel, Wolfe asks the receptionist to take a message and insists it's written down and pushed under the door to their room. Yushkov is unlikely to check the hotel's telephone messaging system. She stresses the urgency.

Leaving the comparative warmth of the phone box, Wolfe looks up and down the road, then heads for the hotel. Soon, she is near enough the elegant Georgian hotel to observe the comings and goings through the front door. Diagonally opposite, on the other side of the road, is a designer lighting shop. Wolfe feigns interest in the contents but uses the glass as a mirror. The hotel's grand entrance has a huge stone portico with two sets of stone steps. Warm light spills from the windows into the street, and a dusting of snow gives the building a fairy-tale quality. Nobody else is crazy enough to dawdle outside, but is a reception committee waiting for her in the lobby? By now she is shaking uncontrollably. If she doesn't warm up soon, she'll get pneumonia.

A hotel of this size is bound to have a back entrance, for staff and deliveries. So she walks around the block and finds herself in a street running parallel to Great Portland. All she can see are row upon row of magnificent white Edwardian houses with white pillars and black balustrades. She almost gives up when she sees an archway, leading to yet another mews, similar to the one she hid in earlier. This lane is one-way and U-shaped, the back of the hotel at the end. It is mid-afternoon and the grey skies, laden with snow, have ushered in an early twilight. The street lighting has not yet switched on. Creeping into the mews, Wolfe peers into indistinct corners and down basement steps that disappear into gloom. Cars and a small van are parked on one side of the mews, providing her with cover. The hotel has a number of rear entrances, all down wrought iron steps and through basement doors. Polished brass signs direct staff and deliveries to the correct entrance. Steam and cooked food smells belch from a humming kitchen extractor fan.

Out of the corner of her eye, a figure moves, then another. She scrambles down steps to a private basement flat then, keeping low, pops her head up enough to see at ground level. Three men appear from the last of the hotel's basement exits, used for refuse management. One person walks ahead, hands in jacket pockets. The two men lagging behind are silhouetted against the hotel's harsh exterior lighting and, when the tall one turns, his profile shows a distinctive kink in his long nose. Sergey Grankin catches up with the first man and offers him a cigarette, which he takes and they light up. They talk in hushed Russian, too far away for her to hear more than the occasional word. The third man walks up and down, keeping watch.

Grankin and the other smoker walk along the cobbled street in her direction, heads close, deep in clandestine conversation. She ducks and holds her breath as they pass by her hiding place.

When she dares to look up, they have paused, a van's length away. But it's not until Grankin's companion peers at an illuminated phone screen that Wolfe's worst fears are confirmed.

The man on the receiving end of Grankin's friendly embrace is Vitaly Yushkov.

42

I've always had an addictive personality. As a teenager it was alcohol, pot and a teacher I obsessed over. As an adult, I moved on to stronger substances. Anything to get that high. To feel invincible. You picked up on my habit, didn't you, Olivia? Called me out on it. Begged me to stop. I lied, said I was clean, but you knew. The euphoria, the confidence, the bounce in my step.

What started with you as revenge has become my need. You are my drug of choice these days and I need a regular fix.

Not knowing what you were doing was driving me crazy. I screamed and railed against Jerry fucking Butcher and his Cyber Crime bitch. My only information came from news reports. When I heard about the shooting in Cambridge, I thought I'd lost you. The dickhead reporter said there had been a fatality. Later on, she changed her story. Moron. When I thought you gone, my world imploded. I couldn't breathe. The walls closed in. I felt alone. Terrifyingly alone.

Now some Russian thugs will take you from me if they see you. Always poking your nose into a hornet's nest, aren't you, Olivia? Although, I suppose I am partly to blame. I sent that email to Yushkov in Antarctica warning him about you. I'd forgotten I'd done it until I combed through my diary. I've provoked the Russian bear and I have to set things right.

I am tucked into a recessed doorway, five parked cars away from where you hunker down on the basement steps, behind the hotel. I've been following you since the British Museum. I just knew you'd contact Butcher. He's the one person you still trust. So all I had to do was watch him and wait and let him lead me to the British Museum, where you were staring at a repulsive mummy. What's so fascinating about preserved bones and flesh? Were you considering your own mortality? Only I decide when it is time for you to die. Not the Russians. Me.

The three men move perilously close to you. Do you recognise Yushkov? Do you see him for the liar he is? A spy? One of them. The lookout has a gun and a knife. He killed that journalist on York Bridge and would have killed you if the park ranger hadn't turned up when he did. I wish now I hadn't texted a photo of you with Harvey to that trashy tabloid claiming I saw you stab him. I've gone too far. What was I thinking?

I start to panic. I don't know what to do. I can't lose you. If you're spotted, they'll kill you. No ranger to save you this time. Do I call the police? No, no. They'll take too long. I start gulping like an idiot. My chest feels crushed. The ground seems to shift. Am I going to black out? Think of happy moments, my psych used to say. I think about the laughing kids I saw earlier, playing with snowballs. My lungs fill again, my head clears. The wooziness passes. I know exactly what I must do.

I raise my coat hood and step out from my hiding place and walk nonchalantly towards the hotel kitchen entrance, just some kitchen hand or cleaner about to clock on. I walk right past you, but all you will see is a hoodie. Being this close to you thrills me. Your stalker is now your saviour. Who'd have thought? I feel strong. Empowered. Taller. I hold my head high. No more confusion. For the first time since I left hospital, I don't have a mind-fuck.

I catch a glimmer of you retreating further down the steps, sinking into the shadows. All three men tense. The two in conversation are immediately silent. The tallest one – I'm betting he's Sergey Grankin – takes his arm off Yushkov's shoulders and places his hand inside his open coat. Yushkov freezes. Behind them, leaning against the railings, the lookout moves in my direction, as if to stop me entering the hotel. I walk straight up to the tall one and ask for a cigarette.

'Sure,' he replies, and offers me one from his pack.

The lookout has come up behind me.

'Thanks, mate,' I say, and shuffle off towards the goods delivery entrance trying not to choke. It's been a long time since I had a fag.

All three watch me go, their backs to you, their focus on the immediate threat. The lookout follows me, ensuring I don't loiter. So I enter the hotel kitchens. The prep chefs are busy. One looks up, but none challenges me. I disappear down a corridor before anyone has the chance to accost me.

But have I done enough to save my little robin?

43

Wolfe waits in darkness, her back pressed against a basement door. Nobody's home. She shivers uncontrollably – never has she been this cold. The creak of boots on snow recedes, as does the soft drone of voices. They have gone, but she doesn't move. Salty tears threaten; she clenches her fists, refusing to succumb. She struggles to fathom why she feels so betrayed. It's not because Yushkov has revealed himself a traitor. It's not because she's been made a fool of and feels used. It's because she believed in him. She believed he tried to protect the innocent in Chechnya and Afghanistan and that he deserved someone to champion him. How could she have let her guard slip like that? She has foolishly tarnished her professional reputation and placed herself in mortal danger. Cohen was right: never get involved.

Her back slides down the door and she hugs her knees to her chest. What to do? Wolfe can't go into the hotel. She probably wouldn't leave it alive. Pride prevents her from calling Butcher – he was right about Yushkov. Does she contact Casburn? Informing feels dirty and she'll be interrogated for hours. Days. No, Yushkov has played her. She's going to return the favour.

Her muscles complain as she stands and moves stiffly up the steps to street level. The lane is empty, save for footprints left by Yushkov and his comrades in the snow. Leaving the mews, she heads back to the phone box, but she's low on change, so she ducks into a coffee shop and buys a hot chocolate, getting change from a fiver. The woman behind the counter hands her a raspberry muffin.

'On the house,' she says, looking Wolfe up and down with pity in her eyes. She thinks she's homeless.

Wolfe smiles and takes the muffin, but the kindness reminds her how far she has fallen from grace. Accused of being a traitor and harbouring a criminal; her face plastered all over the media; hunted by Casburn, the police and security services; unable to go to her flat or even hear Cohen growl, I told you so.

It's barely above freezing inside the phone box as she gulps down the hot chocolate and shovels large chunks of muffin into her mouth. The hot liquid burns her tongue and thaws her stomach. Wolfe dials Daisy O'Leary's personal mobile number, which her friend guards like a jealous lover. If Casburn's had her phone tapped, it's more likely to be her business line.

'Dais, it's Olivia. I need your help.' Her teeth chatter as she tries and fails to speak clearly.

'Liv? Is that you?'

'Yes, sorry, I'm cold.'

'Oh my God, I've been so worried! What in God's name is going on? The cops've been all over your flat – that Casburn creep too. And *UK Today*'s calling you a traitor. The bloody hide!'

'Dais, this has to be quick. I'm in a phone box. Can't use my mobile. Have the cops searched your flat?'

'Not yet.'

'Have you left home since they went through mine?'

'No, why?'

It's unlikely, then, O'Leary's flat is bugged.

'Will you do something for me?'

'Of course.'

'Can you leave my bike outside the garages at the junction of Dr Johnson Avenue and Elmbourne Road? The spare key and helmet are in the hall cupboard. You okay so far?'

'Shit, Liv, are you running from the cops?'

'The less you know the better. Can you then tape the bike keys under the park bench at the junction of Dr Johnson and Hillbury Road and put my helmet inside a bag and leave it under the bench too? Can you do that for me?'

'Sure. When do you need it?'

'Now?'

'Right, okay.'

'If you think you're being followed, ride around for a bit, then go home. If I don't find the bike, I'll know you're being watched.'

'Jesus!'

'You still with me?'

'Yes.'

'I need somewhere to lie low. Do you know anywhere?'

'Um, well, one of my clients is on holiday until the New Year. I know his house is empty.'

'He gave you a key?'

'No, but he's a regular. Sometimes he phones me from work and tells me to go round there and chain myself to his bed and wait. So he gives me the security code. He changes the code weekly, but he only ever uses three. I can get you in there, for sure.'

'Where is it, Daisy?'

'In Chiswick.'

'Any cameras?'

'Don't think so. Just an alarm system.'

'No family staying?'

'Never! His wife doesn't even know about it.'

'I'll write down the codes. Wait a tick.' Wolfe pulls a notebook and a pen from her bag. The pen still works but the notebook is soaked and useless. She uses an escort's business card stuck to the phone box window. 'Fire away.'

'Why don't I meet you there? Sounds like you need a friend.'

'No, Daisy, this is risky enough. I've already seen one person murdered today. Just the access codes, please.'

O'Leary hesitates but gives them to Wolfe. 'You gotta make sure when you leave he's got no idea you've been there. Everything washed, clean and tidy. You hear?'

'Thanks, mate. I owe you.'

'You owe me nothing. That's what mates are for.'

'Promise me you'll stay away. You won't try to see me.'

O'Leary sighs. 'I promise.'

Wolfe walks down Balham High Street. Home turf, but she can't go home. It's rush hour and the Tube was so packed nobody paid any attention to a slightly bedraggled fellow passenger. The overheated carriage helped her warm up, but as soon as she is outside her damp clothes bring on a fit of shivering.

Turning left into Ritherdon Road and right into Manville, she sees the nine garages at the corner of Dr Johnson Avenue and Elmbourne Road belonging to the residents of an adjacent block of flats. Wolfe stops at the crossroads and looks around. There are people about, wrapped up in thick coats and scarves, heads down, heading home. None shows any interest in her. She pays special attention to parked cars. At either end of the row of garages are plane trees, and under one is her Harley-Davidson Sportster 883. She breathes a sigh of relief. Now to find the keys. Heading down Dr Johnson Avenue, Wolfe enters the park and makes a beeline for the bench.

'You're a godsend, Daisy,' she mutters.

There is no lighting over the bench and a leafless horse-chestnut tree overhangs it, keeping her in shadow. Under the wooden slats Wolfe finds a small bulge stuck to the wood with masking tape. She rips off the tape, kisses the keys, and shoves them in the front pocket of her leather jacket. Next, she kneels and opens the plastic bag, checking its contents: her leather gloves and a black helmet with a white skull painted on it.

Wolfe is grabbed from behind and yanked up. A gloved hand covers her mouth; an arm grips her round her chest so tightly she can barely breathe. Wolfe writhes and struggles, elbowing her assailant in the ribs. He barely responds, so she uses the bench as leverage, pushing her feet hard against it. Her assailant staggers backwards but doesn't loosen his grip.

'Olivia,' he whispers in her ear, 'Vitaly.'

She swings her bike helmet up and over her head and smashes it into his forehead and nose. He roars with pain and releases her. His hands fly up to his face. Wolfe bolts down the road towards the garages, her fingers in her jacket pocket as she struggles to pull out her bike's key. She is fast but her backpack and the helmet are cumbersome and heavy. She slips on an icy patch, but manages to right herself. Behind her, Yushkov's heavy footsteps approach fast. She sees her Harley-Davidson. On gravel now, she only has a few more feet to go. A puddle's icy surface shatters, just as Yushkov throws himself at her, grabbing her waist and pulling her down in a rugby tackle. She hits the ground hard, winded, pinned down by Yushkov's dead weight.

She is done for.

44

Before Wolfe can muster enough breath to scream, a bloody hand covers her mouth and grips her chin. For one terrifying moment she thinks he is going to snap her neck.

'Quiet!' Yushkov hisses in her ear.

Wolfe's crash helmet has rolled away and she can't reach it. She lashes out with her fists, but Yushkov pins down her wrists.

'They're here.'

Who is here?

In the distance, Wolfe hears the tap of high heels on the pavement. She tries to scream but Yushkov ensures she makes no sound. Somewhere nearby a car is remotely unlocked. Wolfe forces her jaws apart and bites into Yushkov's hand. He grunts but doesn't release his grip. A door slams and the car engine growls into life.

'Listen to me. SVR watch your flat. I'm here to help you.'

The driver revs the engine and takes off. Wolfe's only hope now is to feign submission and then try to catch him off guard to attack or flee. She lets her body go limp.

'Do you understand?' he says.

She tries to nod.

'Don't scream. If you do, we both die.'

His fingers slowly release their grip on her mouth.

'Grankin is here,' Yushkov says. Blood trickles from his nose.

'What is this crap, Vitaly? I've seen you! With Grankin. Arm in arm, the best of buddies. You make me sick!'

Yushkov shakes her like a rag doll.

'Listen! Grankin find me at the hotel. I pretend to co-operate. I had no choice.'

'Liar! You're SVR! You always have been.' Wolfe screams. 'Help!'

Yushkov grabs her tight as if in a lover's embrace and shoves her face into his coat to stifle her cries.

'Olivia! Stop!' he says, his breath warm on her damp hair. 'We are going to die if you don't shut up. Why would I try to save you if I am working for them? Please, listen. When you did not show at the hotel, they go to your flat. They leave one agent with me – he is now in the hotel garbage bin where he belongs. That is why I am here. It is lucky I found you first.'

He pulls her up to a sitting position and rocks her in his arms, his face pressed close to hers. He could have killed her; he hasn't. He could have alerted Grankin; he hasn't. His hold on her relaxes enough so she can lift her head and look at him.

'Let me go, Vitaly.'

'I got your message. I tried to run but Grankin was waiting. He takes me out the back, shows me a video of my sister, Renata. Grankin promises he will get her to England. I have not seen her for sixteen years.'

'Go tell your sob story to someone who cares. I'm done. Now let me go.'

His arms tighten like a straitjacket.

'*Nyet*. You must listen. Grankin, he says I must steal the bacteria.'

'And me?'

'I must kill you. You know too much.'

'And?'

'And I will not kill you.'

A black Porsche Cayenne with dark tinted windows crawls along Elmbourne Road. It is moving too slowly. Yushkov lies flat on the ground, Wolfe held to his chest, the shadows their only protection. The car crawls up the road and away from them. Yushkov waits until it has turned a corner, lets go of her and sits up.

'You must decide, Olivia,' he says, wiping his nose with a sleeve. 'I walk away now, you never see me again.'

Wolfe clambers up on unsteady legs and brushes herself down. Dirt clings to her damp jeans. He remains on the gravel, looking up at her. 'You tremble. '

'I'm cold, Vitaly. Cold and wet. And I've had enough of your lies.' She picks up her helmet. 'I'm going to get on my bike and I don't want to see you again. Do you understand?'

Yushkov nods.

The Harley-Davidson starts first time and she pulls on the helmet and gloves. Yushkov watches in silence. Revving the engine, Wolfe accelerates away, racing down Elmbourne Road, past the park on her left, towards the junction with the A214. As she waits for a gap in the heavy traffic, the same Porsche she'd seen earlier turns into Elmbourne Road. The passenger stares at a smartphone, his face illuminated: Sergey Grankin. In less than a minute, they will drive past Yushkov.

That's his problem.

But Wolfe doesn't make the turn. Why didn't he kill her? Why not hand her over to Grankin?

If Yushkov is telling the truth, he's a dead man.

Wolfe does a three-sixty and guns the bike. She overtakes the four-wheel drive and skids to a halt outside the first garage. No Yushkov. Where is he? She hears the huge V8 accelerate. She spies Yushkov walking down Manville Road. She shoots over the crossroads and screeches to a halt alongside him.

'Get on,' she shouts. 'Grankin's coming!'

Her backpack is in the way so she rips it off her shoulders.

'Put this on,' she says.

He's ready in seconds and slides on to the seat behind her.

'Hang on tight,' she says, burning rubber.

45

The house in Berrymede Road, Chiswick, is not only architect designed, it is architect owned. The owner clearly likes his privacy because the three-level house is tucked away down a narrow path, hidden from the street by another – less avant-garde – house directly in front. The land was subdivided so the architect could build two houses and live in the one at the back. Wolfe pushes her bike down a path of square limestone pavers, the gaps between each stone slab filled by polished white marble pebbles. Yushkov is close behind. A motion-detecting exterior light switches on, illuminating a small courtyard and a façade entirely in glass. It's like looking into a doll's house with the front open. The house is open-plan and looks to have nothing to soften the sharp angles and hard surfaces – all beech, stainless steel and yet more polished limestone. There is a void from the ground floor right up to the mezzanine master bedroom on level three. There are no curtains or blinds, which might be a problem for two fugitives if the wall of glass didn't face the rear of the other house. Three metre-tall bamboo grows in a semi-circle around an earthenware pot – a water feature that's switched off. To be sure nobody is home, Wolfe rings the doorbell. No response, so she heaves her Harley-Davidson up on to its kickstand.

Wolfe taps in one of three possible entry codes. The second attempt unlocks the door and she switches off the security alarm in the cloakroom, just as O'Leary told her to do. Exhausted and chilled to the bone, she leans against the hand basin. Spying the switch for the underfloor heating, she clicks it on.

Yushkov is in the open-plan stainless steel kitchen, head under a swivel tap, washing the blood off his face. He reaches for a tea towel and wipes his face.

'Did I break anything?' she asks.

'Maybe my nose, but it will mend.' He smiles at her. 'You fight well.'

'Next time, I'll hit harder.'

He laughs.

The home seems scoured of any extraneous matter, with only the essentials for living in evidence. Square orange leather armchairs and a white leather sofa and glass coffee table face a steel and glass TV unit upon which three soccer trophies and some architectural books are displayed. There are no cushions or rugs or shoes lying around or letters that need reading or perishable foods in the fridge. The kitchen bench tops are a mottled white Caesarstone and as bare as an ice sheet.

'Soak that towel in cold water and bleach, will you? We have to leave everything exactly as we found it. The owner doesn't know we're here.'

Yushkov raises an eyebrow but sees the exhaustion in the tightness of her face and slouching shoulders.

'I cook a meal,' Yushkov says. 'It will warm you.'

She watches him open the freezer door and shakes her head. 'What in God's name am I doing here with you?'

Wolfe wearily climbs the open wooden stairs up to the next level: a mezzanine office space with draughting table and framed awards on the pristine white wall.

'I'm taking a shower,' she calls down.

The spare bedroom, with white-painted wrought iron bedhead and mirrored wardrobes, floor to ceiling, is where she guesses O'Leary handcuffs herself to the bed and waits to be beaten. It distresses her to think about it and she keeps moving, heading up to the top floor. Wolfe has lost count of the times she has tried to persuade her friend to change her line of work.

The master bedroom has an en-suite bathroom with sliding

doors opposite the king-size bed. A solitary plastic tree sits in a pot near the glass doors to the roof terrace.

In the bathroom, Wolfe turns on the shower and leans for a moment against the wall-hung heated towel rail, but she is so cold she can barely feel its heat. It's painful to remove her damp biker jacket, which she hangs on the back of the door to dry. It smells of damp dog. She drops the rest of her clothes on the floor and steps unsteadily into the stinging spray.

The hot water pounds her body but she still shivers. She feels like a frozen slab of meat. A wave of dizziness hits her; she pushes her hands against opposite ends of the glass enclosure to steady herself. The bathroom seems to shift, tilting slightly, as though she's had too much to drink. Head bowed, she tries to take a deep breath and doubles over in a coughing fit. The room stops spinning but, as she defrosts and sensation returns to her skin, it feels as though the water is gradually getting hotter and hotter, until it's almost too uncomfortable to bear. She finds some shampoo in a steel basket and pours some into her trembling hand. She tries to massage it into her scalp, but the dizziness returns, together with nausea. There's enough shampoo in her hair to remove most of the dirt, so she leans back and lets the stream of water wash the grime away. Suddenly the contents of her stomach forces its way into her mouth and she doubles over again, vomiting, one hand pressed against the glass, the only thing keeping her upright. She coughs and splutters, then spews again. Her stomach feels as if it's turning inside out and she moans, watching the mess disappear down the drain. The room spins. She has to get out of the shower. Blindly, she fumbles for the mixer tap, knocking bottles to the floor. Her vision blurs and her knees buckle.

Wolfe feels someone's arms under hers, pulling her up. She can't hear the splash or feel the water's heat. She is being lifted, her head flopping over his shoulder. It's like being a little girl again, when her dad would carry her to bed and tuck her in. She loved resting her cheek on his shoulder, her young arms around his neck, breathing in his aftershave. Wolfe is gently seated on the granite tile surround of the bath, her back to the wall, but she flops forwards. She's too weary to open her eyes. She has to sleep. A towel strokes her face, the touch very light, then dries her hair. He holds her close to him as he wraps a dry towel around her body and lifts her.

'Olivia, did you hit your head?' Yushkov asks.

She tries to open her eyes, but it's as if her body is shutting down. Her head lolls back over his arm. He carries her to the bed and somehow manages to pull back the duvet and lower her on to the sheet, covering her quickly with the bedding. She rolls to one side and curls into a tight ball, the shivers coming in violent surges, her eyes clenched shut.

'Cold,' she says. 'So cold.'

The light is switched off. She hugs the duvet tightly around her, desperate to stop the convulsions, frightened by the alternating waves of chills and overheating. She moans.

The duvet is moved and for a moment it seems as if it is floating above her. Yushkov cuddles up behind her, wrapping her in his arms, his legs mirroring the position of hers. Yushkov's warm skin is both unbearable and comforting. Her mind tells her she should be afraid. He could hurt her, rape her. But Wolfe feels safe for the first time in as long as she can remember and relaxes in his embrace. He holds her close, his body still, as hers shivers. She feels his breath on the back of her head, calm and even.

'Sleep,' he says. 'I will keep you warm.'

She drifts into unconsciousness.

251

46

Catherine Wolfe has hardly moved or eaten for three days. She's sobbing into another soggy tissue and hasn't changed her clothes since Dad called Mum a stupid bitch and boasted he'd found someone else. The curtains have remained drawn and windows shut, despite the June hot weather, and the room smells stale and sweet. Fruit flies hover over the rotten apples in the fruit bowl. The phone rings and Catherine doesn't answer it. Doesn't even seem to hear it. Olivia guesses it's her school, wondering where she is. Again. She tiptoes into the room, clutching a plate of Marmite on toast.

'Here, Mum, I made this for you.'

Wolfe stares at her tissue, picking holes in it, ignoring her daughter and the toast. Fourteen-year-old Olivia sits next to her mother, who no longer smells like talcum powder and peaches but of sweat and sour breath. She tries to hug her but is shoved away.

'Leave me alone,' her mother yells. 'It's all your fault!'

Catherine jumps up, tears threatening. She doesn't know what to do. She wants to get help but her mother guards the phone, waiting for her dad to ring and apologise and say he's coming home. But even Olivia knows, this time, Dad isn't going to call. The front door opens and for a second her heart lifts; maybe he has come back after all? Her mother jumps up, blotchy face now beaming with hope. Her brother, Davy, walks in. Eighteen years old and always the joker, always with a girlfriend or two in tow, he is five foot seven and seventy kilograms of muscle, has the same large round dark eyes as Olivia, his coal-black hair cut short. She rushes to him and throws herself into his arms.

'How you going, tiger?' he asks, grinning at her.

But he knows the answer. He lives with them. Olivia's grip tightens around his waist, desperate for reassurance.

He looks at his mother. 'I can't do this any more, Mum. All this misery. The bastard's gone! Get used to it and move on.'

'No,' Catherine says. 'He'll come back. I know he will.'

'Mum, you've got be strong for Olivia.'

Her mother snorts derisively and turns her back on them.

'For fuck's sake, Mum, look at you! You're disgusting. Liv should be at school.'

'No!' her mother screams.

Davy sighs in exasperation. 'Fuck this, I'm outa here!'

He pulls away from his sister's embrace and stomps upstairs to his bedroom. Olivia races after him.

'Where are you going?' she asks, as he pulls a dusty olive-green canvas holdall out from under his unmade bed.

'Joined the Army, Liv.' He stops what he's doing and looks into her sad eyes. 'I'm sorry, mate, but I can't stick this.'

Olivia grabs his back and squeezes tight. 'Don't leave me. Please. Not you too.'

She is bawling her eyes out when she wakes up and looks out through glass sliding doors on to a terrace she doesn't recognise and a view across London's rooftops she's never seen before. Where is she?

She sits bolt upright. The uncertain sun infuses the bedroom with an insipid, grey light. She looks down; she's naked. Beneath her is a scrunched towel. On the other side of the bed, the thick duvet is folded back and the bottom sheet is rucked. Someone has slept there. She rubs her forehead, trying to remember, and then catches sight of her image in the mirrored wall above a bathroom vanity. She blinks at her dark bob sticking out at odd angles, like a fledgling blackbird's feathers. On the floor, next to the shower cubicle, her muddy boots. Then she remembers: jumping into the lake, seeing Yushkov with Grankin, her battle with him as she tried to collect her Harley-Davidson and their arrival here. After that, her mind is fuzzy. Why is she naked and where is Yushkov? She was shivering and dizzy. Yes, that's it. The hot shower was supposed to warm her. She collapsed. She stares at the used pillow next to hers. He wouldn't, surely?

'Oh no!'

Wolfe leaps out of bed and dives for the bathroom, to find her freshly laundered clothes drying on the hot towel rail along with Yushkov's. But she doesn't recall putting them there. Covering her nakedness with an oversized man's white towelling robe, she listens for Yushkov and hears pots clanking. Leaving the bathroom, Wolfe peers over the glass balustrade and down into the void. Two floors below, Yushkov is making coffee. He's bare chested and bare footed, wearing nothing but boxers. As he locks the portafilter into the espresso machine's group head, his back muscles tighten. He put her to bed. She was shivering with cold and burning with heat. He got in with her, using his body to help her through the hypothermia.

Yushkov hums as the espresso machine splutters and the thick coffee drips into a small cup. He drinks the short black as if it were a vodka shot, head thrown back, not a care in the world. Wolfe studies him, still unable to decide if he's a well-trained spy or a victim.

There's a beeping sound, but not from the coffee maker. Yushkov picks up his phone from the island bench: the same cheap brand of pay-as-you-go phone they both bought in Cambridge. Hers is waterlogged. Only Wolfe has his number, so who is texting him?

Wolfe jogs down the stairs and finds Yushkov with his back to her, leaning against the island bench.

'Who's the text from?'

His shoulders tense and she notices for the first time the exit wound left from his commander's bullet, the skin raised, the scar shaped like an exploding star. He doesn't turn around or reply. Instead, he moves to where his coat hangs on a hook by the front door and drops the phone into a pocket.

He pauses, his back still to her.

'You will doubt me again if I tell you.'

Wolfe moves closer and smells eucalyptus and citrus shower gel on his skin. His hair is still damp and a trickle of water runs down the back of his broad neck.

'I will doubt you more if you don't.'

He exhales loudly, then takes the phone from the coat and faces her. The entry wound on his chest has left a pale, ridged scar.

'Here.' Yushkov hands her the mobile and she reads the message.

'Samples moved to Porton Down. You know what to do.'

Protected by the military, Porton Down's Defence Science and Technology Laboratory in Wiltshire is a Level Four facility, famed for its biological warfare research, including experiments with anthrax and smallpox.

'You know how to find this place?' Yushkov asks.

'What I know doesn't matter. Is this from Grankin?'

He nods.

'Are you going to Porton Down?'

He hesitates. 'Yes.'

'No,' she exhales. Placing the phone on the workbench, she tries to gather her thoughts. 'Last night, in the park, you said you wouldn't—'

'Kill you.'

She takes a step back. 'And the bacteria?'

He tilts his head to one side. 'You will never trust me. It is best I leave.'

Wolfe shakes her head. 'I don't know what to believe.'

Yushkov picks up his phone.

'Why?' Wolfe asks. 'Why did you . . . take care of me last night?'

He moves close and reaches out his hand, as if to stroke her cheek. She grabs his wrist and holds it there, barely a few centimetres from her face.

'Don't,' she says.

Yushkov doesn't resist her grip.

'I like your company,' he says.

There's a momentary shock, when her chest feels too small for her heart. But her emotional defences go up. He's messing with her head. She flushes, embarrassed she is so easily swayed.

'Stop your mind games. I'm useful, that's all.'

Instantly his stare is hard. He yanks his wrist free, reminding her she only held it because he let her. He takes the stairs two at a time and is in the bathroom by the time Wolfe catches up. He steps into his jeans and does them up.

'Tell Grankin you won't do it. Walk away.'

He pulls on a T-shirt in silence.

'Do you have any idea how well protected Porton Down is?' she asks.

'Yes.'

Wolfe blanches. 'How do you know?'

This doesn't make sense. Earlier he asked how to find the place. Yushkov glances at her in the mirror and gives her a knowing smile. She sees a man she hasn't known before and the blood drains from her face.

47

'I'll leave you to get your gear together,' Wolfe says, stepping away from Yushkov. His back to her, he watches her in the bathroom mirror as he buttons up his shirt.

When he can no longer see her, Wolfe dashes down the stairs, through the kitchen, scanning surfaces. Where is his gun? It won't be long before he is dressed and ready to leave. She can't let that happen. She rummages through his jacket, hung on a hook near the front door. She finds a Glock 19, Gen 4, semi-automatic pistol in an inner pocket. In the same pocket is a full magazine. Glancing up, she sees Yushkov is dressed, but preoccupied with his phone. She loads the magazine and hears it click, then releases the slide to chamber a round. One of the first things she learnt reporting in war zones was how to load and fire a gun. He is coming down the stairs. She needs a phone to call for help. Yushkov has the mobile. Where is the landline? Desperately scanning the open-plan space, she realises, with a sickening feeling, she is too late. Wolfe grips the pistol in both hands, her arms straight out in front of her. She aims at Yushkov's chest, the largest target.

When he sees her, he stands stock-still, one foot on the bottom stair, the other in the living room.

'I can't let you go to Porton Down. Give me your phone,' says Wolfe.

Yushkov's face is devoid of any emotional response. It frightens her. He is scrutinising her face, then her hands, as if he's assessing her capability to fire. He flicks a look at the exit, gauging the distance. Calculating and controlled.

'You won't use it,' Yushkov says.

He takes a step towards her. She looks down the pistol's sight at him, forcing her hands to hold the weapon steady.

L. A. LARKIN

'So after all we've been through,' she says, 'you think I'm some kind of pathetic female who won't shoot? You patronising sod! Now give me your phone!'

'I don't think you are pathetic. I think you are brave, Olivia. But . . . ' Yushkov takes another step. 'You are not a killer.'

One more step and she fires, aiming wide. The report is astonishingly loud, amplified by the room's hard, bare surfaces. The bullet passes his left elbow and slams into the wall with an explosive thud. She expects him to back away. But he doesn't. Rushing her, he seizes her hands and forces the gun down. Unable to stop him, Yushkov peels Wolfe's finger off the trigger.

'Drop it,' he shouts. 'Don't make me do this.'

Wolfe brings her knee up sharply to his groin, but he blocks the move. Yushkov slams her hand into the wall. She shrieks and drops the weapon to the floor. He lets her go and leans down to pick it up. She tries to knee him in the throat but he's too quick again. He yanks her leg to one side, toppling her, and she lands heavily on the hard stone.

'Stop this, Olivia!'

'No, you stop!' she yells, flat on her back.

The pistol is almost within reach. She rolls to one side and lunges for it. Yushkov gets there first and tosses it under the stairs. He straddles her, pinning her arms to the ground.

'What are you going to do?' she screams, 'Kill me?'

Yushkov freezes. He stares down at her, the muscles of his jaw bulging with the force exerted to keep his mouth clenched. His lips are pressed together so tightly, they almost disappear. Wolfe turns her head away, squeezing her eyes shut. She doesn't want to see the blow coming.

'I can't believe you accuse me of such a thing,' he says.

Wolfe opens her eyes. Yushkov lets go and gets up, grabs the pistol, puts on his coat and walks over to where his boots lie on the floor. He releases the magazine and pockets the pistol and bullets, his movements unhurried. Without the gun, she is no longer a threat. Wolfe scrambles up, her hand throbbing from the blow. All she has left is the power of reason. She sits on the coffee table as he kneels and laces up his boots.

'I was wrong to say that. I'm sorry.'

Yushkov doesn't look at her. 'War is brutal. It dehumanises. I obeyed orders and killed my enemy. This doesn't make me a murderer. I tell you I am an outcast, my life is always threatened because I try to stop the slaughter of innocent people. And yet you think so little of me.' He stands. 'Get out of my way.'

Wolfe feels a stab of shame. She stands too and places a hand against his chest.

'Whatever your reasons for going to Porton Down, please don't do it. Too many people have died already. Leave the gun and walk away.'

'I go to stop Grankin, not to help him.' He looks down at her hand. 'Get out of my way!' he says, louder.

'To stop him?' she repeats, stunned. Her hand falls to her side. His stare doesn't flicker. A bubble of truth bursts from her mouth. 'I believe you.'

'Is this a trick?'

'No trick.'

Wolfe stretches up on her toes and places both hands behind his neck, pulling him down to her. Her lips touch his and she tastes coffee, cigarettes and toothpaste. Yushkov pulls back, frowning.

'What is this?' he asks.

'You are either the best liar I have ever met or one of few truly honourable men in this world. Almost every man I've ever known has betrayed me, but I'm staking my life that you're not like them.'

He studies her face. She holds his gaze.

'It is only men who have betrayed you? You are lucky,' Yushkov says, with a hint of a smile.

She tries to kiss him again but he jerks his head away.

'You want me to fuck you?' he asks.

'No,' she says, 'I want you to make love to me.'

He shuts his eyes and takes in a deep breath, as if preparing for a difficult conversation. Wolfe thinks he doesn't want her. Then his mouth is on hers, his tongue parting her lips, tilting her head back, pressing her close to his body. His stubble scratches her face but his rough lips are surprisingly gentle. He kisses her cheeks and chin, her nose, her temples, then finds the tender nape of her neck. She wants more, but is suddenly released from his embrace.

Wolfe opens her eyes. Yushkov holds the tie of her robe, his eyes asking permission. She gently pushes his hands away, undoes the tie, takes his hands again and places them on her hips. Yushkov parts the robe, finding her breasts, his touch feather-light. He pulls her to him, inhaling her scent for a moment, then tugs the gown down her arms and on to the floor. Stepping back, he gazes at her, taking his time, his eyes savouring her body. She flushes, unused to such scrutiny, aware of the harsh daylight exposing every flaw. He runs the tips of his fingers over each nipple, sending pulses through her. His tongue plays with the silver ring through each dark areola, then he takes one swollen nipple after the other in his mouth and pinches it between his lips. She moans. Kneeling, he kisses her firm stomach, pausing at the pearl on her belly button ring.

'Why a pearl?' he asks.

'It fits nicely.'

'It does,' he says. 'You are very beautiful.' He looks up and grins. 'But I already know this. I have slept with you. Remember?'

Yushkov's kisses continue down to her mound, running his tongue along the smooth skin either side of her dark strip.

'Sit here,' he says, leading her to the sofa.

He removes his jacket, throwing it behind the sofa.

'Let me,' she says, pulling his T-shirt over his head and dropping it.

Wolfe's tongue traces the contours of his neck and his chest muscles, then the skin round his scar. He sighs.

'I like the feel of your tongue piercing,' he says, cupping the back of her head with one hand and pulling her hips into him, momentarily lifting her off the floor. His hard-on presses against her and she wants him badly, but she won't rush.

'Put me down,' she says softly.

Yushkov releases his hold. She kneels and runs her tongue along the exposed skin just above his belt. His abdomen muscles contract with every lick. Slowly she undoes the belt buckle and his zipper, aware he is watching her, then pulls his jeans and boxers to the floor so he can step out of them. She takes his swollen cock in her hand and gently massages it. Eyes closed, Yushkov clenches his fists, his breathing heavy. She sucks the very tip, then tenderly runs her tongue in circles around the shaft. He gasps, and lays his hands on her head, but doesn't force her closer. As she traces the underside with her tongue, he gently pushes her away.

'It is too much,' Yushkov says.

'Let's see how you cope with this.'

Wolfe takes as much of him in her mouth as she can, moving slowly. The urgency of her movements grows. His grip on her head strengthens.

'Stop, not like this,' he says.

She pulls away from him and he opens his eyes.

'Lie down,' Yushkov says.

'No, I want to see you enter me.'

She sits at the sofa's edge, a pile of cushions at her back.

Yushkov kneels and parts her legs, kissing her inner thighs. She melts into the cushions. He finds her clitoris with his tongue, his touch as light as a feather, her arousal intense. Head thrown back, Wolfe luxuriates in the ripples moving up her body, the heat building. She arches her back and, nearing orgasm, he stops.

'I was about to come, you bastard!' she says, giving him a playful slap on the arm.

'Not until I am inside you. I want to feel you come.'

Yushkov stands and lays her lengthways on the sofa, his powerful thighs forcing her legs wide. He parts her softly with his engorged cock, then plunges into her, his restraint lost. She cries out, clinging to him, digging her fingers into his back. He pushes deeper into her, then holds still, his breathing rapid.

'You feel so good,' Yushkov whispers in her ear.

His mouth devours hers, demanding her acquiescence. His teeth hit hers, but he doesn't stop and she doesn't want him to. He slides in and out of her, slow and deep, and she responds, her muscles clenching his cock. She returns his violent passion, probing his mouth with her tongue. She bites his lower lip, drawing blood, tasting its metallic tang.

'You bitch,' he whispers, gripping her wrists above her head and driving into her faster.

Wolfe cries out and Yushkov lifts his mouth away from hers. 'Do you want me to stop?'

'No, I want to feel.'

She runs her fingers up and down his spine, relishing their connection. She knows he feels it too: the outsider, the man who belongs nowhere. He needs this intimacy as much as she does. Their hips move in sync and his urgency grows.

'Not yet. I want to be on top,' Wolfe says.

He slows, but she feels his reluctance to leave her.

'Hold on to me,' he says, letting go of her wrists.

She wraps her arms around his neck. His hands beneath her, Yushkov lifts her up and stands with her legs wrapped around his hips, then sits on the sofa, with Wolfe straddling him, his mouth a whisper away from hers.

'You make me suffer,' he says, smiling.

She runs her fingers through his short hair and kisses his eyelids, his lips, slowing the pace. Neither of them can hold out much longer and she wants to remember this moment before their world flies apart as it surely must. Wolfe has never let her guard down like this, never given herself so completely. He must never know.

Seeing her far-away look, Yushkov lifts her chin, kissing it.

'Have I lost you?' he asks.

Wolfe wants to say, Never.

'Savouring the moment,' she says.

Cupping a swollen breast, she offers it to him, and he takes her engorged nipple in his mouth and sucks so hard, it's almost unbearable. She rides his cock slowly, clenching tight, pulling him into her, wanting to hang on to the memory long after he's gone. Wolfe leans away from him, arching her back, her hands on his knees, his cock angled slightly forwards.

'No further,' he says.

She stays where she is, the tip of his erection just where she needs it: on her G-spot. Yushkov's fingers softly massage her clit as she moves her pelvis back and forth in short, jerky motions. A wave of heat rushes up her body and she throws her head back, making deep, primordial cries, mouth wide, eyelids fluttering, a flush racing across her skin like wild fire. She squeezes down on his cock in rapid bursts, then her release is like a star exploding in her belly. Now, Yushkov rams into her, pumping faster and faster, jaw clenched, his eyes never leaving hers. He roars as he comes inside her, thrusting again and again until he is spent and so is she.

48

Wolfe is still holding Yushkov close. She focuses on the rhythm of his slowing breath, his powerful arms around her, his head buried in the nape of her neck. She is not thinking about the people chasing them. She is happy to imagine she is safe and they might become more than lovers, even though she knows they only have this moment. Their intimacy is shattered by Yushkov's phone. He lifts his head and kisses her once more on the lips, then pulls away.

'I must get that.'

Wolfe reluctantly rolls off him and goes upstairs to shower. When she returns in a bathrobe, he has his bare back to her and is leaning over the kitchen's island bench, his focus on the mobile's tiny screen, hands balled into fists. He suddenly slams them down on the bench surface. The fruit bowl jumps. So does she.

'Vitaly?'

Still naked, Yushkov walks to the vast wall of glass and looks out at the bamboo and paved courtyard as if she isn't there, running his hands over his scalp. Wolfe picks up his phone and sees a video clip. The final frame, frozen on the screen, makes her stomach churn. She hesitates, but she has to know and touches the play button.

The woman's mouth is open, twisted downwards and bloody, one eye red and swollen, almost shut. Her beaten face is contorted in terror. Tears have left stains on her grimy cheeks. The camera angle is tight and the lighting bright, reflecting off the damp and shiny brick walls. The sound of water dripping echoes, as if she is in a cavernous space. The woman in her thirties is chained to a bed with nothing more than a stained mattress for comfort, her jumper dirty, her jeans soiled.

'Please don't,' she pleads in Russian.

Someone slaps her so hard across her face that her head almost hits the wall, and Wolfe thinks he's killed her. But the poor woman whimpers.

'Your sister is a whore!' the man yells off-camera in Russian. Yushkov's sister, Renata.

A man in a balaclava waves a transparent plastic bag in front of the camera as if teasing a dog with a bone. He approaches the bed and tugs the bag down over Renata's head. She screams, kicking and writhing against her chains, but cannot escape. He holds the bag tight around her neck. Wolfe watches in horror as the woman's eyes bulge with panic and the bag steams up. As the oxygen disappears, the bag is sucked into her mouth. Just as her body goes limp and her eyelids flutter closed like dying moths, the bag is ripped away. Renata gasps, coughing and retching.

'Yushkov, you lie to us. You run and hide. Always a coward!' the masked man sneers, then points at the tortured woman. 'You have done this. But you can save her. Get us the Ellsworth bacteria and we release her.' He looks at his watch. 'Eight sixteen, GMT. In forty-eight hours exactly you stand under the clock at Waterloo Station. We will contact you. If you are not there or fail to deliver, Renata dies.'

Wolfe's empty stomach heaves at the brutality. She takes a couple of deep breaths, then moves close to Yushkov, peering up at his contorted face, the veins on his neck raised like cords.

'What do you want to do?' Wolfe asks.

'I . . . will . . . kill . . . them.'

'Are you sure she's your sister? You haven't seen her for years. This could be a trick.'

'She is my sister.'

Wolfe touches his arm. He yanks it away.

'It's a suicide mission,' she says. 'Don't throw your life away.'

Yushkov turns from her and picks up his clothes. She follows.

'Wait! We need a plan, to think this through.'

'I cannot let her die.'

'I get that. But we need to be smarter than them if we're going to save her life.'

He dresses in a hurry.

'Any idea where they're holding her? Here or Russia?' she asks.

'Russia. It is too much trouble to smuggle hostage into this country.'

'Okay, how can we help the Russian police find her?'

Yushkov shakes his head. 'You do not understand. These men are SVR, or maybe Federal Security. The police will not interfere. I have no choice. I must give them what they want.'

'No!' She doesn't mean to shout. 'The very fact it's been moved to Porton Down tells us it's a biological weapon. You cannot hand it to the Russians.'

'I have no choice.'

'You do. Just make them believe you have it.'

'How?'

'Give them another water-borne microbe. Nothing dangerous. We know plenty of scientists who can help. Scientists at Porton Down.'

He glances up at her as he pulls on a boot.

'Too risky.'

'It'll work. We hand Grankin a canister. He won't know if it's the real thing or not. He'll have to take it to a secure laboratory to find out. By then, Renata will be free.'

Yushkov grabs his coat. Wolfe cannot let him leave without her. He will do something reckless.

'Give me five minutes. I'm coming with you.'

'Earlier, you say to me I should walk away from this trouble.'

He touches her face and strokes it. 'I now say to you the same. This is not your battle.'

'I'm making it my battle.'

Wolfe turns, ashamed at her half-truth. She will do anything within reason to save the life of Yushkov's sister, but she will not let him hand the Lake Ellsworth bacteria to the Russians.

All she has to work out now is how to stop him.

49

Whore!

I saved you in that freezing alley, ungrateful bitch. I risked my life for you. And how do you repay me? Yushkov will betray you. Can't you see that? But you don't run from him. Oh no, you fuck him! Christ!

I clutch a downpipe, shaking with fury. The blood in my ears is screaming, my heartbeat pounding like a home invasion battering down the door to my self-control. I bash my fists on the rendered bricks, trying to control my urge to destroy – anything, everything; you. I press my back against the architect's front door, partially hidden by the tall bamboo, my breathing as ragged as a chainsaw.

You hide away in houses and hotels and think I cannot find you, yet here I am looking straight at your Harley-Davidson. It was like a beacon, beckoning me here. Its GPS was so easy to hack. I bet the braking system can be hacked too. Hacked to fail.

I'm not thinking straight. Rabid. Must slow down. Stick to the plan.

The best way to hurt you is to take away everything you hold dear. And I've succeeded. My diary tells me you no longer have a home you feel safe in. And your career is about to flame out, your reputation gutted. Granted, you did most of the work for me; I just had to give it a little nudge in the right direction, heighten your insecurity.

I feel calmer. I shouldn't be so hard on myself.

And that Russian scum? You won't have him long. I didn't save you from the SVR so you could then go and fuck one of them.

I creep down a narrow path to Chiswick High Street, then run, crashing into pedestrians. I'm blinded by images of you screwing a man who's probably raped his way through every war zone he's been to. My head feels as if it's imploding. If only the pigs had reached the hotel faster, then you wouldn't be with him now. I should have made that 999 call earlier.

You know what? Fuck control. You're all convinced I'm a nutter anyway. I might as well give into it. Fuck all my months of planning. Let it take me. Let revenge have me.

At a bus stop I sit, wild-eyed, panting, face slick with sweat, and pull out my iPad, barely able to touch the right keys, my hands shake so much. But I must write it down. My new plan. I've barely managed to write a line, the pain in my head is so agonising. I clench my eyes shut, holding the iPad close to my chest, and rock backwards and forwards, groaning.

'You all right?' asks a pretty teenage girl with long blonde hair.

Her boyfriend, no more than eighteen, calls her away, wary of me.

'Not feeling well,' I say, 'I'll be okay, thanks.'

He takes her arm and leads her away from the stranger in a hoodie, making weird noises. He thinks I'm strung out. I shouldn't draw attention to myself like this. I force myself to stop rocking.

Rummaging in my coat pockets, I find a brand-new burner phone and call emergency services. I ask for the police.

'I heard a gunshot,' I say, my voice full of alarm. I give them the address and tell them I'm a neighbour. 'There's a man waving a gun about.' I want an armed unit blasting Yushkov to kingdom come. 'A woman's in there, screaming. But the owner's away and the house is supposed to be empty. Hurry!' Then I add. 'He looks like the photo in *UK Today*. You know, the Russian spy.'

I drop the mobile, used only once for this call, into a bin.

It feels so good to let go.

50

It is the crunch of a misplaced step on gravel that stops Wolfe in her tracks. Her head snaps round and she catches the briefest glimpse of someone in a hoodie, a tendril of blonde hair whipping over their shoulder, before the figure disappears down the narrow path.

'Someone's here!' she says, rushing to the door and opening it.

Yushkov is instantly by her side. 'You sure?'

But the intruder has turned into the street.

'Yes. We've got to get out of here.'

Wolfe races upstairs and dresses. Her boots are still damp, but her leather jacket is almost dry. A used razor lies on the basin vanity with Yushkov's stubble on it. She grabs it and shoves it in a pocket to be thrown away later. She uses a towel to remove some of their fingerprints from taps and handles but she doesn't have time to do a proper job. No time to wash the bedding and towels. No time to repair the bullet hole, but she'll prise the bullet from the wall to stop the police identifying the gun and, perhaps, who sold it to them. She charges downstairs. The bloody tea towel is on fire in the sink as Yushkov uses a clean one to wipe down his fingerprints on the espresso machine.

'Our DNA is everywhere.'

'I have the pistol, and this,' Yushkov says, holding up what is left of the bullet, as well as the spent casing.

'You must've read my mind,' she says, grabbing her bike keys. Somewhere in the house a phone rings.

'Don't answer,' says Yushkov.

Wolfe follows the sound to a wall-mounted phone near the front door.

'Could be Daisy trying to warn us.'

'No!'

But Wolfe has already answered on loudspeaker.

'Olivia, is Yushkov with you?' asks Casburn.

Yushkov's face darkens as he recognises the detective's voice. He raises a finger to his lips.

'How did you . . .?' Wolfe begins. Police sirens wail in the distance.

'We know he's armed. Can you get away from him?'

She blanches. How does he know?

'You're hunting the wrong man.'

Yushkov makes cutting gestures. He wants her to end the call.

'Listen!' says Casburn. 'He was seen yesterday with an associate of Kabir Khan.'

'What?'

Yushkov snatches the phone and slams it into its cradle.

'He's stalling us,' says Yushkov. 'We leave, right now.'

The sirens are piercingly loud, the armed units almost upon them. But Wolfe doesn't move. The house walls feel as if they are closing in on her.

'Is this true?'

'I bought a gun from a man who once saved my life. Not this Kabir Khan.'

'Why does Casburn think you did?'

He takes her arm. 'It is a trick. We must go.'

She studies the face of a man she has just made love to. A man she thought she knew. A man she felt safe with. And now? She's blind-sided by an improbable yet terrifying connection she never imagined Yushkov had.

'Will you come, or will you stay?' he asks.

All Wolfe can think of is saving Renata and stopping a desperate Yushkov from giving the Russians what they want. She daren't imagine she may be nothing more than a pawn in Yushkov's dangerous game.

'I'm coming.'

Running from the house, Wolfe turns the ignition and the Harley roars to life as Yushkov puts the backpack over his shoulders and gets on the back.

The bike shoots off down the narrow passage and on to Chiswick High Street as a police car slams on its breaks. Wolfe easily dodges it and disappears down a narrow lane as another police vehicle screeches to a halt outside the architect's house. She zigzags her way through Chiswick's backstreets but she doesn't take the turn for the M4 motorway. Instead, she heads for a quiet residential road that runs parallel to the River Thames. She parks the Harley between two cars and kills the engine.

'What are you doing?' asks Yushkov.

'They're looking for two people on a motorbike. So we take a car.'

Within a few minutes she has broken into an old Fiesta and they head west on the M4 in the direction of the UK's most infamous military research site – Porton Down.

As Wolfe drives, she considers their target.

Nestled in the idyllic Wiltshire countryside near the village of Porton, on seven thousand acres, and run by the Ministry of Defence, Porton Down employs three thousand people. The entire area is surrounded by a no-go zone. Between the fencing and the actual buildings is a gamut of motion detectors, security cameras and dog patrols. Wolfe suspects Heatherton and his team will be at the Biomedical Sciences Department, or BSD, in a high containment lab. A few years back, a group of animal liberationists cut through the wire-mesh fence and managed to reach the BSD building. They were shot dead. Wolfe investigated the story but wasn't allowed to publish it.

She wants to save Renata but not if it means handing over LE31S. They must persuade one of the scientists to give them a vial of substitute bacteria. She prays there won't come a time when she must betray Yushkov to Casburn. She isn't sure if she can do it.

As they race past cars and lorries, she goes over Casburn's words in her head. Is he right about Yushkov and Khan? Who is lying? She hopes to God it's Casburn. Because, as her grandmother used to say, she's made her bed and, however uncomfortable that bed may be, she must lie in it.

Snow, like a dusting of icing sugar, softens the flat, barren fields that surround much of Porton Down. There is a section of the perimeter where high evergreen hedges run parallel to electric fencing, shielding the site from prying eyes. Signs, at regular intervals, warn of 'Danger of Death, Do Not Enter'. Wolfe and Yushkov have chosen a spot behind tangled hawthorn bushes that gives them a rare view across a field into Porton Down. They are hoping to spot Heatherton, Price, Sinclair or Matthews.

Through binoculars Wolfe sees a conglomeration of ugly buildings from different eras: red-brick fifties-style two-storey structures with grey tiled roofs; industrial warehouses; row upon row of rectangular buildings with corrugated iron roofs that remind Wolfe of battery hen sheds; Portakabins that have far exceeded their temporary usage; seventies-style low-rise concrete and glass office buildings, and aircraft hangars that look large enough to swallow the *Queen Mary*. Roads traverse the site linking the various groups of buildings. The 'face' of Porton Down is a three-storey brown brick building with hundreds of white framed sash windows, as long as two soccer fields. A sweeping semi-circular driveway leads to the main entrance, where government ministers and weapons manufacturers greet each other before discussing the sale of weapons over tea on manicured lawns.

They watch a man in army uniform patrolling with a German Shepherd.

'This is hopeless,' says Yushkov. 'Let's take a look at the main entrance.'

Wolfe drives slowly past the main gates. A sentry box, with electronic boom gates, manned by two armed guards and featuring a big red 'Police. Stop' sign, isn't promising. A car pulls up at the gate. The driver produces ID but isn't waved through. His car is searched first.

'Police car,' says Yushkov, nodding at one coming their way.

Wolfe takes off and heads for Porton village, only a few miles down the road. Pulling into the rear car park of the Porton Arms, she cuts the engine. There's a chalkboard sign outside announcing the pub is open for breakfast. They remove their helmets and pull on woollen beanies and scarves, so they are harder to recognise.

It's not yet midday and the pub is empty of customers. The publican, a florid, balding man in his forties, is wiping glasses with a tea towel. When they order two full English breakfasts and coffees, he shows them to his 'best table' near the window, which suits them because it is furthest away from the bar.

The publican bellows, 'Martha! Two big brekkies, love.'

Wolfe sees a flash of Martha in the kitchen as she grabs a frying pan with one hand and waves a 'Got it' at her husband with the other. Yushkov sits opposite Wolfe. Their coffees arrive and they wait for the publican to resume his glass polishing.

'How are we going to find Heatherton and the others?' Wolfe asks.

Yushkov leans across the table and keeps his voice low, conscious of his accent and the proximity of a stranger.

'Everything is possible. It is just knowing how.'

'Porton Down is like a maximum-security prison. Except it's guarded by the Military. Your mates won't be allowed out unescorted, and we can't get in.'

'Why can't we get in?'

'People have tried before and failed.'

Yushkov drinks scalding hot coffee. 'Who tried and failed?'

'Activists. To rescue the animals. Thousands are blown up, poisoned and gassed there each year.'

Yushkov whistles through his teeth.

'And Casburn will also have his own people protecting them.'

Cold air creeps through the gap between the window and the frame and she shivers.

'I think Toby, he will help me.'

'Why him? He's frightened of his own shadow.'

Martha delivers two plates of fried eggs, bacon, pork sausages, black pudding, baked beans, fried mushrooms and two slices of toast, steam curling up off the hot food. 'There you go, my loves. That'll warm you up.'

They eat in silence for a while.

'Toby will do it. Once he knows about Renata,' says Yushkov, mid-chew.

She puts down her knife and fork, holding his gaze. 'Vitaly, I need to know we are talking about finding substitute bacteria to hand to Grankin, not the Lake Ellsworth one? Even to save Renata.'

Their eyes are locked.

'Then we must hope Toby helps us.'

He hungrily finishes his breakfast. She has gone off hers.

'Perhaps the publican knows where Toby is staying?' Yushkov says. 'I think you should chat him up.'

'I'll have a go,' Wolfe says, pushing her plate away. She wanders up to the bar.

'Great breakfast, thanks.'

'On holiday, are we?' he asks, grabbing a box of salted peanuts. Christmas is only a week away. She'd forgotten.

'That's right, got family in Salisbury. So tell me,' Wolfe leans closer to him, 'what's with the big hoo-hah? There are police cars everywhere.'

'Something to do with some lethal bug from Antarctica. Not good for trade, I can tell you. Like the time we had that anthrax scare.' He gazes wanly around the near-empty pub.

'But your B and B business must be doing well, what with those scientists staying here.'

'I wish! My pub's apparently not good enough for them. They're over at the Fleets Motel. Pisses me off something rotten.'

'Sorry to hear that,' Wolfe says, delighted. 'Anyway, thanks again.'

Wolfe sits back down with Yushkov.

'We're in luck,' she whispers, and explains. 'Motel security won't be nearly as tight as Porton Down.'

51

The CCTV camera on his narrowboat still feeds live images to his smartphone, despite the muddy water lapping at the underside casing. The boat's kitchen and dining area is three-quarters full of canal water and rising fast. It seeps under the glass of a framed family photo, erasing their image with its dirty embrace. A child's pink plastic beaker floats listlessly on the surface. There's a sudden gush of water as the boat finally sinks and the submerged camera ceases to function. The man holds back a sob; surely his loved ones will forgive him?

The bacteria have performed exactly as he expected. The so-called expert microbiologists at the lab are wasting their time researching its potential for human infection. He alone knows how it could destroy civilisation itself. But not in the way the scientists believe.

Buried beneath three kilometres of ice, living in a permanently dark environment, with no sunlight or warmth, the ancient subterranean bacteria survived on the iron minerals in the lake's rocky bed. It lay fallow, cut off from the rest of the world, as enormous changes took place at the Earth's surface. Dinosaurs came and went, Australopithecus took the first upright steps on a path that led to revolutions which changed the face of the planet irrevocably: agricultural, urban, and finally, industrial. Iron and steel, steam engines, electricity, bridges, roads and cities. Stunning architecture; art and music. But, right from the emergence of the first walled cities almost six thousand years ago, humans have never stopped fighting. War just became more efficient, more brutal and more destructive, culminating in the absurdity of weapons of mass destruction capable of wiping out whole villages, cities, nations, even the planet. And the Lake Ellsworth bacteria remained in virtual suspended animation under the Antarctic ice, waiting for centuries in the dark, until some egotistical fools brought them to the surface.

Because sunlight is the trigger.

In sunlight, it becomes highly aggressive, reproducing at a rate never seen before. Like so many scientists before them, the Lake Ellsworth team never questioned what they were doing. Too wrapped up in a quest for glory, too obsessed with proving they could, rather than considering whether they should. Will those brilliant minds work out in time how to stop it wreaking havoc?

Maybe. Maybe not.

52

Porton Down, Wiltshire

Fleets Motel on the A345 to Salisbury is in the middle of nowhere, surrounded on three sides by fields scraped bare by uninterrupted winds. A sprinkling of snow reinforces the monochrome starkness of whitewashed walls, grey slate roof tiles and an asphalt car park encircling the building like a skirt. Wolfe can see why it's been chosen for Heatherton and his team: open fields in all directions provide no cover for surveillance or an unannounced approach.

It's four in the afternoon and it's already dark. Wolfe checked in hours ago under a fake name and bribed Martin, a bored teenage receptionist who managed somehow to take her details and conduct a conversation without looking up from his smartphone once, into giving her an adjoining room to Toby Sinclair's. Yushkov crept past reception when Martin was in the back and joined Wolfe in room 202 on the first floor.

Now all they have to do is wait.

Except for the cleaners vacuuming and the occasional door banging, it has been quiet. An ill-fitted window further down the corridor rattles in the wind, grating on Wolfe's nerves. She sits on a sagging double bed, with dated pink and brown floral bedspread, while Yushkov paces the room, twitching back the drawn curtains every now and again. Unable to smoke, he eats a muesli bar and some crisps from the minibar, checking his watch every few minutes. Wolfe has never seen him so keyed up.

'I need a smoke,' he says, and heads for the door.

'You'll be recognised.'

'I hate this waiting.'

He pulls his Glock 19 from the back of his jeans and sits heavily, then removes the magazine and racks the slide to eject a round from the chamber.

'Who did you buy that from?' Wolfe says.

'I thought you didn't want to know.'

There's a quiet click as he dry fires the pistol, pointing it at the wall.

'Was he Afghani?' she persists.

He studies her face. 'Yes.'

'Kabir Khan is suspected of funding an Isil terror cell in this country. If you know this man or where he is, tell me.'

Yushkov exhales loudly. 'I do not support terrorism. I do not know Kabir Khan. I just want my sister safe and to keep us alive.'

They lapse into silence and Yushkov goes back to stripping and cleaning the pistol. Wolfe wants to believe him but, like a mosquito bite, she can't leave it alone.

'This friend of yours. Perhaps he's not the man he says he is? Perhaps he's been radicalised?'

Yushkov cuts her off with a zip-it gesture and nods at the door.

In the corridor outside their door, someone gives the all-clear. The protection detail has arrived. More voices: Heatherton's softened Yorkshire accent is easy to identify. He invites somebody to join him for a drink at the bar later and Sinclair mumbles a 'No, thank you.' The door to 204 clicks shut. Through the spy-hole, Wolfe sees a muscular man with close-cropped hair in a cheap suit, seated on a chair facing Sinclair's door. One finger raised, she indicates to Yushkov there is one agent. He nods. The walls are paper thin: next door, the toilet flushes. The TV is switched on and Sinclair channel-surfs, settling for a news channel.

She mouths, 'Are you sure?'

Yushkov nods, then slips a piece of paper under the door between their two rooms. Its message is brief.

I need your help. Please open the adjoining door.
Kevin would want us to stop this madness.

It snags when only halfway. Eventually he wriggles it all the way through. Seconds pass, then minutes. Perhaps Sinclair hasn't seen it? The paper jerks suddenly, then it is gone. If Sinclair betrays them, they are done for.

There is a click and the adjoining door opens a fraction. Sinclair's flushed face nervously peers through the opening. His hand shoots up to his mouth in surprise when he sees Wolfe. Her finger raised, she silently tells Sinclair not to speak. Yushkov takes his friend in a bear-hug, the smaller man squashed in the Russian's embrace until he is steered to the window where they stand in a huddle, as far away from the corridor, and the agent, as possible.

'What are you doing here?' Sinclair whispers.

Yushkov places his hand on the scientist's shoulder. 'I need your help.'

'Everyone's saying you're a traitor. It's all over the news. I don't believe them.'

'It is lies. I did not take the missing sample . . . '

Sinclair blanches. 'You know about that?'

' . . . and I do not spy for Russia.' He pauses a moment to let this sink in. Then he tells Sinclair what Renata's captives want.

Sinclair wriggles free from Yushkov's grip, shaking his shaggy head. 'But I can't, you know that. I . . . I . . . you know I can't.'

More unkempt than Wolfe has ever seen him, the dark semi-circles under Sinclair's eyes betray his exhaustion. Thinner and gaunter, he smells of sweat that deodorant has failed to mask.

'Listen, my friend,' says Yushkov. 'Do not look so worried. I not ask you for Lake Ellsworth bacteria. Not the real thing. You understand?'

Sinclair's eyes dart from her face to Yushkov's and back. 'No, I don't. I don't understand anything. The whole world's gone crazy.' His voice is squeaky with panic.

'Take a seat,' Wolfe says, trying to calm him.

Wolfe explains their plan to hand over bacteria that can pass off as the real thing. He blinks rapidly.

'Yes, yes, I get that, but you want me to steal from Porton Down! I'll go to prison. I can't, I just can't.'

'It's the only way to save my sister,' Yushkov says.

Sinclair shakes his head furiously. 'It can't be. Tell the police. They'll find her.'

'SVR will stop them. She will die. Toby, I wouldn't ask if there was any other way.'

Sinclair rocks himself back and forth in agitation. 'Oh no, no, no!' He's getting louder. 'I don't do this sort of thing. Don't ask me to.'

'Take a look at this,' Wolfe says, handing Sinclair their mobile with the video of Renata ready to play.

Sinclair watches it. By the end, he is trembling. 'Bastards!'

Yushkov covers his mouth.

'Shush!'

Sinclair nods and he removes his hand.

'My friend,' Yushkov whispers. 'Renata is my sister. My only living relative. They kill her if I do not make them believe I have given them what they want.'

Sinclair hides his face in his palms. They wait. Then he suddenly jerks his head up.

'I need to be absolutely clear. I will never give you Psychosillius.'

'Psychosillius?' Wolfe asks. 'Is that what you've called the Lake Ellsworth bacteria?'

He nods.

'Why is it at Porton Down?'

'Oh dear me, no. That's now an official secret. I can't even talk to my family.'

'Is it germ warfare?' Wolfe perseveres.

Sinclair shuts his mouth and shakes his head, like a child trying not to betray a secret.

'Come on, Toby, tell us something. Why do the Russians want it so badly?'

'Because they think they can use it as a weapon.'

'Can they?' she asks.

'Stop pushing me!' he says, raising his voice again. 'I wish to God we'd never found it.'

'You're scaring me. What does it do?'

'I can't, I . . . ' Sinclair is rocking again.

'Stop, Olivia!' says Yushkov. 'It does not matter.' He leans down so his face is at Sinclair's level. 'All I need is something to give Grankin.'

'Vitaly, there's nothing harmless at Porton Down,' Sinclair says. 'That's the point. It's a godforsaken germ-warfare factory.'

'I have to give him something,' says Yushkov. 'Please, Toby?'

'If I do this, you'll leave me alone?'

'You have my word.'

He stares at Wolfe. 'I don't want you coming anywhere near me again. No phone calls. No questions.'

'Understood,' she says.

Sinclair scratches his chin through his messy beard. 'I could get you a vial of Necrotising Fasciitis.'

'Which is?' Wolfe asks.

'Flesh-eating disease. It's a highly aggressive bacterial infection. When it enters the body, the bacteria multiply and release toxins that kill tissue and cut off blood flow. It's nasty. Limbs and tissue sometimes have to be removed.'

'That's the least harmful thing you can think of?' asks Wolfe incredulously.

'Antibiotics and amputation of infected limbs ensures recovery. So, yes.'

'It sounds horrible,' says Wolfe. 'We can't hand that to the SVR.'

'No, no, they already have it. It's no great secret. There've been cases in the US, in Africa and in Eastern Europe. At first glance, though, it looks remarkably similar to Psychosillius.'

'I need it tomorrow,' says Yushkov.

'Tomorrow? Oh God, that fast? Um, okay, I'll bring it here.'

'Take this mobile number, but don't give it to anyone, okay?' says Wolfe. 'In case we need to change the meeting place.'

'No need to write it down. I'll remember,' Sinclair says, 'And after this, you leave me alone, you promise?'

Yushkov nods. 'We promise, my friend.'

53

Atlantic Ocean, off the coast of Morocco,
05.04 hours

The young technician in the main engine room of aircraft carrier, HMS *Queen Elizabeth*, stands in a narrow space facing a wall of over forty brand-new dials that shine in the harsh fluorescent lighting. Leading Hand Sam Boothby turns a wall-mounted wheel a fraction and watches the dials closely. It's hot and claustrophobic but Sam takes great pride in his job, knowing that he must open and shut the throttle valves at a certain pace, otherwise the combustion control system, as well as the boiler water feed and water level controls, won't keep up. Left alone by his supervising officer who is attending to a problem somewhere else, Sam enjoys this moment of solitude: a rare thing on a warship carrying almost fourteen hundred crew. The new ship creaks and the floors and surfaces shudder and the engines roar but, with ear protectors on, he barely notices.

A diehard Whovian, he imagines he's inside his very own Tardis and that the dials, like clocks, enable him to travel backwards and forwards in time and to visit alternative worlds. His favourite Doctor is Matt Smith, maybe because he was one of the youngest in a long line of Doctors, or maybe just because he thinks Smith, like his bow tie, was cool. He starts to hum the theme tune to the programme and doesn't care if anyone hears. Sam's nickname is Geronimo, one of the young Doctor's favourite exclamations, and his obsession is well known on board.

He hears a loud clank, as if someone has dropped a spanner, and peers down the passageway into semi-darkness. There's not much down there, save for the valve above the sea chest: perhaps somebody is checking it? As a boy, he imagined a sea chest was where pirates hid their treasure, but now he knows that beneath the valve is a vast chamber filled with water, providing direct access to the sea beyond the ship's hull. There are several around the ship. Sam hears a loud crack from the same direction, and then a popping sound. He removes his ear protection. The steel floor shudders as if some giant beast is trying to break through the steel floor. Has he lost his mind? Stumbling backwards, he breaks out in a sweat. A new ship shouldn't make noises like this. As Sam fumbles for the intercom, the floor beneath him rips apart and sea water shoots up, hurling him into the low roof with such force his skull splits like a watermelon sliced with a machete. His limp body falls back to the flooding deck, staining the water red. Barely conscious, the last sound Sam hears is the valve, all fifty tonnes of steel, blow off the entrance to the sea chest, like a cannon firing.

07.11 hours

'Circle the ship but don't land. I'll contact you when I'm ready to leave,' Casburn orders the helicopter pilot.

As he is lowered in a harness from the hovering Merlin chopper on to the ship's brightly lit runway, he feels sick to the stomach, like the worst hangover. Not because he's seasick – he's been on carriers many times when he was in the SAS – but because this is his nightmare come true. A terrorist attack on the pride of the Royal Navy. An attack he should have prevented. With him is Professor Matthews and a team of disease control and quarantine experts. Matthews will be winched aboard after him, followed by the others. Free of the harness, the detective from Counter Terrorism Command is led off the aircraft carrier's runway, where he awaits Matthews.

It is barely controlled chaos on board.

Two hours ago, Commodore James Stirling issued a mayday signal and set a course from West Africa back to Portsmouth

Harbour. The vastness of the ship rules out closer ports – there are few deep enough to handle her size. Shadowing her is the destroyer, HMS *Dauntless*. But *Dauntless* has been ordered to stand by and not to attempt to board the aircraft carrier.

The runway is frenetic. In an attempt to save the aircraft, the entire on-board fleet is being scrambled to nearby NATO air force bases in Portugal. Casburn and Matthews hasten to the navigation bridge on the forward island. This new breed of aircraft carrier has two control centres rather than the traditional one, both forward and aft islands protruding from the deck like stacked grey shipping containers. Once on the bridge, they find the white-haired commodore huddled with his officers, staring at the ship's instruments.

'Commodore?' he says, striding up to Stirling. Casburn introduces himself and Professor Matthews.

'Detective, do you mind telling me what you are doing here?'

'We believe this may be a terrorist attack.'

'By whom?'

'I'm not at liberty to say, sir.'

The Commodore takes a deep breath, his white eyebrows so deeply furrowed they almost touch. 'For God's sake, Casburn. Don't be obtuse. My ship is sinking and I want to know why.'

'Sir, that's what we're here to find out.'

They are interrupted by the Captain. 'Sir, we've been refused entry to Portsmouth Harbour and rescue ships have been ordered to stay away.'

The Commodore glares at Casburn. 'What the hell is going on, Casburn?'

'It's a security issue, sir.'

'What in the blazes does that mean?'

'It means that whatever agent has been used to attack your ship, it must not be allowed to reach land.'

Stirling and the Captain exchange wide-eyed, incredulous looks.

'You mean some kind of biological weapon?' asks Stirling.

'It's a possibility, yes. Professor Matthews and his team need to act quickly to establish the cause. Is she in immediate danger of sinking?'

'The lowest deck is flooded but she's designed to withstand that. She'll float as long as the next level isn't breached.'

'Where did the problem start?' asks Casburn.

'Front engine room. Ruled out a torpedo attack. My next thought was a bomb, but nothing indicates an explosion. She has heavy side armour, built to withstand air, sea and torpedo attacks, with thousands of watertight spaces so we can isolate sections of the ship, should she take on water. But something or someone is destroying the hull from the inside.'

'Can you be more specific, sir?'

The Commodore directs Casburn and Matthews to a sweep of polished wood beneath the bridge's windows. On display there are several pieces of metal that look as if they've come from the wreck of a car accident. The edges are jagged, the metal full of holes. It is not warped and blackened by a bomb blast, nor has it rusted or discoloured as if chemically corroded.

'See these holes?' says the Commodore. 'Never seen anything like it.' The holes are circular and perfectly formed, as if something has eaten into the steel. The rest is covered in blisters, like a person suffering from smallpox.

Stirling points at the steel bubbles. His finger is too close. Matthews speaks up. 'Don't touch it.'

Stirling jerks his hand back as if he's touched a hot pan.

'They're all over my ship, working up from the lowest levels. It's like acid eating through her. What do you make of this?' he says, giving Casburn a hard stare.

The detective has seen such holes before: at Porton Down: but in a controlled environment. Not in a 65,000-tonne warship as long as twenty-eight London buses, threatening the lives of 1,397 men and women. Fourteen casualties have been confirmed. Thirty-seven dead. So far.

'Professor Matthews?' Casburn says.

'I'd say it's Psychosillius all right, but I can't be certain until I've done some tests. Where can I set up?' Matthews asks the Commodore.

Matthews places the samples in a sealed container and follows an officer to a room behind the bridge.

Casburn clears his throat. 'Commodore, Psychosillius must not be allowed to reach land. Therefore, I need you to hold your position and to cease immediately all flight operations. Any aircraft attempting to land on foreign or British soil will be shot down.'

'Are you out of your mind?'

'No, sir, I'm deadly serious.'

'You're asking me to sit by and watch the pride of the Royal Navy disintegrate? Do you have any idea how many billions it cost to build her, let alone the aircraft?'

The furious captain can't keep quiet any longer. 'The Commodore is the authority here. You have none.'

Casburn ignores him and addresses Stirling. 'A quarantine ship will be here within the hour. If we establish Psychosillius is the cause of the breach, the ship must be abandoned and every person aboard this carrier will go through decontamination.'

'I'm doing no such thing—'

'Sir?' The Lieutenant Commander interrupts Stirling, holding up a phone. 'The Admiral. He wants to speak to you.'

Stirling blinks twice, then takes the phone. The exchange is brief. 'Yes, Admiral,' concludes Stirling. When he turns to face his officers, his complexion is almost as pale as his hair.

'If the scientists confirm Psychosillius is aboard, we abandon ship in an orderly fashion. Everything, I repeat everything, must be left behind. We leave only with the clothes we're wearing.'

Stirling turns his back on his officers and places his hands on a console for support, shoulders hunched and head hung.

54

Wolfe is jolted from her sleep by men's voices. She is out of bed in seconds. The angry red numbers on the nineties-style digital clock radio tell her it's 7.11; their wake-up alarm hasn't gone off. She shakes Yushkov. His eyelids spring open as fast as a flick knife.

'What?'

'Listen,' she whispers.

The man is outside their door. 'Hurley! Lewis!' he calls. She imagines him pointing at them. 'Don't let them out of your sight, not even when they take a piss. You got that?'

'Yes, sir,' Hurley and Lewis say in unison.

'Get on with it then.'

Doors are knocked upon, then opened. Sinclair leaves his room quietly but Heatherton demands to know how long they will be kept 'like prisoners', while Price refuses to leave her room until she speaks to her husband and kids. The man in charge pacifies her, promising her he'll see what he can do. Matthews tries to keep the peace as they all head to the restaurant for breakfast.

'You and you, come with me.' Two other agents. 'I want this hotel scoured. Top to bottom. I want the names of every guest. I want every door opened.'

'Wake everyone up, guv?'

'I don't care if we wake the dead! Now get on with it! You do level one, and you, take this floor.'

Wolfe and Yushkov dress quickly, in silence. If Sinclair had turned them in, their door would have been kicked in by now, but something has spooked the spooks. Have they been spotted? The window is their only escape route. Locking the adjoining door to Sinclair's room, Wolfe helps Yushkov strip the bed and tie two sheets together, which he then loops around the radiator beneath the casement window. The rest of the makeshift rope hangs down the exterior wall, falling short of the rear car park by about six feet.

'Will it hold?'

'I hope. I go first. Then I can catch you.'

The sun hasn't risen yet, but the dangling sheet will soon alert their pursuers. Yushkov is out of the window and disappears into the darkness, their bag with him. It's her turn. She clambers down the rope easily, then lets go; Yushkov breaks her fall, catching her around her waist.

'The fields,' he says.

Avoiding the car park's pools of sodium lighting, they scramble over a wire fence into a muddy field and crouch low as they follow the bramble bushes running parallel to the main road. The field is sodden, the mud sucking at their boots. Their stolen Fiesta is half a mile away, hidden from view by a clump of beech trees. Each time a vehicle goes by, they duck, their progress sporadic. Finally, they reach their car.

'We need somewhere to lay low until Toby gets back to the hotel.'

'How about our friend at the Porton Arms?' Wolfe suggests.

Yushkov nods.

Five minutes later, the bleary-eyed publican is welcoming them, even if he has only just opened for business. With no overnight guests, he's had a lie-in. They tell him they'd like a room and order the same coffees and breakfasts as yesterday. He's delighted when they hand over cash.

'Here, compliments of the house,' the publican says, handing Wolfe the latest *UK Today*, rolled tight in an elastic band, only just delivered by the newsagent.

Wolfe is tempted to throw it away, but curiosity gets the better of her. Once seated, she unrolls the paper and instantly wishes she hadn't.

'How the hell did he get that photo?'

'Show me.'

'"The Black Widow claims her next victim",' Yushkov reads the front-page headline aloud.

There's a photo of her and Charles Harvey on York Bridge in close conversation. Her hat hides her hair and her scarf, most of her face.

'Could you recognise me from this?'

'*Nyet*. Even I couldn't be sure.'

Nails claims a witness took the picture shortly before Olivia Wolfe 'stabbed Harvey to death'.

'This reporter has got it in for you,' says Yushkov.

The anonymous witness also claims he overheard Harvey tell Wolfe that Yushkov, who is described as her 'lover', killed Kevin Knox.

'This witness gives you motive to kill Harvey,' says Yushkov. 'To protect me. They are framing you.'

'Who? Who knows we are lovers?'

'Whoever you saw running from the house in Chiswick.'

Wolfe feels sick. She can't remember any bystanders near the park bridge, let alone anyone near enough to take photos. And someone must have followed them to Chiswick. The same person? How could she have failed to notice?

The article continues over the page. Wolfe knows it's not going to be nice. But she is stunned by what she finds.

All the colour drains from her face. 'Oh no!'

Across the double-page spread are photos of Wolfe and Yushkov having sex. Graphic photos, in chronological order, at the most intimate moments, shot through the glass windows at the front of the house. She tries to swallow, but the lump in her throat is as hard as an ice cube. Even though some parts are pixelated, there is no mistaking who they are; from height, build and hair colour down to the minutest and most private details, like her bellybutton piercing and Yushkov's scarred shoulder.

'You were right,' says Yushkov, shaking his head. 'We were being watched.' He nudges her playfully, then notices how upset she is. 'You look very beautiful. There is nothing to be ashamed of.'

Wolfe stares fixedly at the table.

'Olivia, in a few weeks, nobody will remember this,' he says, flicking the page derisively with his fingers.

'I'm a private person, Vitaly . . . ' she begins, then fades away. 'I have never been so humiliated.'

'We should focus on who took this and why.'

'You don't get it, do you? What we did was private. It was beautiful and Nails has made it filthy, making me out to be a cheap slut.'

'Don't let this scumbag get to you.'

'I'm being accused of murder!'

'I think SVR does this to deflect attention, so police focus on you.'

'Perhaps I should turn myself in? Tell them what really happened in the park,' she says. 'There has to be a trail linking Harvey to the SVR somewhere – payments, emails, that sort of thing.'

Yushkov shakes his head vehemently. 'That's how you go to prison for something you didn't do.'

She gets up. 'I need to clear my head.'

'I come with you.'

'No, please. I need some space to think.'

'Keep out of sight,' Yushkov says, rolling up the paper, then stuffing it inside his jacket. The publican must not see it.

Through the back door, Wolfe finds several picnic benches on a patch of muddy lawn. Rabbits hop away as she sits, the bench damp with dew. She takes some deep breaths.

'Well, Mum,' she says aloud. 'Thank God you never saw this.'

There's a rustling in a rhododendron bush and she finds she's being watched by a rabbit. A momentary distraction before her mind returns to the explicit photos, imagining fellow journalists snickering, Cohen scowling – furious at what he will see as her stupidity – and, worst of all, Jerry Butcher's profound disappointment. After all he has done to steer her along the straight and narrow, will the man she loves as a father lose faith in her? Butcher has never once reminded her of how he almost wrecked his career to give her a second chance. Her one and only true friend.

Wolfe tries to think logically. What would Butcher do, the man who is always calm in a crisis? He'd break things down into manageable tasks. She and Yushkov have a deadline: hand the bacteria to the SVR and save Renata. It's now up to Sinclair to deliver. Her next task is to find who stole the canister from the camp. Since the Russians don't have it, then who does? Wolfe needs the intel Butcher promised her. But, after seeing the paper today, will he still help her?

55

In the ancient city of Salisbury, Wolfe and Yushkov are outside an internet café. Her hair is tucked under a woolly hat so not a strand can be seen. Yushkov's height and bulk is more difficult to hide, but they have both purchased entry-level, off-the-shelf reading glasses, which Wolfe might find comical if their situation wasn't so desperate. The pedestrian-only street is narrow and the original Tudor buildings lean into the walkway, their small lead-light windows bowed with old age. Nearby, a magnificent Norway spruce twinkles with Christmas lights and red and white baubles.

'His phone will be bugged,' says Yushkov, hands deep in his coat pockets.

'That's why I'm not using mine.' Wolfe purchased a new burner phone a few minutes ago.

They head for a public phone box outside a chemist.

Yushkov persists. 'The more contact you make, the more likely we will be found.'

'We need the information.'

Yushkov sits on a nearby bench to keep watch and lights a cigarette, looking perfectly relaxed, but his eyes are alert, watching, assessing. Wolfe dials Butcher's mobile. She will keep the call to less than thirty seconds, making it harder to trace. Butcher answers after just one ring, as if he is waiting for her call.

'Have you seen today's paper?' Wolfe asks, her voice strained.

'I have. How are you bearing up?'

'Embarrassed. Angry. I feel I've . . .' She struggles to find the right words. ' . . . let you down.'

'Never.'

'I don't know who to trust.'

'Trust me.'

'Is your mobile tapped?'

'I honestly don't know.'

'Then this must be quick. I did not kill Harvey.'

'I know you didn't.'

'Have you got the background checks I asked for?'

'I have.'

'Then put everything in Dropbox. Can you write this down?'

'Yes, fire away.'

Wolfe spells out the account name. 'Got that?'

'Yes.'

'Can you do it now?'

'Yes.'

'Thank you, Jerry.'

'Liv?'

She ends the call after twenty-six seconds and joins Yushkov.

They walk to a tiny internet café that's an odd marriage of twenty-first-century technology and sixteenth-century architecture, tucked down a narrow lane. A Japanese girl in pink woolly dress and UGG boots continues playing a violent video game as she takes their money and nods at a vacant computer.

'What is this Dropbox?' Yushkov asks.

'It's a way of receiving large documents and images. I have several accounts. The one I gave Jerry hasn't been used before, so hopefully the spooks won't know about it.' She taps in her password. There's nothing in her account. Her stomach twists. She peers anxiously through the lead-light windows at all the shoppers streaming past, like debris caught in a flood. To kill time she asks for a mug of tea and a chocolate muffin but, as the girl doesn't budge, Wolfe suspects they will be gone before it arrives.

Back at the computer, a zip file appears, titled simply 'LE'. She opens it. Inside is a file on each member of the Ellsworth team, including the now deceased Harvey. She downloads everything on to her USB stick, but as she doesn't have a computer any more, she prints too. Wolfe hovers over the printer so that neither the girl nor other users can see the contents. To her surprise, she's handed a mug of weak tea and a muffin. The printing complete and the muffin eaten, Wolfe logs off and they leave.

'I've one more call to make,' Wolfe says.

'We should keep moving. We stay in one place, we get noticed.'

'Okay. I'll make it quick.'

It's market day and stalls are piled high with Christmas fare: cards and wrapping paper; dog beds and dog chews in red Christmassy bows; free range turkeys and beef joints; locally made chocolates and cheeses; sheepskin coats and woolly jumpers. The market is buzzing with happy chatter and smiling faces as the Salvation Army band plays carols. For the first time since she read Nails's article, Wolfe feels hopeful. Surely her ball-breaking editor will think she is worth fighting for? Inside the phone box, she dials Cohen's mobile.

'Yup,' he snaps, clearly not recognising the Salisbury phone number.

'Moz, it's Olivia.'

Silence.

'Somebody with you?' she asks.

'Well, you can be sure somebody, a.k.a. those fucking eavesdropping spooks, is listening, even though, of course, wire-tapping like this is illegal, since I'm not a fucking terrorist!' he yells down the phone, as if trying to deafen the said spooks. 'You sure you should be calling me?'

If Cohen is right, she has to talk fast and get off the line.

'Moz, I'm not a killer. I'm being framed.'

'And the photos?'

'Somebody's out to destroy me.'

'Sheesh!' The silence makes her nervous. No cutting remark.

No yelling or swearing. All of which are bad signs. 'You're too hot to handle, my love. I can't help you. You're wanted for murder, for Christ's sake!'

'Except I didn't do it. And Vitaly did not steal the bacteria; nor, it seems, did the SVR.'

'Got any proof?'

'Not yet.'

'Seriously, you need to hand yourself in. Or talk to Casburn. You'll get yourself killed and drag this paper down with you.'

'Not until I've cleared my name.'

Another silence. When he speaks, it is quiet and controlled. 'Olivia, the MD summoned me this morning. There have been meetings. About you. I don't have a choice.'

'A choice about what?'

'I'm making you redundant. It's the best I can do, considering.'

'No bloody way, Moz! You can't. You know Nails makes up shit.'

'I'm sorry, Olivia. Controversial is one thing. Hated by the British public is another. I warned you not to get involved.' He lets the last comment hang in the air. 'It's my duty to protect the *Post* and a killer on the payroll isn't good for business. I'm sorry.'

Cohen puts the phone down on her. Wolfe stares at the receiver. She guessed this might happen, but knowing doesn't make it any easier.

Furious, Wolfe dials Nails's mobile number. Yushkov shakes his head at her. 'No more calls,' he says.

She's beyond reason. Nails answers.

'Who took those photos?'

'Olivia Wolfe, how the devil are you? Out of a job yet?'

'You've trashed my life. The least you can do is tell me who.'

'No, love, you trashed your own life. Maybe you can take up a new career as a porn star, 'cause you ain't getting no reporter's job.'

She can hear him snickering. 'Tell me, Olivia, what attracts you to the scum of the earth?'

She looks at Yushkov, tears stinging her eyes.

'People are trying to kill me, Eric. Just give me something.'

'Go fuck yourself!'

56

Commodore Stirling is on the bridge, but not of the *Queen Elizabeth*.

The last to abandon ship, Stirling has been fast-tracked through decontamination and, declared clear of Psychosillius, now stands next to Captain Steven Cooper of HMS *Dauntless*, wearing borrowed civvies. His uniform has been incinerated. Through binoculars, he stares out at his ship some three nautical miles away, half submerged, her runway pointing skyward, the bridge protruding above the waves by only a few feet. Smoke still pours from her funnel, as if she's exhaling her last dying breath. News media choppers circle outside the exclusion zone, reminding Stirling of vultures circling a carcass. The lines around Stirling's eyes and mouth appear deeper and his stiff posture is a little stooped. He can't remember ever feeling so bereft. As Commodore he is responsible for ship and crew. He has failed in both. For evermore he will be known as the man who lost the biggest Royal Navy warship ever built. And not even in combat. His career is finished.

'Captain?'

Instinctively, Stirling turns round, but it is Captain Cooper who receives the report.

'How many?' Stirling asks.

'One hundred and forty-two dead.'

Stirling looks away. Men and women trapped in flooding decks. A horrible death. Their families must be told. He will do it personally. It's the least he can do.

Stirling lifts the binoculars again and looks to port where the last of his crew leaves an orange lifeboat and climbs the gangplank of a United Nations quarantine ship, her yellow and black Lima flag flying high, warning of contagion. To starboard, the USS *Theodore Roosevelt* awaits. He knows Captain Ron Hart well and has huge respect for the tough Texan. They served together during the invasion of Iraq in 2003.

'Commodore? Captain Hart is on the line.'

Stirling takes the phone. 'Ron?'

'James, I won't ask how you're doing, under the circumstances. We've fought side by side many times, but I have my orders. Your government has asked mine to assist. You understand?'

'I do. Yours is the nearest carrier?'

'She is.'

'I never thought I'd see my ship sunk by an ally.'

'God be with you, James.'

The call over, Stirling knows what is coming, even before he hears the roar of the FA-18 Super Hornets of the Thunderbolts – a Marine Strike Fighter Attack Squadron. This is not about sinking her: she's doing that all by herself. No, this is about obliterating her contagion. The Mark-77 incendiary bombs turn the sky livid orange, then thick black smoke shrouds the remains of the aircraft carrier. More ordnance hits the target, the shock waves rolling across the water until it seems the very horizon is on fire and the sky has turned black.

'God save us if that plague is ever let loose.'

57

Their room at the Porton Arms is at the front of the pub. Yushkov leans against the curtain and keeps watch through a grimy window. They wait for Sinclair's call, fearful of showing their faces.

Wolfe is cross-legged on the bed with documents laid out in neat piles on the chintz bedspread. Somehow Butcher has accessed the Police National Computer, as well as bank statements and medical records. Documents on Dr Stacy Price, Professor Gary Matthews and George Beer are in a separate pile: read, considered, and crossed off her suspects list. The lunchtime crowd arrives downstairs, their greetings and conversations, the clank of glasses and the clatter of plates, filtering up through the floorboards.

Yushkov abruptly pulls back from the window.

'What is it?' she asks.

'Plumber's van. Could be surveillance. Back windows are tinted.'

Wolfe gathers up her papers, ready to flee. Yushkov's body relaxes.

'It's okay. He is alone.'

'How do you know?'

'He opened the rear doors. Just his equipment.'

Wolfe breathes a sigh of relief.

Yushkov nods at the printouts on the bed. 'You read my file?'

'I have. There's very little in it.' Wolfe pauses. 'You and Renata were adopted?'

Yushkov shifts his feet and nods once, clearly uncomfortable.

'To the same family?'

'Yes.'

'Copies of your birth certificate, adoption papers, your army enrolment papers, then nothing until you pop up in Antarctica as ship's engineer on the *Professor Basov*. No asylum application. Just your British citizenship certificate. The rest of it is boring bank statements and employment records at British Antarctic Survey. There are more holes in your life than a shower head.'

Yushkov shrugs.

'Don't you think it's weird? For most of your adult life you don't exist.'

'It is not easy to get information on foreign nationals.'

'A source told me the Foreign Office fast-tracked your citizenship and quashed everything about your life in Russia. Is that true?'

'Then your source knows more than me.'

'Come on, Vitaly! You must have some idea who's suppressed this information.'

Yushkov stares out of the window. 'I do not know. I sought asylum. I got it. I am good engineer, so I get a job quickly.'

Wolfe feels uneasy again. Why is such a huge chunk of Yushkov's life unaccounted for?

'When you deserted in Afghanistan, where did you go?'

'Olivia, please. I do not wish to talk about this.'

'Why?'

'It is best you do not know.'

He turns his back on her.

Frustrated by his reluctance to talk, Wolfe picks up Harvey's file and skim-reads it.

'Do you remember Harvey was one of the first aboard Trankov's plane? He could have handed the stolen cylinder to the pilot.'

'*Da*. But Grankin does not have it.'

She sighs. 'Let's hope the answer's in here somewhere.'

Going through Harvey's bank statements, Wolfe notices a

payment of fifty thousand pounds to Tonbridge School and numerous wedding-related outgoings totalling over thirty thousand. The mortgage is in arrears. Wolfe finds two deposits of twenty-five thousand each, from a bank she has never heard of, made just over a year ago and then one month ago.

'Harvey was drowning in debt. Expensive school fees, I'm guessing a daughter's wedding. Look.'

She passes him the statements.

'I think he was spying on us from the beginning,' says Yushkov.

'How do you mean?'

'Harvey wrote an article on the project from the day Heatherton announced it. He followed our progress as we designed and developed the drill and probe. Then Harvey suddenly says he is not coming with us to Antarctica. Michael is very upset. Then, at the last minute, Harvey changes his mind. He gives no reason.'

'So Harvey was paid to steal your designs a year ago and then again to sabotage the project?'

'This is what I think.'

'But I can't help thinking he had an accomplice.'

Wolfe turns her attention to the pile of documents on Michael Heatherton. Butcher has managed to secure a private detective's surveillance report, proving Heatherton had an affair with a Maggie Cameron. His wife commissioned the PI and confronted him. Heatherton seems to have ended the affair before departing for Antarctica, his desire for respectability and success outweighing his need for a bit on the side. But his wife knows, so there's not much blackmail potential.

The next file is Bruce Adeyemi. Born in London, parents of Nigerian descent, he studied medicine at University College London but dropped out in the second year and enrolled at the University of York, gaining a Bachelor of Engineering. He's worked at Southampton's National Oceanography Centre ever since. His credit card receipts make colourful reading: every Saturday he spends large sums at casinos. He has lost thousands at Southampton's Grosvenor, Maxims and Mint casinos. But his favourite is clearly the London Hippodrome. On top of that, he's paying a mortgage in Southampton, rent for a studio flat at a new Canning Town development, and a car loan. Adeyemi is living way beyond his means.

'And he's got a medical background,' says Wolfe out loud, remembering that Knox was injected with midazolam.

Adeyemi had the right motivation and the know-how to kill Knox.

Her mobile rings: a local area code. It has to be Sinclair.

'Hello?'

'It's me.' Sinclair's voice is shrill. 'I've got it.'

He's put on loudspeaker.

'Good work, Toby. Just tell me whose line you're using?'

'Oh, um, a PA's, in another department. Out to lunch.'

'Good. Is it in a steel container?'

'N . . . no. Glass vial. It's small.'

'We need it in something that can be thrown from your hotel window.'

'Are you mad? What if it breaks? I can't do this. I just can't.'

His voice trails off as he moves the phone away from his mouth.

'Toby! Don't hang up on me.'

'I've got to go. They'll find me.' He pants with fear.

'It's okay. Bring it to the hotel tonight. At nine exactly, open your window. One of us will stand below and catch the vial.'

'But if it breaks? It's flesh-eating.'

'That's our problem. Please, Toby. Promise me you'll do it.'

'Oh God! All right.'

Sinclair ends the call.

'So, who will catch the vial?' asks Yushkov.

'I will,' she says. 'Good hand-eye coordination.'

'You sure?'

'Yes.'

She explains to Yushkov her theory that Adeyemi worked with Harvey to kill Knox and steal the missing canister, perhaps double-crossing Harvey and the Russians. But Yushkov is preoccupied with something outside.

'It is possible,' is all he says.

Setting aside Adeyemi's file, Wolfe grabs the nearest one: Toby Sinclair. She doesn't open it; she can't stop thinking about Adeyemi. Muscular, he'd have no problem getting an unconscious Knox on a snowmobile. He'd also know how to disable the boiler. The more she thinks about it, the more she's convinced. But where is Adeyemi now? Sinclair would know.

The stuffy room is making her lethargic and, like Yushkov, she's getting cabin fever. She stretches, then skims the documents on Sinclair. Born and educated in Edinburgh, worked in environmental microbiology, microbial biodiversity, environmental genomics, and life in extreme environments since graduating. Shy and socially inept, Sinclair has barely got his feet on the bottom rung of the career ladder, despite his brilliance. Both his parents are still alive. Brother, Hector, joined the Royal Navy and at the end of his commission moved to Sydney, Australia. Toby met his wife, Huma, at Edinburgh University. The name sounds Afghani to Wolfe and, as she reads on, she discovers Huma and her family were Afghani refugees who settled in Scotland. Sinclair's life is organised, routine and suburban. Nothing out of the ordinary. The mortgage and credit cards are paid off each month. One speeding ticket and two parking fines. Bored, Wolfe is about to move on to another file when she notices photocopies of three death certificates.

Her phone rings again. Yushkov leaps at it and answers. 'Okay, we will come now,' Yushkov says. 'It is the same plan, okay? You will throw it down to Olivia. But one more thing. Can you bring sulphur powder? Enough to fill a food tin?'

Toby sounds flustered.

'When you get to the hotel, leave it under the van you arrive in. Okay?'

The call over, Yushkov fills her in.

'They are all being moved. Your calls from Salisbury, they were traced.'

'Shit!'

'They go to the motel now to pack their things, then to a safe house. We must get the vial from Toby now.'

'Are you out of your mind? In broad daylight?'

'We have no choice.' He shrugs. 'I need an empty food tin and aluminium foil. Can you ask the publican?'

Yushkov undoes one of his boots and removes a shoelace.

'What are you going to do with that?' she asks.

58

The Ford Transit van is stolen. Wolfe drives, Yushkov in the passenger seat. The van belongs to U-Bend Plumbing and has two tinted windows in the rear doors. When the plumber leaves the Porton Arms after lunch he's going to get a nasty surprise. Wolfe feels bad about this; when they no longer need it, she plans to phone the number painted on the van and tell him where to find it. A large police van pulls into a parking spot at the front of the motel and half a dozen uniformed officers spill out.

'Jesus!' Wolfe says. 'We can't get near.'

Wolfe drives past, watching the activity in her rear-view mirror. A grey Ford Galaxy MPV pulls up. The doors open and two plain-clothes officers step out, followed by Price, Matthews and Sinclair. Heatherton appears reluctant to leave the car, and the officer takes his upper arm, applying unmistakable pressure.

She glances at Yushkov. 'I like a challenge, but this?'

'You do not have to do this. You can stay in the van.'

'You're a stubborn bastard.'

'How do you say? We are peas in a pod.'

She can't help but smile. 'Okay, what's your plan?'

He points to their right. 'Pull into the petrol station.'

She parks near the tyre pump, as far away from the CCTV cameras and the shop as possible.

'We attack the air conditioning. The pumps are around the back. We park next to them. I will put this tin inside the unit and light it. The sulphur stink will reach every room. People will leave the hotel, I promise you.'

'A diversion?'

'Yes. You wear this.' He points to a fluorescent yellow hi-vis vest with reflective silver stripes and the logo of U-Bend Plumbing. 'If somebody challenges us, you do the talking. Yes?'

'I'll be recognised.'

'*Nyet.* You look like a plumber, you behave like one. Then you are one. Just act the part.'

'But this only works if Toby's dropped the bag of sulphur?'

'Correct. We swap now. I drive. I park next to the Ford Galaxy. The cops will come up to us, tell us to move on. You must distract them.'

'I'll think of something.'

They swap seats and Yushkov sets off.

'Here's hoping the space next to the Galaxy is still available,' she says.

But it isn't. There are cars either side.

'I must block them in,' says Yushkov. 'You talk on the phone.'

Yushkov parks across the Galaxy's rear, gets out, leaving the engine running. Wolfe, hair tucked under her woolly hat and wearing glasses and plumber's vest, jumps down and starts a loud, fake conversation with a distraught, fake customer.

'You can't park there,' shouts one of the plain-clothes officers, jogging towards them. 'Move your van!'

'So where's the water coming from?' says Wolfe into the phone.

'Move, now!' says the officer, holding up his warrant card.

Wolfe puts her hand up to tell him to be quiet and turns away from him. 'Water's all over the floor, you say? Do you know where the stopcock is, Mrs Brown? You need to turn it off.'

'Hey!' says the officer. 'End your call, and move your van. Now.'

Wolfe covers the face of her phone. 'All right. Keep your shirt on. Her kitchen's flooded, poor lady.' She then calls over the top of the van at Yushkov, who is hidden from view. 'Time to go, mate. Coppers want us gone.' Then she directs herself back to the officer. 'We're going now, officer.' She gets back into the passenger seat and pretends to continue talking to Mrs Brown. Yushkov gets in and drives around the back of the hotel, never making eye contact.

'Do you have it?' she asks.

'I do,' he says, as he parks next to the air-conditioning unit.

He pours the sulphur powder into the empty food can, covers the top in aluminium foil, then sticks a severed section of his shoelace through the foil and into the sulphur, which now resembles a wick. Checking his pocket for his lighter, Yushkov leaves the van and opens the back of the air-conditioning unit. He lights the wick, checks it's burning, then shuts the door so that pumps and stink bomb are hidden. He gets back in the van and drives further along the rear of the hotel until they are directly beneath room 204: Sinclair's room. They both get out and light up. A casual smoke break.

'Don't drop the vial,' he jokes. 'I don't want my legs falling off. I need them.'

At the second-floor window, she spies Sinclair's nervous face. She catches his eye and he drops his chin once.

'Hey! You two! What're you doing?' calls one of two uniformed officers just turning a corner.

Toby disappears from view.

'Just having a smoke, mate. Been a busy morning,' Wolfe calls out.

Yushkov leans nonchalantly against the side of the van, head down. The officer doing the talking is in his thirties and his sidekick looks as if he's still in training.

'Look, normally, we wouldn't care. But today we need the car park clear of all vehicles.'

He glances at her cigarette. Wolfe looks down at his hands and sees nicotine stains. 'Like one?' She offers him the packet.

'I'm on duty.'

'Can I just finish this?'

They're interrupted by a voice through his Airwave, ordering an evacuation.

'Get moving, will you? Possible gas leak,' the officer says, as he and his young mate run off.

As soon as they have gone, the curtain twitches and a flushed-faced Toby slides open the window. His eyes dart from her face to the length of the car park and back again. Wolfe stands directly beneath his outstretched arm and gives her undivided attention to the test tube in his trembling hand. He screws his face up and coughs at the sulphur fumes. The vial of flesh-eating bacteria jolts, almost giving Wolfe a heart attack.

'I'm ready,' she calls.

But he doesn't release it. He's frozen.

'Just let go,' she encourages.

Toby looks down at her and shakes his head. He slides the window shut and moves out of view.

Panic rising, Wolfe shoots a look at Yushkov, but he's fixated on another window, two rooms along. Through his window, Heatherton stares straight at her. No, not at her, *through* her. He's not calling for an officer. He's not scrambling to evacuate his room. He's still. Wolfe recognises that look: empty, hopeless eyes, slumped shoulders. She's seen the same expression on civilians brutalised by war, who think there is no end to the atrocities. It's utter despair. She wants to tell the once-proud Dr Heatherton that it will be all right, but Yushkov drags her away.

'We go.'

Wolfe resists. She can't take her eyes off Heatherton, who rolls up his sleeve and then plunges a syringe into his vein. Wolfe cries out a stifled, 'Don't!' but it's too late. Heatherton screws up his face in sudden agony. He starts to shake and falls to his knees, his forehead slamming against the windowpane. He looks at her and opens his mouth, as if trying to speak. His spittle bubbles, then slides down the glass. Heatherton collapses out of sight.

Wolfe rips Yushkov's hand away. 'We have to help him.'

'It's too late. He knows what he's doing.'

Yushkov tugs a struggling Wolfe to the van, shoves her into the passenger seat and drives off at a measured pace so as not to draw attention.

'What's he doing?' says Yushkov, frowning into his rear-view mirror.

Wolfe peers round and sees Sinclair fleeing down the fire exit steps and heading for the neighbouring field.

'He's running! Turn back.'

'Get down!' yells Yushkov, swerving.

Armed officers open fire. A bullet hits the front bumper, another tears through the side of the van, slamming somewhere into the plumbing gear stacked on shelves in the back. Bullets pepper the tarmac. They're aiming for the tyres. Yushkov accelerates into the road, narrowly missing a Renault Clio. The driver honks. More gunfire. Yushkov floors the accelerator as he weaves in and out of the oncoming traffic. It doesn't take long for a white, unmarked BMW 330d Interceptor to come tearing after them.

'They'll catch us. We don't have the speed,' Wolfe says.

Yushkov's eyes dart from the rear-view mirror to the road ahead. The BMW swerves into oncoming traffic, its siren blaring and lights flashing, to overtake a lorry labouring under a load of steel beams, narrowly missing a woman and her two children in a silver Peugeot 308. The road is long and straight with grassy verges and barren hedges on their side. The BMW is specifically configured for high-speed pursuits. The heavily loaded van rolls around like a boat.

They approach a crossroads.

'Take a right here!' shouts Wolfe.

'Sure?'

'Yes!'

Yushkov yanks the steering wheel to the right at the last moment and the van takes the turn on two wheels. Wolfe is convinced they'll tip over, but Yushkov manages to keep control. Loose tools and PVC pipe offcuts fly around the back of the van. The BMW misses the crossroads and has to do a U-turn in a cloud of blue-grey tyre smoke. Yushkov and Wolfe hurtle down the single-track lane surrounded by high grassy banks. If they meet a car coming the other way, they will collide. The van bounces and sways as the road meanders downhill. Wolfe looks to her left and sees a railway track that crosses the road at the bottom of the hill and a freight train on a collision course with them.

They race through Westbury village. Signs tell them, in vain, to drive carefully. Behind them, the police siren gets louder. The village is little more than a few houses, a pub and a railway crossing. No barriers or train station. Amber lights start flashing and a warning bell sounds.

'Pull up on the line but keep the engine running,' says Wolfe.

'Are you crazy?' demands Yushkov.

'The driver will slam on the brakes. Just when it's about to hit us, drive off. It can't stop immediately. It'll block the road.'

Yushkov shakes his head.

'What? You never played chicken as a kid?'

'You are craziest woman I ever met.'

He slows the van as they approach the crossing. Wolfe looks to her left. The train is hurtling towards them. It sounds a horn. Yushkov stops the van in the middle of the track but keeps the engine idling.

'If she stalls, we are dead,' says Yushkov.

The train keeps coming. The horn screams, louder and repeatedly, then brakes screech. Wolfe sees the driver in his cabin, mouth open, horrified. Yushkov revs the van's engine.

'Not yet,' says Wolfe.

Sparks shoot out from the train's wheels, metal screeches in protest, there is a deafening gushing sound as the braking system dumps air, and the stink of diesel exhaust almost makes Wolfe gag.

'Now!' she yells, and Yushkov accelerates.

The van leaps forward and the train misses smashing into them by a matter of feet. The locomotive comes to a halt six or seven wagons later, completely blocking the road. 'They'll radio for help. We have to dump this van,' says Yushkov, his accelerator foot on the floor.

More sirens, from all directions. They pass a stand of beech trees on the right and a farmhouse. No opportunity to hide the van: the farmer is in the yard.

'We split up. They search for a man and woman together,' Yushkov says.

They stop at a T-junction to a main road. A sign indicates Salisbury is to the left and London to the right. Yushkov hesitates.

'Go to London,' says Wolfe. 'We can hide at my grandma's old bungalow. The Excalibur Estate in Dulwich Hill.'

'Why there?' Yushkov looks to his left, Salisbury way.

'It's a village of prefabricated houses earmarked for demolition. Almost everyone's left, so there are streets of empty houses.'

'Which house?'

'Two, Mordrid Street.'

The question is unnecessary if they stick together.

'Don't even think about Porton Down. They'll shoot you on sight.'

'I have nothing to give SVR. Renata will die.'

Yushkov stares at the sign, gripping the steering wheel so tightly his knuckles are white. A driver behind them honks in frustration.

'Please, Vitaly! We'll find another way.'

Yushkov slams the steering wheel with both palms. 'I have to give them something. She dies tomorrow.'

'You can't help her if you're dead.'

Traffic is building up behind them. More drivers sound their horns. Wolfe glances back, frantic.

Yushkov takes the right turn to London. Police sirens are louder and closer.

'Look!' says Wolfe, into the sky.

In the far distance, a police helicopter bears down on them.

They approach the village of Boreham Woods. Outside the village shop is a delivery truck. The man unloading from the back lifts a box on to a hand trolley and wheels it into the shop.

'We dump this van and hide in that truck,' says Wolfe.

Further up the street is Holy Trinity Church, a Norman building with a bell tower and a small car park surrounded by conifers. 'In there!' she says.

'You get out here,' says Yushkov. 'I'll hide it.'

He pulls in to the side of the road.

'You won't make it in time.'

'I will. Go!'

Wolfe jumps out of the van, throws her pack over her shoulder and runs across the road to the parked delivery truck. Yushkov starts up the hill. She checks nobody is looking, then crawls into the back of the truck. Only a few boxes remain and she hides behind them, listening for the sound of Yushkov's footsteps. The sirens are deafening. Tyres screech, doors slam, people shout.

'What's going on up there?' a man says. Wolfe catches a glimpse of the delivery man through the open door.

'Oh my goodness,' says a woman. 'They've got guns.'

'Hands above your head!' someone yells.

Wolfe creeps forward so she can see better. The U–Bend Plumbing van is in the middle of the road, engine running, door flung open, and Yushkov stands with his hands above his head. Two armed officers have guns trained on him. Police cars block either end of the street.

'Kneel!'

Yushkov hasn't even attempted to hide the van. He has surrendered.

59

At Heathrow's Terminal Three, the man behind the destruction of the *Queen Elizabeth* sips a weak tea in a takeaway cup as he reads the front page of the *Post*. He stares at the image of the sinking aircraft carrier engulfed in flame; death toll 142. So be it. All his life he has felt powerless, struggling to be taken seriously. Only his wife believed in him. Now even the unflappable Royal Navy is in turmoil. The exhilaration of revenge is like fire in his veins.

But his aim is to save civilisation, not destroy it. Politics is broken, protest useless. He has exhausted all other avenues. It's time to move on to bigger targets. Then, finally, they will have to listen. The only way is to disable the war machine, to force a halt to the billions upon billions wasted on finding increasingly efficient and more horrific methods to kill.

He glances at the carry-on bag at his feet. Inside is more than enough Psychosillius. He's developed his own mutation. Stronger. Faster. And he's found a way to fool airport security.

On page four he reads of Yushkov's capture. He feels sorry for Vitaly. A man, like himself, who never fitted in. His 'accomplice', Olivia Wolfe, is still on the run. She's too smart to get caught and he knows it won't be long before she works out who he is and what he plans to do.

He's banking on it.

His flight is called. He stands in line, ticket and passport in hand. He shows both to a smiling female flight attendant and boards the plane.

60

Dulwich Hill, South London

The café in Dulwich Hill is popular with cabbies and clubbers and is open all night. Wolfe sits at the back, making her meal last as long as possible before she makes her way to her grandmother's derelict bungalow. It's warm inside, the tea's hot and there is a television. The volume is turned up loud so Dot, the café owner, can keep abreast of the latest news on the sinking of the UK's largest warship.

Dot shakes her head. 'Those poor lads. And the humiliation. First frigging trip! We look like right pillocks!'

Dot slaps the counter with a tea towel.

On screen are re-runs of HMS *Queen Elizabeth*'s grand departure from Portsmouth Harbour, escorted by a flotilla of boats and pleasure craft, a brass band parading up and down the quay as families and well-wishers wave Union Jacks.

'It didn't sink though, did it?' says a cabbie, who's just finished his plate of sausage, beans and chips, his black cab parked outside. 'They bombed it. Now what did they go and do that for, hey?' He taps his nose conspiratorially. 'Something's just not right.'

Wolfe can tell the TV commentators are getting stone-walled by the Royal Navy and the Ministry of Defence, because the same old theories are running on a loop – anything from a Russian submarine torpedoing the pride of the Royal Navy to an Islamic State terror plot involving some kind of biological weapon. She finds it hard to believe the Russians would act in such a nakedly aggressive way. If Isil has committed an act of bioterrorism, then the already febrile Middle East might explode into full-blown conflict. Either way, the attack is an act of war, and Wolfe's stomach knots as she imagines the consequences.

'It's a plague ship, that's what it is,' an old bloke in the corner pipes up. 'Germ warfare.'

Wolfe glances at the old fellow and guesses he is probably at least partly right. She's convinced somebody has used Psychosillius, but as she doesn't know how it affects people, her guess is as good as his. She is sure of one thing, though. This attack is just the beginning. Who or what is next?

Counter Terrorism Command, MI5 and MI6 have failed to stop this plot, and Casburn is at the centre of it all. He will be furious. Humiliated. Desperate. Unless he captures who did this, he will likely serve out the end of his career in the most godforsaken shithole the British Government can find.

God help the person Casburn believes responsible.

61

Yushkov tastes the blood in his mouth and feels the sting of his smashed lip. But he doesn't spit out the blood. Instead he sucks on the wound, creating a ball of rusty-tasting saliva, so desperate is he for something to drink. Since his capture, he has been hooded, driven to a location he estimates is some two hours from Porton Down, hands and feet bound to a metal chair that's welded to a thick metal sheet, which in turn is screwed into the concrete floor of an abandoned warehouse. When his hood was removed, the brightness of the four powerful pedestal lights, angled so they seared his eyes, made it impossible to see his interrogators. This place had been prepared for him.

The last time he'd been interrogated, he'd been in a sterile white box of a room, subjected to sleep deprivation and inter-mittent blasts of hot and cold air, but the 'little chat' had been terribly British. Civilised even. Casburn had played the nice guy, Flynn the threatening one. When the good cop, bad cop routine failed, they'd threatened to revoke his British citizenship, to give him back to the Russian military. When this failed, Flynn lost control, giving Yushkov a solid punch or two to his stomach. Yushkov had kept his cool. Nothing they did surprised him. He had survived far worse.

But this is different. The balance of power has shifted to Flynn and MI5. Casburn is little more than a spectator. There are no video cameras or voice recorders. His interrogation never happened and he does not exist. The stench of desperation oozes from their pores and drips on to his face as they lean over him, trying to intimidate. They attempt to hide their alarm, but Yushkov knows something bad has happened. It is Yushkov's silence that's led Flynn to violence, pulverising his captive's body like steak with a tenderising hammer. The agent is all muscle and knows where to land his blows for maximum effect. Yushkov's left eye is so swollen, it has closed up. Breathing is difficult, his ribs almost certainly broken. The drug – probably sodium amytal or sodium pentothal – keeps his vision blurry and his head lolls like a newborn's. At least it dulls some of the pain.

Flynn and Casburn leave, but somebody watches him, hiding in the darkness behind the floor lamps. How many hours has he been here? There is no clock. He's begged them to tell him the time but Flynn uses it as a bargaining chip, demanding he gives them something useful, before they give him what he wants. When they leave for a break, Yushkov looks up at a shattered skylight and thinks he can discern a purple tinge to the night sky. If it's dawn, Renata doesn't have long to live. At 08.16 the SVR will kill her. Why won't Flynn listen?

Yushkov is sweating profusely, his T-shirt and jeans soaked, thanks to the drugs and the intense heat from the lamps. They are deliberately cooking him. Dehydration, lack of sleep and the drugs make it hard to think.

Yushkov tries to wriggle his wrists free of the handcuffs, hoping the blood from his lacerations will lubricate his skin. He's already dislocated one thumb, but the cuffs' grip is vice-like. He throws his head back and roars in frustration, then coughs as he nearly chokes on his own blood.

'Casburn! I will tell you something. Casburn!'

Olivia has a connection with Casburn. Yushkov is more likely to convince him than Flynn.

Shoes on concrete, glass snapping underfoot. Then chewing. That eternal chewing. Casburn's face appears. Grey eyes, hard as granite. A crew-cut. He's got to be ex-military.

'This better be good, Vitaly, cause we were having a coffee break.'

Yushkov blinks his one good eye, as sweat drips down his temples.

'You save Renata. She is innocent. Contact SVR. Please. Buy her some time.' His words are slurred. His mouth isn't co-operating with his brain.

Casburn stops gnawing on his Nicorette gum and sighs. 'With what? You've gotta give me something.'

'I arrange meet with Sergey Grankin. Pretend I have what he wants. You capture SVR agent. You get answers to your questions. You tell SVR, if they want him back, they give you Renata.'

'Fuck this!' Flynn says, throwing his arms up in exasperation.

Casburn tries to keep his voice calm. 'We've been through this, Vitaly. We thought the Russians had the canister. Now we know they don't. So I don't give a shit about Grankin. Tell me who you gave it to?'

'I never had the canister.'

'Christ! While you sit here feeding us lies, a hundred and forty-two people have died. Look!'

He holds up a photo of a sinking ship. Yushkov squints, trying to focus. Casburn continues. 'The bacteria you stole was released on board a Royal Navy aircraft carrier. Who did this, Vitaly? Who was the buyer?'

'I did not steal it.' Yushkov tries shaking his head but everything spins. What did Olivia say when she was reading the files? 'Harvey was Russian asset—'

'We know. He tried and failed to get it.'

Yushkov is grasping at straws. 'Bruce Adeyemi gambles. Money problems—'

Flynn slams a punch into Yushkov's jaw. 'What is the next target?'

Yushkov spits out blood. 'I do not know. I will do anything, anything you ask to save my sister, but I cannot tell you what I do not know.'

'Tell me about Kabir Khan,' Flynn demands.

'I do not know this man.'

'Liar! March 2000, Afghanistan, before you murdered your commanding officer.'

Yushkov swallows. He daren't look up in case Flynn sees his rising panic. It was a black operation.

'You were sent to assassinate a Taliban leader named Fazi. You slaughtered a whole village.'

'No, no. Captain Razin did this. I try to stop him.' His head bobs weakly.

'You run. A boy helps you. Hides you from the Taliban.'

Yushkov squints at Flynn in disbelief. 'How do you know this?'

'Who was the boy?'

'The boy? I don't understand—'

318

'His name!'

'Gull Zaman.'

Flynn glances at Casburn and runs his tongue over his dry lips.

'Why did he help you?'

'Because I tried to stop Razin butchering his village. He led me to safety. Hid me. His uncle dug out the bullet in my shoulder. Gull Zaman helped me cross the border into Pakistan.'

'And in return for his help?'

'Nothing. He showed compassion.'

'Compassion!' Flynn scoffs. 'This man is Isil. He doesn't know the meaning of the word. He's behind the attack on the aircraft carrier. He's going to kill again—'

'No. He's a good man. He is shopkeeper in Hounslow. He came here as refugee.'

'Did you train with him in Pakistan?'

'No.'

'Your mate Gull Zaman did. He came to this country as part of a sleeper cell.'

'You lie.' A sudden surge of energy fuels Yushkov's outburst.

'He was radicalised.'

'No!'

Casburn is suddenly in his face. 'Recognise him?'

He holds a photo of a bearded man in his late twenties in traditional Pashtun dress, outside a London mosque.

'It is Gull Zaman.'

Flynn grips Yushkov's face, shaking him. 'Liar! That's Kabir Khan. But you know that, don't you?'

62

Yushkov squints at the photo Casburn holds up. 'I tell you, this is Gull Zaman.'

'When did you last meet him or his associates?' Flynn demands, tightening his grip on Yushkov's jaw.

Yushkov knows where this line of questioning is going and he sees the train-wreck that is his life finally coming to an end.

'A few days ago. I buy a pistol.'

'Truth at last!' Flynn says, releasing his hold on Yushkov's face. 'He sold you an illegal firearm.'

'Yes.'

'And why would a shopkeeper sell you a gun?'

'People want him dead. He is protecting his family.'

Casburn holds up a photo of Yushkov sitting next to a young Middle Eastern man at a café. In exchange for the Glock 19, Yushkov handed him four hundred pounds in cash. 'This man you're with,' Casburn says, 'is Samad Sayyaf. He is part of Kabir Khan's terror cell.'

'I did not know this. I bought a gun for protection. That is all.'

Yushkov knows his protestations are useless. They have evidence linking him to a man they claim is an Isil terrorist. But he may still be able to free his sister. 'What do you want? I will do it. Anything. Just save Renata.'

'Kabir Khan has disappeared. Tell us where he is and we talk to the Russians about Renata.'

Despairing, Yushkov slumps forward as far as his bound hands will allow. 'I meet him once at his shop, and another time at his house for a meal. That is all I know.'

'Then we've no reason to help your sister.' Flynn makes a show of looking at his wristwatch. 'Oh dear. It's seven fifty. How long has she got?'

'Help her, please,' Yushkov pleads.

'How fucking long?' Flynn yells in his face.

Yushkov wants to rip his head off. 'They kill her in twenty-six minutes. *Please*! Let me go. I will find Gull Zaman for you, just don't let her die.'

Yushkov has never begged for anything, but now he would gladly get on his knees, if he believed it could make a difference. They walk away.

Yushkov yanks at his restraints. 'Help her! *Please*!'

Flynn's face appears like an apparition; his arrogant smirk, dark hair and stubble remind Yushkov of the commanding officer he shot in Afghanistan. Flynn tilts his head as if inspecting a particularly fascinating corpse. 'Think they'll fuck her before they snuff her?'

Yushkov lunges forward and manages to head-butt Flynn's nose. There's a snap as a bone breaks and Flynn leaps back, covering his face.

'Fuck you!' Yushkov yells.

'He broke my fucking nose!' says Flynn, blood pouring down his lip.

'Help my sister!' Yushkov shouts.

'Give him some more,' barks Flynn.

Somebody appears with a syringe. Flynn points a Taser at his chest. 'Stay still,' Flynn orders.

'He's had enough,' says Casburn.

'I have command here. If you don't like my methods – leave.'

Casburn hesitates and walks away.

The cold liquid enters Yushkov's veins and he almost blacks out. Flynn slaps his face and jerks his chin up.

'What is Khan's next target?'

Yushkov is lost in darkness. His jaw slackens. A bloody dribble slips from his mouth and lands on Flynn's hand. Flynn ignores it, pinching his face harder. He repeats the question, yelling into Yushkov's face.

'Don't . . . know,' Yushkov mumbles.

'Where is he hiding?'

'Don't . . . '

'Where is Olivia Wolfe?'

Flynn shoves his watch in Yushkov's face. 'You've got six minutes.'

He cannot tell them about Khan because he has no idea where he is. And Olivia has lost everything because of him: her job, her friends, her reputation. She is despised, tainted by her link, through him, to terrorism.

Casburn appears from nowhere.

'Look at me!' he says. 'Tell us where Olivia Wolfe is hiding, and I'll call my SVR contact.'

Yushkov barely hears him. Must he betray the woman who is so much more than a lover to save his sister? There has to be a way to keep both women safe. There has to be.

Somebody is shaking him, calling his name. The room is moving, the walls swaying. He's desperate to sleep. He drops in and out of consciousness.

'You gave him too much, you fucking idiot!' Flynn shouts at someone. He slaps Yushkov across his face. 'Hey! Four minutes left, then Renata dies. Where is Olivia? Tell me.' Flynn turns away. 'Thought this stuff could make a buffalo sing. Why doesn't it work?'

Yushkov doesn't hear the reply.

'Olivia?' he mumbles.

'That's it,' says Casburn. 'Where is Olivia Wolfe? She's in danger. Tell me where she's gone?'

Yushkov can barely move his lips, his tongue like lead. He tells Casburn her location, unaware he has done it.

'Right, I want everything we've got at the Excalibur Estate. Now!' says Flynn. 'This cunt may not talk, but she will.'

Yushkov hears a brief argument but not the words. Casburn and Flynn. Somebody leaves in a hurry. Yushkov blacks out.

He comes round suddenly; a bucket of freezing water has been flung over him. He pants and gasps in shock. Flynn grins, dried blood caked to his nostrils.

'Thought you might like to see this,' he says, holding up Yushkov's mobile phone.

Yushkov blinks water away and cranes his head forwards, trying to focus on the tiny screen.

'Your SVR mates sent you a message.'

The video begins. Renata is tied to the same bed, her stare empty as tears trickle down her filthy face. She whimpers, her mouth taped.

'No!' shouts Yushkov, straining against his handcuffs, jaw clenched, every muscle in his body tensed.

A masked man steps in front of the camera. Holding a GSh-18, a semi-automatic pistol. Yushkov knows it well. Used by the Russian military, he is well aware what it will do to somebody if fired at close range.

'I tell you, Vitaly, you could have saved her. But you failed. You failed your only living relative.' He shrugs, lifting his hands and waving the pistol around.

The masked assassin sits next to the woman writhing on the bed, her eyes wide with terror. He rips off the tape from her mouth and forces the gun between her teeth. 'And now? You are alone.'

The gun fires, the report so loud, so shocking, that Flynn jolts the phone, almost dropping it, even though he has seen the video before. Yushkov's heart feels as if it has been ripped from his chest. He opens his mouth but he can't speak. Her blood and brain matter is splattered over the wall behind the bedpost. The killer gets up, his white shirt speckled crimson. The camera zooms in on Renata's face, her mouth still open. The back of her head has been blown apart and blood spreads out like a red halo over her grimy pillow. The video cuts to black.

For the first time since he was a very young child, Yushkov sobs, his chest heaving.

But there is a second video, taken at a different location.

Sergey Grankin is looking sombre, hands clasped together as if to deliver a eulogy. The camera angle is tight but damask wallpaper and heavy curtains and a delicate floral-pattern teacup on a tray are in view, the room very British. He peers into the lens.

'Yushkov, you have betrayed your country. Again. I missed my mark in Cambridge. I won't make that mistake twice.'

63

Wolfe hides inside the porch of St Mark's church, the only building on the twelve-acre Excalibur Estate exempt from demolition. She's watching her grandmother's empty bungalow, a two-bedroom, single-storey prefabricated shoebox, only differentiated from the other houses by the paint colour and the contents of the now overgrown garden.

Wolfe remembers her grandma Mary as a hard-bitten woman with a sharp nose and even sharper tongue, who offered no sympathy for her daughter, Wolfe's mother, when Wolfe's dad walked out on them. Mary saw depression as an indulgence of the upper classes, and the only piece of solace she could come up with was to tell Catherine to 'snap out of it.'

The dawn light is enough for Wolfe to see the faded yellow exterior, now stained with mould. The chain-link fence is torn and the wooden gate hangs off its hinges at a forty-five-degree angle. She stares at the 'Asbestos, Keep Out' sign; at the steel mesh rectangles that cover every window and exterior door. All the abandoned houses in Mordrid Street are secured the same way. No matter. She knows a way in.

All night she's thought about Yushkov, wondering where they've taken him and what they're doing to him. He's suspected of stealing a deadly pathogen that has been used in a terrorist attack. She imagines him bound and beaten, subjected to who-knows-what torture. She rubs her temples, willing the thoughts away.

'Why let them take you?' she says aloud.

But she knows the answer. Yushkov imagines Casburn will trade him to the Russians in exchange for Renata's freedom. But Wolfe knows Casburn too well. If Yushkov cannot give Casburn the one thing he really wants — the person with the missing canister — he will not save Renata. Yushkov will be 'disappeared'. He has sacrificed himself for nothing.

Wolfe has spent much of her life working and surviving alone, relying on her wits to get out of danger, but now the weight of her isolation is crushing. For the first time in her life, she can barely function. Her interminable journey to this dump, the torturously slow trains, relying on her hoodie to conceal her face, furtively dodging security cameras and avoiding eye contact, made her feel like the criminal she is accused of being.

The site has streetlights, but there is no power to the empty bungalows. A security guard drives around every few hours. A crack of a twig or a fox's scream sends her heart racing, convinced the hunt is over and the police have found her. She told Yushkov where she would be. He will eventually tell them. A man can only endure so much pain.

But she can think of nowhere else to go.

Checking her watch, she bows her head. Renata is dead and, even though Wolfe is not a religious person, she says a prayer for her. With a heavy heart Wolfe darts across the road, down the side passage and into her grandmother's tangled back garden. The roses have grown into crazy stick people and brambles engulf the back fence. Behind the fence is a row of Sitka spruces that block the sunrise. An A-frame swing, rusted, the seat broken, still stands in one corner. She remembers as a little girl calling to her brother, 'Higher!' as she swung through the air.

The house is raised a foot off the ground by breezeblocks. She lies on her back in the dirt and scrambles under the narrow space between gravel and floorboards, dragging her backpack with her. She finds the hatch she's looking for and hopes nobody has thought to seal it. Gas pipes, now disconnected, run under the floor and into the sitting room, where Mary had a gas fire installed. Wolfe pushes upwards against the small door but it doesn't budge. She thumps at the cut lines with the flats of her hands until she finally loosens the seal formed by age, dust and damp. But a rug stops the door from opening fully. She takes a penknife from her pack, opens the longest blade and saws through the rug. Dust and tufts of hessian fall on her face. She coughs and keeps going until the hatch opens enough for her to squeeze through.

The sitting room has no furniture. Wolfe runs her torch beam over the mildewed peach wallpaper and the grimy lace curtains. She slides her back down the wall and sits, her knees bunched up under her chin, running her fingers over the old rug beneath her. She wants to hear Cohen tell her she's a fucking idiot but he'll get his lawyers to sort things out. She wants to hear Butcher tell her to believe in herself, that he'll talk to his mates in the Met and make sure she gets a fair hearing. She wants to hear Daisy's Irish rebelliousness as she tells her to 'Fuck the lot of them!' Most of all she wants to have Yushkov next to her and see his wry smile. She wants him and her life back. And the only way that can happen is to find whoever stole the Psychosillius sample. Apart from a few bank statements that suggest Bruce Adeyemi has gambling debts, she has run out of ideas.

Wolfe curls up on the musty rug, her face not far from a skirting board. She has come full circle, back to the house Social Services insisted she move to when her mother died. She falls into a fitful sleep. In her dreams, faces come and go. She is in the mess tent at Lake Ellsworth, toasting those brave enough to speak the truth. She is thinking of Nooria.

'Sometimes the price is too high, I think,' Yushkov says in a hushed tone. 'Sometimes it is best to walk away.'

Now she is with Trent Rundle in his tractor, crossing the Ellsworth Mountains, listening to his incessant chatter; now she's watching Yushkov expertly handle the hot water drill; now she's in the mess tent, surprised by Sinclair's outburst about the innocent casualties of war.

'Nobody cares, Olivia. What do the military call the women and children killed by drones? Collateral damage. How very compassionate.'

Wolfe opens her eyes and sits up, wide awake. She dives for her backpack and pulls out the printouts in such haste she rips some of the pages, flicking through them, discarding the ones she doesn't want. She opens Toby Sinclair's file and searches for the death certificates. Wolfe finds them in Heatherton's file, crammed there when they left the Porton Arms in a hurry. The death certificates are for Huma Sinclair, aged thirty-four, Sally Sinclair, aged eleven, and Ben Sinclair, aged nine. They all died on the same day, two years ago, in Kandahar, Afghanistan.

She skim-reads a press clipping from the obituaries in *The Scotsman*. Huma Sinclair arrived in the UK when she was seven, with her family, as refugees. Her father was a teacher. His school had been burned down by the Taliban and he'd been almost beaten to death for trying to give girls an education. The family settled in the southern Glasgow district of Govanhill. She studied Medicine at Edinburgh University, met and married Toby Sinclair and became a family GP. They had two children. Huma had returned to Kandahar several times as a volunteer despite death threats. Two years ago she took the children with her, keen for them to meet her family. Toby was meant to accompany them, but could not because of his work. Huma and the children had been in Kandahar for a week when a US drone destroyed the house they were in and four surrounding buildings. The official statement claimed they were harbouring Taliban fighters, which neighbours and surviving family denied.

She reads a quote from Toby.

'I have died with them. I will never see my children grow up, never hear their laughter again or tuck them into bed at night. My wife was a beautiful, kind, giving person who died needlessly, trying to help the poor and sick in Kandahar. She wanted to inspire women there and encourage female education. She hated what the Taliban was doing and she would never have harboured terrorists. The Americans won't admit they made a terrible mistake. They murdered my wife and children and I want them held accountable.'

64

Dr Stacy Price and Professor Gary Matthews are escorted down the narrow corridor of the Biomedical Sciences Department by two soldiers whose job it is to protect Porton Down and its lethal pathogens confined within. Wall-mounted cameras monitor every corridor and inside every lab.

'I'm worried about Toby,' Price says to Matthews.

Matthews places a reassuring hand on her shoulder. 'They'll find him.'

Price looks up at her much-taller colleague. 'You don't think he'd, you know, commit suicide like Michael?'

'He'll be okay, Stacy.'

They turn a corner. Ahead is a hermetically sealed steel door with one circular window. On the door a sign says Caution! Authorised Personnel Only. BSL-4. Beyond that door is a changing room and shower facility where they will don their positive pressure personnel suits, affectionately known as 'space suits', with breathing apparatus. They must then pass through another hermetically sealed door, a vacuum room, and an ultraviolet light room before finally entering the lab currently dedicated to finding a way to kill Psychosillius. The doors are synchronised so that, if one is open, the other stays closed, like an airlock on a spaceship.

Off other corridors, similar high-containment labs hold stocks of drug-resistant tuberculosis, exotic strains of flu, the SARS and MERS viruses, plague, anthrax, botulism, ricin and the Ebola, Marburg and other haemorrhagic fever viruses. Deliberately infected animals ranging from mice to monkeys, in cages, are on the floor below, and, below that, the huge steel vats of the effluent decontamination and self-contained waste disposal system.

Dr Price and Professor Matthews are early, the first to arrive. They are ten feet from the first door to their lab when Price stops so suddenly, the soldier behind ploughs into her.

'What's that?' Price asks.

The mid-section of the door looks as if it has been in a fire, the steel charred.

Matthews peers over the top of his bifocals. 'It can't be, can it?'

'What's wrong?' asks the senior ranking soldier.

Price swallows hard. 'A possible leak. Stay where you are.'

Price edges closer, followed by Matthews. The steel has blistered, as if it were suffering from smallpox, and through a three-centimetre hole they can see into the room beyond.

Price's hand whips up to her mouth as she gasps.

Matthews swivels round to the nearest soldier. 'Alert security. Psychosillius is no longer contained. Every lab in this facility is threatened.'

The soldier responds by smashing the glass wall-mounted box and presses a red button as the other soldier uses his two-way radio to alert his commander.

Security roller doors above the main entrance and exit to the building slam to the ground. They cannot leave. Claxons wail all over the seven thousand-acre site. At the perimeter fence, red lights flash. All hell breaks loose.

The Secretary of State for Defence, Harold Brennan, taps his pen on his green gilded leather desk blotter as he contemplates his impending meeting with the PM regarding the sinking of the *Queen Elizabeth*, and how in God's name it was allowed to happen.

There's a knock at the door and the Permanent Under Secretary, Jillian Warwick, pokes her head round the door.

'Apologies, sir. There's a problem at Porton Down.'

Forty-year-old Warwick is built like a tank and isn't the slightest bit fazed by Brennan's scowl.

'Very well. Come in and shut the door.' Warwick does as she's asked. 'Well?'

'Psychosillius is no longer contained. It's eaten through a BSL-4 lab door. The site is in lockdown, but it can't be secured. Doors, fences, even CCTV cameras are corroding.'

Brennan stares at her. 'And? The pathogens? Are they secure?'

Warwick shakes her head. 'Afraid not, sir. The glass and sealants will remain intact, but anything steel is collapsing – biolab doors, storage canisters, even the air filtration and effluent systems.'

'Jesus!' says Brennan. 'I'll get on to Thorneycroft. You contact every BSL-4 lab in the UK. Find out what they can take from Porton Down. But keep this under wraps. If it gets out, we'll have a nationwide panic.'

'I think that's going to be hard to avoid, sir.'

'And convene COBRA.'

'Yes, sir.' Warwick races from the room.

Brennan picks up the phone and uses a secure line to dial General Sir Charles Thorneycroft, the Chief of the Defence Staff and head of the British Armed Forces.

'Charles,' says Brennan, 'We have a national security issue.'

65

There can't be a man, woman or child in this country who doesn't know your face and yet you have disappeared. Not even I can find my little robin. All night I've been at my computer, scanning news bulletins, listening to police radio.

Distant acquaintances and even so-called friends are falling over themselves to do the 'I knew her when . . . ' and the 'I always knew she was a bad one . . . ' interviews, supplying the worst photos of you they can find. There's a hideous one of you as an angry teenager. If this ever gets to court, they're going to have to empanel a jury of people who've been living under a rock. Good luck with that.

'We have breaking news,' says a TV reporter. 'Armed police have surrounded a derelict house on the Excalibur Estate in Dulwich Hill. Fugitive Olivia Wolfe is believed to be hiding there.'

I catch my breath and lean closer to my monitor. Armed officers in bulletproof vests carrying semi-automatic carbines. Tangled garden. House all boarded up. I inhale, imagining I can smell the damp and see the broken tiles and peeling wallpaper, and you hiding inside.

A memory goes off in my head like a mortar round, splattering primary colours across my vision. I blink rapidly, and grip the desk, battling dizziness.

I have my hand on your shoulder, as you sit at your laptop. I don't know where we are; the room is unfamiliar. A hotel room. Outside, there's shouting in the street and car horns honk and the air is thick with dust. Suddenly I know I'm in Mosul. Before we ran for our lives. Before the grenade attack.

'You're good at this stuff,' you say, looking up at me. Your hair is shorter – a pixie cut. How I prefer it. 'Please, just take a look. It's running so slow.'

I'm going to be late. For what, I can't remember. But I nod and we swap seats and I catch a glimpse of myself in the mirror. I am whole. No scarring. My long blonde hair falls over my shoulders. I have make-up on, the lipstick a pale plum: I've just recorded a news update for CNN. Our eyes meet and you smile at me in the reflection.

'I'll miss you,' I say.

You don't know how difficult that was to say. You're not listening.

You peer at the small screen over my shoulder, pointing at something, your cheek close to mine. I turn my head and kiss your translucent skin. You pull away as if I've given you an electric shock, rubbing your cheek, shock in the O of your perfect lips. It was then I knew you would never love me the way I loved you.

Is it me, or because I'm a woman?

The memory evaporates like steam from a kettle.

My stomach heaves as if it is trying to vacate my body, to physically expel my humiliation. I collapse on to all fours and spew up last night's meal; then, when there is nothing left, a trickle of yellow bile.

If I can't have your love, no one can.

66

A voice from a police officer's Airwave tells Wolfe she has company. She reacts instinctively, cramming the papers into her bag and diving through the floor hatch. From beneath the bungalow, she peers out at the tangled rear garden. They haven't reached the back of the house yet, so she bolts for the spruce trees, clambering over the bramble-clad fence and into their welcoming darkness. Once through the closely planted trees, she's on a public footpath that runs between two rows of houses. She jumps over the next waist-high fence and yanks open a side door to the garage. There she finds her grandmother's Toyota Yaris; Mary's neighbours let her park it there and Wolfe has never got around to selling it.

Concealed inside a tin of rusting screws, old screwdrivers and secateurs is the car key. Wolfe opens the two wooden garage doors on to Guinevere Street, wincing at the squeak of a rusty hinge, then ducks into the driver's seat and turns the ignition. Nothing but a whine. She turns the key again. A sustained whine.

'Come on!' she breathes.

She pumps the accelerator. The engine coughs into life. Wolfe accelerates into Guinevere Street. The tyres drag, the pressure low. There is shouting. She's been spotted. Wolfe aims for an old picket fence that divides the estate from a park and rams it, denting Mary's pride and joy. The soft turf makes for hard going, but she hurtles across the open playing field, past a play area, and does a sharp turn on to a main road, the nose scraping the tarmac as she careens over the gutter. She hears sirens, but won't give up. Not now she has a purpose – she can save Yushkov and redeem herself. She knows who stole the missing canister. In a multi-storey car park she dumps the Yaris and steals a 2002 Honda Civic.

Wolfe doesn't stop until she reaches Toby Sinclair's house in Sturton Town on the outskirts of Cambridge. His Volvo XC90 is not there, nor is he answering his mobile. The house is an end terrace, tucked into a right-angle bend. Brick walls, tile roof with chimney, blue door, lace curtains: just an ordinary suburban home.

Wolfe rings the bell. Nobody comes to the door. She calls through the letterbox. Down a side passage she finds the back door, picks the lock and slips inside. In the sink are dirty dishes and there's a sour smell of rotten food coming from the bin.

'Toby? You home?'

It's colder inside than out; the heating has been off for a while. In the lounge room, Wolfe recognises the distinctive red octagonal elephant's-foot pattern of a rug made by the Afghani women of Bukhara. There's a pot-bellied stove in the chimney alcove, a white sofa with red cushions, red curtains, and wicker armchairs. Hanging from the length of the mantelpiece is a red ribbon, from which hangs a selection of bird feathers in black and brown, grey and white, russet and pale blue, in varying shapes and sizes, all sticky-taped by the quill to the ribbon. A child's handiwork.

Framed family photos adorn the mantelpiece; one she suspects was taken some time ago, of Sinclair's mum, dad and brother. She's struck by how alike the brothers look. Next to it is a photo taken on a narrowboat, presumably on the local Fens. The boat looks new, its blue paint glinting in the sun, the brass porthole and window frames polished to a high shine. Sally and Ben wear yellow life jackets. Behind them, Toby and Huma pose arm in arm. They are laughing. The smiling man in the photo is very different from the one she has met. It's not just that Sinclair is clean-shaven and slimmer, but he looks straight at the camera too. The Sinclair she knows avoids eye contact and camera lenses. Stuck into the back of the frame are two tiny blue and yellow feathers. Perhaps the kids loved collecting them?

With a sinking feeling, Wolfe remembers a solitary out-of-place feather stuck to the ice-cave wall at Camp Ellsworth, the first batch of samples destroyed. All bar one.

In the kitchen, Wolfe combs through drawers and a notepad by the fridge. She pokes her head into the downstairs bathroom and moves on. There's a door beneath the stairs she assumes leads to a storage cupboard, but discovers wooden steps leading to a basement. To her left is a circular Victorian light switch with a brass knob; she flicks it on and finds herself looking down into a state-of-the-art, pristine, fully equipped laboratory, with white walls and concrete floor.

'Toby? It's Olivia.'

She hesitates, then takes the creaky steps down to the surprisingly warm, windowless basement. She checks the door at the top of the stairs is still open. Cellars unnerve her. A portable hyperbaric chamber is set up on the floor: exactly what Sinclair would need to keep Psychosillius at the right pressure. She's drawn to a shelf of Petri dishes with lids taped on. Suspended from the shelf above are a tubular light and a wide silver reflector that focuses the hydroponic light down to the Petri dishes. It is on a timer and emanates considerable heat.

Each dish holds creamy blooms of bacteria. Some are in a clear solution. But in the dishes with labels there is additional matter. Those in the first row contain fragments of copper, iron ore, steel, aluminium, titanium, silver and other metals. In each dish, the fragment is clearly visible. Except for iron ore and steel. Inside these dishes, the bacteria have multiplied, filling the whole dish, the lids now opaque.

Wolfe checks the second row: these dishes contain pieces of concrete, brick, cement, wood and various glues and sealants, all still present inside the dishes. The third row of dishes holds a bizarre selection: a piece of plastic, a fragment of glass, a strip of latex, even a cigarette butt. The specimens that really disturb her are animal tissue, probably rat: skin, bone, muscle, various tiny organs, an eye, hair. Wolfe backs away and pulls on surgical gloves and face mask.

Humming away in a corner is an old, dented refrigerator. She opens the door slowly, nervous of its contents. The fridge light has been disabled; the specimens are in total darkness. On the first shelf, the Petri dishes contain tiny pieces of metal identical to those under the hydroponic lighting, except the metal samples are all intact, even the iron ore and steel. Wolfe works her way down the shelves, each set of dishes mirroring those she has just inspected under the lighting.

What concerns her most is the hundred-millilitre plastic sham-poo bottle with black plastic screw-top lying on the workbench near Sinclair's computer. It's the maximum size liquid container permitted on a commercial flight. Is an airport his next target?

With a shaking hand, Wolfe switches on Sinclair's computer. It's slow to respond.

'Come on.'

Wolfe's challenged for a password. Trying to guess it will waste precious time. Instead, she searches through a white filing cabinet for any hints on Sinclair's plans. All she finds are bank statements, bills and printouts from previous research projects. One project catches her eye because it relates to a ship: the *Titanic*. Sinclair was the scientist who identified the deep-sea bacteria eating away the remains of the *Titanic*. Stuck to the front page is a faded handwritten Post-it note:

'Don't work too late, my darling. Night night, Huma x'

Wolfe frowns. Did Sinclair steal the canister to exact revenge on those he feels responsible for the death of his wife and chil-dren? With renewed urgency, she yanks open the drawer under the workbench to find stationery, memory sticks, some mints and, right at the back, a curling Post-it note. On it is written 'Eisenhower1961'. The password? Why would someone with an almost photographic memory write it down? The handwrit-ing is identical to Huma's note. His wife needed to jot it down, not Sinclair.

The password is accepted.

Wolfe trawls through Sinclair's emails, skim-reading: spam, messages from friends, invitations to birthdays and Christmas parties, a message from his mum, Gladys, urging him to join them in Edinburgh for Christmas. His brother, Hector, and his family are flying in from Australia on Boxing Day. Sinclair hasn't replied.

One email exchange stands out. There is a brief note of condolence from someone calling himself Jock007, sent two years ago. Then no further communication until Sinclair contacts him from Lake Ellsworth. Sinclair says he's run down and needs a holiday, and when the project is over he'd like to visit Jock in Indian Springs, then spend a few days in Las Vegas. The email was sent the day after the canister was stolen. Jock replies with excitement.

> But I'm not single any more, mate, and would you
> believe we met at Creech? Louise works for the
> HMO – that's the Housing Management Office to you
> civilians. But if I can get time off to join you in Vegas,
> it'll be just us lads. What goes on tour, stays on tour.

Wolfe googles 'Creech Indian Springs'. She finds Creech Air Force Base: a United States Air Force command and control facility, home to the Hunters of the 432d Wing and 432d Air Expeditionary Wing. It is famed for the remote piloting of armed drones in countries such as Iraq and Afghanistan. Ground crews launch drones in the conflict zone, then their operation is handed over to controllers hundreds of miles away at Creech. It is also where the next generation of combat drones is tested.

'Oh shit!'

Sinclair's reply was sent yesterday from his smartphone:

> Boarding flight. See you soon, Toby.

Wolfe's mind is spinning. First Sinclair slips his protection detail. Then the sinking of a Royal Navy aircraft carrier. And now he's heading for the United States' control centre for overseas drone missions. She stares at the Petri dishes under the hydroponic light and the penny finally drops: Sinclair isn't releasing a pathogen to make people ill.

Wolfe stares at the dish marked 'steel': the steel has disappeared.

She looks around. Steel is everywhere. Skyscrapers, bridges, stadiums, airports, hospitals, cars, trucks, pipes, railway tracks, nails and screws. But Sinclair is targeting the military. Anything with steel in it: guns, bullets, knives, rocket launchers, rockets, tanks, bomb casings, submarines, ships, stealth bombers . . . and, of course, combat drones. All it takes is one tiny steel component.

Wolfe fumbles for her mobile but there's no signal in the basement. She copies Jock's cell number into her phone, then searches Sinclair's emails for flight information, boarding passes, anything that will tell her where and when he flew. She guesses Las Vegas, the nearest commercial airport to Indian Springs. She checks his browser history. Nothing except for Purple Parking at Heathrow Airport. But Heathrow is one of the largest and busiest airports in the world. She needs more than that.

Wolfe is panicking, her breathing fast. Racing up the basement steps two at a time, her phone gets a signal in the hall. She dials Jock's number. It goes to voicemail.

'Hi, this is John Lindsay from Logan Aeronautical Systems. Please leave your name and number and I'll get back to you as soon as I can.'

Wolfe leaves a message, trying not to betray her fear.

'Hi, my name's Olivia. I'm a friend of Toby's. I think he's staying with you? He's in terrible trouble and I need you to call me urgently. It's an emergency.'

She leaves her mobile number, then searches for Sinclair's passport. Inside the hall table drawer Wolfe finds passports for Huma, Sally and Ben and two empty plastic passport covers. Two? Regardless, Toby's is missing. Wolfe phones Stacy Price.

Her call will be traced, but she has to know if she's right about Psychosillius's destructive power. Price answers.

'Stacy, it's Olivia. Please don't hang up.'

'I can't—'

Wolfe takes the plunge. 'Toby stole the missing canister—'

Price cuts her off. 'Don't be ridiculous!'

'Is Psychosillius corrosive?'

'Oh God, no, no, no.'

'No, what?'

Price gulps. 'He's going to use it, isn't he?'

'Stacy, how do you know that?'

'He never got over their deaths. Blamed himself. He should have been with them. He found out it was a drone strike that killed them. It infuriated him they wouldn't admit responsibility. He changed after that.'

'Psychosillius doesn't attack people, does it?'

Price is crying. 'Michael's dead. Committed suicide.'

'I know, I'm sorry. Stacy, I—'

'Michael was so ashamed. His greatest discovery.'

Wolfe checks her watch. If the spooks don't yet have a fix on her location, they soon will. She must hurry. 'Stacy, I can help Toby, but only if you tell me what Psychosillius does.'

'It doesn't corrode.' A moment's silence.

Wolfe relaxes.

'It devours. The speed. I've never seen anything—'

'Devours what?' Wolfe asks.

But Price isn't listening.

'We ignored the drill. Then the tractor blades. We shouldn't have; they were a sign. In Cambridge, we confirmed the bacteria's hyper-activity is triggered by sunlight. That's when it feeds and grows. If it's kept in the dark, it's dormant and harmless. We wasted valuable time testing it on rats. Toby worked it out way before the rest of us. He knew, or at least suspected, even at Lake Ellsworth. He was the first to notice the rats' steel feeder-bottle spouts had disintegrated; simply disappeared within an hour.'

'An hour?'

'Unbelievable. isn't it? That's why we had our doubts. It's all very well attacking living organisms, but steel? And so fast!' Price pauses for breath. 'Look, the reality is we know very little about Psychosillius except it destroys steel, and iron of course, even alloyants, like manganese. Our models show that a capful can destroy the steel in an armoured tank in two days; the iron in the Eiffel Tower in four days; the 76,000 tonnes of steel supporting the Sears Tower in Chicago in seven weeks.'

Somebody shouts at Price. A man's voice, ordering her to put the phone down.

' . . . we don't know how to stop . . . ' Price doesn't finish There's a scuffle.

'Who is this?' a man demands.

Wolfe cuts the connection, heart thumping. If Sinclair is already in the USA, somebody must alert the FBI. But nobody will believe her.

There is only one person she knows who can trigger the necessary emergency protocols. Somebody the FBI will take seriously.

Dan Casburn.

67

'Stop dicking me around. Tell me where you are.'

Wolfe's call to Casburn hasn't started well. She watches the wall clock's thin red seconds hand jerk a fraction. When it has completed one revolution, Casburn will know she is at Sinclair's house; five or ten minutes later, unformed officers will storm the place. If she's going to hand herself in, she has to be sure Casburn believes her.

'Dan, we've known each other a long time, so please hear me out. Toby Sinclair stole the canister of Psychosillius. He's been testing it, modifying it in his basement lab. He used it on the *Queen Elizabeth*. He wants revenge: a US armed drone killed his wife and kids in Afghanistan two years ago. I think he's on his way to Las Vegas and he has Psychosillius with him.'

'What are you talking about?'

'Listen! His target is Creech Air Force Base.' No response. 'Dan? Did you hear what I just said?'

Wolfe hears his agitated breathing and wonders how many others are listening in. She checks the clock.

'Where is this crap coming from?' Casburn says.

'Emails with John Lindsay from Logan Aeronautical. He works at Creech, probably a contractor. Yesterday, Toby told him he's boarding a flight and will see him soon.'

'So? He's hooking up with a buddy in America. Proves nothing.'

'He escaped your protection detail.'

'You scared the little twat.'

Her head is pounding. She has to convince him.

'Take a look in his basement. He's been experimenting with the bacteria. And he's using hundred-millilitre shampoo bottles to carry it on board.'

'The local uniforms are on their way. Stay where you are.'

'Check the passenger manifests.' Wolfe is almost out of time. 'He's probably used Purple Parking.'

'I'll pass that on.' He sounds distracted.

'And? What happens to me?'

'You're a murder suspect. You know the drill.'

'And you? What are you doing?'

'I'm doing my job.'

'Which is?'

'Focus on protecting this country from an Isil terrorist attack.'

'You don't get it, do you? Sinclair is the imminent threat. He is the terrorist!'

'Olivia,' sighs Casburn. 'This bullshit won't save Yushkov. It just makes things worse for you.'

A man says something unintelligible in the background. Wolfe slams down the handset. Casburn doesn't believe her. Will he even check Heathrow's passenger manifests? She is left with no choice: she must get to Las Vegas and find Sinclair. It is for just such an unexpected departure that she always carries her passport in her Go Bag.

Running out of the back door and through the garden gate, Wolfe dives into her car and heads for Heathrow Airport. She calls Butcher.

'Liv, are you okay?'

'Do you still have faith in me?'

'What? Of course I do.'

She swallows. 'I need your help.'

'Go on.'

'I know who stole the canister, and I think he's taken it to America.'

'Slow down. What's in the canister?'

'Steel-eating bacteria.'

'Steel?'

'If it's exposed to sunlight it becomes a steel-saw on steroids.' She explains what Dr Price told her.

'Seriously? That fast?'

'According to Dr Price. I think his next target is Creech Air Force Base.'

'Jesus! Is he mad?'

'He's angry. His wife and kids were killed by a drone strike in Kandahar. He's hitting back, targeting the military and manufacturers of combat drones.'

Silence. His unresponsiveness worries her.

'Jerry?'

'Liv, this is too big. Tell Casburn. He'll notify the right people.'

'He doesn't believe me.'

'Then maybe you've got Sinclair wrong?'

'And what if I'm right? What if he releases it at Creech? Or Heathrow? Or takes it to a city like Los Angeles? Imagine buildings collapsing, machinery failing. The devastation. The deaths.' She takes a breath. 'Can you find out if he flew to the USA yesterday? Probably Las Vegas.'

'I know Inspector Walker at Heathrow, but he'll tell me bugger all. You forget, I'm retired.'

'Please, just call him. If I'm wrong, where's the harm? If I'm right, maybe this Walker will take action.'

Butcher sighs. 'His full name?'

'Tobias Arthur Sinclair.'

'I'll call you back.'

By the time he does so, she's already on the M25, approaching the T3 Heathrow exit.

'Anything?'

'Spoke to Walker. He was reluctant to co-operate.'

'Is Toby on a passenger list?'

'No.'

'No?'

'No, Liv. He did not fly from Heathrow or any UK airport yesterday and he's not on any list today.'

'That can't be right.'

'Guess Casburn was right.'

She falls silent. 'Wait! Can you do one more thing? Ask Walker to check for Hector Mark Sinclair?'

'Who's he?'

'His brother, lives in Australia. If Hector has become an Australian citizen, he won't need his UK passport. They look alike, so Toby could've used his brother's passport.'

'A long shot but I'll check.'

Wolfe takes the Terminal 3 turn-off and pulls over as soon as she can. A few minutes later, Butcher calls back.

'You're right. Hector Sinclair flew to Las Vegas yesterday, landing at 7.26 in the evening. Could it be the brother?'

'As far as I know, Hector's in Australia.'

'You want me to talk to Casburn? He'll listen to me.'

'I'll do it.'

Before she can dial Casburn's number, he calls her.

'Meet me at Heathrow's police station. I need everything you know about Sinclair.'

68

Wolfe leans against her car outside Heathrow's police station, ill at ease. Where is Casburn?

Located on the outskirts of the airport, the station is home to a specialist armed unit known as Aviation Security Command, or SO18. The building's silver exterior resembles the large overlapping plates on knights' armour, but the interior – she's read – is modern, well lit and well ventilated, and is therefore unlike any other nick Wolfe has ever seen. It has thirty custody cells comfortable enough to rival rooms in a budget airport hotel, a high-tech Command and Control Centre and an armoury that would make any gun fanatic green with envy.

Someone ploughs into Wolfe, shunting her sideways into a wall. Her wrist is grabbed from behind. Instinctively, she bends the wrist and grips the hand that holds her, at the same time stepping away from her captor and turning to face him. The arresting officer is looking down at the handcuffs he's pulling from his body armour pocket. Seeing his colleague in difficulty, the second officer lunges at her, but she has already taken the arresting officer in a painful wrist lock, forcing his hand down to a ninety-degree angle from the wrist. He winces and releases his grip. She bolts. This is not what she and Casburn agreed.

Wolfe is rugby-tackled to the ground. Two other armed officers point MP5s at her.

'Police! Stay where you are.'

Wolfe freezes and raises her arms. The arresting officers don't make the same mistake twice: one holds both her arms behind her back as the other handcuffs her, then they both drag her up to standing.

'Olivia Wolfe, I'm arresting you for the murder of Charles Harvey.'

Wolfe senses somebody close behind her and smells stale breath barely masked by mint. 'Dan, there's no need for this.'

She's escorted in silence to a table-less interview room and the handcuffs removed. In theory, the absence of a table enables them to watch her body language.

'Where's Flynn?' she asks Casburn.

He folds his arms.

She folds hers.

'He doesn't know you're here, does he?'

A man in his mid-thirties with receding hairline enters the

room. His shirt is creased from wearing a bulletproof vest he's only just removed. Inspector Doug Walker announces himself, the time and date and who else is present in the room – DCI Casburn.

Wolfe glances at the video camera recording them, then at Casburn, who wears a shirt too big around the collar. She guesses he's borrowed a clean shirt from somebody at the nick. There are three rust-coloured stains on his jacket lapel. Possibly blood spatter: Vitaly's. She feels a sudden surge of anger.

'Dan, you promised me—'

'I promised nothing. Now explain why you think Toby Sinclair is headed for Creech Air Force Base?'

Wolfe tells them everything she knows. She pleads with Casburn. 'You know how destructive it is. Why aren't you stopping him?'

Casburn remains poker-faced. 'I'm waiting for confirmation Sinclair has it.'

'Of course he does!' she shouts in exasperation. 'You just don't want the Americans to know you've messed up.'

Casburn lifts his chin a fraction. That's it. He doesn't want to admit to the FBI he's failed to contain Psychosillius. If it reaches the USA, his career is over.

'If Sinclair has it,' says Walker, 'is it possible he's used it at this airport?'

'I don't know, but I don't think so. He's not targeting civilians, just the military.'

They get up to leave.

'What are you going to do?' she asks.

They ignore her.

'Inspector Walker! A man posing a major threat to the United States has already sunk an aircraft carrier. At least warn Creech and the FBI.'

'Have you any idea how many apparent threats we deal with

every day?' says Walker. 'Ninety-nine per cent a waste of time. I need more than the word of a murder suspect.'

'But you know Hector's in Australia, right?'

Walker nods.

'Don't you find Toby travelling on his brother's passport a little suspicious?'

There's a knock on the door and a female PC enters, handing Walker a note. 'Okay, keep it muted and bring it to me.'

Then to Olivia, 'John Lindsay's returned your call. You take it on loudspeaker.'

The PC returns with Wolfe's mobile. Walker drags a spare chair into the space between them, puts the phone on the seat and takes the mobile off mute.

'John, this is Olivia. Sorry to keep you waiting.'

'It's three in the morning. This'd better be important.'

'Is Toby Sinclair with you?'

'I don't mean to be rude, but I don't know you from a bar of soap. Why do you want to know—'

'Enough!' cuts in Casburn, who moves close to the phone. 'John, I'm DCI Dan Casburn, with Counter Terrorism Command in London.'

'Is this a wind-up?'

'No, sir.'

'What's this got to do with Toby?'

'Please, just answer the question. Is Toby Sinclair with you?'

'Look, this isn't right. You could be anyone.'

Walker interjects. 'John, my name is Doug Walker. I'm a police inspector at Heathrow. I'll give you our number. Call me back. But be quick. This matter is extremely urgent.'

Lindsay hesitates. 'Err, well, okay, I guess. Look, something weird's happened.'

'What?' demands Casburn.

'I picked Toby up at the airport, brought him home, had dinner. He looked like crap so we had an early night. I hear a bang, get up to check it out and Toby's gone.'

'Gone where?' asks Casburn.

'I thought maybe a walk. You know, jetlag and all that. But he took his stuff with him.'

Walker blinks rapidly. Casburn shifts in his chair and clears his throat.

'How long ago?'

'I don't know, twenty minutes.'

'Is he on foot?'

'Guess so. Hold on, I'll just check . . . ' They hear footsteps. Casburn's jaw is locked so tight, the veins in his neck bulge. 'Shit! He took my damn car.'

Casburn stands abruptly and leans over the phone. 'Where's he gone?'

'No idea.'

'Is anything else missing?' asks Wolfe. 'Security pass, passport?'

'You're kidding, right? Toby's not a criminal.'

'Check now, sir,' snaps Casburn.

The knot of anxiety in Wolfe's belly tightens as they wait. Casburn paces, Walker stares at the phone.

'I can't find my Creech security pass.'

Casburn finally glances at Wolfe. There's fear in his eyes. 'Could Toby use it to get on to the base?'

'In theory, yes. He'd have to switch the photo. But he'd never do—'

Casburn closes his eyes for a few seconds, takes a deep breath, then just as quickly opens them. 'Mr Lindsay, I have reason to believe Sinclair will try to enter Creech. I'm contacting the base. The police will be with you shortly. Stay where you are and do not attempt to contact Sinclair. Do you understand?'

349

'Yes, but—'

Casburn pockets Wolfe's phone and leaves, hastily followed by Walker. A police officer stands near the door watching her.

At last, they believe her. But after thirty minutes of waiting and no news, she's going crazy, chewing her fingernails to the quick.

The door bursts open. Casburn enters with two officers armed with MP5s. He handcuffs her.

'You're coming with me.'

'Where?'

'Creech Air Force Base.'

69

Las Vegas, USA

Wolfe has been handcuffed to Casburn for the entire flight and the constant focus of nervous glances from fellow passengers. Occasionally he yanks her wrist towards him, reminding her he is in control, as if she were a dog on a leash. When by accident the detective's hand brushes hers, she shudders, repelled. She doesn't trust him.

'Are you wearing Vitaly's blood?' she asks, nodding at his jacket, unable to keep the anger from her voice.

Casburn swivels his head to look out of the window, ignoring the question. But she knows the answer and feels sick. Casburn sleeps most of the journey, except for brief phone calls. From these it's clear that twenty-four hours after his arrival in the United States, Toby Sinclair is nowhere to be found.

As they disembark at McCarran International Airport, they're met by two FBI agents who introduce themselves. Anthony

Garriola, Special Agent-In-Charge, in his early forties, has a narrow face, deep-set eyes under heavy brows, and salt-and-pepper hair. Baron Banks, six foot four with a linebacker's build, is in his late twenties.

'We don't want her here,' Garriola says, jerking his head in Wolfe's direction as they head for Passport Control.

'*I* want her here. She knows Sinclair. We may need her to talk him down.'

'We have professionals for that, sir.'

'He trusts me,' Wolfe says. 'Let me help.'

Garriola doesn't even look at her.

'Sir, every goddamned law enforcement agency wants in on this one. USAF police, local cops, marshals . . . ' Garriola stops himself, giving Wolfe an unfriendly glance. There's something he doesn't want her to know. 'Then there's the military pulling rank. It's like feeding time at the fricking zoo. So we don't need you interfering. You understand what I'm saying?'

'Here to help,' Casburn replies. Handcuffed to him, Wolfe feels his arm tense. 'But let me remind you the suspect is a British national and our involvement in this operation has been cleared at the highest levels.'

Garriola shakes his head. 'Let me remind you that you're the ones who let a biological weapon get into the hands of a terrorist. You've done enough.'

Garriola flashes his badge and paves their way through border security.

The brightly lit red and yellow 'Welcome to Las Vegas' sign in Arrivals does little to cheer Wolfe. This is not a good start. Casburn and Garriola need to co-operate if they're going to find Sinclair in time. As they exit the terminal, the freezing night air makes her shiver. She and Casburn pile into the back of a black Chevy Suburban for the thirty-five mile journey through the desert to Creech Air Force Base. Garriola drives.

'I need an update,' demands Casburn.

'Sinclair's flight's been quarantined and we're locating all the passengers,' Garriola says, his left arm resting on the doorframe, the window down despite the cold. 'Got the best bacteriologists and germ warfare experts all over it. Your two scientists, Matthews and Price, and some other guys from Porton Down land in an hour. They'll be escorted to the base.'

'Good. Any news on Sinclair?' Casburn asks.

'Lindsay's pickup's been found in a car park. Must be driving something different. We're following up on reported car thefts in the area. You sure about his target?'

'All the evidence suggests he's planning an attack on Creech.'

Garriola whistles through his teeth. 'You'd better be right. Stirred up one hell of a shit storm.'

'He wants revenge,' says Wolfe. 'A drone strike killed his wife and kids. A drone controlled from Creech. Creech has to be his target.'

'Did I ask you a question?' Garriola snaps, flicking her a look in the rear-view mirror.

Casburn squeezes her arm. A warning. Wolfe opens her mouth to object, then thinks better of it. In their eyes she's a murder suspect.

'Well, he ain't been on the base, that's for sure,' Garriola continues. 'Lindsay's pass hasn't been used and there's no way he could break in. Maybe we scared him off?'

'I doubt it,' mutters Wolfe.

Once they are beyond the bright lights of Las Vegas, the straight road leads into an engulfing darkness with only dusty saltbush either side of the asphalt illuminated in the headlights. The silence is only broken by the rumble of the tyres. Soon, though, a wide arc of light brightens the horizon and street lighting lines the road once more. From a distance Creech is unassuming, a collection of nondescript hangars and low-rise administration buildings, surrounded by high mesh fences, razor wire and perimeter walls. Despite an almost full moon, Wolfe cannot see the barren hills surrounding the base or get any sense of the almost four square miles the site covers. The floodlit car park is a hub of activity: soldiers with dogs patrol the perimeter; the local police in their beige uniforms gather near one of the many parked black and white police cars as they're briefed by an officer leaning over a map; and, as their car slows, NBC, KTNV and Fox News reporters rush towards them. Garriola weaves past the crash barriers and pulls up at the main gate, shows his badge to a female air force police officer in blue uniform and cap, and is waved through.

'Who's in overall charge of this investigation? You?' Casburn asks Garriola.

The FBI agent shakes his head. 'It's never that simple.'

The motel was cheap, the clerk took cash and didn't ask for ID. Sinclair sits on the sagging bed ignoring the loud hum from the mini-fridge, eating a take-out cheeseburger and fries as he watches the news on TV. There are often protests outside Creech, anti-war hippies with placards who get arrested. Well meaning but ineffective. Sinclair plans to use stealth. Surprise his enemy.

Local news reporters are filling air-time until they can discover what the unspecified 'threat' is at the base. The big question on every reporter's lips is: will the special visitor arriving at Creech tomorrow still show? Sinclair is in no doubt. Of course he will. He's not a man who scares easily.

Cameras flash and reporters scramble to see inside a black Chevy Suburban that's just arrived at the base's main gate. Sinclair leans forward, straining to see who has caused such excitement. There's no mistaking the FBI vests worn by the men seated at the front, but it's the person handcuffed in the back who draws his interest, her pale face and startled wide brown eyes recognisable in the glare of broadcast camera lights.

'Ah, Olivia. I knew you'd come. Too smart for your own good.'

Sinclair looks at his padded backpack on the floor containing the hundred-millilitre shampoo bottles of Psychosillius. Of the twelve containers he brought with him, one is now empty, used to fill the fountain pen's cartridge. He will keep one other for an unforeseen opportunity. The rest of the destructive bacteria he will transfer into a single glass bottle tomorrow.

I miss my little robin. I have nothing to do all day. Nothing except read my diary.

I've seen your face flash across every news channel, entering that American base, the media surrounding your car. What's it called? Stupid name, rhymes with screech. Doesn't matter. They say you're a killer assisting the authorities with their enquiries. I feel bad about that. Time to set them straight. Eyewitnesses change their stories all the time. I don't want you in prison for murdering Harvey. Where would be the fun for me?

I was surprised to see Casburn with you. Trying to save the world, Olivia, even if it means dancing with the devil?

Don't bother. It isn't worth it.

Just come home. Be mine again.

The holding cell is spartan: concrete floor, breezeblock white walls, a steel washbasin and toilet, bed base with anorexic mattress, and chair fixed to the floor. At least it's heated and she's had a meal. Wolfe is collected by a USAF police officer in camouflage battle-dress and blue beret, and taken to an equally barren interview room, where Garriola sits, arms folded, tight-lipped as if he's sucked a lemon. Next to him is a military USAF police investigator who is introduced as Hendrix. No Casburn. Wolfe suspects he's on the other side of the large two-way mirror.

A man in his late thirties with shaved head in a dark suit wearing an earpiece, the spiralling wire disappearing behind his collar, strides into the room. From the tips of his polished shoes to the sunglasses poking out from his top pocket and the bulge in his loose jacket due to the gun, radio, handcuffs and badge he inevitably carries, Wolfe is in no doubt he's Secret Service. The one in charge.

But what is he doing here?

'Special Agent Pine,' he says, sitting on the table edge. He holds a bulging A4 manila envelope. 'May I call you Olivia?'

'Yes. Why is the Secret Service involved?'

He ignores the question. 'How well do you know Toby Sinclair?'

'We first met in Antarctica a bit over two weeks ago and we got to know each other pretty well in the five days I was there.'

'And you helped him escape his protection detail at Porton Down?'

'That wasn't my intention.'

Pine raises an eyebrow.

'Like to explain why we found this in the glove compartment of Lindsay's car. It's Sinclair's handwriting.'

Pine places the envelope on the table. One side has been

carefully opened. It has something rectangular inside. On the envelope is written:

Olivia Wolfe, my thanks. You of all people will understand.

She inhales sharply. 'How could he know?'

'Know what?' says Pine, leaning closer.

Wolfe looks up, frowning. 'That I'd be here. I didn't even know until Casburn decided.' She shakes her head, baffled.

'You told him you'd be here.'

'No.'

'You're working with him?'

'What? No. Of course not.'

'Then how did he know you'd come to this base?'

'He must've guessed I'd work it out and follow him.'

'What do the words mean?'

'If he means I'd understand him using a biological weapon to destroy a military base, he'd be wrong. Utterly wrong. I want to help you stop him.'

'Why is he thanking you?'

'I don't know. I mean . . . ' she rubs her temples. 'He knows I champion women and children in war zones, the forgotten victims. Perhaps he's thanking me for caring? I just don't know.'

'Look inside,' says Pine, nodding once at the envelope. 'Forensics has been over it.'

Wolfe doesn't touch it. She peers into it and sees a slim rectangular black box. She hesitates. 'Is it safe?'

'You tell me,' Pine replies.

Wolfe nervously pulls out the black box and fumbles with the lid. Inside is a Sheaffer fountain pen engraved with the words 'Collateral Damage'.

'What does he mean?' Pine asks.

Wolfe clenches her eyes shut, trying to remember her conversations with Sinclair.

'Hey!' shouts Pine, clicking his fingers in her face. 'Answer me!'

'I'm trying to think,' she retorts, opening her eyes. 'Women and children caught up in war? Maybe he means the families of the men and women stationed here? If he releases Psychosillius, they could get hurt. Collapsing buildings, cars malfunctioning.'

Wolfe holds up the pen and pulls off the lid, searching for an answer. She stares at the nib. A hint of blue on the tip.

'Oh no.'

Her mouth dry, her hands shake.

Pine sees something is wrong and takes the pen from her just as she lets go of it. 'Oh no, what?'

'Did you check for Psychosillius?' Wolfe croaks.

Garriola pipes up. 'Of course we did. You think we're stupid?'

'Look at me!' Pine demands. 'Why did he send you the pen?'

Wolfe isn't listening. Why would Sinclair address it to her? What does he want her to do?

'It's not me,' she whispers.

'It's got your name on it,' Pine barks, losing patience.

Wolfe looks up at him. 'It's you.' She looks around the room. 'All of you.'

'What the hell are you talking about?' says Garriola.

Wolfe rubs her forehead. 'The cartridge. You tested it? You're sure?'

Garriola blinks rapidly. She sees doubt in his eyes. 'Forensics said bacteria-free.'

Pine turns on him. 'You better be one hundred per cent sure. That stuff could melt this whole base!'

'I'll get the report,' says Garriola, heading for the door.

'Wait!' calls Wolfe. 'Has anyone used this pen? Triggered the ink?'

Garriola screws up his face as if he has a stabbing headache. 'Shit!' Then he yells at the two-way mirror. 'Banks! Get in here now.'

Banks shuffles into the room. 'It was cleared by the lab. I just wanted to see how it would write, is all. Never used a fountain pen before.'

'Where? Where did you use it?' Wolfe says, standing up.

'Sit the fuck down!' Garriola grabs her shoulder and forces her to sit.

'Answer her,' Pine tells Banks.

'At the lab,' says Banks. 'As I said, it was cleared.'

'And here?'

'No, just the lab.'

'This was his plan all along,' says Wolfe. 'Sinclair knew you'd test it, and he guessed you wouldn't test inside the sealed cartridge. He knew you'd confront me with it. Here. At Creech.'

Wolfe stares at the three men in the room.

The USAF investigator, who has remained a taciturn observer, bolts from the room, presumably to alert his commanding officer.

'Son of a bitch,' exhales Garriola.

'He was never going to break in. You did it for him,' Pine shouts at Garriola. 'The pass was a fake out!'

'Now wait a minute—' Garriola begins.

'Get on to the lab now!' Pine yells. 'Lock it down. Nobody leaves. I want everybody who touched that envelope tested! That pen's a biological weapon.'

70

Since he entered Wolfe's cell, Casburn hasn't spoken. He is seated on the chair that's screwed to the floor, leaning his forearms on his thighs, staring at the concrete beneath him.

'Dan?'

'Creech is Psychosillius free. It's been confirmed,' he says without looking up.

'That's good news.'

Wolfe aches with exhaustion. Sunrise is only an hour away; she hasn't slept and is too anxious to try. She sits on the bed cross-legged, wrapped in a blanket, and tilts her head to one side. He clearly has more to say. She waits. Casburn wearily runs a hand over his crew cut.

'You did well, Olivia.' He doesn't look at her, uncomfortable with the admission. 'Looks like your reaction saved the base from contamination.' He shakes his head. 'At least I was right to bring you here.'

Wolfe has never seen Casburn doubt himself. She leaves her blanket and stands in front of him. He looks up, eyes bloodshot.

'Sinclair was right under my nose,' he says. 'I should have known.'

'He fooled us all.' She pauses. 'Dan? This one time, will you trust me?'

Casburn gives her a hint of a smile. 'You know I'll never do that, Olivia.'

Wolfe gently rests her hand on the detective's shoulder. His hand immediately clamps down hard on hers. She doesn't flinch.

'Then believe me,' she says. 'Believe me when I say Yushkov never had the stolen sample and never gave it to Kabir Khan. And nor would Toby. He'd never support Isil. This is personal.'

His grip on her hand softens but it remains holding hers.

'Sinclair's a terrorist,' says Casburn, 'just as much as Khan.'

'Except, he'll still listen to reason. I can talk him out of it.'

'You're convinced there's another target?'

'I am. And please believe me when I say I will do all I can to stop him.'

Casburn looks away.

'For once,' Wolfe continues, 'let's forget our differences and work together.'

Casburn gives a brusque nod and lets go of her hand. She turns back to the bed.

'So, with the Secret Service involved, I'm guessing somebody important is coming here?' Wolfe asks.

'I guess you'll know soon enough.' Yet he pauses, uncertain. 'The President is inspecting Creech. Today.'

'You've got to be kidding!'

'Do I look like I'm kidding?' Casburn gets up. 'The Secret Service wants to cancel. The President won't.'

'What does Pine have to say?'

'If the President insists, then all Pine can do is ramp up the protection detail.'

Wolfe stares at Casburn. 'When was his visit made public?'

'A good few weeks ago. And the advanced detail would've vetted the location three months ago so word could've got out earlier.'

'Tell me they realise the President has to be the target?'

'Sinclair would be insane to try. He's the most protected person in the world.'

'Yes, but—'

'How, Olivia? Toby isn't a sniper; he's unlikely to have explosives. He has no history of violence. All he has is bacteria.'

'How many steel components do you think are in Air Force One? All it takes is one serious malfunction.'

'He'd never get near Air Force One.'

'Really? Like he'd never smuggle bacteria into a highly secure US Air Force Base? But he did.'

Wolfe spies the pale blue nose of Air Force One low in the hazy sky as it approaches McCarran. The Presidential plane is headed for a secluded part of the airport, cordoned off and under tight security, well away from the passenger terminals. Through a chainmail perimeter fence they watch Secret Service agents and the twenty-five cars of the Presidential motorcade move into position. Neither Casburn nor Wolfe is allowed near the President. Behind them are two armed FBI agents. Wolfe mustn't leave their sight even though her arms are handcuffed in front. If it weren't for Casburn vouching for her, she'd still be in her cell.

'Keep an eye out for anyone who looks like Sinclair,' Casburn says.

The hot wind blows dust in her face. She's frustrated. Nervous. Sinclair is out there somewhere. 'I can't see much from back here. I need to be closer.'

'No chance.' Casburn hands her binoculars. 'Use these.'

'There's a Presidential back-up plane?'

'Always.'

She does a sweep with the binoculars. Counter snipers armed with Wing Mag rifles are in position. Police officers form the outer defence; general Secret Service agents cover the middle sector. The Presidential Protective Division agents form the inner guard, with Cadillac One at their centre.

Air Force One glides to a gentle landing, the magnificent blue and white, shiny Boeing 747-8 glinting in the sun. Wolfe turns the binoculars to her left. Behind half a dozen uniformed officers and barricades, carefully selected media crews excitedly jostle for position, giving live coverage of the President's arrival.

'Every journalist and cameraman has had to pass rigorous background checks for the second time, their equipment taken away, inspected and returned to them,' says Casburn.

'Dr Price is here?'

'Somewhere. She'll test for any signs of Psychosillius.'

'And Professor Matthews?'

'At Creech.'

To Wolfe's right is the motorcade of black Suburbans, Cadillacs and support vans, parked at the side of the runway, where numerous agents in suits and sunglasses watch, ever vigilant. Police dogs have already checked each vehicle for explosives. The heavily armoured cars will be escorted by police officers on motorbikes. Marksmen are positioned on rooftops. An armed team in black, wearing bulletproof vests, waits in their SUV, parked some distance from the main activity; they are the Counter Assault Team or CAT and will take down any threat. Casburn sees where she's looking.

'If those guys leave their car, dive for cover,' he shouts above the roar of Air Force One's engines. 'That's when all hell breaks loose.'

'The President's still going to Creech?' Wolfe asks.

'Yes, but his route's changed and he's an hour early. Sinclair couldn't possibly anticipate this.'

'Who are they?' she asks, pointing at a small delegation waiting to greet the President.

'The Colonel, a senator, local bigwigs.'

'Will he meet the public?'

'Nope. He's going straight to Creech. His wife and daughters are off to the Hoover Dam, then the Grand Canyon.'

Wolfe snaps her head round. 'The First Family? They're here too?'

Casburn picks up on the alarm in her voice. 'They don't go anywhere near Creech. They'll be fine.'

Wolfe watches Air Force One taxi slowly towards them, the powerful engines thrumming.

'Airspace has been shut down over a thirty-mile radius,' says Casburn. 'Incoming flights have been delayed or diverted, and departures are grounded until the President leaves.'

'So no private planes? No tourist flights? No media helicopters?'

'Nothing, and the airport connector tunnel is closed. It runs under this runway so no traffic's going through. Toby won't be able to get near him. Apart from anything else, the roads are gridlocked.'

'What about on the way to Creech? It's pretty exposed.'

'Agent Pine knows what he's doing.'

'But Toby is brilliant. He's not your average criminal.'

The blue and white plane's engines have been cut and the mobile staircase is being pushed towards the plane's front exit. A swarm of agents move in and, as the official state car pulls up near the stairs, they position themselves around it, looking outwards.

'Cadillac One,' Casburn remarks. 'Seats seven. Built on a truck chassis. Five inch-thick glass. Armour plated. Biochemical protection. Petrol tank's wrapped in fire-retardant foam, tyres have a Kevlar inner tube so, if they're shot, it still runs.'

'I've heard they call it The Beast.'

Casburn nods.

The President appears at the top of the stairs in a navy blue suit, white shirt and cobalt tie, holding the hand of his six-year-old daughter, Melanie, who's in jeans and mauve T-shirt. She's petite like her mother, who follows her husband down the stairway in a yellow dress and matching jacket, clutching the hand of their eight-year-old son, Thomas. The First Family waves at the camera crews in the distance.

'Their codenames?' Wolfe asks.

'The President is Socrates. The First Lady is Stardust. Daughter, Snowdrop, and son, Solar.'

After a short meet and greet, the President kisses his wife and children, waves to the onlookers and gets into Cadillac One. The Colonel joins him. The Secret Service moves like clockwork. A second limo, identical to Cadillac One, pulls away at the same time to act as a decoy, shifting positions with Cadillac One. Two other limos join the manoeuvre, making it difficult to know which one has the President, and the motorcade moves off, lights flashing.

Through the binoculars Wolfe watches the First Lady, Elizabeth, and her children, escorted to a waiting VH–3D Sea King helicopter, its distinctive green and white colours recognised the world over as Marine One. But for this trip, the helicopter's call sign will be Executive One Foxtrot, the F indicating the First Family is aboard. The son, Thomas, is clearly excited, and races up the steps and into the helicopter first. Their Secret Service detail joins them and the Sea King takes off, followed by three similar military helicopters. Once airborne they shift formation, then head for the Mike O'Callaghan-Pat Tillman Memorial Bridge, better known as the Hoover Dam Bypass Bridge.

Wolfe stares after them, a knot of worry in her stomach.

'Hey!' says Casburn, trying to get Wolfe's attention. 'In the car. We're going back to Creech.'

She's missed something. Casburn's right. Sinclair has no chance of getting to the President, his limousine or his plane. So what is his target?

Casburn grabs her binoculars. 'Your job's not done until they're back in D.C. Let's go.'

He takes a step in the direction of the car that's waiting for them, but she doesn't budge. Casburn turns, irritated. She tracks the disappearing helicopters.

'Collateral Damage'. Why bother to engrave the pen? Does Sinclair somehow want her to stop him?

Then, in one horrifying moment, Wolfe knows.

She swivels her head and raises her handcuffed hands to point at the helicopters. But they're grabbed by one of the FBI agents assigned to watch her, and yanked down. It shocks her out of her stupor. She finds her voice.

'The First Family!'

'What about them?' says Casburn.

'They're the target!'

71

Inside the McDonnell Douglas police helicopter Special Agent Pine has commandeered, the rotor noise sounds like angry hornets. They have been granted special permission to fly through the thirty-mile no-fly zone surrounding Air Force One. Pine sits next to the pilot.

'Appreciate you doing this,' says Casburn into his headset.

'I've stuck my neck out on this one, so she better be right,' Pine says, jerking his head towards the back, where Wolfe, Casburn and Dr Price are seated. They're all wearing headsets so they can talk to each other.

'Why don't you stop the tour?' Wolfe asks. The juddering of the helicopter makes her voice sound shaky.

Pine cranes his neck so he can eyeball her. 'Because I'm not cancelling the trip on a hunch.'

'So their itinerary hasn't changed?' Casburn asks. 'Hoover Dam then the West Rim of the canyon?'

'Changed flight paths and landing points.'

'That may not be enough.'

Pine doesn't respond.

'I can't believe this is Toby we're talking about,' says Price, the freckled skin on her face taut with stress. 'But Olivia's theory makes sense in a perverse sort of way. He's lost his wife and children, so he plans to hurt the President's. It's the way his mind works. Precise and balanced.'

'Balanced?' says Pine. 'We get ten threats a day minimum against the President and the First Family. Some are just dumb fucks mouthing off. This Sinclair? He's our worst nightmare. A whack job armed with a biological weapon and he knows how to use it. He sure as hell ain't balanced.' Pine pauses. 'If he uses this Psychosillius, how do we kill it?'

'Incineration,' says Price. 'But we don't yet know if that's one hundred per cent effective. We're monitoring the ocean where the *Queen Elizabeth* went down.'

'We've had to incinerate the infected aircraft carrier and a military research facility at Porton Down,' says Casburn. 'Cost us millions. Hundreds dead. Caused a major panic. People have gone into siege mentality and won't leave their homes.'

'At all costs we must stop it getting into the Colorado River,' says Price. 'If it does, we don't know how to stop it spreading. It'll move too fast.'

'At least we know what Sinclair looks like,' Wolfe points out, trying to stay positive. 'We find him and talk him out of it.'

'You help us find him. That's it.'

The semi-circular Hoover Dam looms large in the distance over seven hundred feet tall and, behind its curved barrier, Lake Mead, the darkest of emerald greens. Beyond, the arched Hoover Dam Bypass Bridge spans the Colorado River, providing tourists with a bird's-eye view of the dam.

'Stunning,' says Price.

'Where's the First Family?' Wolfe asks, peering through the glass.

'On the bridge taking happy snaps,' says Pine, pointing. 'Over there. Traffic on either side's been stopped.'

Wolfe peers down, scanning the barren, red rocky terrain, hoping to glimpse the car park where they are going to land. They swoop over the compound of tour operator, Dam Helicopters, all their choppers grounded. Rumours have spread of the First Family's arrival, and pedestrians race for the bridge. A Secret Service helicopter hovers above and she can just make out a man armed with a rifle on a café roof. On the ground is a line of stationary vehicles on Route 93. In the middle of the bypass bridge, lined up in perfect precision like green and white stripes on a tie, are the four Sea Kings.

The road crossing the bridge is divided in two by a concrete median strip so the landing space for the choppers is tight. There is only one walkway across the bridge and it's accessed on the Nevada side, separated from the road by a concrete barrier running its whole length. Except, today, a central section of the barrier has been removed to allow Elizabeth, her children and their protection detail to move easily from the road to the footpath. From this vantage point they get a spectacular view of the Hoover Dam, five miles up the river. To the First Family's left, the narrow footpath is a bottleneck of onlookers behind waist-high crowd-control barriers. Facing the crowd are two Secret Service agents.

Their chopper hovers over a car park. Police cars have been moved to allow them room to land.

'This is as close as I can get you,' says the pilot.

The chopper's downwash blasts grit into the air and police officers shield their faces against the dust and debris.

'It's tight,' Casburn says.

'I've landed in tighter,' responds the pilot.

As soon as they've touched down and the pilot's killed the engine, they hasten from the helicopter and, keeping low, head for a broad man in a suit with Marine-style haircut wearing mirror sunglasses. 'Ron Lightbody heads up our Nevada office,' says Pine. 'This is DCI Casburn from Britain's SO15, and murder suspect Olivia Wolfe. She's helping us find Sinclair.'

Lightbody glances at her handcuffed hands.

'I'll bring you up to speed as we walk,' says Pine. 'Let's go.'

Pine and Lightbody lead. The others follow.

'Should she even be here, sir?' Wolfe hears Lightbody ask.

'Her hunches are good. She thinks FLOTUS is the target. So she stays.'

FLOTUS being the code name for the First Family.

Pine updates Lightbody as they climb zigzagging steps and then race along a cliff-edge footpath towards the bypass bridge. High above them in the cliffs, a Secret Service sniper lies flat, peering down the sight of his rifle. Wolfe spots another on the Arizona side. Next to him, an agent with binoculars. All are in black with bulletproof vests.

Lightbody leads them to the Hoover Dam Police's operations centre, a flat-roofed, single-storey building with viewing platform which the Secret Service has taken over for the duration of the First Family's visit. Inside, agents watch CCTV feeds from cameras covering the bridge and surrounding area.

'Let me get this straight,' says Lightbody. 'This Sinclair has a biological weapon that erodes steel and he'll try to use it to harm FLOTUS? How?'

'We don't know. That's the problem,' Pine replies.

Price clears her throat and speaks up. 'Um, I have an idea.'

'Go on,' directs Pine.

'The Hoover Dam Bypass Bridge is a steel-concrete composite, right?'

'Right.'

'I've done some calculations, and at 23,000 cubic metres of concrete and 7,258 metric tonnes of steel, and given Toby's modified bacteria devours steel almost twice as quickly as the original specimens, a cupful could corrode the bridge enough for it to collapse in twenty-four to forty-eight hours.'

'FLOTUS will be long gone by then,' says Lightbody, arms folded. 'A collapsed bridge is not our problem.'

'That's just the beginning,' says Price. 'If it gets into the river, it'll be washed downstream, corroding any steel it comes into contact with. Pipes, turbines and gates will collapse. Downstream at the Davis Dam, they'll close the gates, but that won't stop its progress. Psychosillius will eat through those gates, and the next gate, and the next.'

'How many states get their drinking water from this part of the Colorado River?' asks Wolfe.

'No idea.' Lightbody calls over Hoover Dam police officer Bohannon, and repeats Wolfe's question.

'Approximately eight million people,' Bohannon replies. 'That includes residents of Arizona, Nevada and California and, because of seepage from the All-American Canal, there's Mexico too.'

'And that's just the people impacted by the water-borne bacteria,' says Price. 'Psychosillius can travel on people and cars and trucks and planes. This is more destructive than any bomb. It will level cities. Skyscrapers will collapse. Flights won't take off, ships won't sail. We're talking about a global economic collapse and the death of millions.'

'Okay,' Pine says, 'I get the picture. Our job is to protect POTUS and FLOTUS. Nothing else.'

Wolfe's heart is pounding. She's terrified she is right about Sinclair and they can't stop him. She's also terrified she's wrong and therefore leading the Secret Service on a wild-goose chase and making enemies of the most powerful law enforcement agencies in the world.

'Has the crowd been screened?' Pine asks Lightbody.

'Initially,' says Lightbody. 'But we had a bottleneck along the walkway. Kids getting crushed, so we let some through un-magged.'

Pine frowns. The magnetometers detect guns.

'Could Sinclair be armed?' he asks Wolfe.

'Normally I'd say no way. But his plan to infect Creech has failed. That could destabilise him. So, yes. Yes, he could.'

72

Wearing a Nevada Wolf Pack black baseball cap and sunglasses, Sinclair stands just forty feet from his target.

Pretending to take photos with his phone, his focus is on the President's six-year-old daughter, Melanie, zooming in on her face, her blue eyes wide with wonder as her mother, Elizabeth, points out a feature on the dam. The daughter has a blonde bob held back by a mauve hairband and freckles on her nose. She can't stay still, bouncing from foot to foot, just as his Sally used to. He feels a stab of guilt like heartburn in his chest. But Sally won't get to see the Hoover Dam, or go to university, or fall in love.

The First Lady moves, momentarily blocking his view of Melanie. Sinclair lowers his phone. His stomach somersaults when he realises the small group is heading his way. The shift agents react instantly. The one closest to Elizabeth says something over the air to the shift leader. It's rare for the protection detail to speak so, if they do, they have a problem. This kind of impromptu move is exactly what the Secret Service hates and what Sinclair had hoped for.

There must be a hundred onlookers jostling around him on the narrow walkway and hundreds more heading their way. People scream and wave, desperate to grab Elizabeth's attention and get that once-in-a-lifetime photo. Between Sinclair and his target are families, backpackers, couples, and twenty or so Girl Scout Juniors, easily identified by their jade green vests covered in badges and patches over white polo shirts.

Earlier, at the Hoover Dam's High Scaler Café, where he'd bought a coffee and killed time staring at the T-shirts, key rings and other memorabilia, he'd overheard one girl tell the woman at the till they were the Girl Scouts of South Nevada. The Girl Scout standing directly in front of Sinclair, wearing a pink daypack and pink clips in her long dark hair, looks to be no more than nine. She squeals with excitement and jumps up and down at the First Family's approach.

'Holly! They're coming! They're coming!' she says.

Holly is dumpy and bespectacled, with a wiry plait down her back. She sees her friend jumping up and down and follows suit.

Being short, Sinclair doesn't stand out. He's made sure he is next to a Canadian family of five holidaying in Nevada so he doesn't look like a lone male. He's read how the protection detail scrutinises crowds, looking for anyone out of place or behaving oddly. In his right pocket is a glass laboratory bottle with a unique red cap he's invented. Sinclair takes care not to put a hand into his jacket or to look down. He doesn't want to look suspicious. Like he's drawing a weapon. He keeps his eyes on his target.

Twenty feet away and closing.

The President's daughter has honed in on the Girl Scouts at the front. Sinclair has studied his target and knows Melanie is a Girl Scout 'Daisy'. A few months ago, the Girl Scouts from Maryland, Virginia, West Virginia, Oklahoma and Washington, D.C. had a slumber party on the White House lawn. Elizabeth had come up with the idea and some lucky girls even got a group hug from the President, who dropped in to say hi. Melanie joined her mother at the camp singing songs around a makeshift campfire of battery-operated lanterns.

'She looked at me! She did! I've got to get to the front,' says Holly's friend, 'You stay here.'

The dark-haired girl squeezes between the two in front, ignoring the angry shove she receives.

Holly holds up her phone to take a photo, attempting a selfie with the First Family in the background, but she's being jostled and is too short. Sinclair looks over her shoulder as Holly inspects the photo: all she's managed to take is herself and the crowd.

'Please don't die on me!' she mumbles, shaking the phone.

Sinclair can see the battery is almost flat. Holly slides a finger behind her glasses and rubs a tearful eye. Sinclair knows that feeling. The loser. Never cool. Overlooked.

'Excuse me,' Sinclair says. Holly looks behind her, startled, her plait flicking around. 'Would you like me to take a photo of you and them?' he asks. 'I can text it to you.' He holds up his mobile phone.

She blinks at Sinclair, uncertain. 'I'm not supposed to talk to strangers.'

'Okay,' he says, smiling, then looks ahead, ignoring her. She'll change her mind, just as Sally used to do.

The protection detail is as close as it can get to Elizabeth, Melanie and Thomas, without blocking their path to the well-wishers. The lead agent at the barrier directs a police officer to move so the First Family can stand at the barriers.

'Sir?' says Holly, tugging at Sinclair's jacket. 'Please will you take a photo?'

'Sure.'

He raises his phone high and takes a photo of the President's family, then of Holly smiling, making sure it captures a glimpse of Melanie through the crowd.

'Here, have this,' Sinclair says, offering Holly his phone.

Holly holds it in her open palm, confused.

'You want me to take a photo of you?'

'No, you have the phone. It's yours. I don't need it any more.'

'You mean it, sir?'

'I mean it.' She takes his phone. 'Hey, I got an idea,' Sinclair continues.

He opens his other hand; resting in his palm is a metal, circular key ring with a colourful vintage Hoover Dam travel poster image on the front.

'I bet Melanie would like a souvenir. I just bought this at the shop. You give it to her. Go on. Follow your friend. You can do it,' he encourages.

'Thank you, sir,' Holly says, beaming. Then, just as quickly, her shoulders slouch and she looks defeated.

'I'll never get through.'

'Course you will. Come with me.'

From the raised platform outside the Secret Service's operations centre, Wolfe and Casburn scan the crowd on the bypass bridge. Casburn has an earpiece so he can communicate with Pine. Price is running tests for Psychosillius at the side of the bridge. Lightbody and Pine are in the control room.

Where is Sinclair?

Wolfe leans on the platform's metal rail. She can't see the onlookers' faces: they have their backs to her. So she searches for a man of the right height and build. On the edge of the tightly packed throng, a dark-haired man in a denim jacket moves his head constantly, scanning the crowd.

'Can I have the binoculars?' she asks.

Casburn hands them to her but the handcuffs make them difficult to use. 'For God's sake, Dan, get these cuffs off me! I'm not going to do a runner.'

He looks her straight in the eye. 'You run and I'll kill you myself.'

She holds out her wrists and he removes the handcuffs.

Through the binoculars Wolfe focuses on the suspicious man. She can just make out a coil poking out of his jacket collar and up into his ear. Relieved, she realises he's Secret Service.

There's a bit of shoving near the cordon as a young girl in a green waistcoat with a chunky pigtail pushes to the front, followed by her father. The little girl stretches out a plump arm over the barrier towards Melanie. The agent assigned to Melanie has grey short-cropped hair and sunglasses. He instantly steps between them.

The girl with the plait hangs her head and pulls back her arm, clearly crestfallen. Melanie pouts, upset she can't accept the gift offered, and pleads with the agent, who has a brief conversation over the air, takes the gift, inspects it, then hands something small and circular to Melanie. She gives the agent a big smile and moves closer to the gift-giver for a chat. Cute, but Wolfe reminds herself not to get distracted. She refocuses on the men in the crowd.

But the Girl Scout chatting to Melanie draws her attention once more. Another agent moves in and takes what looks like a souvenir key ring from Melanie and walks away with it. He heads towards a support helicopter. Melanie chats to her new friend, who gestures to her father in a black baseball cap to take a photo of them both, handing him the phone. The man takes the photo but seems distracted by the agent walking away. He isn't even looking at them when he takes the picture and then shoves the phone back into his daughter's hand. Why is he annoyed?

A long-haired man next to the annoyed father looks down. He's undoing his jacket and slides his hand inside. Even if Sinclair was wearing a wig, the man is too tall to be him.

Wolfe's eyes move back to the Girl Scout's father. On his back is a navy blue backpack. She uses the binoculars to zoom in on it. Is that a tiny teddy bear dangling from the top handhold?

He's not the father.

Wolfe grabs Casburn's arm.

'Toby! There!' She points.

'Imminent threat! Snowdrop!' shouts Casburn into his sleeve's microphone.

Wolfe doesn't hear any more. She jumps the handrail and runs as if her life depends on it.

73

Wolfe sprints down the bridge's footpath and throws herself into the closely packed crowd.

'Stop him!' she yells. 'Sinclair!'

Her shouts go unheard above the raucous gathering. Between her and Sinclair are a hundred or so people. The Secret Service will react in a matter of seconds. The counter assault teams armed with fully automatic Stoner SR-16 rifles and flash-bang grenades will spill out of the Suburban and wherever else they're hiding. The snipers will be ready to take the shot. She hopes to God that Pine will tell them she's not the threat. But she knows that if she gets in the way, they will shoot through her.

Melanie is still at the barrier with her new friend. The agent in the denim jacket shoves through the crowd towards the long-haired man reaching inside his coat.

'Gun!' the undercover agent shouts, then clutches the man in a bear hug, pinning his arms so he can't move.

At the word 'Gun', the agent protecting Melanie snaps his head round and sees the undercover agent grappling with a suspect.

The young girls at the front shriek and try to run, but they are pinned against the barrier.

Each shift agent runs to shield their protectees. Distracted for a second, the grey-haired agent swivels to grab Melanie, but Sinclair has jumped the barrier, snatched the President's daughter and holds a gun to her head. It looks like a Glock, a pistol easily bought from any gun shop on the Strip.

The shift agent draws his pistol and points it at Sinclair.

'Drop your weapon,' he bellows. 'Do it now!'

Sinclair grips the terrified child around the waist with his left arm, ducking low, using her to shield his torso from a bullet. If snipers try to shoot from behind, there's a risk the bullet will travel through his body and kill Melanie too.

Sinclair shuffles backwards until his rear is against the white rails that run the length of the bridge. They are the only thing stopping him and Melanie from plummeting into the Black Canyon, nine hundred feet below.

Wolfe battles a tsunami of terrified people fleeing, her progress agonisingly slow. She's almost knocked to the ground, staggers and pushes on.

Elizabeth screams as she's forcibly removed from the scene.

'No!' she cries. 'Not my daughter!'

'Mummy!' Melanie wails. 'Mummy!'

Thomas is picked up and thrown over an agent's shoulder like a sack of beans and carried to the nearest chopper, the blades on all Sea Kings already turning, readying to leave.

Sinclair sits the little girl on the rail, her legs dangling, her back to the dam and the deep ravine below. He grips her tightly with one arm and tilts her slightly backwards. Melanie gives an ear-piercing scream. If he lets go of her, she will plummet to her death.

The CAT team from the Suburban has taken up a semi-circle formation around Sinclair and the President's daughter, their R-16s trained on him. But they can't take a shot and risk losing her. Close behind Wolfe, the heavy rapid thud of boots: a second CAT team. Wolfe fights her way closer.

'Don't come any closer! I'll push her over!' says Sinclair. 'Shoot me and she dies!'

Wolfe has reached the crowd-control barrier that's been opened to let the CAT team through.

'Stay back!' says a uniformed officer.

'Let me through! I can stop him.'

Over the cop's shoulder she watches Sinclair slowly put the gun away in his jacket's upper pocket. The movement causes Melanie to jolt a fraction. With his free hand, Sinclair takes from a hip pocket a glass bottle with a red cap and lever, and holds it over the rail.

'See this? Psychosillius. The most destructive bacteria known to man. If I drop it in the river, it will decimate your country and turn America into a wasteland.'

'Stop him!' Wolfe yells, trying to dodge the cop.

Suddenly Wolfe is hit from behind and thrown to the ground. A police officer has thrown his weight on her.

'Don't move!' he yells.

She's being handcuffed. Winded, she tries to speak but can't. As she is yanked up to standing, Wolfe hears Sinclair shout, 'Get me Olivia Wolfe. Now!'

74

Surrounded by Secret Service agents and police officers, Wolfe tries taking a deep, calming breath but the bulletproof vest she's been fitted with is like a straitjacket. Her mouth is so dry her tongue feels like Velcro. She wears an earpiece and a microphone hidden beneath her sleeve so Pine can direct her.

Pine wipes sweat from his upper lip with the back of his hand as he uses his mobile phone to talk tactics with his agents back at Creech Air Force Base.

'Get him to Air Force One *now*!' says Pine, ending the call.

Lightbody grabs his attention. 'Sinclair's refused, sir. He'll only talk to Wolfe.'

Pine turns to Wolfe. 'Are you sure you're up to this?'

Wolfe nods, then fiddles with her earpiece. It's a little loose.

'This is all about getting Snowdrop to safety, okay?' says Pine. 'We need her off the rail, feet on the ground. Then we take him out.'

'Sir,' says Casburn, stepping in. 'I don't think you understand how destructive that bacteria is—'

'Not my problem.'

'It will be if he drops it,' says Casburn. 'You'll be responsible for the decimation of your country.'

'Like hell I will.'

Pine steers Wolfe away from Casburn. 'Listen to me,' he says.

'Get Sinclair to release Snowdrop. That's all you need to think about.'

Casburn isn't so easily thwarted and steps between them. 'Inside that bottle is a biological weapon, as destructive as a nuke. Sinclair must stay alive until we have it.'

'I don't have time for this.'

Casburn shoves Pine in the chest. 'Make time! No kill shot, not till we have the bacteria.'

Pine yells at him, 'Get out of my way before I have you arrested!'

Casburn throws his arms in the air and walks away, then pulls out his phone. Wolfe guesses he's going above Pine's head.

'Keep to Sinclair's right, okay?' Pine says to her, pointing up at the ravine wall behind them. A sniper lies prone, looking into the telescopic sight, finger on the trigger. 'Dickson will take the shot as soon as Snowdrop is off the rail. If he can't take it, O'Reilly will.' Pine nods in the direction of another sniper.

She prays they're accurate.

'Give me time to grab the bacteria,' Wolfe says.

Pine shakes his head.

Wolfe persists. 'Imagine a swarm of locusts but, instead of devouring crops, it devours anything with steel in it: cars, homes, offices, bridges, airports. If Sinclair breaks that glass bottle, the United States of America will look like a war zone.'

'Enough! Take this phone. Record what he has to say.'

She's wasting her breath. She takes the phone. 'Why?'

'He wants media coverage. He's not getting it. You make him think he is with that. Ready?'

'As I'll ever be.'

Pine leads her through the throng of uniformed officers and agents, who part like the Red Sea for Moses.

'Get him talking,' Pine continues. 'Don't interrupt. Show him you're listening. Empathise and build rapport. You need his trust to change his mind.'

'Got it.'

'Move nice and slow. Keep your hands where he can see them.'

Pine's mobile rings. He looks at the number and answers.

His eyes open wide in surprise. 'Yes, Mr President.' He hands his phone to Wolfe. 'The President wants to speak with you.'

All her working life, Wolfe has dreamed of interviewing the President of the United States. She never imagined it would be in such dire circumstances.

'Mr President? It's Olivia Wolfe speaking'

'May I call you Olivia?' His voice is deep. It sounds controlled. She cannot imagine the turmoil he must be in.

'Of course, sir.'

'What you are about to do is very brave. I thank you. All I ask is you do everything you possibly can to save my little girl. I don't feel Presidential right now. I'm just a dad who wants his little girl back safe.'

'I will do everything I can, I promise. But, sir?'

'Yes, Olivia?'

'Sir, I'm sure you've been briefed on the biological weapon he's threatening to drop into the Colorado River?'

'I have.'

'Your agents are naturally focused on saving your daughter, so I need to ask, sir, as the President, if I have to choose between saving Melanie and preventing the bacteria's release, what do you want me to do?'

'Dear God!' the President exclaims. Then he's silent. Somebody is talking to him in the background, possibly advising him. 'That's an impossible question, Olivia. As President, I've taken an oath to protect my country, but as a father, there's nothing more important to me than protecting my children.' He pauses. 'I need you to do both.'

Wolfe inhales sharply.

'You have to talk him down, Olivia.'

Her mind has gone blank.

'Can you do that for me?'

She replies without thinking. 'Yes, Mr President.'

'I'd like to speak to Special Agent Pine,' he says.

Wolfe hands over the phone. Pine listens.

'Yes, Mr President, will do,' he says, then puts his phone away.

'He wants me to save both,' Wolfe says. 'Keep the bottle in one piece and Melanie alive. I don't know how . . .'

Casburn steps close. 'Olivia, you can do this.'

'Let's go,' says Pine, leading her to within ten feet of Sinclair.

Melanie clings to her captor, whimpering. His arm muscles must be tired by now, probably shaking with the strain of hanging on to a forty-pound girl. The CAT agents have backed away as Sinclair earlier demanded, but are ready to attack on command. Wolfe reminds herself that she has been in great danger before. She's faced worse and survived. But, if she fails this time, the repercussions are catastrophic.

Pine calls out, 'Toby! We have Olivia Wolfe for you. You want me to send her over?'

'Yes,' he replies.

Sinclair tenses, and Melanie cries out as his grip on her tightens. Wolfe takes her first trembling steps towards Sinclair. She has never felt so alone.

'Hello, Toby,' she says, trying to smile.

'Stop there,' Sinclair says when she is a couple of feet from him. Wolfe does as he directs.

Melanie stares at Wolfe, her cheeks stained with tears. 'Please help me,' she sobs.

'It's all right, Melanie, my name's Olivia and I'm here to help. Just keep hold of this man, okay?'

'I want my mummy,' the little girl wails.

'I know you do, but just hang on to this man while I talk to him, okay?'

'Okay,' Melanie replies, sniffing back tears.

'Toby, tell me what this is about.'

'You're here to make sure the world knows how the United States murdered my wife and children.'

Wolfe remembers when she first met Sinclair. Nervous and uncommunicative. Excited by the prospect of an imminent scientific breakthrough. Unassuming. Now, his eyes are hard as granite. He's poisoned with hatred.

'Pacify him,' Pine says through her earpiece.

'I'm so sorry, Toby. They died needlessly. You must have loved them very much.'

'They were my life . . .' His voice trails away.

'Sally was about the same age as Melanie, wasn't she? Do you really want another little girl to die?'

'The President must feel the pain. Know what it's like to lose a child.'

Sinclair tilts Melanie back further so her head and torso lean out over the ravine. The terrified girl screams. There's a collective gasp. Wolfe instinctively steps forward to grab her.

'No, you don't!' Sinclair shouts. 'Stay where you are!'

'Calm him!' Pine says in her ear.

'Toby, I'm sorry. I didn't mean to scare you. Please don't hurt Melanie,' Wolfe says, holding up her hands to pacify him. 'You want to tell me your story? I'm here. Talk to me. But keep Melanie safe. Please, Toby. She's only six.'

He slowly pulls Melanie towards him so she sits upright on the rail once more. Wolfe notices a dark stain on the little girl's jeans where she's peed herself in terror.

'Where are the media crews I asked for?'

'You're armed. It's too dangerous. But I'm here. Tell me your story. I'll broadcast it.'

'I want you to record it.'

'Can I use my phone's video? It's in my right hand.'

'Show me,' he says.

Wolfe holds out her hand and opens her palm. 'Can I move closer?'

'One step. Just one.'

She does exactly as he asks.

'Move to your right,' she hears through her earpiece.

Wolfe is blocking the line of fire. But if she moves to the right, she will be too far away to catch the bottle if he drops it. She stays put.

'Olivia, if we have to take a shot, you're in the line of fire,' Pine says.

'Olivia, this is Casburn, you have to move.'

Their voices irritate her like buzzing mosquitos. Wolfe presses the record button on her phone.

'Okay, it's recording. What do you want to tell me?' Wolfe says.

'I don't feel. Anything. For two years I've just existed. I died with them. Their needless deaths.' His words catch in his throat.

She remains silent, waiting for him to continue. Her eyes flit to his hand holding Melanie and then to his other hand clutching the glass bottle full of cloudy Psychosillius. His thumb holds down some sort of lever attached to the red lid.

'They were killed by a drone strike in Afghanistan,' Sinclair says. 'A drone controlled by operators at Creech Air Force Base.

They never admitted responsibility. Huma was volunteering at the local hospital. She'd finished her shift and was having dinner with her family. It was the first time the kids had visited their relatives in Kandahar. I'd only spoken to them an hour before. They sounded so happy . . . '

'Huma sounds an amazing woman.'

'She was. Selfless and loving. All my life I've been dull old Toby. Never invited anywhere. Ignored. Overlooked at work, despite my ground-breaking discoveries. But Huma saw something in me nobody else did. She believed in me, in my research. She made everything I did worthwhile. I loved her more than life itself. And still do.'

'What would Huma think of this?'

'What does it matter what she'd think? She's gone!' he yells.

Wolfe sucks in a breath, terrified she's gone too far.

'Please, go on,' she urges.

It takes a few moments for Toby to compose himself. 'This isn't about revenge, if that's what you're thinking. If I wanted to hurt people, I could've engineered a virus. But I didn't. This is about saying, "Enough!" Someone has to do it. Stop the war machine. Destroy their weapons. Psychosillius does exactly that. Tanks, battleships, drones, guns – anything with an ounce of steel in it; they'll all be useless and the world will be better for it.'

'Get him talking about Snowdrop again, then ask him to hand her to you,' she hears through the earpiece.

'You've got everyone's attention, Toby,' Wolfe says. 'You've succeeded. But the best person to convey your message is you. Give yourself up. The coverage will be wall-to-wall. You'll be centre stage. Just let Melanie go and hand me the bottle.'

Sinclair stares at her as if he hasn't heard. 'You know, back in the sixties, Eisenhower warned us about misplaced power, about the military-industrial complex.'

'I know that speech.'

'Then you know he was talking about the military and weapons manufacturers controlling government. What did he say? "We must never let the weight of this combination endanger our liberties or democratic processes." But it's already happened. It's too late. Can't you see that, Olivia?'

'I understand what you're saying, but releasing Psychosillius isn't the answer. It won't just attack military targets. It'll hurt innocent people. Children will die. Homes will collapse, sports centres, schools, playgrounds. Surely you don't want that?'

Sinclair looks down and his shoulders shake and for a moment she wonders if he's laughing. When he looks up, his eyes are watery and their expression has softened.

Through her earpiece she hears the sniper, Dickson, complaining he can't get a clear shot and neither can O'Reilly.

'Give Melanie to me,' Wolfe urges, trying not to betray her rising panic. 'You have my word nothing will happen to you.'

'As soon as I let her go, I'm dead.'

Wolfe is so close to Sinclair she can smell his fear, his vinegary sweat. His voice is weary. She takes a gamble. She puts out her arms. Sinclair doesn't stop her. She lifts the girl off the rail. When Melanie's feet touch the ground Wolfe tells her to run. Arms wide, she races for the grey-haired agent, who scoops her up in his arms and runs to a waiting helicopter.

'Good work,' says Pine. 'Now, talk him into giving you the bottle.'

'That was good, Toby. Very good,' she says. 'Now hand me that bottle. If you want change, you need to speak up, but nobody's going to listen if you release the Psychosillius.'

'Know what this is?' Sinclair says, holding the bottle up.

His thumb holds down a plastic lever connected to the bottle cap.

'No.'

'A dead-man's switch. You or anyone tries to grab it, I release the lever and the glass explodes.'

'Please, Toby, just give it to me.'

'Do you know what our government intends to do with Psychosillius? Hmm?'

Wolfe hears Casburn shout, 'Shut him up! She can't know this.'

'Don't say any more, Toby. You'll get us both killed.'

In that second she's aware of a terrible irony. All her career she has sought out the truth and now she is begging a man not to tell her.

'Just hand me the bottle,' Wolfe begs.

'They're going to use it as a WMD. To my eternal shame I've helped develop the most dangerous biological weapon the world has ever seen.'

'Stop him!' yells Casburn.

'I don't want to know,' Wolfe screams at Sinclair.

'Take him out! Now!' Pine orders.

Wolfe lunges at Sinclair, seizing the hand clasping the bottle, and wraps both her hands around Toby's fist, squeezing tight. Startled, he yanks his hand away, leaving her gripping the dead-man's switch.

She hears the unmistakable fut, fut of a rifle firing twice in rapid succession. Then nothing.

Casburn hears the wet thwack and the crack of a sonic compression wave he remembers all too vividly from his SAS days, as the bullets hit.

Sinclair's body jolts as his head explodes. Blood and bone and brain matter sprays up and outwards like a Catherine wheel, crimson and grey against the pale blue sky. He sinks to the ground; Wolfe staggers, then collapses on top of him.

Casburn sprints over to Wolfe and skids to a halt on bloody concrete. He can't see the bottle. He slides his hand between Wolfe's body and Sinclair's, and finds her hands. She still grips the dead man's switch, hands clasped tightly. The bottle is in one piece.

Wolfe lies face down in a burgeoning pool of blood, hair slick with gore, eyes shut. Motionless.

75

Two weeks later, on a bitterly cold, grey day, Jerry Butcher stands outside the crematorium chapel smoking a cigarette. At least he's not back to twenty a day. He can't. If he did, his wife would never have him inside the house again. But since he heard about what happened in Nevada, he finds that only a cigarette settles the shakes. Strange really. He can only remember suffering the shakes after one, maybe two, particularly gruesome cases. But this was personal.

As he blows smoke up towards the 1930s slate roof, he watches his nicotine-stained fingers tremble, like the almost imperceptible pulse of a butterfly's wings. Emma wants him to get tested for Parkinson's but he doesn't want a doctor asking questions he doesn't want to answer. Like, how did he fail Olivia so badly? He should never have let her get into such a terrible mess.

Only ten or twelve people have turned up. He expected more. The emptiness of the chapel reminds him how easily we are forgotten and how little we are forgiven.

Butcher squints into the drizzle, beyond a neat circular patch of grass around which the drive sweeps and down the road, lined with barren, leafless poplars standing to attention like sentinels. Everything feels damp – even his mac seems to hold him in a wet embrace. He stamps his feet, which are numb with cold. Organ music pulsates through the open door, which reminds him of the Dracula films he saw as a boy, then immediately he feels guilty. He is being disrespectful. A pallbearer pokes his head out and nods at Butcher.

'Service is starting.'

'I'll stay here for now.'

The doors shut with a clunk.

After thirty years in the force, Butcher thought he'd seen everything. Some cases were worse than others, child murders the most harrowing. But he'd always kept his emotions under control, always stayed focused. That was his job and the best way to bring some resolution for the grieving relatives. But when he heard about Olivia's bravery and the shooting, he realised how deeply he loves every rebellious, impulsive, adventurous, argumentative bit of her.

A car races along the crematorium drive, gravel flying. It takes a right turn before it reaches the chapel and heads for one of two car parks. He drops his stub and stamps it out. If he leaves it there, he'll get an earful, so he picks up the crushed stub and places it inside the cigarette packet. He hears the crunch of boots on gravel, his view of the late arrival hindered by a tall, manicured yew hedge, so smooth it resembles a vertical carpet.

'Traffic was a nightmare. Has it started?' she asks.

'Just. We can probably sneak in the back.'

She is at the door, twisting the horseshoe-shaped doorknob.

'Olivia?'

'Yes?'

She glances at him, impatient to get inside. She's wearing a long black coat, her biker boots protruding under the hem, and a black felt 1930s-style bell-shaped hat. He's never seen her wear a smart hat before.

'How's the head?'

'Throbs.' She touches the white dressing, partly hidden by the hat sitting low on her head. 'They had to shave above my ear. Looks like Edward Scissorhands got me.' Wolfe grins.

Butcher doesn't move. He looks back down the drive and watches a blackbird swoop low. 'I thought I'd lost you.'

Wolfe steps away from the door and squeezes his arm. 'But you didn't.'

'You were lucky. Another millimetre or two, and that bullet would've shattered your skull.'

'We should go in,' she says.

Butcher still doesn't budge. He wants to say more, but can't find the words.

He looks beyond the hedges and cars and can just make out the cemetery, like a meadow full of neatly placed white mushrooms.

'Come on,' Wolfe says.

She takes his gloved hand in hers and twists the handle. The door opens and they step inside to bid goodbye to a man reviled.

76

Wolfe is packing boxes in her flat when Casburn rings the bell. She knows it's him because, for once, she invited him. Most of her fragile and precious possessions are already packed, including the framed photos that normally hang behind her desk. She moves tomorrow and has told nobody where she is going.

Wolfe lets Casburn in and leads him into her sitting room

in silence. She has no interest in attempting their usual banter. Gesturing for him to sit, she takes the sofa, he the armchair. She anticipates he will try to take control of the conversation, and she's happy to let him: he has something, or rather someone, she wants.

'I can't free him,' Casburn says.

'We both know he's innocent.'

Casburn sighs. 'What do you want, Olivia?'

'A deal. I persuade Vitaly to hand you Kabir Khan. You give him a new ID, a new start. No record.'

'I'm here because of what you did, but I have no intention of trading Yushkov.'

Wolfe leans forward so her elbows rest on her thighs, hands clasped so he can't see them tremble. 'I made you look like a hero, Dan. You owe me. The President owes me. Do I have to talk to Garriola? Or the President himself?'

Casburn's eyes narrow. 'Yushkov claims he has no idea where Kabir is.'

'And I believe him. But he can find him for you.'

'How?'

'He puts it out he's turned. Wants to join their cause. I suspect he has enough hatred for you and this country to be thoroughly convincing, and his injuries will leave Kabir in no doubt he's been tortured.'

Casburn lifts his chin a fraction and blinks once – his tell. The confirmation sends her heart rate into overdrive.

'Kabir will suspect a trap. He'll kill Yushkov.'

'If Vitaly is prepared to take that risk, what have you got to lose?'

'I can't risk him disappearing.'

'Put a tracking device on him. It's not like you've got any other options, is it?'

'Yushkov won't do it. He's protecting him.'

'He'll do it for me.'

Casburn snorts derisively. 'You think he gives a shit about you?'

Wolfe flushes with anger, but she keeps her voice level. 'He'll do it for me because I have proof of Kabir Khan's guilt.'

Wolfe is escorted into Belmarsh Prison's high-security unit; a gaol within a gaol, for those deemed an escape risk or too dangerous to mix with other offenders. It has housed IRA prisoners, KGB agents and 9/11 terror suspects. Now, Vitaly Yushkov is an inmate in this special unit.

Her boots and belt removed, she has been through a metal detector, had her fingerprints taken, and passed through fifteen security doors, monitored at all times by CCTV. Each time a door clanks shut, it chills her. The guards eye her with curiosity and suspicion.

'Don't know what strings you pulled to get here,' the guard says. 'Hope it's worth it.'

She's shown into a surprisingly large exercise yard, surrounded by high fences, topped with barbed wire.

'I'll stay close by.' He leads her in. 'You have ten minutes. And no touching.'

There is only one man in the yard, watched by two more guards. In polo-neck jumper and jeans, his hands are cuffed in front. Yushkov walks towards her, smiling, but his movements are slow and he leans forward slightly. When they are but a few feet apart, he stops. She doesn't. Her escort moves between them and tells her to step back. She obeys.

'I want to wrap my arms around you,' Yushkov says, 'Kiss you. But they will take you away if I do.'

All that remains of his black eye is some yellowing skin, but the cut along his cheekbone will take longer to heal. He finds it hard to catch his breath. She guesses broken ribs.

'I miss you,' she says.

Wolfe wants to ask a myriad of questions but the clock is ticking. 'We only have ten minutes. I'm here to help you. To get you out.'

Yushkov shakes his head. 'That will never happen. But I thank you.'

'Let's walk,' she says.

They head off slowly, the guard close behind. 'Casburn is offering you a clean slate. A new identity, no record. In return, you will be fitted with a tracking device. Contact Kabir Khan. Ask for his protection. Tell him you want revenge for what SO15 has done to you.'

'Betray a friend? A man who saved my life? Showed me forgiveness? I will not do it.' He stops walking and faces her. 'I cannot believe you ask me this.'

'Vitaly, please listen. Kabir Khan is not the boy you once knew. In Pakistan he was radicalised, filled with hatred. He's funded by a man I've spoken to you about: Colonel Lalzad.'

'Olivia, please stop! My freedom has been taken; my sister has been taken; I cannot be with you. I have nothing left but my integrity. I will not betray an innocent man.'

'He's not innocent, Vitaly. I can prove it.'

Wolfe turns to her escort. 'Can I have my phone, please?'

He hands it to her. 'No photos, no recording. Just play the audio, as agreed.'

Wolfe faces Yushkov. 'Remember I told you about a young Afghani girl who was murdered by Lalzad's lieutenant in Kabul. Nooria Zia was her name.'

'I remember.'

'She was murdered to protect Khan and his terror cell. I recorded our conversation. Listen to it. Please.'

Wolfe holds up her smartphone; the chip inside it is from the phone that was in her dress pocket when Nooria died. She plays the audio recording.

The squeak of a gate opening.

'You must leave,' a woman says with urgency, her accent thick. 'Mina is watching.'

'Can you meet us at the market later?' Wolfe asks.

There is a loud crack. A gasp. Then a thud. Wolfe remembers shoving Shinwari to the ground.

'On the roof opposite,' Wolfe pants. 'Sniper.'

The crunch of snow underfoot.

'Help me!' Wolfe calls. Then a scraping sound as Wolfe drags the fatally wounded Nooria behind a pillar.

'What do we do?' screams Shinwari, terrified.

A pause, then the girl speaks. Yushkov turns his head to hear better.

'Kabir . . . Kabir Khan . . . '

The girl chokes.

'Nooria!' Wolfe says.

' . . . bomb London.' A pause. 'Da'ish,' she says. Another shot booms out.

Wolfe stops the audio recording and studies Yushkov's face. He backs away.

'Vitaly?'

Yushkov bends over as if he's been punched in the stomach, then stands tall and roars, 'No!'

The guard nearest Wolfe steps in. 'Time to leave.'

'Wait!' Wolfe says.

'Please,' says Yushkov, putting out his hand. 'A few more minutes.'

She pulls away from the guard. 'I'm sorry you had to hear it from me, but Khan has been recruited by Isil. He's Da'ish.

393

He's planning an attack in London, but we don't know where or when and we need your help.'

'We? You work for them now?'

'If you help them, you will be free.'

'I do not want to help the people who tortured me.'

'Then do it for a young girl who made a stand against Isil.'

'*Nyet.*' He shakes his head slowly. 'I will do it for you.'

'Thank you.'

But her elation is short-lived.

'There's a catch,' Wolfe says. 'You'll be a free man but . . . you can't stay here. You'll get safe passage to wherever you choose. But you must leave England and never return.'

She looks down so he cannot see her pain.

77

It is a cold blustery Christmas Eve and Wolfe looks through a mesh security fence at the London Gateway Container Terminal, a deep-water port in Essex that handles the largest container ships in the world. She peers up at a 398 metres long, black, white and red monster that sits low in the water, fully loaded. Enormous grey cranes tower over the vessel. But they are still, their booms lifted high into the air and clear of the ship, their job complete.

Further down the quay another ship is still loading. The crane booms extend over its deck, the trolleys trundling back and forth with a lumbering grace, spreaders locked on to brightly coloured steel containers, piling them on the deck like a toddler's brick set. Yellow straddle carriers, like fifteen metre-high mechanical insects, trundle around at the feet of the giant gantry, incessantly ferrying the containers back and forth between the quay line, the storage yard and waiting trucks. The machines on the quay are a mechanical marvel, an engineered dance devoid of people.

The wind buffets Wolfe's face and the intense cold makes her eyes sting. The air is thick with salt blown off the sea and brings with it the distant metallic thunk of container touching container, the constant burr of engines and the stink of bunker fuel and diesel. Wolfe wears the black bell-shaped felt hat and long coat she wore to Sinclair's funeral a week ago. She has said her goodbye to Sinclair. Now she must say goodbye to Vitaly Yushkov.

He walks down the metal stairs from the terminal's control room, wearing an all-in-one blue boiler suit and dark blue beanie. He waves, his smiling eyes never leaving hers. She waits, hands in pockets, on the other side of a full-height security turnstile, listening to the clomp of his boots. She knows they don't have long. The crew is aboard, and a HiLux waits for the newly appointed ship's engineer.

Vitaly swipes his security pass over the reader and the cumbersome turnstile clicks as he pushes through. Wolfe closes the distance between them and he wraps his arms around her. His broad back shelters her from the wind and his body emanates heat through his overalls. She listens to the quickening beat of his heart.

'I have missed you,' Yushkov says.

Wolfe looks up. His split lip has healed well but the cut across his cheekbone has left a vivid scar.

She takes his face gently between her hands and lightly kisses his lips.

'Thank God you're now safe,' she whispers.

'I have you to thank, not God.'

His tongue parts her lips, his grip around her body tightening, and he kisses her with a passion more intense than the pain he must feel from his slowly healing ribs.

'I want you,' Yushkov whispers.

'I wish we had more time.'

He strokes her cheek then touches the white dressing partially visible from beneath her hat. 'Does it heal okay?'

'I'll be fine.'

Yushkov looks around him, wary. 'Let's walk. I don't have much time and who knows who may be listening.'

He takes her hand and they follow the line of the perimeter fence, the wind behind them. 'You are like a cat, Olivia. Many lives,' he says, smiling. 'Please do not run out of them.'

She stops. 'Vitaly, there must be another way? I'm a journalist. I can work anywhere in the world. Surely we can be together.'

'I would like this very much, but it is not possible, Olivia. The work you do makes you easy to find and, if you are with me, you will always be in danger. If I stay away from you, don't contact you, then you will be safe. It is the way it works.'

'I'm prepared to take the risk.'

Yushkov hugs her again. 'It does not matter where we are, my enemies will find us and they will kill us. You first, so I see you suffer. I will not place you in this danger.'

Wolfe is silent for a while, her mind searching for a solution she already knows doesn't exist.

'So when you reach Durban, will the SVR be waiting?'

'Perhaps. I will be careful.'

A seagull screeches overhead. 'How can I contact you?'

Yushkov takes her hand as they head back to the turnstile.

'Just keep walking and look straight ahead. I have dropped a phone in your pocket. There is just one number in the directory. Only use this phone to call me and nobody else, and only if it is an emergency.'

'That makes long-distance dating kind of hard,' she jokes.

But she feels crushed. She wants to beg him to stay, just as she had begged her dad to stay when she was young. But she knows the words are futile. Wolfe stares down at the wet concrete. For once in her life she is lost for words. He lifts her chin gently, his brow creased with concern.

'I will see you again one day. I promise.'

'I know,' she says, 'but right now one day seems like infinity.'

Yushkov tilts his head to one side. 'I think it is best if I go now.'

He kisses her one more time and walks away.

'Vitaly!' she shouts.

He turns.

'Happy Christmas!'

'And you!'

He waves, then turns into the wind.

'Vitaly!'

He looks over his shoulder.

'You're a man of integrity and never forget it.'

He nods once. She watches him go through the turnstile. He doesn't look back again. He gets into the waiting vehicle and a flashing orange safety light on the cabin roof switches on when the engine starts.

Wolfe makes her way through the car park. Her walk becomes a run, and she keeps running until she is inside her grandmother's car, tears streaming down her face.

Her mobile rings, and for one silly moment she wonders if it might be Yushkov. She checks her pockets and finds the mobile phone he gave her. But it is not ringing. She rummages through her bag and finds her smartphone. It's Casburn. She hesitates.

'Yes?' She sounds weary.

'Thought you might like to know we've got enough to put Kabir Khan away for life.'

She holds the phone away and covers it with her hand so she can sniff back a tear without him hearing.

'Hello?' she hears him say. 'You there?'

When she's ready, she replies. 'That's great news.'

There is an awkward silence. She is waiting for the real reason for his call.

'I'm changing jobs. Heading up a new command.'

'Congratulations. Don't suppose you'll tell me what you're doing there?'

'It's classified.'

'Of course it is.'

Another pause.

'Don't I get any thanks?' Casburn asks.

'For what, dropping the charges? I was innocent.'

She can hear him chewing gum. 'I saw you at Sinclair's funeral.'

'You were there?' Wolfe immediately wonders if he is at the port too. 'Why, for Christ's sake?'

'Just dotting i's and crossing t's.'

'Don't be so irritating, Dan. Why have you really called?'

'Now, now, no need to be like that.'

'Why don't you just tell me what you called about?'

'Thought you'd be interested to hear that a certain SVR agent has been found dead, floating in the Thames near Battersea Bridge.'

'Sergey Grankin?'

'Yes, Sergey Grankin, with a bloody great big cut across his throat.'

'You think the SVR did it?'

'No, I don't, and nor do you. We both know who did it, but the body's been in the water too long. Forensics could find nothing useful.'

Wolfe touches the pocket holding Yushkov's mobile phone, her only connection to the man.

'No, I don't know who you mean. Tell me.'

Casburn sighs. 'All right, have it your way. But be careful, Olivia. Vitaly Yushkov is a trained killer. He's not the man you think he is.'

'He's everything I believed him to be.'

Wolfe has had enough of Casburn's games. She ends the call, throws her phone into her bag and turns the ignition. It's a long drive home. But she doesn't put the car into gear. Instead, she pulls out Vitaly's mobile. She stares at it, wondering how he would react if she told him about Grankin. Would he tell her the truth?

She shakes her head.

'Best not to know.'

78

Snow has settled overnight, enough to fill the gaps between paving stones and coat the grassy zones of Collinson Court, a sprawling council estate in Southeast London. Children scream with delight as they scoop up the snow in mittened hands and throw it at friends, hitting their targets in explosions of white. Wolfe can't think of the last time London had snow on Christmas Day; even though the streets are eerily empty, driving on icy roads has made her journey difficult. Not that it was ever going to be easy. She hasn't seen her brother, Davy, since he was sentenced. As she watches a little boy chase a girl with pink earmuffs and hurl a snowball at her, Wolfe can't help wondering if the boy might be Joe Wolfe, her nephew.

She remembers playing such games with her brother, who also taught her how to build a snowman.

'Mel, come inside now, we're doing presents,' calls a neighbour.

The little girl in pick earmuffs skips to her mum, the game forgotten, presents her only thought. For a moment, Wolfe feels very alone. No family to share Christmas with.

'Snap out of it,' she tells herself.

Wolfe kills the car's engine and looks up at the sitting room window of Davy's first-floor council flat. A small, fake, green Christmas tree is decked with a string of flashing lights, framed by beige curtains that haven't been hung properly, sagging at the top in uneven waves. Someone moves behind the tree, but it's little more than a human shape. She shouldn't be here. She's violating her protection order and Davy's parole. But the decision is made; she has to know. She reluctantly leaves the warmth of the car and trudges along the icy pavement towards the blue door of number forty-two. She rings the doorbell and hears it chime, then the creak of somebody coming down the stairs.

'This is my house.'

Standing next to Wolfe is a boy with large brown eyes, and hair as dark as a blackbird.

'Joe?'

'Who wants to know?' The boy gives her a cheeky, lopsided grin.

The door opens. The woman has short bleached-blonde hair, with dark roots, a puffy face and bloated body. She's in a red sweatshirt and grey tracksuit pants. Between her chapped lips, a cigarette dangles. As warm air escapes through the open door, Wolfe smells the delicious gamey smell of a turkey roasting.

'Well, bugger me,' says Claire Spiers, taking the cigarette from her mouth. She's wearing chipped black nail polish. 'Look what the cat dragged in.'

'Hello, Claire. I'm here to see Davy.'

Spiers raises her eyebrows in disbelief. 'You've got a fucking nerve!' Then she notices the boy. 'Go play with your mates,' she says, shooing him away.

Joe gives Wolfe a quizzical look, then runs off to join the other children. He looks like Davy when he was that age.

Spiers – taller and wider than Wolfe – steps into the doorway, blocking it.

'Who the hell do you think you are, turning up like this, after what you did?'

She flicks ash into the air.

'Claire, it's up to Davy, not you. Will you go ask him if he wants to talk? Please?'

Spiers juts her neck forwards. 'Don't tell me what to fucking do!'

'Who is it?' says a voice she barely recognises from the top of the stairs.

'Your fucking sister!' she shouts over her shoulder. Then, at Wolfe, 'Now get lost!'

The children stop playing and stare in silence. Wolfe doesn't want to cause a scene, but she's not going to walk away because Spiers says so.

'Davy!' Wolfe calls. 'Can we talk? Just five minutes. Please.'

Spiers gives Wolfe's shoulder a solid shove. Before Spiers realises what's happening, Wolfe grips the woman's hand to her chest, squeezing her thumbs under Spiers's palm, and applies pressure to the already partially bent wrist, forcing the hand back at a right-angle.

'Ow!' Spiers squeals.

'Do that again, and I'll break it,' says Wolfe, releasing her grip.

Spiers steps back, surprised, clearly used to throwing her considerable weight around.

'Let her in,' calls Davy, his words slurred.

As Spiers steps aside and follows Wolfe up the steep stairs to their first-floor flat, she wonders if Davy has been drinking. But when she sees him standing in the sitting room, she realises her mistake. His stocky build is slightly stooped and his hair has turned pepper and salt. But this is not what causes her to stare. His left eyebrow and eye socket have dropped a fraction, and his eyelid is lazy and stays half closed. Butcher had warned her about the attack on him in prison, but she can't hide her distress.

'Look nice, don't I?' He takes a few steps towards her. 'You did this.' He points to his face. 'You put me through hell.'

'I didn't know, Davy. Until you were released, I didn't know.'

He turns his back on her and sits down in a sagging, pale green armchair. Wolfe follows, keen to move away from Spiers's laboured breathing on her neck.

'Your mate, Jerry, tell you, did he? How fucking thoughtful of him.'

Wolfe sits opposite, on an equally sagging two-seater sofa. She glances at Spiers, who stands in the doorway, arms folded, like a bodyguard.

'How are you going?' she asks.

'Fucking dandy, can't you tell? I talk like a fucking retard and look worse.'

His hand shakes with fury as he pulls out a cigarette and lights it.

'Are you working?'

Davy takes a deep drag, then exhales. 'Why?'

'Just asking.'

'Yeah, a bit of IT. Subcontracted stuff I do at home. But if it wasn't for Claire, we'd be well and truly fucked.'

Wolfe takes a deep breath. The room is overheated and the roasting turkey's aromas are so strong, she feels she's going to choke.

'What's with the dumb hat?' Davy asks.

Wolfe removes it.

'Well, aren't we a matching pair?' She swears Davy almost smiles. 'Heard you got shot. Been all over the news. Shame that sniper wasn't a better shot.'

Wolfe clasps her hands together. During the drive there, she had rehearsed what she was going to say. Now she isn't sure how to begin. She glances at the Christmas tree and sees discarded wrapping paper and opened presents lying next to the plastic three-pronged stand: an aftershave gift set, a cheap brand of tablet she's never heard of, some DVDs, a pair of women's pyjamas and fluffy slippers. Wolfe feels like an intruder.

'Davy, there's no point in going over old ground. You did what you did, and I did what I did. I'm sorry you went to jail. I'm sorry you were beaten up. But can we start again? You're all I've got.'

She sounds pathetic. She hadn't intended to say this.

'You want family? Go find the old man,' he replies.

Wolfe swallows. 'You heard from him?'

'Course not. And if I did, I'd tell him to go fuck himself.'

She pulls from her pocket a small box, wrapped in red paper covered in smiling snowmen. 'For Joe.'

Spiers can't stay quiet any longer. 'How dare you come in here expecting to buy your way into our family! Get out! Go on, get the fuck out!'

Davy stares at the TV, which isn't on. Wolfe gets up, leaving her gift on the sofa cushion, and pulls on her hat. She has to ask the question she came there to ask.

'Did Freddie Glenn teach you to hack computers?'

She has Davy's attention. 'What?' he asks. 'You trying to frame me for something else?' Davy is up and standing over her, his chin jutting forwards, his mouth curved into a sneer.

'Someone's hacked my computer. Stalking me.'

'Oh, and you think that's me, do you?' He yells. 'Get out! Don't ever come here again.' He grabs the gift and hurls it across the room. It hits the radiator with a clang.

79

Your visit was unexpected.

It's Christmas night, the turkey's been eaten, the telly's on, the Queen has made her speech; all is right with the world. But it isn't, is it?

I'm fucked up and you're fucked up. But I will always bear the visible scars.

You'll recover from the bullet wound, your hair will grow back and – in a few months – nobody will ever know. The mind heals more slowly. Will you ever forget the moment Sinclair's skull exploded? His blood and brain on your face? Do you wake at night in a sweat, reliving your failure to save him, a man who had lost everything? Or is he already compartmentalised? Locked away, forgotten, as I suspect I am?

Ah, but the heart is slowest of all to heal. Yushkov is gone. He will never contact you and, should you ever call him, his silence will crush you.

I still watch you. But I keep my distance. GPS trackers. Your new phone, your bike, your grandmother's car. That's enough for now. With Yushkov out of the picture I can relax, re-read my diary, relive my successes and learn from my mistakes. Each time, the experience is exhilaratingly new, like the first time you leave home, go overseas, or lose your virginity.

Moz Cohen is a disappointment. I guess he had to reinstate

you. How fickle is the public: one minute you're hated; the next you're a hero. Even if the subtext is, 'Not bad for a slut'. You can't take back your filthy secrets. Do people look at you differently now, Olivia? Do men give you the once-over, remembering those photos of you with Yushkov? Or do you get the cold shoulder? Respect is so fragile. You can be sure that video will follow you wherever you go, just as I do. The golden girl of investigative reporting is tarnished.

I lean back in my armchair, feet up, and savour the moment, knowing that in the morning I will have forgotten the part I played. You may not have fallen as far as I'd hoped, but there's time, and I have plenty of it.

Yes, your visit today was unexpected. Futile. You are none the wiser. But I am.

I know you suspect the wrong person.

'Hello, Olivia.'

She is signing the removal company's inventory. The van is loaded, the rear doors closed. Olivia looks up and at first doesn't recognise me. I've made sure I look my best: even got my hair done. Her brow creases. I decide to help her along.

'It's been a while,' I say, and smile.

I haven't been within arms' reach of Olivia since she visited me in hospital. I've forgotten – as I do most things – that I am a good foot taller than she is.

'Annabel?'

Olivia still sounds unsure. Her eyes flick around my face and land on the scar and my lame eye, partially hidden by my glasses. 'Annabel Maine! Well, I'll be. How are you?'

She smiles, clearly delighted. I feel lighter, warmer, happy. She envelops me in a hug, leaning her head against my chest, and it takes every ounce of self-control not to stroke her hair or lift her chin and try to kiss her lips.

Releasing me, Olivia says, 'You look really well.'

'Thanks. I'm getting there. Slowly. How's Moz?'

'As cantankerous as ever, still reducing trainees to tears. You know how he is.'

'Vaguely. There's still a lot I can't remember.'

'So what are you doing here?' Olivia asks, so close I can imbibe the perfume I know so well.

I study her face. There's no hint of suspicion. Just surprise.

'Meeting a friend for lunch,' I lie. 'She suggested the Bombay Palace.' It's Olivia's favourite. I've watched her eat there often enough. 'You're a curry fan, as I remember. Why don't you join us?'

A heavy-set man in a Big Ben Removals T-shirt interrupts. 'All right, love, we'll meet you there in, say, half-hour. All right?'

'Yes, thanks,' she says.

The driver and his mate get into the truck and drive off, thick black smoke belching out of the exhaust pipe.

'Moving house?' I ask.

Indecision flits across her face like a dark cloud. 'Time for something new. A change.'

'Where you going?' I keep my voice light, as if I don't care.

Olivia frowns, then looks to her right, watching the truck disappear down the road with everything she possesses inside.

'Give me your number,' she says. 'Gotta get going, otherwise the removal men will get there way before I do, and I'm paying by the hour.'

Ah, so she's not going to tell me. Never mind.

'Sure.' I pull a pen and notepad from my satchel, tear off a page and jot down a mobile number.

She takes the scrap of paper, shoves it in her jeans pocket, then holds my hand.

'Once I'm settled in the new place, I'll call you. Lovely to see you. Bye for now.'

Olivia jogs up the path and waves at me as she closes the communal door to her flat on Elmbourne Road.

I wave back. The door shuts with a click.

'Goodbye, my little robin. For now.'

Acknowledgements

The story of *Devour* was inspired by a British expedition to Antarctica in 2012 led by Professor Martin Siegert, who kindly shared his adventures with me over many cups of coffee in Bristol. He and his team were attempting to drill through three kilometres of ice to reach the subterranean Lake Ellsworth, hoping to discover new life. Despite a Herculean effort, they did not succeed in their mission, but thanks to the information Professor Siegert shared with me, I was able to bring to life the imaginary Camp Ellsworth, the drilling operations, and the dangers the team faced. I must stress that the scientists and engineers in *Devour* in no way resemble any of the British team, and the character of Professor Heatherton is entirely fictitious. Any deviation in camp layout, equipment or drilling techniques was my decision.

Some years ago I was lucky enough to be in Antarctica, and it was on an ex-Russian scientific research vessel, the *Professor Multanovskiy*, that I encountered the inspiration for the character of Vitaly Yushkov. He was the ship's engineer, a man seemingly impervious to the bitter cold and who spoke with a wry smile and in the stilted English I have endeavoured to convey in this thriller. Antarctica is not only a place of stunning beauty, it is also the last true wilderness left on our planet, and long may that last. Antarctica is not owned by any one country. It is protected by a goodwill treaty between numerous nations, known as the Antarctic Treaty, that forbids weapons, nuclear testing and mining, and proclaims the continent to be a place for peaceful scientific research and co-operation. However, there are countries already exploring ways to exploit its resources. I ask those Antarctic Treaty signatory nations to hold strong. Protect Antarctica, for all our sakes.

Retired Detective Chief Superintendent of Sussex CID, David Gaylor, is not only an invaluable advisor on all British policing matters, but also a great friend, and I thank him from the bottom of my heart for his support and guidance. I have huge respect for the British police and must stress that my fictional retired detective, Jerry Butcher, bears no resemblance to David, and nor is DCI Casburn from Counter Terrorism Command based on anyone living.

If you haven't already read the book, here is a spoiler alert. I wish to thank Ronald Kessler for his insights into the United States' Secret Service in his books *In The President's Secret Service* and *The First Family Detail*. I would also like to thank Dan Emmett for his first-hand description of life in the Secret Service in *A Secret Service Agent's Definitive Inside Account of Protecting the President*.

Thank you neuropsychologist Jenni Ogden for helping me understand brain disorders and how those affected manage their lives. Her book, *Trouble In Mind*, and our conversations, enabled me to create the damaged stalker character in *Devour*. Any deviation from scientific studies is entirely my choice.

I'd like to touch on the character of Olivia Wolfe. *Devour* is the first book in a series of action and conspiracy thrillers featuring this resourceful and resilient investigative journalist. Wolfe is inspired by American journalist Marie Colvin. Marie was killed in the bombardment of Homs in Syria in 2012, along with French photojournalist, Rémi Ochlik. I used to read Marie's articles, amazed at her courage and determination to tell the world what was happening in war zones such as Iraq,

Afghanistan, Kosovo, Chechnya, Zimbabwe, Egypt, Libya and Syria. Wolfe is entirely fictional and her looks, relationships, morality and actions have nothing to do with Marie Colvin. Her self-defence techniques are thanks to demonstrations and advice from barrister and martial artist, Craig Everson.

Thank you to my wonderful husband, Michael, for your encouragement and honest feedback when editing early drafts. Your input has made this a much better book. Thank you Phil Patterson, the best literary agent anyone could ever wish for. And huge thanks to Krystyna Green from Constable/Little, Brown UK for your passion and drive, and for championing Olivia Wolfe. And the team at Hachette Australia, thanks so much for embracing *Devour* with such enthusiasm.

Finally, to you, the reader, thank you for joining Olivia Wolfe on her first adventure. Watch out for the next in the series – *Prey*. Coming soon!